Praise for *A Single Source*

'Hugely accomplished, brilliantly plotted'

Irish Independent

'Topical, authoritative and gripping'

Charles Cumming

'Tight, pacy and strong on atmosphere'

Michael Palin

'Completely unputdownable'

Seb Emina

'A compelling story set against some of the global forces shaping our times'

Mishal Husain, *BBC Today* presenter

'If you love le Carré, were gripped by *Homeland* and couldn't get your nose out of *A Dying Breed*, here's another thrilling read for you'

Dame Ann Leslie

'Draws you in from the first line and keeps you guessing until, literally, the very last'

Allan Little

'An enthralling read'

Roy Greenslade

'Peter Hanington is entirely in command of this thrilling story and tells it with great verve'

Kirsty Wark, author of *The Legacy of Elizabeth Pringle*

'Hanington has a knack for telling the stories of the lives behind the news headlines in a way that invites you, the reader, to care about his characters'

Fi Glover, *Fortunately* podcast

'An intelligent, spellbinding thriller'

NB Books

'Another absolutely outstanding addition from an author who spins an almost Kipling-esque story with insight, humanity, humour and, at times, near fury'

Crime Review

Praise for *A Dying Breed*
Sunday Times Thriller of the Month

'There are nods to John le Carré, but his impressive debut is its own thing, with three radio men at its centre, not spooks or civil servants'

The Sunday Times

'Thoughtful, atmospheric and grippingly plotted'

Guardian

'An impressive debut by Peter Hanington. The multi-layered plot, set in Afghanistan and BBC headquarters, moves excitingly and entertainingly but also raises serious current issues about dodgy political and commercial interference with the search for truth by journalists . . . Hanington has true talent'

The Times

'A tremendous novel – shot-through with great authenticity and insider knowledge – wholly compelling and shrewdly wise'

William Boyd

'*A Dying Breed* is an enthralling page-turner, and, as befits an author steeped in newsgathering, there's a real sense of authority and authenticity at work in this quality thriller'

Michael Palin

Also by Peter Hanington

A Dying Breed

PETER HANINGTON

A SINGLE SOURCE

First published in Great Britain in 2019 by Two Roads
An Imprint of John Murray Press
An Hachette UK company

This paperback edition published in 2020

1

Copyright © Peter Hanington 2019

The right of Peter Hanington to be identified as the Author of the Work has been
asserted by him in accordance with the Copyright, Designs and Patents Act 1988.

All rights reserved. No part of this publication may be reproduced,
stored in a retrieval system, or transmitted, in any form or by any means without
the prior written permission of the publisher, nor be otherwise circulated in any
form of binding or cover other than that in which it is published and without a
similar condition being imposed on the subsequent purchaser.

All characters in this publication are fictitious and any resemblance to real persons,
living or dead, is purely coincidental.

A CIP catalogue record for this title is available from the British Library

Paperback ISBN 978 1 473 62548 8
eBook ISBN 978 1 473 62547 1
Audio Digital Download ISBN 978 1 473 67445 5

Typeset in Fournier MT by Palimpsest Book Production Limited, Falkirk, Stirlingshire

Printed and bound in Great Britain by Clays Ltd, Elcograf S.p.A.

John Murray policy is to use papers that are natural,
renewable and recyclable products and made from wood grown in sustainable
forests. The logging and manufacturing processes are expected to conform
to the environmental regulations of the country of origin.

John Murray (Publishers)
Carmelite House
50 Victoria Embankment
London EC4Y 0DZ

www.tworoadsbooks.com

For Jack and Martha

CONTENTS

News stories should be multi-sourced. That said – single-source stories are sometimes unavoidable. In these circumstances, the source must be authoritative, a participant involved in the action or with first-hand knowledge of the event. Above all, both reporter and source must have a track record of telling the truth.

The Journalists' Handbook

Prologue

The man Gabriel wanted his grandsons to meet wore an electric blue-coloured business suit with wide lapels, a white shirt and thin red leather tie. He had a chunky steel watch that was too big for his wrist and that he looked at repeatedly.

'I see you notice my watch? It was your grandfather that got me this watch: Tag Heuer. It is real, I have had this checked. I thought he might try and cheat me . . .' – he looked at both brothers in turn – '. . . but he did not.' There was a hint of disappointment in the man's voice. 'So, I owe old man Gabriel the favour and he says that you two are how I am to repay.' The name on his embossed business card was Adam Adonay but the man had asked that the boys refer to him only as Mr Adam. 'Like the first man – you understand?'

The boys nodded.

Mr Adam glanced around the room, the look on his face suggesting that he found nothing there that met with his approval. Gabriel had arranged for the meeting to take place in the home of a mutual friend, someone who both he and Mr Adam agreed could be trusted. The house turned out to be only a few streets from the boys' own home in the rundown district of Godaif. 'I live in the European section, you know it?' This question was directed at Gebre, who nodded. 'It is a good area, not like this. This house has nothing – a few sticks of furniture is all, not even a picture on the wall. Look!' He waved a hand in the direction of the nearest wall and Gebre looked. Mr Adam was not wrong. He pointed at the table in front of him, an old tea chest covered in a yellow cloth. On it were some papers, a litre bottle of beer and three glasses. 'They do not even have a proper table!' He refilled his already half-full glass to the brim, leaving his guests' glasses empty. 'I have asked around about you two boys. The police find no fault with you, no one else either, so tell me, why do you need to leave?'

Gabriel had told the pair to expect this question and provided them with a prepared answer but Gebre chose to improvise.

'There is nothing for us here, Mr Adam. We live in a house like this house – just me, my brother and our mother. We have no work, no hope of decent work. In Europe we can work and improve our lives, send money back to help our mother and grandfather too.'

The man shrugged, this answer seemed satisfactory.

'I understand. But let us not talk about Europe just yet. One footstep at a time as they say. First we have to get you across the desert . . . Eritrea to Sudan and Sudan to Libya. Then the sea. Then Europe.' He took a gulp of beer and again refilled his glass. 'I told old Gabriel that I would treat you well; that the price he has paid will be the total price. I promised him this.'

Gebre studied Mr Adam. He wondered what this man's promise was worth.

'So, you two will not get the normal trip . . . you will get the VIP trip, you understand?'

The brothers shook their heads. Mr Adam smiled and Gebre saw the flash of a gold tooth.

'Very Important Passenger trip, this is what I have arranged for you. I will tell you how it works. As I said to your grandfather, nothing will happen for two days, but then everything will happen. Things will move very quickly, and you will need to be ready.'

He told them they'd be picked up in a regular taxi and taken an hour or two out of the city; here they'd meet up with their fellow travellers and the men who'd been paid to drive them across the desert. 'This letter, this is your passport.' Mr Adam handed Gebre a single sheet of paper. In typewritten script were three lines of text and under that a telephone number. Each line contained the same message: once in Arabic, once in Tigrinya and once in English.

Mr Adam does guarantee good character and cost of transport for the two boys holding this paper: Gebra and Soloman Hassan.

Gebre turned the paper over. The reverse was blank.

'This is all?'

Mr Adam sucked his teeth, clearly offended.

'That is all you will need, I wrote it out myself. It is more than most people have. Much more. That is my personal mobile phone number on this paper. Where you are going this piece of paper is worth more than an Italian passport or a German passport or any other passport you can name. Do not ever lose this.'

Gebre handed the piece of paper to Solomon.

'Both of our names are spelled wrong.'

Mr Adam snatched the paper back and held it close to his face.

'I do not have my typewriter with me; it is only a small difference, it will not matter. *My name* is the important thing for these people.'

The boys were silent, they knew how much it had cost their grandfather to arrange this trip: ten thousand nakfa or six hundred American dollars – more than two years' pay for most Eritreans and this piece of paper and a promise was what they got in return.

Mr Adam picked up a clear plastic wallet from the makeshift table and inserted the boys' travel document with a certain amount of ceremony. 'As I say before, do not lose it. This is your future.' He handed it across the table to Gebre and clapped his hands together. 'I believe that is all. Your grandfather will be told when the first car will come.' Mr Adam stood and the brothers followed suit. 'He is a good man, your grandfather., I told him he should come into business with me, he knows a lot of people, he knows how to make things happen. Do you know what he said?'

Gebre nodded.

'He always says that he prefers to move objects . . . not people.'

Mr Adam smiled.

'This is exactly what he says to me . . . that if he loses a sack of grain, a bicycle or even a fine watch, it is shame but still he can sleep at night. I told him I understood this problem well – I find it very, very difficult to sleep at night.' Mr Adam finished the beer. 'My doctor says it is the gas but I am sure it is more than this.'

PART ONE

@tsquarelawan

The black and white days are coming. There will be no more grey and everyone must choose . . . which side are you on?

1 The Listening Room

DATELINE: Highbury Fields, London N5, December 27 2010

William Carver stared at the long line of London plane trees, stretching from the bench where he sat, all the way up the Fields to the clock tower at the top. Each tree wore a snowy skirt around its trunk; each looked the same as its neighbour. It was more than thirty years since he'd first set eyes on them, yet the trees seemed unchanged. Carver wondered how far back you'd have to go for the trees to have looked much different. When were they saplings for instance? Maybe all the way back, when these Fields were where London's rich came to hunt stag and fornicate? Carver nodded to himself; trees like these certainly made you think about the passage of time. He took his mobile phone from his anorak pocket and poked out another message: *Get a bloody move on.*

Patrick was pulling the front door to his flat shut when he felt his phone buzz; he ignored it and sloshed his way across the snowy road, greeting Carver with a wave.

'Merry Christmas.'

'What the hell are you wearing?'

Under his long black raincoat Patrick had on an eye-catching red and green sweater featuring a drunk-looking reindeer and several elves.

'It's my Christmas jumper. Me and Becs both bought each other one. Hers is even funnier than this.' Carver remained unsmiling. Patrick noticed that instead of his usual uniform of jeans, black trainers and white shirt, William had a suit on underneath the anorak. 'How come you're so smart?'

'It's just a suit and tie.' His hand went to his collar as though to check this fact. 'McCluskey is a bit of a stickler for smart.'

Patrick grimaced. 'You should've said. Shall I go and change?'

Carver shook his head. 'No time.' He picked up his plastic carrier bag and stood.

They'd walked a few steps when the sound of frantic tapping at a top-floor window stopped them. Rebecca was standing on the sofa, wrapped in a white towel. Whatever urgent thought had occurred to her, had occurred while she was halfway through drying her hair – her blonde bob stuck out at a variety of angles. Patrick grinned at his girlfriend; she looked like a scarecrow – an incredibly pretty scarecrow.

She was mouthing something: '*Ask him.*'

Patrick shook his head.

She pointed at Carver and tried again: '*Ask him.*'

Patrick shrugged and continued pretending not to understand. He sensed Carver losing patience.

'She wants you to ask me something. But you obviously don't want to, and I don't care either way, so shall we just leave it?' He gave Rebecca a wave and dragged Patrick away. 'We've got a train to catch.'

As they walked along the wide pavement that ran down the side of the Fields, Carver reminisced. Back at the beginning of his career – before switching to radio – he was junior crime reporter for a popular north London local tabloid and Highbury Fields was on his patch. 'Christmas week was always good. Drunken scraps at the Lord Nelson . . . bottlings . . . joy-riders. You even got the odd murder-suicide if you were lucky. My editor always gave me extra pages Christmas week.'

Patrick had heard some of William's gory stories before, but he didn't mind hearing them again. They were riding the escalator down to the Victoria Line before he could get a word in.

'So where are we going? You said you'd tell me on the way.'

Carver glanced at his colleague. 'We're off to Caversham, the BBC Monitoring station. I got a call from McCluskey, I've been summoned.'

Patrick nodded; he'd always wanted to see Caversham. 'Cool. And who's McCluskey?'

Carver smiled. 'McCluskey is a legend.'

The train to Reading was one of the modern types: moulded plastic fittings and seats like sandpaper. Carver found an empty table and took the window seat, facing backwards. He watched London recede and slowly the blocks of grey and brick and graffiti made way for trees and irregular-shaped patches of green. The taxi rank at Reading was empty and the station guard advised them that the best way to travel the last leg to Caversham was by bus.

The pink-coloured single-decker wound its way out of town and dropped them a ten-minute walk from the stately home. The cold sky shone as they walked past well-tended allotments and then a field, empty apart from a brown horse, its nose buried in a broken bale of hay. By the time they reached the tall iron gates, Carver was breathless; they stopped and admired the grand-looking facade in silence before William pointed out a few things to Patrick.

'See the sat dish over there? The big green one?'

Patrick looked where Carver was pointing and saw the largest dish he'd ever seen, painted green to help it blend with the gardens but obvious nonetheless.

'They used to have loads of short-wave aerials all over the front of the building, but they took them all down.'

'I guess they don't really need that old stuff anymore?'

Carver shrugged. 'Opinions differ.'

Caversham was an impressive sight, Italian baroque made from stone and steel. 'It was designed by the same bloke who did Tower Bridge.' What Carver's tour lacked in detail it made up for in enthusiasm. Patrick could tell that his colleague felt at home here. 'I used to come and hang out with McCluskey and a few of the others when I was on leave.'

'Isn't that a bit of a busman's holiday?'

'Best sort.'

They walked around the building, past a stone temple, frozen flowerbeds and laurel hedges until they reached the back. 'This is the old orangery.' Carver put his face to a window and pointed. 'And that's the listening room.'

Patrick took a look. This was home to a group of people that Patrick had long considered the most intriguing of BBC employees: the *Monitors*. 'Great. Are we going in?'

Carver shook his head. ''Fraid not, all shut up for Christmas. But I thought you should get a look at it.' He turned to leave. 'McCluskey wanted to meet *away* from work anyhow. It isn't far.'

The red brick, two-up, two-down was on a small estate halfway between Caversham and the local golf course. Patrick had an idea which house they were heading for from some distance away, the clue being a thicket of short-wave aerials poking from the eaves. As they drew closer he saw a white-haired woman kneeling on the grass on the other side of a low flint wall.

Carver called out. 'Hello, McCluskey.'

She ignored him. The woman was crouched above a frozen fishpond with a claw hammer raised high above her head. Patrick saw half a dozen blurs of orange beneath the ice.

'Are they alive?'

10

'Shut yer mouths. I need to concentrate on this or I'll brain one of my fishes.'

She smacked the ice with the hammer and the orange blurs flicked back to life. 'There we go.' She glanced up at her visitors. 'You're early, Carver, but then you're always early. Help me up, will ya?'

She had a thick Glaswegian accent. As William went to help, Patrick studied her. McCluskey wore a black polo neck jumper, green quilted jacket and tweed skirt. Her hair looked like white candyfloss and she had the most enormous ears Patrick had ever seen. Carver huffed and puffed as he pulled McCluskey to her feet.

'Christ. You're not getting any lighter in your old age.'

'You can talk, you fat bastard.' She shot Patrick a look. 'Who's this? Your carer or your grandson?'

Carver smiled. 'That's Patrick.'

William and Patrick sat in the living room while McCluskey went to make tea. The furniture and decor reminded Patrick of his old nana's house, oversized, floral-patterned armchairs and side tables all over the place, although in McCluskey's house every table was in use. There were snow globes everywhere – side tables, windowsills and every other flat surface. The pick of the collection was lined up on the mantelpiece either side of a gold carriage clock. Patrick stood and took a closer look: there was a New York skyline with the Twin Towers still intact; the Sydney Opera House; Paris at night. He picked up the Great Wall of China and gave it a shake; it was still in his hand when McCluskey appeared pushing a tea trolley.

'It's a terrific collection.'

'Yes.'

The woman glanced at the gap on the mantelpiece where the Great Wall globe belonged; Patrick took the hint and put it back down carefully. Carver's attention was focused on the tea trolley.

11

'Have you got any of those little cakes? The kind you had last time?'

'Fondant fancies.'

'That's them.'

While she went to find the cakes, Carver gave Patrick a little of Jemima McCluskey's background. Scottish dad and Polish mum, she'd been raised speaking both parents' native tongue as well as Russian. She learned French at school and whichever part of the brain needs to be exercised in order to master a new language was so well developed by the time she went to university that she had no trouble adding Italian and Spanish. She joined Caversham with these six languages then learned Arabic when it looked like Arabic would be useful. 'It was McCluskey who saw what Pope John Paul's visit to Poland would mean for the Soviet bloc.'

Patrick gave Carver a blank look.

'She knew the Berlin Wall was coming down weeks before anyone else and she was on duty when it fell.' It was clear that he could have gone on and would have done so if their host hadn't returned with a plate of brightly coloured cakes in one hand and a pile of papers in the other.

'Have a cake and then take a read of these.' She handed Carver the untidy sheaf of A4 photocopies.

From where Patrick sat he saw that each page had a different dateline at the top. The dates were recent – all within the last month – but the locations various: Tunis, Tripoli, Algiers, Cairo, Rabat, Sana'a, Riyadh . . .

Carver read in silence, pausing occasionally to help himself to another cake.

'They let you take all this stuff out of Caversham?'

'No, 'course not. All our emails are monitored these days too. I copied them on the quiet and tucked them inside my undies. Security would rather swallow a gob-full of polonium than search me down there. What do you think?'

'Not very interesting individually, but I guess when you put them all together . . .'

McCluskey nodded. 'That's right.' She paused. 'I can usually tell I'm on to something when those spooks up on the top floor start showing an interest and they're very interested in all this.'

Carver stopped reading and waved the papers in her direction. 'So you think all this adds up to something?'

'I wouldn't drag you out here if it was nothing. It's *something*. Maybe one of those somethings that changes everything. Take it all away with you if you like. Just don't show anyone else.'

McCluskey refilled the teapot and replenished the plate of cakes. Patrick and Carver emptied it while he and Jemima chatted around the general theme of things not being what they used to be. Carver had heard rumours that the BBC might even consider closing Caversham. McCluskey enjoyed a good rumour but she didn't like this one.

'Nah, bollocks they will. The boss class are stupid but they're not that stupid. They'll never sell that place. There's no room for us in W1 and not a hope in hell they'd persuade all those spooks up on the top floor to move anywhere else.'

'I hope you're right.'

'I am.'

Patrick cleared his throat and risked an opinion. 'I suppose the problem is the technology is changing so fast. Everyone is a monitor now . . . or can be. Anyone with a mobile phone in their pocket?'

There was an agonising silence before McCluskey spoke. When she did Patrick was relieved to see she was nodding.

'It's a fair point. A bog-standard smartphone can access as much information *now* as all the gizmos in Caversham could a few years back. That's not the hard part anymore. The hard part's knowing what's important. Monitors filter as much as monitor – tell you the difference between the cream and the crud. The truth and the lie.'

Carver stood; he could feel the tea swilling in his stomach, his mouth claggy with fondant fancies. He asked to use the bathroom and suggested that he and Patrick should leave before too long. As soon as he'd left the room, McCluskey took the chair closest to Patrick's. She spoke in a low whisper.

'Carver looks like he's put on a few pounds. That dreadful suit looks even worse than last time I saw it. He's all right, is he?'

Patrick tried to reassure her and he did a fair job. When he'd finished speaking he looked over and saw that she was smiling.

'It's interesting . . .'

'What is?'

'Carver's been the rogue male so long . . . do you know that term?'

Patrick shook his head.

'A solitary beast . . . widowed or wounded usually.'

'I see.'

'Anyway, he's been that way so long. I never thought he'd end up with . . .' McCluskey examined Patrick over the rim of her teacup, trying to work out what he was.

Patrick tried to help. 'A partner?'

'A cub.'

There was a farting sound of trombone-like proportions from the toilet and then the sound of flushing and an air freshener being sprayed. Carver returned a little red in the face.

'We should make a move . . .' He retrieved the papers. 'Thanks for this, McCluskey. I'll check it out.'

'You do that. Bring me back a snow globe.'

Carver smiled. 'I'm not sure they do snow globes in North Africa.'

'They do snow globes everywhere.'

Patrick laughed. 'That's globalisation I guess?'

The carriage clock on the mantelpiece chimed the hour. Eventually McCluskey spoke. 'I believe there's a train at half past. You might make that.'

*

Back at Paddington station, they were about to go their separate ways when Patrick cleared his throat and muttered.

'William . . . earlier, when Rebecca was shouting down at me.'

'Yeah?'

'She wanted me to ask you for dinner. You know? Like a late Christmas dinner? At our place?'

Carver nodded. 'Right, I see.'

'So what do you think?'

Carver paused. 'Thank Rebecca for the thought, Patrick. But I'm busy, other plans, you know?'

''Course, 'course, yes. I thought you'd probably . . .'

'Some other time. Have a good evening – the pair of you.'

Patrick nodded.

'And call me tomorrow, first thing. We need to start making travel plans.'

'Sure. Hey, William, thanks for today. I mean thanks for asking me along.'

Carver was pulling his tie from his collar; he stuffed it into his pocket then zipped up his anorak. 'No problem. Merry Christmas.'

Carver did his best thinking on the move. He took the Bakerloo Line down to where it connected with the Northern Line. Opting for southbound, he walked to the end of the platform and when the next train drew in he settled himself in the last carriage, next to the locked driver's cab. He read through McCluskey's collection of stories slowly and in date order. When the train reached Morden he got out, crossed the platform and took the next train north, back the way he'd come. On the return trip and on a whim, he got off at Embankment. He walked along the river for a while, quieter than usual, although a few tourists were braving the cold. At Westminster Bridge he cut up on to Whitehall and headed north. It was almost dark, the sky a midnight blue and a few stars visible in the cold air. Government business had stopped for the

Christmas week. The only sign of life – one bright rectangle of light from the office building opposite Horse Guards. Carver glanced up at the uncurtained window and then looked around to get his bearings: the Ministry of Defence.

2 Kifaya

DATELINE: Tahrir Square, Cairo, Egypt, January 25 2011

Nawal tried to remember when she'd stopped being scared. A few weeks ago she would have turned tail at the sight of a police van – the smallest hint of trouble. Now, when she heard sirens and the swell of noise coming from the other side of Tahrir, from close to the governing party headquarters, she shouldered her rucksack and practically ran in that direction.

The square concrete block of a building was alight, the windows at the top spitting broken glass down on to the street below. Nawal moved closer, near enough to feel the heat of the fire on her face. A looting operation was under way with a steady stream of people running in and out of the tall black doors at the front of the party HQ. Those on their way out of the building carried wooden chairs, desks, photocopiers and more old-fashioned-looking pieces of office equipment. A man walked past her carrying a mechanical adding machine; another was struggling under the weight of a golf-ball typewriter. The women involved in the looting had different priorities: they seemed to be more interested in official files than office furniture. One group of women – several generations of the same family – strode from the building carrying armfuls of grey box files. Nawal knew the reason why – inside these files they hoped to find answers to questions they'd been asking for years: information about missing husbands and brothers, daughters and sisters and sons. She got out her phone and started typing.

A Day of Anger some were calling it but Nawal felt no anger, she was euphoric.

By the early evening, the worst of the fighting in and around Tahrir Square was over but there was no clear winner. The police had managed to push the protesters back from the centre of Tahrir, but they still held one corner of the square – an area the size of half a football pitch or maybe slightly more. The demonstrators were regrouping inside that space.

Standing on the steps up to the Omar Makram statue, Carver surveyed the scene. He counted three armoured personnel carriers, burned black and upturned like dead beetles. A couple of ambulances had found a way through the barricades that both sides had set up to control access to Tahrir and paramedics were dealing with the casualties. Ten yards from where he stood, Carver saw one of these medics kneeling over a young man with a stomach wound; the medic's green tunic was sleeved in blood. Carver had counted seventeen injured so far, eighteen including this kid. Eighteen protesters and three police.

He reached into his yellow plastic bag, pulled out his reporter's notepad and jotted down these numbers. Usually he'd trust this sort of detail to memory, but it had been a long day and he was tired – tired and hungry. He took another look inside the bag and saw the chicken shawarma sandwich he'd bought for breakfast; the brown paper wrapping was stained dark by the grease and it smelled a little ripe. Carver decided to give it a go anyway.

Patrick arrived in time to see his colleague gobbing a masticated mouthful of chicken on to the ground. 'Lovely.'

Carver shrugged and put the sandwich back in the bag. 'How many injured have you seen?'

'I counted nineteen protesters, three police.'

'Nineteen? You're sure?'

Patrick nodded and watched as Carver corrected the tally in his notebook.

'Okay, we better update that last bulletin piece then.'

Patrick stared at his colleague. Carver's face was grey, his voice thinner than usual. 'Why don't you have another blast of the inhaler first, William? There's still a bit of tear gas blowing about. You're sounding wheezy.'

Carver found his puffer and took a gulp, and within a minute or so his voice was back to normal. He nailed the forty-second-long bulletin piece first time.

'We'll need to check in with the hospitals. I've seen a couple of nasty-looking injuries. One kid I saw looked like he might be bleeding out.'

Patrick nodded. 'I can do that.' He got his phone out and checked his Twitter feed, looking for any recent posts from a pro-democracy campaigner he'd started following. Sure enough:

@tsquarelawan
| New Cairo Hospital needs help. Anyone with blood
| type O please go. Big shortage of type O!

Patrick would try the New Cairo first, then the others. He checked the time and saw to his surprise that it had already gone seven. They'd been working for ten hours solid, filing bulletin pieces for the top of each hour and collecting more than enough material for their longer *Today* programme piece. He glanced across at Carver, who was flicking through his notebook; he looked knackered. 'How about you knock off for now, boss? Nothing else huge is going to happen here. I'll check the hospitals then meet you back at the hotel?'

Carver reluctantly agreed to call it a day. He set off walking east on Al-Bustan; his plan was to move away from Tahrir Square and the worst of the traffic before doubling back in the general direction of the river. He had half an eye out for a taxi although he knew the chances of finding one were slim. He walked the back streets, the hot stink of human excrement, rotting rubbish and petrol thick in the air. It was a smell he'd got used to – perhaps even rather attached to – on his visits to Cairo. Certain things about the city had changed down the years, but the smell had not.

Carver emerged from the back streets close to the Kasr Al Nil Bridge. This wasn't where he'd expected to find himself – Cairo's labyrinthine streets never seemed to take you the same way twice – but it was in broadly the right direction. Halfway across the bridge, his legs started to feel heavy and he decided to take a rest. Down on the wide, yellow-brown Nile, a brightly lit party boat was chugging by, Egyptian pop music blaring from its speakers. It seemed odd that ordinary everyday life could be carrying on when so much of the city was in turmoil. Carver reached into the plastic bag for his MiniDisc recorder; he knew that Patrick would be able to do something interesting with the sound.

He was standing with his back against the cold stone, his headphones down around his neck and the tape machine running when he heard a single exuberant voice shouting, calling out in time with the boat's loud music.

'*Kifaya . . . Kifaya . . . Kifaya.*' Looking to his right, Carver saw a young man walking at impressive speed up the middle of the pavement, singing as he came. He had a strange gait, both arms and one leg swinging wildly as though he were marching in a military parade. As he drew closer, Carver saw first the boy's clubfoot and then the broad smile, so bright that he could not help but smile back. The policeman was walking in the opposite direction, away from Tahrir and the disabled kid clocked him more or less at the same time as Carver did. He stopped singing but kept walking. As the two came closer, just as they were about to cross, the boy raised his hands – a gesture of conciliation or understanding and smiled again, broader still. What happened next happened quickly and just a few yards from where Carver stood. The policeman snatched the baton from his belt, lifted it high and brought it down hard on the side of the boy's head. Carver winced and turned away.

The noise was unlike anything he had ever heard. It was the sound of the hardest kind of plastic that man could make, hitting and breaking a boy's skull; it was the sound of someone's brain shifting in its housing and spilling out. The young man's scream was like an animal in pain. The baton broke the thin bone at the boy's temple, tearing the artery. The kid performed a macabre, jolting dance and then fell to the floor. The policeman stood above him for a moment, then glanced at the baton, seemingly surprised at how effective his single blow had been. His arm was still raised and he appeared to be in two minds about whether to hit the boy again. He tucked the baton back into his belt and walked on.

Carver threw his headphones down and walked quickly over to the boy, knelt by his side and put his ear to the kid's lips, listening for breath. There was something – and then nothing. A trickle of thick red blood ran from his ear, down his cheek and Carver wiped it uselessly away. William had seen dead bodies but for some reason this felt different. He lifted one of the boy's eyelids and then dropped it again, frightened by the size and darkness of the pupil, pitch-black and empty of anything. Carver held his hand.

And then the father came. The man must have been following his son; unable to keep up perhaps, as he was old. He arrived at Carver's side and stood staring for a moment, saying nothing, then he knelt and slapped at the boy's cheek to wake him, first softly, then harder. He mumbled a name.

'*Adjo.*' Then he shouted it. He put his hands under his son's shoulders and lifted his head. Carver feared that he might try and shake him back to life but instead he slowly lifted him. He held him upright, carrying him gently to the side of the bridge and sitting down against the stone wall, cradling his dead son in his arms and crying.

The piece of radio that Carver and Patrick filed to London later that evening was short. They began the report with the sound of the boy's last minute of life: the sound of a party boat pushing up the Nile, of pop music, of his simple chant and then his killing. Carver followed it with a short piece of script:

'*This is the sound of Egypt's revolution, of the latest chapter in the Arab uprising. The word being sung is* kifaya, *which means "enough" and that was the last thing this boy said before he was killed with one blow from a policeman's baton.*'

They put the report together in Carver's hotel room and after they'd finished, Patrick suggested they order some food.

'I'm not hungry.'

'Okay, well . . .'

'I need a drink.'

'Yeah, but you asked me to help . . .'

'You're my producer, Patrick, not my fucking mother. I need a drink. Just something to take the edge off.'

Patrick nodded. 'I'll find something.'

'Thank you.'

Carver sat down on the bed and opened the file on Patrick's laptop; he stared at the jagged waveform for a while and at one section in particular. Near the top of the piece, a single spike, representing the moment the baton connected with the boy's head. He played the piece through a couple of times, wincing each time and then moved the cursor to a point just to the right of the spike.

Carver played the audio backwards. And then again, and then again. But it did no good. He pushed the laptop shut.

Patrick poured a splash of the cheap Polish vodka he'd bought from the hotel barman into his Coke and kept Carver company while he drank the rest of the vodka neat. Before leaving, Patrick sat down at the hotel room table and logged in again; he wanted to check that their report had filed in full and that London was happy. When he turned back around, Carver was asleep, still fully dressed, sprawled diagonally across his double bed and snoring. The air conditioning had turned the room cold. Patrick pulled the duvet and sheet over his sleeping colleague and flicked off the bedroom light.

'Night-night, William.'

3 Lying for Your Country

DATELINE: Old Kent Road, London SE11, January 26 2011

Rob Mariscal stretched a wet arm around the side of the shower cubicle and turned the radio up.

'Let it run,' he muttered, as Carver's final line of script faded into the sound of a crowd on the Cairo street. They let it run. 'Quality,' Rob said to no one in particular.

As the piece finished there was a second of respectful studio silence before a deep, Welsh-accented voice back-announced the report: *'That's our man William Carver, in Cairo.'*

A second male voice, this one with rather less authority picked up: *'Yes, he's having quite a run of it, isn't he?'*

Mariscal shook his head. 'Dickwad.'

Rob turned the shower off and poked his head round the corner of the cubicle in search of a towel. The radio was informing him that they'd be discussing the implications of the worsening situation in Egypt later in the programme. 'Great, can't wait. Lindy? Lindy baby, have you got a dry towel in there?'

His girlfriend arrived, fully dressed and unsmiling, finished drying her hair with the towel and handed it to him.

'Thanks.'

Lindy glanced at the radio, which was covered in soapsuds. She hesitated a moment then turned it down. 'You're going to electrocute yourself on that thing one of these days.' Her tone suggested that this was more an observation than a concern.

'Yeah, well, I did ask you for a waterproof radio. For my birthday, you remember?'

'Yes, and I asked *you* for a walk-in shower.'

Mariscal pulled a face; this was familiar ground. 'This *is* a walk-in shower, Lind. I walked into it five minutes ago and I'm about to walk out again now. Look, I'll show you – you just need to lift your beautiful size fives.'

'And you just need to go screw yourself. I don't know why you won't spend some of that redundancy money making this place half decent.'

Mariscal sighed and turned the radio back up; he needed to hear the news bulletin and he didn't want another argument about money.

The half seven bulletin reached a big audience. It was only a couple of minutes long, included only a handful of stories and was a hard target to hit, but Mariscal was hopeful. He wrapped the damp towel around his midriff and listened. The top story was Egypt, then a quick trot around the rest of the Arab world before the newsreader cued into an item about the Cabinet reshuffle.

'Here we go.' Rob had spent most of the previous day briefing journalists about the new Secretary of State for Defence – his new boss. He leaned closer to the radio.

'More details are emerging of the ongoing Cabinet reshuffle with changes at several key departments including Treasury, Home Office and Environment.'

'Fuck the environment.'

'One of the most notable new appointments is at the Ministry of

Defence where Martin Whitewing has been named as the new Secretary of State. Mr Whitewing was previously a junior minister at the Foreign Office and has a military background, having served in both Iraq and Afghanistan.'

Mariscal's bellowed laugh was loud enough to attract the attention of his girlfriend, who walked back into the bathroom with her hair freshly blow-dried and make-up applied.

'What is it?'

'Oh, nothing – just further confirmation that I'm brilliant at my job.'

Lindy nodded. 'Lying for your country.'

The grin slid from Mariscal's face and he gripped his towel a little tighter. 'What?'

'That's what you called it – last night. You were drunk, and late and I asked you where you'd been. You said you'd spent fourteen hours on the phone, slogging your guts out, *lying for your country*. You thought it was very funny.'

'Right. I remember.'

'Is it still funny?'

'Sure, sure it's funny. What else would it be?'

Rob dried himself and got dressed. Every other senior manager at the Ministry of Defence wore a suit and tie and after a few weeks of resistance when he first started the job, Rob had fallen into line. The only remaining sign of sartorial defiance was his fondness for black. Both of the new off-the-peg suits he bought were black, as were all his shirts, socks and shoes. Some mornings he would glance in the full-length hallway mirror and imagine he still saw a hint of Johnny Cash but today, like most other days, his glassy doppelgänger looked more like a struggling, high street undertaker. He had an early meeting with his boss, the permanent secretary, and he needed to look presentable.

'You look fine.' Lindy brushed a few flakes of dandruff from her boyfriend's shoulder and pushed him gently to one side. She wanted to check her own outfit and that was fair enough, the mirror was hers really.

Rob watched her study herself. The mirror was Lindy's friend; occasionally it might suggest a change in her choice of top or shade of lipstick but most of the time the mirror simply told her how great she looked and wished her well. Mirrors told Mariscal to go kill himself. He left her to it and stepped out of the flat and into the shared hall for a cigarette. The floorboards beneath the thin carpet were spongy with woodworm; he paced up and down checking the emails on his phone and puffing away. He selected the radio app and stuck an earphone in just in time to hear the promised discussion about how to deal with the *Egyptian situation*. An academic and a well-known Egyptian novelist were suggesting everything from stiff letters and special United Nations sessions to sanctions and a tightening of the export ban. Mariscal rolled his eyes.

'The export ban's already tighter than a duck's arsehole, you idiots.' The Welsh-accented presenter thanked them for their suggestions. 'Yeah, great idea. Let academics and novelists decide government policy . . . we'd be bankrupt in a week.' He was about to phone and check if his car had arrived when Lindy appeared at the door.

'Smoking in the stairwell still counts as smoking in the flat. The draught from the street blows the smoke straight back in.'

Mariscal nodded and made a show of smoking the cigarette at speed, taking several quick, deep pulls before lifting his foot and stubbing the butt out on the bottom of his shoe.

Lindy watched, unimpressed. She ran a protective hand down over her still-flat stomach. 'For every five cigarettes you smoke, the baby smokes one.'

'That explains why I keep running out of fags. I gotta go.' Mariscal moved to give his girlfriend a goodbye kiss and was offered a dusty cheek, which he dutifully pecked.

Rob and Lindy's flat was situated just off the Old Kent Road.

This part of south London had so far stood firm against gentrification and it wasn't hard to see why: their front door was fifty yards from a flyover. The traffic was heavy this morning; roadworks meant that two lanes were being siphoned into one. Drivers approaching this obstruction over-revved their cars, changed lanes and then skipped back again in search of some small advantage. Rob stood on the pavement, stamping his feet against the cold and cursing his missing driver. He was about to reach for his phone to give the cab company an earful when he saw his car, a black Ford C-Max, double-parked outside the fried chicken shop on the other side of the road. He dodged through the traffic, wrenched open the door and collapsed into the back seat.

The driver turned to greet him. 'Good morning, sir.'

'Morning. Do me a favour and switch the radio to shuffle, will you?'

His driver glanced down at the digital display and pushed the shuffle function. 'I do not use this button.'

'No? It's a blast, have a listen.'

The radio retuned itself to a classical music station and Mariscal heard a few seconds of an inoffensive sonata before the announcer picked up with the weather; after ten seconds the radio switched again, this time finding Radio 1 where a much younger voice was already reading the news bulletin against a bass-heavy backing track. The presenter was talking about last night's shock defeat for Manchester United. Rob tapped his foot impatiently. He didn't have to wait long, next up was the news he'd been waiting for: there was a new man in charge at the Ministry of Defence, the first in decades who'd done active service. 'Bingo!' Rob was particularly pleased with this mention since Radio 1 was the station of choice for a large number of squaddies. The radio changed again and then again – Gold, Magic, Heart – and by the time his car had reached Waterloo, Mariscal's new minister had completed fourteen tours of duty.

This small success had unlocked Rob's appetite and he asked the driver to stop outside the takeaway bakery near Waterloo so he could buy a cheese and onion slice. Mariscal was back in the car, a paper napkin on his lap and about to tuck in when his phone rang. The caller display announced it as *Fox – Standard & Guardian*. 'Bollocks, better take this,' he muttered to himself.

Even down a scratchy mobile line the man's voice was loud as a bell. 'I've heard what you're trying to sell, Mariscal, and I'm not buying. *Two tours of duty?* He's a bloody part-timer, a reservist. And from what I hear, a rather reluctant one at that.'

Rob laughed. 'Nonsense, he's done two tours, Richard, it's all in the records. One in Iraq, one in Afghanistan.'

'Tours? Pull the other one, Rob, it's got bells. Those were more like long weekends than tours and it seems his main job was to see that our brave boys didn't run out of biscuits.'

It was inevitable that someone would work out that there was less to the new minister's military career than met the eye and unsurprising that it was Richard Fox who had done the job. Rob decided to bluster it out. 'An army marches on its stomach, Richard, good supplies are essential, you know that.'

'I'll tell you what I know. I know you've got a bloody cheek. He's a part-time soldier and a big risk in an important job like this, especially now. What was wrong with the old Secretary of State?'

'Not dynamic enough.'

'Ha. Not pliable enough more like. Your new man's a novice. That's what I'll write.'

'Fair enough. I can live with that, Richard.'

Having proven his point the old defence correspondent softened a little. 'He does look the part, I'll give you that.'

'He does, doesn't he?' The new man had a moustachioed and military air to him. 'Very charismatic too.'

'God save us from charismatic politicians. Well, he's going to need more than charisma to stop the Treasury cutting your budget to buggery, I'll tell you that for nothing.' Fox paused. 'I'll write that your new man's an unknown quantity.'

'That's kind of you, Richard. How about we sit down for lunch sometime soon?'

'I'm not biddable, you know that.'

'And I'm not buying. I don't *want* anything, Richard, I just like having lunch with you. Shall I book a table at the Academy?'

'Why not? Mondays and Tuesdays are good.'

'How about Wednesdays, Thursdays and Fridays?'

'Ha, those are good too. Tell them you're coming with me and they'll give us a decent table.'

Mariscal's driver dropped him outside the Ministry of Defence employees' entrance. Rob took a moment to brush the pastry from his shirt and trousers before heading in.

Walking down one of the long and over-lit corridors he saw a middle-aged woman in a dark green suit and high black heels coming the other way. The woman wore a fixed but friendly smile, which slipped from her face the moment she saw Mariscal. Rob stopped walking and waited for her to do the same.

'Good morning, Minister, I just wanted to say how . . .'

The woman lowered her head and kept walking.

'So, our new Secretary of State is already a fan of yours, Robert. A *big* fan.'

Mariscal arranged his face into something that he hoped conveyed both modest surprise and appropriate gratitude. There were a lot of idiots working at the Ministry of Defence but the man sitting on the other side of the old oak desk was not one of them.

'That's good to hear, Permanent Secretary.' Rob had realised within days of arriving at the ministry that the permanent secretary preferred to be addressed by title rather than name.

'Isn't it?' Leslie Craig had been living in England for thirty years, but his Northern Irish accent was still strong, and it always took Rob a while to tune his ear. 'I've just had a quick *how d'you do* with him. I was telling him who's who and what's what – all that sort of thing. I made it *very* clear to him what an asset you are.'

'Thank you, Permanent Secretary.'

'It's a pleasure, I was simply speaking the truth. He didn't need a lot of persuading – that's quite a sales job you've done on him this morning. Every radio station and telly show I saw had his name all over it.'

Mariscal nodded. 'His appointment's gone down pretty well, I think.'

'It certainly has.' Craig folded his hands into a steeple shape in front of him. 'Perhaps too well. Your man was strutting around like he's General George Patton – and he's only just got here.'

Rob smiled. 'The *Evening Standard* might take some of the wind out of his sails.'

'Good. His main mast was billowing away like nobody's business. The *Evening Standard* you say?'

Rob nodded.

'Will that be Mr Fox giving the snake oil an extra sniff?'

''Fraid so. I just spoke to him, he's not buying much of what I'm selling.'

Craig shook his head. 'No bad thing; a confident minister is a good thing, a cocky one is not. I take it you heard your old radio show this morning? The latest from Cairo?'

'Yes, sir.'

'Those good old tectonic plates our political masters like to talk about are on the move.'

Mariscal nodded. 'Sounds like it.'

'We have a dynamic new Secretary of State in place, now we need something for him to say.'

'What kind of thing?'

'Nothing fancy. A cautious welcome for the winds of change. Maybe mention we're taking another look at export controls.'

'The export controls are already as tight as a duck's . . . I mean they're already very tight.'

Craig agreed. 'I know, but that's the way we're headed. Better to say it now and appear to be ahead of the game than wait and look like we've been forced into it. Wouldn't you say?'

Mariscal couldn't argue with that.

'Downing Street wants us to take the lead on this.'

'Why?'

This was a question too far. Craig pretended not to have heard and, pushing himself up out of his black ergonomic chair – the only concession to twenty-first-century working practices visible in this office – walked over to the long picture window. From here, he had the best view of Horse Guards in Whitehall; significantly better than the Secretary of State whose office was one floor below.

Rob studied the permanent secretary's profile. His face was of a shape and pallor that brought to mind certain church gargoyles – not the monstrous kind, more the comic sort. Mariscal felt sure that he'd seen the civil servant's stony twin on the side of an Oxfordshire church: bulbous eyes, wide nose and fleshy mouth. He hadn't mentioned this to his boss.

'Where was I? Ah, I remember, I was telling you how important you are to us, Robert. The best head of comms we've ever had, that's what I told the Secretary of State.'

'I'm very grateful.' Mariscal wondered whether he might take advantage of his newly acknowledged importance to leverage another five grand. Now was probably not the right time to raise the matter, but maybe later. 'By the way, I saw the previous Secretary of State stalking the corridors on my way up here. I thought for a minute the Prime Minister had changed his mind – decided to give her another go?'

Craig snorted and walked back to his desk. He took a pair of half-moon glasses from his breast pocket, balanced them on his broad nose and examined a sheet of headed notepaper. Underneath the departmental crest and that day's date was a list of his appointments. 'No danger of that, no second chances for her. But yes, I see that I'm due to meet with her later.'

'At twelve forty-five for fifteen minutes.'

Craig looked up sharply. 'How the devil do you . . . ?'

Rob jutted his chin in the direction of the list of appointments. Age and every available excess had taken a toll on Mariscal in many ways, but his eyesight was still twenty-twenty and he'd always been able to read text as easily upside down as the right way round. It was not a particularly useful talent; rather like being double-jointed or speaking Esperanto but Rob was proud of it anyway.

'Just because you retain some of those shady journalistic skills, it doesn't mean you should practise them. Especially not on me.'

'Sorry, old habits . . .'

Craig turned his list of appointments over. 'I'm seeing the former minister at a quarter to one. My guess is that she's arrived early so she can sit for her portrait.'

'Her what?'

Craig smiled. 'I don't believe you've been with us long enough to observe the tradition. Every serving Secretary of State at Defence is asked whether they'd like to have a portrait done, captured in oils once their term in office is complete.'

'You're kidding? That's fucking ridiculous.' The permanent secretary flinched at the profanity and Rob chided himself for using it. 'I'm sorry, but a portrait? What a waste of public money.'

'Yes, that's what most of the ministers say when I tell them about the tradition. Still, so far none has refused to sit – when the time comes.'

'What happens to the pictures?'

'Well, we hang them on a stretch of wall near the canteen for a few weeks and the old minister comes and takes a look; usually they bring their family and a photographer from their local newspaper. After that, we put them into storage. We've got scores of them in bubble-wrap and brown paper, somewhere in the basement.' Craig pushed his glasses up his nose. 'A couple of the better ones are still hanging – here and there.'

'The better ones? Better ministers?'

'No, Lord, no – the better painters. We used to have some rather renowned artists do the job. Now we just use whomever the Society of Portrait Painters pushes our way. There've been some dreadful efforts recently; hopefully this latest fellow they've given us will be better. I know the minister has said that she's happy to sit for as long as necessary.'

This was not a surprise to Rob; in his experience, sitting very still and worrying about the world was the former Defence Secretary's absolute forte. If the artist in question wasn't confident about painting her, then maybe he could just trace her? Rob decided to keep this idea to himself.

'A picture of every politician, I had no idea. I'll look out for the good ones while I'm doing my rounds.'

'Do. You have to go back a fair few years for anything of quality; keep an eye out for frock-coats and telescopes is my advice.' The civil servant took another look at his list of appointments, and it seemed that the meeting might be over. Mariscal was on his feet when Craig cleared his throat. 'One more thing, Robert, before you go.'

'Certainly, I'm sorry, I thought we were done.'

Craig smiled. 'Not quite. I wondered whether you'd mind taking a look at something for me?'

'Certainly, Permanent Secretary.'

'It's a copy of next year's budget, a draft of what I plan to send over to the Treasury.'

Rob nodded. 'You mean my part? The communications department budget?'

'No, I mean the whole budget – the Ministry of Defence budget.'

'I see.' Mariscal was aware that his boss was watching him, gauging his response to this unusual request. He had no idea what sort of test it was that the permanent secretary was setting him but he knew better than to ask.

'Well of course, I'd be happy to take a look.'

'Good, ask Miriam for the file on your way out and we'll talk about it at our next routine.'

'That's tomorrow.'

'Yes, tomorrow. Problem?'

'No problem.'

The main purpose of the meeting done with, Craig relaxed, leaning back into his chair.

'What sort of story *did* you spin around the ex-minister's removal, by the way? I didn't see much mention of her in the news.'

Mariscal smiled. 'No, there wasn't meant to be. I've been preparing people for her sacking for a while now, dropping hints: *Not across the brief . . . struggling with the detail . . .* that sort of thing. She's got teenage kids too – that helped. No surprise equals no news.'

The civil servant nodded. 'Very clever. You have a talent for stories, Robert.'

Mariscal shrugged. 'It's obvious really: people are busy, there's a lot of competition for their attention. If you tell them one good story about someone, then they're usually happy to take it.'

'And believe it?'

'Why not?'

Craig stood and walked towards his office door, opening it for Rob. 'What *one* story would you tell about me? I wonder.'

Mariscal shook his head. 'I wouldn't be so presumptuous,

Permanent Secretary. You're a very complicated character, I'm not sure one story would do the job.'

The civil servant made a barking sound that Rob had come to recognise as laughter. 'Craven flattery, Robert, craven flattery. Take the file from Miriam, have a good read and we shall talk about it tomorrow.'

On the way back down to his desk, Rob saw the sacked minister again; she was standing outside the Secretary of State's office, watching a man in blue overalls scratching her name from the office door. The gold leaf came away easily. There *was* one story that helped explain the permanent secretary: it was a story that his secretary had told Rob not long after he arrived in the job. Leslie Craig was born and grew up in Belfast, where his father was governor of the Maze Prison and as a result his name was right at the top of an IRA hit list. Monday through Friday, Governor Craig would drop little Leslie at school on his way into work at the prison. It wasn't a long car ride but it was a potentially dangerous one and from the age of seven it was Leslie's job to hold his dad's old service revolver while his father drove the car. He had his instructions, he knew what he had to do if there was trouble: a hold-up or an accident of some sort. His father made it very clear.

'If you've got the gun, Leslie, and you can shoot them, you shoot them, you understand?'

'Yes.'

'But if they take me, if they are dragging me off, shoot away, son. I'd rather be shot than taken. Repeat that to me please.'

'I shoot away, Da. You'd rather be shot than taken.'

'Good boy.'

Craig's secretary had told Rob this story with a tear in her eye and Rob had reacted accordingly. But for Mariscal the moral of the story wasn't that Leslie Craig should be pitied, it was that he should not be underestimated.

4 Dreamers

DATELINE: The Taxi Café, Asmara, Eritrea, January 26 2011

The air is hot, the light brilliant. Gabriel Hassen sits in the window of the Taxi Café watching the city he's known all his life vibrate in the haze. Asmara is unique – despite all the effort Mussolini and his fellow fascists took to make it seem like somewhere else, the Eritrean capital looks only like itself.

Gabriel Hassen will tell you the story – if you sit down with him and drink a beer he'll give you chapter and verse.

'Our Italian masters wanted *La Piccola Roma* but they ended up with something much more interesting than that.'

In Gabriel's version of Asmara's history, architecture is key. He always began his tours by explaining how Il Duce's imperial ambition led to some of Italy's most ambitious architects arriving here at the very north of the rift valley. 'An architect's playground, that's what we were. Neo-classical, Novecento, Monumental – do you know these terms?'

Gabriel's main work was buying and selling, acquiring things that most Eritreans found it difficult to come by. His second job and the one he enjoyed significantly more was as Asmara's least official but most authoritative tour guide. Given the choice he would have quit the buying and selling business and dedicated all his time to tourism but this was not practical – tourists were extremely hard to find and he needed to make money; he had two grandsons and a daughter-in-law to support.

The last walking tour was a month ago now and it hadn't gone well. Gabriel knew what the problem was: the tour was too long, but with thousands of historic buildings in Asmara, making the walk any shorter than five hours seemed impossible. The group of middle-aged Germans had asked for a comfort break at the art deco Cinema Impero and then given up altogether after seeing the old Fascist Party headquarters. Gabriel pointed out that he was at least twenty years older than any of them and was walking just as far, but it did no good, they were hot and their feet hurt. They tipped him generously but that in no way made up for the fact that the tour had ended before they had reached the Fiat Tagliero garage. The next tour he led would start at the Taxi Café. There was an excellent view of the Tagliero from here.

Gabriel stirred some sugar into his dark beer and flicked through the newspaper, starting with the sports section and paying particular attention to any football or cycling stories before working his way backwards through the paper until he got to the Eritrean and international news. He found these pages useful – not as a source of accurate information but as an insight into the preoccupations and psychological state of the government. The protests in Egypt, Tunisia and elsewhere in the north had been given a reasonable amount of coverage in recent weeks and this had surprised Gabriel. Popular protest of any sort anywhere was usually ignored. He had even joked with his grandsons that maybe the official censor had run out of red pencils. However, as the number of stories of Eritreans and other sub-Saharans caught up in the growing chaos grew, it became obvious that for the newspaper's editor and his political masters the Arab uprising was a useful cautionary tale. Difficult as things were *inside* Eritrea, *outside* it was worse.

Gabriel folded his paper and stared out of the window; a man of similar age to himself but in a wheelchair was propelling himself down the pavement using ski poles. It was too hot for anyone sensible to linger long outside but a group of taxi drivers were sitting in the shade of a date palm, drinking coffee and waiting for a fare. The traffic was steady, with old Volkswagens and Fiat 500s chugging up and down the Dekemhare Road, occasionally overtaken by a Land Cruiser or yellow taxi. Each time a cab passed close by, the driver would toot a greeting to his colleagues who were setting up the board for a game of gebeta to pass the time. Business was slow, everything was slow – the heat was such that it seemed to slow the clock. Gabriel looked at his watch; soon his two grandsons – Solomon and Gebre – would join him for a plate of pizza and some coffee. He looked forward to their regular catch-ups although today's meeting might be more difficult. He had things he needed to say.

Gebre sat as close to his girlfriend as the armrest would allow, watching curls of cigarette smoke twist in the projector light. The pair had chosen the back row of the Cinema Impero and neither was that interested in the film: an old Indian musical that the management had screened so many times that the film stock had faded and the soundtrack crackled. Gebre had seen the musical ten times at least but he didn't mind; the tickets for Indian films only cost a few nakfa and he got to sit in the cool dark next to Martha for two precious hours. His mother referred to the cinema, somewhat dismissively, as *a house for dreamers* and Gebre didn't argue. Up on the screen the action shifted from indoors to out and as the auditorium brightened, Gebre stole a sideways glance, admiring the elaborate braiding in Martha's hair. She smiled and turned her head, and she reached over and took his hand. She pulled it gently towards her and brought it to rest at the point where the hem of her short cotton dress met her thigh. Gebre tried to control his breathing and stared wide-eyed at the screen.

Solomon shifted gears and kept an eye out for potholes. Cycling through the unmade roads of his own neighbourhood of Godaif was no fun – the one part of his regular training ride he did not enjoy. He rode as quickly as he dared and before long the tin shacks, with bright laundry hanging on lines strung from house to house, were replaced by brick-built two-up two-downs and then much finer properties. The dirt roads became proper tarmac-adamed streets that widened as he reached the old European section of Asmara. Solomon shifted down through the gears, increased his speed and put his head down; the honey- and pink-coloured art deco buildings went by in a blur.

Gebre arrived at the Taxi Café first and so Gabriel sent his younger grandson out on to the street to look for Solomon and hurry him up. Gebre was reaching for his phone when he heard a bike brake hard at his back and turned to see his brother, a broad grin on his face.

'Feel this!' Solomon grabbed Gebre's hand and pressed it against his chest. 'Can you feel it?'

'You sweat like a sow, man, let me go.' Gebre was grimacing.

'Do you feel my heart?'

Gebre nodded; of course he could feel it, his brother's heart was pumping like an engine beneath the bright cobalt-blue cycling shirt.

'I did more than forty kilometres this morning; it took me two hours and my heart was never beating faster than this – one hundred beats in a minute. It is the same as Miguel Indurain.'

'Another cyclist?'

'Not *another* cyclist, the *greatest* cyclist. Do not tease me, brother, you know about Indurain.'

Gebre grinned, he knew.

'Tour winner five in a row. I will do what he did, maybe not five but I think I will do it once. I will cycle under the Eiffel Tower, I will stand on the top of the stage, kiss the pretty girls and spray the people with champagne. You believe me, don't you?'

'Of course.'

'I mean, you believe I will do it?'

Gebre saw the flicker of doubt on his brother's face, and smiled broadly. 'I *know* you will do it, brother. If you put your mind to it, you will do it.'

'Yes.' Solomon dropped Gebre's hand and looked across the wide cobbled pavement for a place to chain his bike, somewhere where he would still be able to watch over it from inside the café. His bicycle rarely left his sight; it slept in the same room as the boys, attached to a bracket on the wall above a collage of colourful pictures of their various heroes: footballers and cyclists mainly. 'Where is the old man? Inside already?'

'Yes.'

'Drunk already?'

Gebre shook his head. 'No, he's okay. He is only drinking beer today.'

'He has a hangover then.'

'Maybe. He went to watch the football at the Impero last night. Manchester United versus someone . . . I don't remember who, but he won some money, a big bet I think.'

'Great, maybe he will be in a good mood then? A good mood means more food and not so many stories . . . I am hungry.'

Gebre watched his brother walk the sleek racing bike across the road in the direction of some metal railings. His brother loved Miguel Indurain in part because of his sporting success but also because of his size: the Spaniard was big, like Sol, six feet two

41

and heavy with it – heavy but powerful. Their mother used to joke that Solomon must have queued up twice when God was handing out muscles to his Eritrean children, but because of that he had arrived too late to receive a share of common sense. She would console Gebre with the suggestion that for him, the opposite was true. Gebre tried to remember when their mother had last joked with them like that. A long time ago.

While Solomon un-snaked the long bike lock and fussed with his machine, Gebre glanced idly into the window of the El Dorado Boutique, a clothes shop one door down from the café and owned by the same family. The window display – old-fashioned ladies' shoes, dresses and men's jackets faded by the sun – offered little, except perhaps a rather stark reminder of the hard economic times that Eritrea was enduring. But one item did catch Gebre's eye: a brightly coloured shawl, wrapped loosely round the neck of a pink-skinned mannequin. The shawl was right at the back of the display, out of direct sunlight and the flowers embroidered across the white cotton had held their colour. It was their mother's birthday soon. Gebre doubted whether Solomon had much spare cash but he had a little and if his grandfather spoke to the owner and they clubbed together, then maybe they could afford it. His mother's shawl was ancient and, frankly, so worn that it looked more like an old dishcloth than an item of clothing. She wore it all the time and although it didn't seem to bother her, Gebre felt embarrassed every time he saw her in it.

'Come, let's eat.' Solomon's big hand landed on his brother's shoulder, pulling him back to the present and in the direction of the café and their grandfather.

As the brothers entered the café their grandfather was addressing a young man no older than Gebre, a new member of the waiting staff and so, for Gabriel, a new audience. He was pointing a bony finger in the direction of the Fiat garage.

'I helped to build that building. A garage made in the shape of an aeroplane, wings longer than an aeroplane: unsupported, made from stone but hanging in the air . . . like magic.' He broke off from the tale to greet the boys. 'I will tell you the rest of this story later, you will be amazed. These are my grandsons: Solomon and Gebre.'

The pair nodded a greeting.

'Sit, boys, sit. What will you have? Pisseti yes? And coffee or something else?'

Solomon looked back towards the bar; behind the zinc counter was a tinted mirror flecked with gold. This mirror served the dual purpose of making the room feel larger than it was and of doubling the number of drinks on offer. It was a necessary doubling, the choice was small. They ordered two bottles of orangeade along with a plate of the small pizzas and their grandfather nodded his approval.

'You can always order some more later, you can have everything you like today.' He grinned at Solomon. 'Did Gebre tell you? I won big money on the football.' Gabriel reached into his jacket pocket and pulled out a roll of brown notes secured with a green rubber band and some coins which he deposited on the table. 'Manchester United versus Bournemouth.'

'United won?'

'No!' The old man laughed. 'Thankfully for me – and for you – they lost. I bet my money on Bournemouth. I like to back the underdog sometimes; you don't win that often but when you do win, it feels *very* good.' Gabriel poured an inch of beer into both the boys' water glasses and lifted his own drink. 'Let us drink a toast to the underdogs.' The three of them clinked glasses and drank.

As he put his glass down Gebre caught the eye of a thin, middle-aged man sitting alone at the table behind his grandfather with an empty glass in front of him. The man wore a tired-looking brown suit and, as Gebre watched, he took a notebook and pen from his pocket and started to write.

Gabriel saw the look of concern on his grandson's face and, turning in his seat, he jutted his chin in the direction of the man's notepad. 'We are just chatting about football here, my brother, nothing else. No need for you to be concerned.'

'I don't know what you're talking about, old man.'

'Is that right? Then put the pen and paper back into your pocket.' He turned back to Gebre. 'Grandson, why don't you take some of my money and buy our friend here a beer.'

The man gave a nod of thanks and put his notepad away. He rose and followed Gebre to the bar to make sure that the beer he'd been promised was imported and not the local Suwa beer.

Gabriel turned towards Solomon with his eyebrows raised. 'Even here it happens.'

Solomon nodded. 'Everywhere.'

'Last week I went to try and find your grandmother, up at the graveyard. She was not where I left her – always on the move, that woman. It took me a good long time to find her and when I did I swear to God that there was a fellow at the next grave, listening to every word I said to her. That is how things are in Eritrea now; you can't even talk to your dead without the government listening! No wonder the young leave.' He drained his drink. 'Damn them all. Please cheer me up, big grandson; tell me where you have been cycling today, tell me what you've seen.'

Solomon beamed as he described that morning's cycle ride to his grandfather: all the way from Asmara down to Port Massawa and back again without a stop. The route took him over the mountains, a hard ride but also the one Sol loved best. 'I was moving through the clouds for a mile or more, Grandfather. Coming down the mountain into Massawa you feel like you are flying.'

'I believe you. Maybe I can come with you one of these days; you can put me on the handlebars.'

Solomon grinned. The plate of pizza arrived and he cut one in half and ate hungrily.

'I am still trying to acquire that bike helmet you told me about, Sol, and the shoes too.'

Solomon shook his head. 'Do not worry, I am doing fine with what I have. My latest times are as good as anyone else's – on the track and on the road.'

His grandfather nodded. 'Eat, eat. I need to talk to you about this some more but we will wait for your brother.'

In time Gebre returned with another bottle of beer for his grandfather and the orangeade. 'I'm sorry. That man didn't just want to drink your money, he wanted to justify himself as well.'

Gabriel nodded.

'He says there are reports of illegal meetings here – people who harbour ill will for the government.'

Their grandfather gave a snort of laughter. 'Almost every man and woman walking down the Dekemhare Road fits this description.'

Gebre smiled but lowered his voice. 'I suppose, but you should be careful, Grandfather, he says they are investigating economic crime too. Information about people bringing things over the border . . . stealing from Red Sea Shipping.'

Gabriel gave a shrug. The ruling party owned and ran the Red Sea Shipping Corporation – but not very well, they often lost track of shipments and some of the things they lost ended up in Gabriel's hands. The boys' grandfather glanced back at the man in the brown suit, who was bending the ear of the barman while glugging his second free beer.

'I am not so worried. Remember what I tell you, boys: *when thief robs thief – God laughs.*'

5 Arabs Got Talent

DATELINE: The Seti Hotel, Cairo, Egypt, January 26 2011

It had seemed like a good deal at the time, but now Carver wasn't so sure. Patrick had offered to record all the interviews they needed; in effect, do almost all the work. In return William would swim the twenty lengths his doctor had recommended. Carver had spent the day in bed, sleeping off a hangover – a real humdinger. Now Carver came to think about it, the hangover was partly Patrick's fault. It was Patrick who'd bought the piss-poor Polish vodka and Patrick who'd watched while he drank the whole damn bottle. Now here he was, trunks on underneath his trousers and more or less ready to go; he just needed the other hotel guests to bugger off. Swimming was bad enough without an audience – the idea of being watched as he wandered around half naked and waded into the shallows was unbearable.

At least the pool at the Seti Hotel was decent: thirty metres long and clean, though slightly over-chlorinated in Carver's opinion. It was flanked on both sides by palm and pine trees and when the wind blew, the higher branches swayed and showered pine needles across the water and the surrounding garden. Carver looked at his watch then lay back on the sun lounger and stared upwards; a gust of dry Cairo air moved through the trees displacing a handful of needles, which dropped, bouncing off the roof of his sun umbrella. The sound reminded him of light English rain and he let his mind wander.

They'd been schlepping around North Africa for a month now, working seventeen- and eighteen-hour days with barely time to stop or think. The Seti was the first decent place they'd stayed in, or rather the first decent place *he'd* stayed in. Patrick was staying elsewhere – in a crappy little hotel down in the centre with nothing to recommend it other than it overlooked Tahrir Square. He felt a little guilty about this arrangement but he'd won the coin toss fair and square and Patrick didn't seem to mind. Carver had been bitten to hell by bed bugs in Tunis and got food poisoning for breakfast in Casablanca; maybe he deserved a little feather bedding? A gentle breeze ruffled the swimming pool; most of the other hotel guests had packed up for the day but there was still a group of women, Russian he thought, sitting down in the shallows, chatting and swinging their feet in the water. They talked loudly and with the confidence that comes from knowing that few others can understand your conversation. Carver stared at them in the hope that this might encourage them to leave; it didn't – they glared back.

The double doors opened with a loud creak and Patrick stepped somewhat gingerly on to the balcony; the wrought ironwork was rusted to green and broken in places but the grey cement floor seemed solid enough. His room at the Royal View was a poky little single at the top of the building with a bare light bulb and the narrowest of beds, but it had a clear view of Tahrir Square and that outweighed all the disadvantages. The plan had been that one of them stay here – with a box seat on what might soon be the biggest story in the world – while the other took a room up the road at the Seti, where they had proper comms: a reliable power supply, Wi-Fi, working telephones and so on. At first Carver had argued that *he* should take the room at the Royal View but Patrick suggested they toss for it, with whoever called the coin correctly getting the more comfortable option. Patrick tossed the coin and when it landed in his favour lied about the outcome. Carver had had a hard time of it in Tunisia and Morocco, he was run down and Patrick thought the rest would do him good. What's more there was a swimming pool at the Seti Hotel and therefore a chance that William might do some exercise. Exercise that had been recommended in the *strongest possible terms* in the doctor's note that Patrick had found stuffed down at the bottom of Carver's plastic bag.

He gazed down at Tahrir Square. A steady stream of people had arrived through the day and a fair chunk of the square – the equivalent of a football pitch in size or slightly bigger, now belonged to the protesters. Patrick smiled as he remembered the recent lecture he'd had from his colleague about using football pitches as a unit of measurement. Patrick had suggested that William might be using it too often.

'*People know how big a bloody football pitch is. You want me to say one hundred and twenty yards by seventy yards?*'

He went on to catalogue the comparisons that were and weren't acceptable as far as he was concerned. Twice the size of a double-decker bus was fine; half the height of Nelson's Column was okay. Using Wales as a standard unit of measurement was not. Patrick had noticed that Wales was now used to measure everything from forest fires to American states to oil slicks and Carver was against it. '*All it tells you is that something is quite big.*'

'*Better to say half a million football pitches?*'

'*Wales is as big as two million football pitches. I checked.*'

Inside the protesters' football-pitch-sized space, tents were being erected and larger makeshift structures built from planks of wood and tarpaulin: they were settling in. Patrick reached for his phone and checked the Twitter feed belonging to Tsquare Lawan, the activist whose posts he'd started following. Dozens of people were posting about the protests but a lot of it was rubbish. Patrick had grown to like Lawan; the information he put out was clear and reliable, and the odd tweet could even raise a smile. Patrick scrolled through to find the most recent posts. He'd grown used to Lawan's habit of posting first in Arabic and then a few moments later in basic but competent English. Sure enough:

@tsquarelawan
> Fellow Egyptians watching Arabs Got Talent . . .
> there's a better show: Tunisia Got Freedom! Watch
> that!

@tsquarelawan
> At school we learn that history is made by powerful
> men or economic forces but . . .

@tsquarelawan
> . . . sometimes it changes because a few thousand
> people can hold on to a square . . . come!

Patrick smiled and gazed down at the square; most likely Lawan was in there somewhere. A couple of bonfires were going now and a string of caged light bulbs marked the perimeter of the protesters' camp. The scene reminded Patrick of Marrakech and the Djema el-Fna market. He'd been there with Rebecca – their first foreign holiday together – and more recently with Carver. The second visit had been significantly more stressful and a good deal less romantic than the first. Patrick made a tally of the last month: four different countries, eight different cities, a dozen flights at least.

They'd started in Tunisia covering the story of a young

street-seller called Mohamed Bouazizi who had set fire to himself in protest at police harassment and political corruption. Bouazizi ran a fruit and vegetable cart and had worked hard for years, supporting his own family from the age of eight as well as giving any spare food he had to people even poorer than himself. His self-immolation had triggered a wave of popular dissent and Carver and Patrick arrived in Tunisia in time to report on the early stages of that protest. William had hoped that he might get a chance to interview Bouazizi and they camped out at the hospital for a few days. When the kid died, Carver and Patrick produced obituary pieces for any outlet that would take them: local radio, national radio and the World Service. The protests grew, as did interest in the story and the Tunisian President ended up fleeing to Saudi Arabia, washing up in Jeddah, the same city where the Saudis had sheltered Idi Amin. Carver and Patrick covered it all and after Tunisia travelled on first to Yemen and then Morocco before Carver decided that Egypt was where the real battle would take place.

The larger part of Tahrir Square that wasn't under occupation remained open to traffic, and volunteers were directing vehicles at several intersections but with mixed success. From where Patrick stood it looked more like a banger race than a working roundabout. No one seemed sure who had right of way. A taxi had stopped in the middle of the road and the driver was making a half-hearted attempt to untwist his car bonnet, which had been dented and distended in a collision with a city bus. The bus had stopped as well and a hastily convened jury, made up of passengers, pedestrians and some of the young demonstrators, was being asked to pass judgement on the crash. Eventually, after much shouting and by majority decision, they agreed that the bus driver should give the cabbie a few notes. This done, the jury turned their attention to the broken car. Using hands and elbows they wrestled the metal back into a shape such that the bonnet would stay shut, at least until the driver could reach a garage.

As the taxi drove off, everyone went on their way and Patrick was left feeling rather impressed that the whole incident had been handled without any police involvement. There *were* police in the square but they were gathered in groups at the main entrances to Tahrir, sitting slumped in coaches resting and readying themselves for whatever the next day might bring. As he'd moved around the city centre that day, collecting material so Carver could rest, Patrick had a feeling that the regime and the protesters were drawing breath, preparing themselves for the next encounter, an encounter that both sides expected to be definitive.

Patrick pulled the doors shut and stepped back inside. He gathered his recording equipment together, checked his rucksack, closed his bedroom door and rode the antique Schindler elevator with its caged doors back down to the lobby. The walk from his hotel to Carver's had been taking him around twenty-five minutes. He bet himself he could do it in twenty, glanced at his watch and set off.

Carver shaded his eyes and stared at the pool – shining that bright particular blue in the low evening sun. The only person doing any actual swimming belonged to the Russian women: a dark-haired girl, three or four years old, who was bobbing about in the deep end, close to Carver, her round face sandwiched in between two inflatable pink armbands. The girl was staring at him and when he nodded back, the look of concentration and twist of the mouth that he received in return made him grateful for the extra chlorine. Carver wagged his finger at the kid and immediately felt the Russian women's attention turn again in his direction; there was another loud exchange of opinion before the girl's mother grudgingly left her sun lounger. She made some minor adjustments to her metallic gold bikini before striding up the side of the pool. Bending low, the woman grabbed hold of an armband and dragged her daughter back towards the shallows.

Carver called after her. '*Spasibo.*'

On hearing this, the woman let go of the armband, turned back and spat one of the few Russian phrases Carver was familiar with plus an unnecessary English translation. He shrugged and turned his attention to the wooden hut with the palm-frond roof that served as the Seti's poolside bar. He wanted a drink but knew that even one bottle of the crappy local beer would put paid to any swimming. And he'd promised Patrick that he'd swim.

The sun lounger Carver had chosen was situated close enough to the bar that he could hear the conversation taking place but not so near that he risked being drawn into it. The half a dozen men and women at the bar belonged to *his* tribe: foreign correspondents working for a range of international papers, radio and television networks. He tuned his ear and caught a mixed bag of accents: American, French and an Antipodean voice that he thought he recognised; he turned and took a look but the woman had her back to him and was wearing a headscarf. His fellow hacks were discussing a Muslim Brotherhood meeting they'd heard was taking place, a key meeting. They all knew it was happening but none of them knew when or where. Carver cleaned his glasses on his shirt-tail and glanced around the gardens. Zahra should be on shift by now; she'd know where the meeting was or, if she didn't, she'd be able to find out.

The sun had left the pool now and the Russian women were on their way too. Carver stood, pulled his white shirt over his head, dropped his glasses on top along with his watch and shuffled out of his trousers. Twenty lengths – he could manage that. Then a beer.

There were several aspects of Cairo's complicated geography that confused Patrick. Top of the list were the pedestrian passageways: narrow alleys that ran in between and sometimes right through the middle of buildings. They were so narrow that it was almost impossible for two people to cross without touching. Emerging from one of these – a clever shortcut, or so he hoped – Patrick stopped. He found himself standing next to a building site; workmen were pouring porridge-coloured concrete into the foundations of another new building. He crossed the road heading away from the commercial centre and into a more residential neighbourhood. The stench of diesel and rotting vegetables was temporarily absent. In its place, wood smoke, grilled meat and garlic. The locals were preparing their evening meals. The stretch of street he was on, with its thick, dark wooden doors and fractured pavement, seemed vaguely familiar but he decided to check the tatty tourist map that Carver had given him anyway.

Standing in the road, turning the map in his hands, Patrick became aware of a noise, louder than Cairo's usual cacophony of car horns, street-sellers and construction work. The tumult – close and getting closer – had a different and more urgent tone to it. A march or demonstration of some sort, and, after a quiet day with little new to report, a stroke of luck. He stuffed the map into his pocket, took his recording machine from his rucksack and waited in a nearby doorway, holding the machine and its large foam-headed microphone out in front of him with both hands.

He didn't have to wait long; the first indication of what was about to arrive came in the form of a muffled pop: a tear gas canister being fired into the air and then the roar of a crowd – more excited than scared. He looked down at the digital recorder: the levels were dancing around wildly from green to red; he tweaked a dial and hoped that the device had captured both the *fump* of the tear gas and the crowd's cheer. Patrick was considering whether to risk checking the recording when, from the top of the street, a ragged group of young people came running, shouting as they ran, tearing down the centre of the road. Several were wearing the football shirts of their local Cairo team; others were dressed in a more practical outfit of thick jackets and scarves.

They wore the jackets to protect against baton blows from the police and the scarves to combat tear gas. Patrick smelled the sharp stink of the gas on the clothes of the people streaming past him. He put the tape recorder in his jacket pocket and one hand over his mouth while keeping a firm grip on the microphone with the other.

The demonstrators shouted as they ran, throwing their words up in the direction of local residents, who were watching wide-eyed from their balconies: '*Enzel! Enzel!*' Come down! Join us! Patrick looked up too and saw a growing number of people emerging from inside their apartments to take a look, some moving pot plants or taking their washing down from the line so they could get a better view. The demonstrators shouted louder, urging their fellow Cairenes to leave their cramped homes and join them in Tahrir Square. Patrick counted sixty or seventy protesters, none any older than himself and most of them significantly younger: teenagers. He saw Egyptian and Tunisian flags being worn as capes or waved in tribute or for inspiration.

He recognised one face, a woman with coal-black hair and green eyes who he'd seen working behind the reception at Carver's hotel. William had mentioned her but Patrick couldn't remember her name. As she sprinted by, the woman glanced at him, smiled and slowed her run; she recognised him too and something about Patrick seemed to amuse her. For a moment he thought she was going to stop and speak but her friend, a short-haired girl in a leather jacket running a few paces behind, caught up, placed a hand on her shoulder and urged her on. The boyish-looking young woman had a mobile phone in her hand and was texting as she ran; she wore a rucksack like Patrick's.

The mob moved on together down the street, their shouting growing louder: '*Enzel! Ghadan!*' *Ghadan* was one of the other Arabic words that Patrick had learned in recent weeks. He had made a list of these words in the back of his black notebook for ready reference. When he read the list it seemed to Patrick that the words had a certain style to them: *ghadan* meant 'tomorrow', *thawra* meant 'revolution', *kifaya* as he already knew meant 'enough'. A lexicon of revolution.

Carver wrapped a towel around his pink, pale freckled shoulders and lay back on the sun lounger, gulping air. The swim had taken it out of him. He retrieved his gold-framed glasses from the pile of discarded clothes and stared upwards. It was getting dark and the trees in the hotel garden had lost their colour; they looked like black cut-outs against the blue night sky. He had the gardens almost to himself: the bar had shut for the night and the skinny lifeguard was clearing up around the pool. He watched as the kid attempted to waltz a reluctant sun umbrella across the floor and under cover for the night. As he set it down, the heavy concrete base caught the boy's bare big toe; he uttered an oath and Carver looked away. When he looked back he saw that someone was offering to help the lifeguard and it took him a moment to recognise that this someone was Zahra, dressed strangely, in a thick puffer jacket and scarf. Carver sat up and waved her over but she shook her head, lifting a hand to indicate that they could talk in five minutes. William nodded.

6 Zahra

DATELINE: The Seti Hotel, Cairo, Egypt, January 26 2011

The Seti Hotel and its manager, Mr Akar, relied heavily on Zahra Moussa. Her job seemed to involve everything from running the reception desk to serving dinner and Carver was sure she was over-qualified for all of it. Zahra had checked him in on the day he'd arrived, and then a few minutes later brought his luggage to the room herself, to the Englishman's significant embarrassment. She took the crumpled notes that Carver offered as a tip but then seemed to loiter. When a confused Carver offered her some more tip money she shook her head.

'*What place in England are you from?*'

'*London.*'

'*I have been to London. Trafalgar Square.*'

This was said with such pride that Carver found himself saying how interesting the square was – so much history, the fourth plinth etc. etc. – in spite of the fact that he loathed the place, avoided it at all costs and thought the plinth was a scandalous waste of public money. She matched him enthusiasm for enthusiasm and when he said he was a journalist, delivered the first piece of useful information he'd received since arriving in Cairo. Zahra told him that the head of Egyptian intelligence was going to make a statement later that evening, that it had just been announced.

Carver decided to test her further, asking if she could draw him a map showing him the best way to get from the Seti Hotel to the Royal View where his colleague was staying. She'd taken the pen and paper from Carver's bedside table and drawn him a map. Her knowledge of the city and the quality of her English – top of her class at school and then a summer scholarship to an English language school on the Kent coast, she told him – convinced Carver that instead of employing the fixer that London had recommended he'd try and persuade this woman to do the odd bit of translation work and provide the local expertise he needed. He rarely used BBC fixers anyway, preferring to find someone local who would work *only* for him. Zahra Moussa might fit that bill.

Carver made the offer the following morning, while reception was quiet and her manager was elsewhere. He promised decent pay and flexible hours that could fit in around her commitments at the hotel. Zahra accepted immediately, her only condition being that no one else at the Seti, neither guest nor staff – and in particular Mr Akar – should know about the arrangement. This suited Carver just fine and they shook hands on it.

While he waited for Zahra and her colleague to finish clearing up around the pool, Carver dressed and checked the contents of his plastic bag. The bag rarely left his side; it contained his MiniDisc recorder, a reporter's notebook and several pens.

It was dark now and the mock-Parisian streetlights around the hotel garden were flickering into life, the air was cool. He wondered whether they might be better off inside the hotel, in the warm, but swiftly dismissed the idea. Better to stay out here, away from Mr Akar and from other sharp-eyed hacks. The Muslim Brotherhood meeting was important, potentially decisive and a significant scoop if he and Patrick were the only ones to find out about it. Carver felt a little guilty for missing a whole day's work and figured that finding out about the Brotherhood's plans might go some way to making up for that.

For all the talk of the Arab Spring being a Facebook or Twitter revolution organised by a bunch of kids with smartphones – an idea that Carver was deeply suspicious of – the Muslim Brotherhood was still key. The younger generation could start something – they had started something – but they wouldn't be able to finish it. For that they would need the Brotherhood. The Brothers had the brawn and the numbers.

He dried his thinning hair with the towel and folded his arms against the chill. A bat dropped from one of the palm trees and swept low across the swimming pool. Carver thought he heard its call – a high-pitched piping sound, two beats long. After she'd finished clearing the sun umbrellas and the gawky lifeguard had sloped inside to help serve dinner, Zahra walked the long way round the pool and over to where William sat.

'Hello.' She sat down on the lounger opposite his. 'Are you not cold?'

Carver looked at her. What light there was left in the darkening garden seemed concentrated on Zahra's open face. Her green eyes were bright, her dark hair shone. Carver looked away.

'I'm fine.' He pushed his glasses up his nose. 'So, listen, I need to find out about this Muslim Brotherhood meeting everyone's talking about. Have you heard anything?'

'Of course, they decide whether they will support Friday's protest. It is an important meeting.'

'Right, and d'you know when it's happening – when and where?'

'People think it will be at the Mosque of the Servants of the Compassionate, near El Hossein Square. But I don't know when; sometime tomorrow or, if not, then the next day. When I find out, I can tell you.'

Carver nodded. He took a pen and the spiral-bound notepad from his plastic bag and handed them to her. 'Write down the name of the mosque, will you?'

Zahra wrote the name and address in careful capitals.

As she handed the notepad back Carver noticed an acrid smell, a whiff of something from the folds of her clothes and scarf. He recognised it straight away. 'You stink of tear gas; where've you been? A demo?'

'A small one only.'

Zahra lowered her voice and told Carver about the demonstration, organised at short notice by a friend of hers and designed to annoy the Egyptian police and encourage more people to get involved ahead of the next big protest. They'd gathered outside a nearby government building with a few handmade placards and despite only a hundred or so people turning up – mainly students – the police had arrived quickly and in force.

'When they started to fire the tear gas, we ran.'

'Good idea. Running is always a good idea. Running away is the first thing they teach you on the riot training course.'

Zahra pulled her sunbed closer to Carver. 'You have been taught *riot training*? What else do they teach you?'

Carver stared at Zahra, the trace of a smile on his face. 'I'm not sure I should tell you; the training's meant to help journalists *report* a riot, not demonstrators *start* one.'

'You can tell me – information in return for information. You tell me this and you do not have to pay me for the details of the Brotherhood meeting.'

He dropped the notepad back into his bag. 'Fair enough.' He knew that Zahra had been sympathetic towards the pro-democracy protesters for a while, but it seemed to him that she'd been attending more meetings since he'd asked her to work for him. He felt increasingly responsible for her safety. 'Let me see what I can remember. The obvious stuff: don't get hit by the grenade, stay clear of the container that spews out the gas, don't try and pick them up or throw them back, they're hot.'

Zahra nodded.

'What else was there? Get yourself upwind if you can, away from where the gas is coming from. Buy yourself a gas mask, of course, if that's possible?'

She shook her head. 'It is impossible; anywhere in Cairo that sold them is stopped. People have been arrested for even asking shopkeepers about a gas mask.'

Carver remembered being advised to wear a bandana or scarf soaked in lemon juice or vinegar in the absence of a gas mask but he got the impression that this was not new information as far as Zahra was concerned.

'Or get yourself some swimming goggles. I saw some of that in Tunisia and years back in Seattle.'

Zahra leaned forward, she found this advice more interesting.

'And if you've got nothing else, no protection, then just try and breathe the air inside your shirt until you can get clear. How's your breathing now?'

Zahra took a deep breath in through her nose, flaring her nostrils, before exhaling through her mouth. 'It is okay.'

'Good.' Carver hesitated. 'If you start getting wheezy, let me know, I've got inhalers. You know? Puffers?' He put a hand to his mouth and mimed the motion.

'I know what this is. They give you these for riots?'

Carver shook his head. 'Not for riots, for asthma. And for being . . . you know . . .'

'Old?'

'Middle-aged.'

Zahra smiled, checked the time on her phone and stood. 'Your friend was at the demonstration . . . Patrick?'

'Was he? That's good news. Did he have his Marantz? I mean did it look like he was working . . . recording?'

'Yes. He was standing against a wall, hiding. Holding his micro-phone up like this . . .' Zahra mimicked Patrick's stance. 'He looked funny, like a little boy with an ice cream.' She glanced back in the direction of the hotel. 'I should go and get ready.'

'Sure. You're doing the dinner shift?'

'Dinner shift and night shift, I am helping Mr Akar out. He is very short of staff.'

Carver watched her walk back across the garden in the direction of the brightly lit hotel. He'd wait a few minutes before making his own way back. Just then something caught his eye – a move-ment, three or four floors up inside the main hotel. A figure, standing silhouetted in a lit window and looking their way, but when he looked again the figure was gone. Most likely one of the maids, turning down the room.

He got out his phone and texted Patrick. He told him he'd heard that his producer had gathered some new audio. He suggested they put the piece together in his room.

'I'll get us some room service. My treat. No vodka necessary.' He pressed send and then a thought occurred. 'PS: I did the bloody twenty lengths so no nagging necessary either.'

7 Firebrands

DATELINE: The Taxi Café, Asmara, Eritrea, January 26 2011

Gabriel twisted the top off his fresh bottle of beer and filled his glass. He stared at his grandsons, a more serious look clouding his old face.

'While I have you both together, before I forget, I need to talk about something.'

The boys put their drinks down and focused on their grandfather.

'I saw your mother today, she came to find me. She was upset . . . worried.'

Solomon could guess what was coming; he continued to eat, leaving Gebre to do the talking.

'Worried about what?'

'About you two of course, about her boys.' The old man shuffled awkwardly in his seat. 'But mainly, Sol, she worries about you.'

'Why? What have I done now?'

Gabriel turned the thick brown beer bottle in both hands and sighed. This was familiar if uncomfortable ground for all three of them. In the absence of a father figure, the boy's mother would call on Gabriel when she had concerns. More often than not, her concerns centred on her elder son. For almost ten years now, Gabriel had been trying to play the part of father and grandfather; he used to tell himself that it would get easier as the boys got older, but in fact it got harder.

'It is your cycling. She worries that if you are selected for the team, if you travel outside the country, you will not come back. She read a report in the newspaper about the Red Sea Camels, the footballers who asked for asylum in Botswana.'

Solomon sucked at his teeth. 'First she hates the cycling because she thinks it is not serious – a waste of time she called it. Now she thinks it is too serious.'

'She is your mother, it is her job to worry.'

'It should be her job to support me, to help me and Gebre, but she will not do that. If I am selected for the cycling team and they travel, then I will go. I have to.'

'I understand, that is good. It's just . . .'

'And whether I come back or not will be up to me. Half of the young people in the country are leaving, or trying to.'

His grandfather glanced back over his shoulder.

'Would either of you blame me if I did the same?'

The restaurant was busier now and Gabriel doubted that anyone other than he and Gebre had heard Solomon's words, but nevertheless he pulled his chair tight to the table and whispered his response. 'This is foolish talk, son, dangerous talk.'

'I'm not your son.'

'I know, but—'

'But nothing, I am not your son, you are not my father, you cannot tell me what to do.' Solomon pushed his chair back; it scraped noisily against the floor and now other people *were* paying attention. The man at the bar had turned and was looking their way.

Gabriel leaned towards Solomon and lowered his voice. 'Please, Sol. Stay and finish your food.'

But Solomon's pride was more powerful than his hunger; he stood up and glared down at the pair. 'No. I have more practice that I need to do.' He waved a hand in the direction of his brother. 'Gebre will stay.'

Solomon and Gebre's father had been gone for nearly ten years now. Missing, but not yet presumed dead, at least not by the boys' mother who continued to hope and pray for his return. She was helped in that respect by the cruel unpredictability and general air of mystery that surrounded the Eritrean judicial system. The husband of one of her cousins, together with his friend, had been hauled off the street by the army in a similar manner to her own husband. Both men had eventually returned, much diminished but alive, several years later. These sorts of stories were common, so who was to say that the same might not happen in her case?

Daniel Hassen had fought with honour during the Eritrean war of independence but his reward for that service had been small. He quickly became disillusioned with the politicians who put themselves forward to lead the newly independent Eritrea and made no secret of his dissatisfaction. Solomon remembered his grandfather's attempt to explain the reasons for Daniel Hassen's regular run-ins with the authorities.

'Your father is a firebrand. Dictators needs firebrands for a time and then, later, they need yes-men. Your father never said *yes* to any man if the word in his head was *no*.' The first three times they arrested his son, Gabriel somehow managed to arrange a release. The fourth time he could not, despite pulling every string he knew and practically setting up camp outside the Justice Ministry.

Losing his son to the system took a toll on old Gabriel and an even heavier toll on the boys' mother. Every time that Solomon or Gebre walked into the house and their mother looked up from whatever it was she was doing – it was disappointment they saw. Disappointment before love. Solomon had it worst. The bigger he became, the more he came to resemble his father: strong in the shoulders, stern in the face. The likeness was so great that it often took his mother a second or two to realise that it was her elder son she was looking at and not her husband.

'No, Mother, I am still not *him*. I am just me.' It was devastating for both of them and every time it happened his mother would cry – with shame and from grief. She would go to her room and stay there for as long as it took Gebre to coax her back.

Back in the Taxi Café, Gebre and his grandfather sat in silence, the boy picking at his pizza. After a while the old man raised a hand and called the young waiter over.

'One more orangeade for my grandson and I think I will have a glass of araki now.'

Gebre gave his grandfather a look of concern, which the old man ignored.

The drinks arrived and Gabriel took a gulp of the spirit, the aniseed taste making him wince. 'I believe your brother is probably right, he is a full-grown man – his affairs are none of my business.'

'He didn't mean to be rude, he is just frustrated.'

Gabriel nodded. 'Does he talk a lot about leaving?'

'We both do, but it is more urgent for Sol. If the cycling team do not take him then next school term he'll be sent to Sawa.'

Gabriel nodded; the Sawa military camp was where almost all Eritrean youngsters were sent in their last year of school. The camp was nearly two hundred miles north of the capital and a byword for hard living and hard luck. Depending on how you did there, how you had performed at school or how well connected your family was, you were either assigned a job back in Asmara or conscripted directly into the army for an unspecified period of time.

'Everyone has to spend some time at Sawa, it is inevitable. I am sure I will be able to help with travel permits, medical leave, things like that.'

Gebre shook his head. 'Sol is not very good at keeping his head down and doing what he's told. Sawa will not suit him, and he knows that. You know it too.'

Gabriel nodded. 'Do you think the cycling team will select him?'

'They have to. His times are easily the best, he works harder than anyone else.' Gebre stared at the old man, who seemed unconvinced. 'But if they don't then he will find another way out.' He paused. 'I have said that I will go with him.'

'How?'

'We could do what others do and walk to the refugee camps in Ethiopia or Sudan. Or find someone to take us north.'

The frown on Gabriel's brow deepened. He had heard stories of young men and women being shot at by their own army as they tried to run over the border into Ethiopia. Some were killed outright, others were badly injured. The lucky ones made it to the refugee camps; the unlucky were eaten by hyenas. As for paying a trafficker to drive you north across the Sahara? He knew the sort of men who organised those trips. Gabriel finished his araki with one swallow and called for another.

'Maybe it will not be necessary, my grandson. Things can change – quickly sometimes – all empires fall, even the strongest. History shows us this: the Greeks, Imperial Rome and fascist Rome.' The old man laughed. 'Manchester United, nothing lasts for ever.' He jutted his chin back in the direction of the gaunt-looking spy, sitting at the bar. 'Not even our current, glorious leader . . . not even he can go on for ever.' His voice was louder now and Gebre was growing nervous. 'Where's my drink?' He looked round and saw that most of the bar was looking his way. Gabriel sighed and turned back towards his grandson. 'You should leave me now, Gebre. The spirit has loosened my tongue . . .' He waved his empty glass in the direction of the thin man at the bar. 'And I'll be damned if I buy that bastard spy another drink. Where is that new waiter? I promised him I would tell him about the Fiat Tagliero.'

8 The Story of the Ship

DATELINE: Old Kent Road, London SE11, January 27 2011

'Have you seen the almond milk?'

Rob looked up from his breakfast, a frown on his face. 'Was it in a green carton?'

'Yes. Did you drink it?'

'I threw it away, I didn't know it was almond milk – I thought it was sour milk.'

Lindy took the regular milk from the fridge and slammed the door shut. 'You've only been watching me drink almond milk for the last two years.'

'I'm sorry, I'll get you some more. I thought it was off, I was thinking of the baby really. Didn't want you drinking something dodgy.'

Lindy's hand went instinctively to her stomach. 'Have you got that list of stuff I need you to get?'

Mariscal smiled and patted reassuringly at his trouser pocket; the list wasn't in there but he was pretty sure he remembered where he'd left it.

'Anti-stretch cream, more of those vitamins: Vitachild, was it?'

Lindy nodded. 'And my baby magazines.'

Rob pulled a face.

'Please – my friends say they're really helpful.'

'Five quid a pop they'd have to be.'

'Don't start.'

Rob finished the last of his coffee, pushed his chair from the table, and dropped his plate and cutlery in the sink.

'I know I go on about it, but five quid? You can *buy* a baby for that.'

'Rubbish.'

'You can.'

'Where?'

'Ethiopia.'

'Don't be an arse.'

Rob took a crumpled packet of cigarettes from his pocket and counted how many he had left.

'You can, I was offered one. It was a few years back but the point stands. I was offered a baby. It was a good baby too – not one of those fat-stomached starving ones.'

'You're an idiot.'

Rob shrugged and took a look at his watch; he was late. He hurried around the flat, gathering together his briefcase, Lindy's shopping list and the thick lever arch file that the permanent secretary had asked him to read. They were due to talk about it at their routine meeting that morning. As he paced up and down the Old Kent Road, looking for his cab, Rob recalled the Ethiopian woman who had offered him her baby: her name was Miracle and she didn't want money, she just wanted him to take her son. It was a long time ago but he remembered how tempted he'd been and tried to remember why he'd felt that way. The thought of doing something good, he guessed. Something unquestionably good.

*

The permanent secretary had held firm against the fashion for open-plan offices. Other people might be happy working that way, his own staff might be forced to work that way but he would not. Rob rapped on the dark wood door and waited. Nothing. The gold lettering spelling out Leslie Craig's name had a good gleam on it, recently polished – possibly by Craig himself. Rob knocked again.

'Enter.'

Mariscal did as instructed. Inside the door there was an umbrella stand stuffed with half a dozen oversized golfing umbrellas and next to that a green foldaway bike, gathering dust.

'Robert. How are you?'

'Very well, thank you, Permanent Secretary.'

'Good, good.' The civil servant glanced at Rob before turning his papers over and rising from his seat. He strode over to the wooden coat rack in the corner and took down a long black mackintosh.

Mariscal stepped to one side. 'Sorry, maybe I misunderstood? I'm here for our routine meeting; did you cancel?'

'No, I didn't cancel, I'm looking forward to it. However I thought we might relocate. I missed my morning constitutional so I thought we might walk and talk. Kill two birds with one stone as it were.'

Mariscal smiled. 'Two birds? That shouldn't be a problem.' Rob waved the file in the civil servant's direction. 'According to this, we spent seventy million quid on ordnance last year.'

'Very droll.' Craig's Belfast accent seemed particularly thick this morning. 'I suggest you bring an umbrella, the forecast says rain.'

Mariscal selected the most normal, least golfy umbrella he could find and followed Craig out the door. They walked side by side through the building, the permanent secretary half a pace ahead of Rob and moving quickly for a man of his bulk. As they progressed through the offices and along the corridors, heads turned. Leslie Craig kept himself to himself; he arrived at work before most of his staff and left well after – a sighting was rare. Several of his employees attempted a greeting but the permanent secretary was moving too quickly for anyone to land a successful *Good morning*. Mariscal nodded to a few people, including Craig's deputy, who observed the pair with interest. The permanent secretary didn't utter a word until he and Rob were through security and outside the building and even then it was small talk – bordering on the banal.

At the corner Craig stopped to retie a shoelace; he wore a pair of stout brown brogues. Mariscal stared at the shoes, polished to a shine and shade that reminded Rob of a freshly fallen conker. This done, Craig stood and stared at Mariscal. 'Good to be out and about, is it not? Fresh air, touch of scenery?'

Rob nodded. As far as he was concerned it was a terrible waste to be outside and not smoking but he knew Craig would not approve. They carried on walking and not really talking until they reached the next corner.

'Here we are – Queen Mary's Steps. She had Sir Christopher Wren design these for her you know?'

Rob nodded. He knew.

'And underneath all this, buried deep beneath, do you know what's there?'

Mariscal knew this too but, not wanting to spoil the permanent secretary's story, he shook his head.

'King Henry the Eighth's Whitehall Palace. His Whitehall pad! How about that?'

'Incredible. It's a fair bit of history we're stepping on here then?'

'No doubt about it.' Craig was heading for a well-situated bench, looking out on to a row of thick-trunked plane trees and beyond that the river.

'Is this a favourite view of yours then, Permanent Secretary?'

'Not really.'

'You prefer your view of Horse Guards?'

'Not too bothered about that one either. The best view of London – in my opinion – is to be had in the rear-view mirror of a fast-moving motor car.' He turned and stared at Rob. 'The sort of panorama I prefer lies elsewhere. Have you ever heard of Kinbane Head?'

'No.'

'Good. The fewer people know about it the better.'

The pair propped their brollies against the bench and sat. The air was thick with unfallen rain – soon it would come, but not yet. Rob put the file down, a boxy grey bridge between the two men.

Craig glanced at it. 'So, you read it?'

'Of course.' Rob had read it first page to last. The thick lever arch file – filled with the names of defence projects, manufacturer details, dates and eye-wateringly large numbers – a file that he'd fully expected to ruin his evening, had instead turned out to be quite a page-turner. At first he thought the nostalgic pleasure he was getting from removing interesting-looking pages and arranging them on the sitting room floor was because it reminded him of his student days, of university. It was the early hours of the morning before he realised that what his increasingly obsessive behaviour was reminding him of wasn't college – he'd never worked that hard at college. What it reminded him of was journalism. 'I read it all. Cover to cover.'

'Good man. And?'

Rob shrugged. 'I guess the headline is we're broke; we've got overspend on our overspend. I think the Department of Health is going to have to close a few more hospitals to make up the shortfall.'

Craig gave a thin smile; his general policy was to acknowledge Rob's humour without actively encouraging it. 'Very funny.'

'Thanks. Anyway, we're overspent.'

'That's true.'

Rob hesitated. 'And that's obviously before you take into account the next round of budget cuts.'

'Obviously.'

'Twenty per cent is what people say the Treasury will go for.' Rob glanced at his boss, who remained stony-faced. 'That's just a rumour of course.'

Craig shook his head slowly. 'It's an accurate rumour. Twenty per cent is exactly what the Treasury will ask for.'

'I see.'

The permanent secretary sighed. The pair sat in silence for a time; the clouds above the Thames were unmoving, their colour darkening with every second that passed.

'It's been the story of my working life: bashing heads with those bean counters at the Treasury.' Craig picked up the file and turned a few pages. 'I sometimes wonder which of the great departments of state has done the *most* damage to this country over the past hundred years.'

Rob gave an encouraging nod.

'Most of the time I reach the conclusion that it's a dead heat between the Treasury and the Foreign Office.'

Rob grinned.

'The main problem with the Treasury is their timeframe, they can only think in financial years; they never see any further than the following April.' Craig closed the file and steepled his hands on top.

Rob shrugged. 'Yeah, but I guess it's like this every year, isn't it? Twenty per cent is just their opening bid. They want a finger, so they ask for an arm. Like any negotiation.'

'That's true,' Craig acknowledged. 'Very true. But there are a few cuts I'm not willing to countenance.' He looked down at his folded hands and wiggled a thumb. 'Some fingers I am particularly keen to keep.'

'Of course.'

'So . . .' Craig turned and met Rob's eye. 'Imagine you were a journalist reading this.'

Mariscal bristled slightly. 'I *am* a journalist reading this. I mean I was, until recently.'

'Apologies, of course. So while you were reading this document –with your journalistic eye – what jumped out? Bearing in mind what the Treasury agenda is, where are we most vulnerable?'

Rob pulled himself a little straighter. 'Well, obviously the bigger ticket items stick out – the stuff that costs billions rather than millions' – his boss nodded – 'so it's the carriers, the aircraft carrier project. If it's twenty per cent the Treasury are after then that's where they'll look.'

Craig smiled. 'I thought that was what you'd say. I feared so anyway. Of course you're right, they'll start sniffing around the aircraft carriers and they'll encourage their friends in the media to do the same. Perhaps they've already started?' Craig gave Rob a questioning look.

'I've heard rumours.'

'Right. So that is where they will push and I will need you to push back, Robert.'

'Push back how, Permanent Secretary?'

'I need you to tell people one of your stories. Your most persuasive story yet: *The story of the ship!*'

He delivered this line with such bombast that Mariscal had to work hard to hold his face straight. 'The story of the ship?'

'That's it. We need to remind people of England's proud history as a sea-faring nation, how no Englishman lives more than forty miles from open water – all that buccaneering stuff: Trafalgar, Admiral Nelson, HMS *Pinafore* . . .'

'"The Owl and the Pussycat"?'

Craig gave Rob a sideways look. 'If it helps persuade the great British public that we need aircraft carriers, then yes.' Craig stood; he looked around on the off-chance that anyone else might be foolhardy enough to be taking the air on such a miserable day. No one was, but he lowered his voice anyway. 'We need a story so powerful that those tooth-combers at the Treasury will be forced to leave the carriers alone and look elsewhere. Do you understand?'

Rob looked past Craig and out across the dirty brown Thames. 'I'm sure I can come up with something.'

'I'm sure you can too.'

Mariscal paused, and then tried his luck. 'Why?'

'Why what?'

'Why is it so important to protect the aircraft carriers?'

Craig met Mariscal's eye. 'They're crucial to the defence of this nation. We don't want China seizing Neptune's trident, do we?' Craig was smiling as he said this but he could see that Rob was unconvinced. 'There are other reasons too and there might well come a time when I need for you to know them. But not now.' He glanced up at the sky. 'It's going to rain. You should get back inside. Return that file to Miriam and start work.'

'You're not coming?'

'Not quite yet.'

Rob walked back, deep in thought. *Imagine you were a journalist*: that's what Craig had said. Rob wasn't a hack anymore; he was a PR guy – *a flack* – albeit a well-remunerated and grandly titled one. He'd been good at the old job and he'd loved doing it but there was no going back. Poacher turned gamekeeper, that's what he was. Or possibly the other way around? Rob was around the corner and twenty yards up the road before he realised he was getting wet. Looking up he saw fat drops of rain exploding off the tops of black umbrellas all around him. He opened his own borrowed brolly, tucked the file under his arm and quickened his pace, back towards the ministry.

9 Sins of the Fathers

DATELINE: The Taxi Café, Asmara, Eritrea, January 27 2011

Gabriel had delivered the new part for the espresso maker that he'd managed to acquire on behalf of the Taxi Café's owner and was sitting watching the man attempt to fix the antique Milano-made machine. His payment came in the form of food, a table filled with all the old man's favourites: injera and chicken stew. The chicken was a little stringy but the pancakes were perfect and he was complimenting the café owner on this when he saw his elder grandson standing outside the café window, his face like thunder. Solomon was looking for his grandfather. Gabriel raised a hand, waved and watched Solomon turn and wheel his bike in the direction of a nearby tree. He left it there – unlocked – and strode back into the bar.

'You do not want to chain your bicycle?'

'No point. Not anymore.'

Gabriel nodded gravely; the coffee machine made a strange growling sound and the smell of roasted coffee filled the room. 'The cycling team did not select you.'

'You heard already?'

75

'No, not heard . . . feared.' Gabriel pushed his glass of beer over towards Solomon who took a long swig.

This seemed to calm him a little; he slumped back into the chair and sighed. 'It is unfair, my times are the best in every kind of riding condition. I work harder than anyone; I arrive early for training and leave last. I am polite to the coach, respectful – even though the man is a complete idiot.'

His grandfather gave a gentle smile.

'What else could I have done?'

'Nothing. I suspect that there was nothing you could have done. What is your coach's name again?'

'Medhanie.'

Gabriel nodded. 'I know him – by reputation. He is not a brave man; I think he will have picked his team not for their *talent* but for *trust*. He has chosen the boys he thinks he can rely on not to put him in any trouble. He has a nice house and an easy job and he doesn't want to lose them. That is more important to him than winning cycling races.'

Solomon glanced at his grandfather. 'I thought maybe *you* could talk to him?'

'Of course. Maybe he will be persuaded, but I don't want you to get your hopes up. He is, as you say, an idiot.' Gabriel called the waiter over and asked for two more beers and an extra plate for Solomon. He piled it high with the spongy pancakes, chickpeas, lentils, cabbage and chicken and watched his grandson eat. 'Have you told your mother yet?'

'No, I can give her the good news later. I've only told you and Gebre.'

Right on cue, Gebre tapped at the café window. He had Solomon's bike by his side. Sol took the bike lock from his pocket, walked to the door and handed it to his brother. Gebre returned moments later.

'How is having your bike stolen going to help?'

Solomon shrugged. 'I have spoken to Grandfather about it. He'll try talking to coach Medhanie but he doesn't think he'll change his mind.'

Gebre nodded and put the key for the lock down on the table. 'I know that he won't.'

'What?'

'I just went to see Medhanie, I thought *I* could try and persuade him. I went as soon as I got your text message.'

'And?'

'And he spoke to me. He said that you had been too angry to talk to, that you had walked away before he could explain.'

The boy's grandfather watched the pair with interest and a slight sense of foreboding. Solomon said nothing.

'He said that it was not your fault, Sol, that you could not have done any more than you did.'

'I know this already, the man is a cheat.'

'I don't know about that. He said that it was not his decision. That it was taken from his hands. He told me that you were suffering because of our father's sins.'

Gabriel dropped his half-empty beer glass on the table and grabbed at his grandson's wrist. 'What did you say?' The old man's arthritic hand gripped Gebre's arm surprisingly hard; the boy could have broken free if he had wanted to but he would not dare. 'I asked you a question. What did you say?'

Gebre blushed before stammering a reply. 'It . . . it was not me, Grandfather. Sol's cycling coach said this, he said that Solomon was being punished for our father's sins.'

'Damned lies. Your father committed no sin.'

Gebre nodded but his grandfather's grip remained firm.

'Let me hear you say it.'

His grandson sighed. 'Our father committed no sin.'

Gabriel let go of Gebre's arm but his face was still set; he stared at his hands. 'Shame enough that they *kill* my son, but then to sully his name as well. They want to kill him twice.' The old man's eyes were suddenly wet.

Gebre and Solomon sat in silence; it was the first time anyone in the family had admitted the possibility that their father might be dead.

Solomon hesitated and then covered his grandfather's papery hand with his own. 'How do you know that he is dead, Grandfather? Who did you speak to?'

Gabriel looked up at the boy. 'I spoke to no one. I know because I know . . .' He sniffed back the tears. Solomon handed him his napkin and he wiped his face. 'I know because he was my son. The last time the army took him; they told me they needed him to confess to something, a minor matter. All he had to do was confess and give them some other names – any names. He refused.' Gabriel gathered himself. 'I broke half a dozen sticks on that boy's backside. I never met a man with half the will that he had. Your father is dead, but know this: it will have taken ten men to do it and whatever lies it was they wanted him to tell – he would not.'

Gebre's mind turned to his mother but he waited a while before giving voice to his thoughts. 'If this is true, Grandfather, then you should tell our mother as well. She needs to know this.'

Gabriel shook his head. 'Your mother knows. She has known for a long time. But knowing something and choosing to believe it are not always the same thing.' Their grandfather started patting at his jacket pockets, looking for something. 'Old people like your mother and I are allowed to look backwards, if backwards is what we prefer. Young people like you do not have that choice. You have to look forwards, no matter what forwards might mean.' He reached into his trouser pocket and brought out a white business card, embossed with thick black lettering. 'There is a man I want you to meet.'

10 A Breath of Fresh Air

DATELINE: The Seti Hotel, Cairo, Egypt, January 27 2011

The loud ring of the hotel room phone hauled Carver from a deep sleep. He struggled to free himself from a tangle of sheets and blankets and reaching over knocked his glasses, watch and a half-full bottle of spring water to the floor before his hand found the phone.

'Patrick?'

'No, it's me.'

'Oh, Zahra, sure. What's up?'

'The Muslim Brotherhood meeting you asked about.' Her voice was little louder than a whisper. 'It will happen today, after midday prayers.' Carver pushed the heel of his free hand against his forehead and tried to focus.

'Oh yeah, yeah, I remember. Am I still the only hack here who knows 'bout this?'

'I have told no one else.'

'Good, great, so after prayers, right, at the Mosque of the something . . .'

Zahra made a tutting sound. 'The Mosque of the Servants of

79

the Compassionate. I wrote it down for you. Mr Akar is here, I have to go.'

Carver hauled himself up into a sitting position; the dark mahogany headboard was cool against his back. He squinted at the bedside table, looking for his watch but not seeing it. 'Wait, is breakfast still—'

But Zahra had gone. He swung his feet from the bed and retrieved his glasses and watch. He pressed his feet into the thick hotel carpet and made a short audit of his various aches and pains. He was sure there'd been a time when a good night's sleep was a reliable restorative, but he was damned if he could remember when. These days it seemed like he woke up each morning in a slightly worse state than when he went to bed. Carver hobbled to the bathroom, filled the tooth glass brim-full with cold water and swallowed a couple of painkillers. He washed his hands, his face, armpits and crotch with a few squirts of the complimentary shower gel then brushed his teeth and flattened and combed his hair using his fingers.

Carver needed to look presentable for the Muslim Brotherhood meeting and selected his blue blazer and a reasonably clean white shirt. He gave his shoes a quick polish with a pair of balled-up socks, grabbed his plastic bag and headed for the door. The remains of the room service burgers he and Patrick had eaten the night before were still sitting in the hall. Carver took a handful of cold French fries, dipped them in the crusted-over ketchup and ate them while waiting for the lift – something to line the stomach in case they'd stopped serving breakfast.

The hotel dining room was empty apart from two of the Russian women who had finished eating and were sitting, staring blindly into their mobile phones. A handful of flies moved in lazy circles around the empty but uncleared tables and the room smelled faintly of burned toast. Carver was about to leave when he noticed someone sitting alone at one of the outdoor tables, just the other side of the French windows. The woman was wearing a loose-fitting headscarf and she had her hand raised in his direction.

'William Carver, man of the hour!'

The voice was the same Antipodean growl he'd heard the night before, from among the group of hacks drinking at the pool bar. He narrowed his eyes and stared at the woman's long face.

'Jean?'

'Well done! Got it in one, Jean it is. As we both live and breathe.' She waved him over. 'Come. Sit.'

Jean Fitzgerald was an old friend; at one point a close one. A fellow foreign correspondent who had a few more years and a dozen more disasters and wars under her belt than Carver. When he was starting out in *the misery business* – Jean's favoured description of the work they did – she had been helpful. Kind, at a time when kindness was in short supply.

'You're not swimming this morning?'

Carver shook his head.

'I was out here last night, asking people where to find you. Next thing I see is *you*, ploughing up and down the pool, didn't want to interrupt you. So what's going on? How come you're swimming?'

'How come you're wearing a headscarf?'

'I'm being culturally sensitive, you prick.'

Carver smiled.

'Plus, my long Titian locks ain't what they used to be.' She lifted a hand and removed the headscarf revealing a still impressive mess of coppery curls. She saw Carver looking. 'I rather enjoyed watching you swim.'

William said nothing.

'Your front crawl reminded me of a deep-sea fishing trip I went on one time. I saw this huge wahoo, hooked hard by its mouth, being slowly dragged to the stern side, flailing all the way.'

'Cheers.'

'Your breaststroke, though – that wasn't bad, almost elegant. So how come you're swimming? Swimming is exercise, not something I associate with Billy Carver.'

Carver looked at his feet. 'My doctor thought it might be a good idea.'

Jean shook her head. 'Doctors! Fifty-plus years I went without seeing one. Now I'm in there every other week.' She saw him look around for a waiter. 'I think we missed the best of breakfast. I hope we did anyway, the coffee tastes like hot mud. You want some?'

'Sure.'

They shared the pot of sulphurous coffee and while they drank, they talked. The last time Carver had seen Jean she'd been married; hitched to an old newspaperman called Raglan Jones, a contemporary of Carver's from back when they'd both worked on local newspapers.

'How's Raglan?'

'He's dead. Heart attack.'

'Shit, Jean, I'm sorry.'

'Don't worry.' She shrugged. 'No one deserved it more than Rags. He really worked at it. You remember how he was: the smoking, the drinking, the eating – especially the bloody eating.' She took a packet of red Marlboro and a book of matches from her pocket. 'You still smoke?'

Carver shook his head.

'Good for you.' She placed a cigarette in her mouth, handed the matches to William and waited patiently while he fumbled around, trying to get the flimsy cardboard match to strike. He managed on the third attempt.

As Jean dipped her face to the flame he studied her: she still had the same dark eyes, long straight face and aquiline nose that had encouraged admirers to compare her with Modigliani's women. He recalled reading a piece recently where Jean had bemoaned the passing of her Modigliani days and suggested that she now looked more like one of Picasso's women, with *bits of face all over the place.*

She took a deep pull on the cigarette, held it then let it go, screwing one eye shut against the smoke. 'Yeah, so Rags fell off the twig two years back. We'd been separated for a while when it happened. He traded me in for a younger model.' Carver was about to apologise again but Jean held up a hand to stop him. 'He was running the obits page at the *Telegraph*.' Jean grinned. 'That was ironic – he used to spend hours polishing his own tribute. In the end he didn't even get a full obituary, because a whole bunch of bishops and air chief marshals died that week. He ended up with one of those little boxes down the bottom. The *also-dead* section he used to call it.' She took a long pull on her cigarette. 'He'd have been bloody furious about that.'

'It's good to see you again, Jean; you look . . . you look well.'

'Give me a break, Carver, we both know what that is: it's a hell of a lot of slap. I had to bring three bags with me on this trip: one for make-up, one for clothes and one for drugs.'

Carver shifted in his seat. The painkillers he'd taken hadn't kicked in yet. 'What kind of stuff?'

'You name it: antidepressants, anti-anxiety, anti-ageing. Anti pretty much anything you can think of in fact. Then there's the sleeping pills, blood thinners . . .'

'Painkillers?' Carver asked casually.

'Are you kidding? Sure painkillers. I've got these Kiwi pain pills – they take everything away.' She blew a plume of smoke up into the sky and stared at the palm trees, spiky silhouettes against the cornflower blue. 'Where does it hurt?'

Carver shrugged. 'The knees. Neck. My back.'

'Ah, the back, tell me about it. My backbone's like the rubble of Tangshan. Hurts like hell in the mornings. I can help you with that, no worries. I wanted to ask a favour anyway.'

'What kind of favour?'

'You've been chasing this Arab Spring thing around a while. I was going to ask you to bring me up to speed, tell me which way Egypt's going to topple.'

Carver grinned.

'What's so bloody funny?'

'I get to bring the great Jean Fitzgerald up to speed? How come? Haven't you had time to sleep with the chief of police or the Reuters guy yet?'

Jean pulled a face. 'I really wish I'd never said that.'

A year or so back, during a long and, Carver thought, rather fawning *Woman's Hour* interview, Jean was asked how she managed to survive and thrive, working in the difficult places she'd worked. She'd been in a playful mood and the answer she gave was that as soon as she arrived in whatever hellhole it was she was reporting from, she would first seduce the chief of police and then the local Reuters correspondent. A bit of pillow talk from these two provided pretty much all the information she needed. Her remarks were widely reported.

'I should've kept my big mouth shut. It was just a joke and now it's the only thing anyone remembers about me. That was never my modus operandi anyway. I've only ever slept with *one* chief of police and shagging the Reuters correspondent rarely gets you anything – apart from a dose of the clap.'

Carver grinned, Jean Fitzgerald was more than a breath of fresh air – she was a force ten gale when she was in the mood.

By the time Patrick arrived at the Seti to rendezvous with Carver, he and Jean had been swapping old stories for over an hour. As Patrick strode across the dining room and out into the garden he saw Carver's shoulders shaking. As he got closer he saw that his colleague was . . . well, the only word for it was giggling – not something Patrick remembered seeing before. Carver introduced him and Jean stubbed out her cigarette, stood and shook his hand.

'So you're Boy Wonder to Billy Carver's Batman. I heard some people talking 'bout you on the plane. Flattering stuff.'

Patrick blushed and was reaching for the right response when Carver interrupted.

'A planeload of hacks was it?'

Jean nodded. 'Yeah, that's the bad news. Yesterday's BA flight was stuffed full of the usual suspects, including your old mate John Brandon. Although he turned left rather than right, of course.'

Carver shook his head. 'The circus has arrived.'

''Fraid so. A hundred or more on my flight and more to come, I reckon.'

Patrick chipped in. 'Another plane arrived this morning, the reception's packed. It's pretty buzzy.'

Carver scowled. The news that a load more journalists had joined the fray helped focus his mind. He swallowed the last of his coffee with a grimace and ordered Patrick to go and see if there were any taxis outside the hotel.

'We'll leave in ten.'

'Where are we going?'

'I'll tell you in the car.'

Patrick said goodbye to Jean.

She waited until he was out of earshot. 'Sweet kid.'

Carver was sifting through the contents of his plastic bag. 'What? Oh yeah.'

'He adores you.'

'Nonsense.'

'He does. I wish I could find a young bloke to look at *me* the way he looks at you.'

Carver was checking his MiniDisc recorder. 'He's the best producer I've ever worked with. Best in the BBC or anywhere else as far as I'm concerned.'

Jean smiled. 'And I bet you tell him that all the time.'

'Don't want him getting big-headed.'

''Course not. So where are the pair of you rushing off to?'

William shrugged. 'Oh, I don't know. Probably head down to Tahrir, see what's going on and—'

'Cut it out, Carver. I know you. You get a certain look about you when you're sniffing down a story. Don't worry, I'm not the competition anymore.'

'Just as well.'

'I'm here for features, not news but don't tell me if you don't want to. I know sharing stories isn't your long suit.'

He lowered his voice. 'You know the Muslim Brotherhood meeting that everyone's talking about?'

'Yes?'

'I know where it is.'

Jean smiled. 'Of course you do.' She put her hand on his and Carver felt a jolt – old, almost forgotten electricity. 'I'll bring my medicine cabinet down later. We'll sort out those aches and pains of yours and talk some more, yeah?'

'I'd like that.'

Zahra was on reception, checking in the new guests. The place was – to use Patrick's word – *buzzy* and every arrival and departure was being carefully observed. As he made his way across the hotel lobby, Carver was aware of being watched. He slowed his pace and tried to appear less purposeful. A pair of winged sphinx statues stood sentry at the entrance to the hotel, one either side of the sliding glass doors, and leaning casually against one of the statues, chatting to Patrick, was Security Steve – all six feet four of him.

'Bollocks.'

Carver noticed Patrick shift position, placing himself between William and the giant who was wearing a safari jacket, camouflage trousers and boots.

'Hi there, William, you remember Steve?'

'Yep.'

Security Steve was the former Special Forces man who the BBC had hired to look after team safety. Carver and Patrick had come across him in Tunisia and he and William had taken an instant dislike to each other. Usually Carver got on well with the former army blokes who did this sort of work but he didn't like Steve. As far as Patrick could work out, William's main objection was his age.

'It's usually the older blokes do the security thing – late forties and fifty-year-olds. He's in his twenties, early thirties tops. Why's he doing this job?'

Patrick had suggested that Steve might have been discharged on health grounds or something similar but Carver wasn't buying.

'Bollocks. Look at him; he's as fit as a butcher's dog. It doesn't add up.'

Patrick exchanged pleasantries while Carver skulked around making his impatience obvious. After a couple of minutes, Steve picked up a clipboard, which looked small and slightly ridiculous in his huge hands.

'So, if you two are heading into Tahrir you'll need to take the flak jackets.' He had a Bristol accent that hardened slightly when he was issuing instructions. He turned to Carver: 'And for you, old-timer, it'll be the respirator, or at the very least your inhaler.' A history of asthma meant that William was entitled, encouraged in fact, to take the respirator if he was going anywhere near tear gas. It was an unwieldy device that he and Patrick had taken out once in Tunis and ended up sending back to the hotel in a taxi.

'I don't want the bloody respirator. And I've got my inhaler.'

'Suit yourself.'

'We're not going to Tahrir anyway.'

'I see. Where are you going?'

The sliding doors were open, with a few people smoking nearby.

Carver had the feeling that other ears were tuned to their conversation and he had no intention of telling Steve anyway.

'Mind your own business.'

The only taxi waiting on the rank was a black and white Lada with dents down the side and at least one hubcap missing. The driver's seat was empty but as they drew closer Carver saw there was a man lying across the back seat of the car, an open newspaper across his face, apparently asleep. He rapped on the rear window and the man pulled the paper from his face and squinted up at him. Sitting up in the seat, he wound down the window and nodded at Carver who leaned in and lowered his voice to little more than a whisper.

'The Mosque of the Servants of the Compassionate, El Hossein Square?'

'I know this place.' He pulled a notebook from his trouser pocket and made a great show of flicking through it. 'It is two hundred dollars.'

'What? Bollocks to that. That's more than you get paid in a month.'

The man shrugged and began winding the car window back up.

Carver jabbed his finger at the man. 'Give me a minute.'

The cabbie shrugged, lay down and pulled the newspaper back across his face. He wasn't going anywhere.

Carver turned to Patrick. 'Go fetch Zahra. The receptionist with the long dark hair?'

Patrick returned moments later with Zahra at his side. She didn't bother tapping on the window but instead simply wrenched the back door of the cab open and started interrogating the taxi driver in a noisy Arabic. The man argued back, but not for long; soon his head dropped and Zahra turned to the two journalists.

'He says there is a new rate for the taxis now. During the *national emergency* he is calling it.'

The man nodded and took his notebook out to show them the new rates.

Zahra dismissed him with a wave. 'It is nonsense. But the American and the Japanese television people paid him four hundred dollars for a day of driving and now he and his friends think they can charge anything.' She turned to the man and spoke again, more softly now.

The cabbie stared at Zahra and glanced briefly at Carver before getting out and walking round to the other side of his car and opening the passenger door.

'What's going on?'

'He has changed his mind. He understands how important your work is. He will charge you what it says on the meter.'

Carver laughed. 'Really? I've *never* seen a Cairo cabbie use the meter. What did you say to the man?'

Zahra lowered her voice. 'I told him about the work you are doing and then I asked him where his shame was.'

The old Lada started on the second turn of the key and the driver slipped it into first gear and crawled down the hotel drive towards the security barrier. A tired-looking guard in khaki uniform waved them through. The footwell on the passenger side was littered with old newspapers, sweet wrappers and cigarette packets; Carver cleared a space with his foot and put his plastic bag down while Patrick arranged his long limbs in the cramped back seat.

After a few hundred yards the taxi stopped at a red traffic light and Carver saw a small crowd, gathered around a pile of rubbish heaped at the bottom of a lamp post. They were staring at the rubbish with looks of wonder and amazement on their faces, pointing at the pile of black bags. The taxi driver rolled down his window and then they heard it: blaring loudly from a speaker concealed somewhere inside the rubbish, came music.

The cabbie banged his hand on the dashboard and laughed. 'It is our song, the old song of Egypt.'

It took Carver a moment to make the connection; he knew the old national anthem had been banned by the government, he just didn't know what the anthem sounded like. He was hearing it now.

Stunts like this, small acts of civil disobedience, had become increasingly common in Cairo. The traffic lights changed colour but the cars did not move; drivers waited and watched and listened to the banned song, and the crowd on the street grew. As Carver and the cabbie watched, a policeman arrived and pushed his way to the front. When all he saw was a pile of black bags he was momentarily confused, then he started digging through the bags looking for the source of the outlawed song. When he finally unearthed the offending item – a bulky silver cassette recorder – he ceremoniously pressed stop before throwing it to the floor and bringing his boot down hard on the tape recorder again and again. The crowd began to boo but when the policeman shot them a warning glare, instead of guilt or fear he saw ridicule. Some of the watching crowd laughed openly at the officer while a group of children mocked him with a stamping dance of their own.

Carver turned in his seat. 'Did you . . .' He saw Patrick, hanging halfway out of the window, microphone in hand.

'I got all that.'

'Good.'

'So where are we going?'

'*I'm* going to this Muslim Brotherhood meeting, but I think it's better if I go alone.'

'How come?'

'Less conspicuous and it means you can go on to Tahrir and get people reacting to whatever the Brothers decide.'

It was clear that Patrick didn't like the plan and Carver sympathised – he wasn't that keen on it himself.

The taxi came to a halt beside a stretch of high white wall; the driver wrenched the handbrake up and pointed out of the passenger side window. 'Mosque of Servants of Compassionate. I will wait?'

Carver shook his head. 'No, take my colleague here on to Tahrir.'

Carver climbed out of the car and nodded at Patrick who watched as William walked across the street, towards the mosque's main gate, and allowed the crowd to swallow him.

11 Citizen Journalist

DATELINE: The Corniche, Cairo, Egypt, January 27 2011

Nawal strode down the corniche. A growing line of TV crews were setting up live broadcast points, jostling for the spots they thought would provide the best backdrop. She walked up and down the line until she found what she was looking for: a pile of placards hidden under a gantry close to where one of the big American networks was broadcasting. Nawal had received a direct message from a follower in New York early that morning. She got out her phone.

@tsquarelawan
| Pro President demonstrations happening @ the
| corniche where western TV stations are working.

@tsquarelawan
| Demonstrating at 0530 in the morning! So they are
| in the background of US primetime news shows . . .
| clever.

@tsquarelawan

> We must be clever too! Let at least one hundred
> people gather @ the corniche tomorrow at 0500!

She gathered the pile of pro-presidential placards together in both arms and dumped them further down the street, burying them underneath a good foot of rubbish and rotting vegetables. Standing back, she caught sight of her reflection in a shop window. Black hoodie under a tatty leather jacket, cropped hair, cargo pants and trainers. She looked tired and about a million miles from pretty. But pretty wasn't important – not anymore. Nawal's thoughts turned to Zahra. She wondered whether her friend felt the same? Zahra never looked ugly, she never looked plain. In Nawal's opinion, Zahra never looked anything other than beautiful. She checked her phone for messages and then set off in the direction of Tahrir Square.

Nawal liked to enter and leave Tahrir using a citizen checkpoint that she'd helped set up close to the Arab League building. The buck-toothed boy who had the job of greeting new arrivals and checking that no one was carrying a weapon had a nice manner. As he nodded Nawal through he grinned and yelled over her head, towards the queue of people waiting patiently to enter Tahrir.

'*Hold your head up high, be proud! You are Egyptian!*'

Staring across the square, Nawal *was* proud. She remembered one of her grandfather's stories: how the stones of the pyramids were cut so well, so perfect was the fit that you could not slip a knife between one stone and the next. Only the Egyptians were able to do this, he said. As she walked across the square, Nawal felt something similar. She got her phone out and typed a couple of lines, not a finished message but something that they could use later: *Here in this square is what we should be, what we once were and could be again.*

*

Carver attracted suspicious looks from the moment he walked inside the mosque's main gates. He hurried, head down, across the courtyard, trying to remain as inconspicuous as possible. The space outside the main mosque building was filled with worshippers unable to find room inside. They were busy arranging their prayer mats around an ancient-looking sundial and compass that stood on a tiled dais in the centre of the courtyard. The sundial looked like it had been cast from solid gold, the compass also gold but with an ivory inlay beneath the delicate magnetic metal needle. Most of the worshippers seemed happy to use these old instruments as a guide to where to place their mat and the correct direction of prayer. Not all, however, and Carver was interested to see some of the younger Brothers consulting apps on their phones and shuffling their prayer mats around accordingly.

It took him some time to work his way through the crowd and into the mosque. Once he had, Carver found a shadowy corner and stood, his back against the wall, trying to get the measure of the place. At a long row of deep ceramic sinks, bearded men, young and old, most of them wearing white jellabiya, were washing themselves: hands and forearms, face, neck and ears before slipping off their shoes and entering the prayer room. In the past, in other countries and at other mosques, Carver had been invited to join them, to perform his own ablutions and take part in the act of worship but glancing around he knew there was little chance of any such invitation today. The atmosphere ahead of the Brotherhood's big political decision was tense and the presence of an overweight westerner, skulking in a corner, wasn't making anyone feel more relaxed. The stares he received ranged from mild suspicion to outright hostility.

He decided it would be better to move around and look like he was expecting to meet someone here and so he did this for a while, edging past tight groups of men deep in conversation. Carver nodded a respectful greeting at anyone who looked his way and muttered the same Arabic sentence at them all: *Hal tatahadath Al Englyzeyah?* He knew that many of the men he asked this question *did* speak some English but none of them wanted to speak it with him – not today anyway.

He poked his head inside the high domed prayer room and took a look. There were a dozen pillars down each side of the carpeted room; it was empty of furniture apart from a platform at the far end where the stoop-shouldered imam was struggling with a microphone stand, attempting to lower it to the correct height. Carver was admiring one of the Koranic verses, painted in beautiful, tall calligraphic script on the honey-coloured stone wall when he felt someone grab his upper arm. A hard hand gripped him and pulled Carver round and away from the room. Carver shook his arm free and stared at his assailant who was a foot shorter than him but stocky. The man wore a white skullcap and dirty-looking dishdasha; he was shaking a fat finger at Carver.

'This room is not for you, it is forbidden.'

'I understand.' Carver moved away from the prayer room in the direction of the front door but the man followed him and blocked his exit.

'What do you want here? What is it you do?'

Carver buttoned his blazer. 'I'm a journalist.'

'You are English?'

'Yes, I'm English. My name's Carver.' He held out his right hand, more in hope than expectation. Sure enough the stocky man ignored Carver's hand, which was left hanging, marooned in mid-air for a time before he let it drop. The man moved closer and Carver could smell him now: his clothes stank of old sweat, his breath was sour. Carver stepped back towards the wall and as he did, knocked against a rack of shoes, spilling them on to the floor.

'You are not a journalist. You are a kafir and a *spy*.' The man raised his voice as he made this dangerous accusation and it worked; half a dozen other men heard his words and Carver felt a crowd start to gather around him.

He put his plastic bag down on the floor and reached into his blazer pocket for his wallet and, inside that, his press card. He found it and held it out in front of him, willing his hands not to shake.

The skullcapped man glanced at it and laughed, pointing his finger again. 'It is *fake*. We have spies outside our house, my brothers, and now we have a spy *inside* as well. What is to be done?' The question was aimed at his colleagues but the man spat the words into Carver's face.

Carver recoiled at the stink of halitosis and the strength of this stranger's hate. He felt other hands on him now, pushing and plucking at him.

Just then there was movement at the back of the crowd and Carver watched as a rake-thin black man in a dark suit and tie pushed his way to the front, mumbling apologies in Arabic as he did so. Arriving at the front of the angry knot of men he nodded at the thug in the skullcap before taking Carver's press card from his hand and studying it. He was a tall, fine-featured man – not an Egyptian, Carver thought: East African perhaps?

The man sucked at his teeth then spoke, first in competent Arabic and then a fluent, heavily accented English. 'This card is genuine. This man is no spy, he is a journalist trying to tell people what is happening here in your country.' He paused and glanced around, judging the effect his words were having on his audience. 'More than this, he is your guest. He has a right to a welcome. You have a *duty* to welcome him, your book tells you this.'

Heads nodded, some in agreement, others in resignation. The thug in the skullcap grabbed the press card and looked at it again before tossing it to the floor and turning away in disgust.

Carver's protector retrieved it and handed it back. He was

smiling now. 'Come, I will take you to see Mr Shalaby, you will be safer in his company.'

'Er, thank you.'

'It is nothing. We outsiders must stick together.'

Carver was unsure what to make of this man. His accent intrigued him and he was keen to ask where he was from, but before Carver knew it he was standing in front of Mr Shalaby. His guardian angel made the introduction and stayed long enough to listen to the journalist explain what he was after, before moving away. When Carver next looked, he had gone.

Shalaby was an unassuming-looking middle-aged man with thick, black-framed glasses and a short grey beard. He said he would be willing to give a short interview on the condition that he was referred to simply as a spokesman for the Muslim Brotherhood. This wasn't ideal but Carver wasn't in much of a position to argue. An interview of any sort was better than none and better than any other hack was likely to get. He agreed and took his tape recorder out.

'There is growing discontent in Egypt, protests like those we've seen elsewhere in the Arab world. Many believe these protests will only succeed if the Muslim Brotherhood gives their support. Will you?'

Shalaby took his time before answering. 'Individuals must use their own judgement, make their own decisions about what to do.'

The men around him were hanging on every word; Carver could see that Shalaby was a man of some authority.

He paused, choosing his words carefully. 'The Muslim Brotherhood believes in order and discipline. Demonstrations can bring disorder and chaos but at certain points in history there is no alternative.'

'And this is such a point?'

'It could be, yes. But, as I say, members of the Brotherhood will decide for themselves.'

Carver nodded. He tried several more questions but Mr Shalaby had said what he wanted to say. Prayers were about to begin and he was happy to let the men around him lead him away.

After the prayers, the political meeting began; Carver took up position just outside the prayer room and surreptitiously recorded the speeches. He needed to know whether what Shalaby had told him squared with the general message of the meeting and although he couldn't understand much of what was said, Zahra would have no trouble.

Leaving the mosque, he looked again for the East African but there was no sign. Instead he saw two of the most conspicuous plain-clothes policemen he'd ever seen, suited figures slouched against the wall of the apartment block opposite. These must be the spies that the thug in the skullcap had spoken of. The smaller of the two was paring his nails and staring openly at certain faces in the crowd; his colleague had his mobile phone out in front of him and was pretending to send text messages while in fact filming. The Muslim Brothers kept their heads down and strode quickly past the police and Carver tried to do the same, though his presence there clearly interested the pair. The plain-clothes man with the mobile dropped the pretence, raising his phone to eye level and turning it in his hand, tracking Carver as he walked down the narrow street in the direction of El Hossein Square.

Nawal was crouched next to a streetlight in the centre of Tahrir charging her phone when she got the message. She was borrowing some electricity that an enterprising individual had managed to re-route from the base of the streetlight to a four-gang plug point. When the message came through from her contact at the mosque, she felt goosebumps rise on her arms. She unplugged her phone and started typing frantically.

@tsquarelawan

Time for a new chant here in Tahrir: the
Brotherhood and the people are One Hand!

@tsquarelawan

With every hour that passes we are more united. If
we believe we will win – THEN WE WILL WIN!

Patrick had been in Tahrir Square for a couple of hours when a
murmur went through the crowd. People in front of him started
reaching for their phones. He was trying to figure out what was
going on when his own phone rang – Carver.

'Hello? I just left. It looks like the Brotherhood are going to
back the protest.'

'That explains it.'

'Explains what?'

'I think the crowd just heard.'

Carver sucked at his teeth. 'That was quick. Bush telegraph
must be working overtime, I guess.'

Patrick smiled. 'If that's what we're calling Facebook and
Twitter this week, then yes.'

'What?'

'Nothing. I better go get some reaction interviews. You want to
meet back at the Seti?'

'Yeah, I need to run this stuff I recorded past Zahra then file it
pronto. We can head back to Tahrir later.'

Carver glanced around his hotel bedroom, unsure where to put
himself. Patrick was at the writing desk unpacking his laptop,
leads, sound card reader and notepad. Zahra was lying on her
stomach on the bed with Carver's MiniDisc player in front of
her and a pair of headphones clamped over her ears. She had her
hands pressed against the headphones as though she were trying

99

to push the sound deeper into her ears and was swinging her legs behind her. When she saw Carver she lifted the headphones from one ear.

'This is what we hoped for. A message to the Brotherhood. A clear message.' Her voice was high with excitement.

Carver just nodded. 'Fine. Keep listening, will you? I need you to check it all.'

He edged past Patrick and into the bathroom, kicking the door shut behind him. He twisted the cold tap on, splashed water on his face and left it running for inspiration while he took a pee. His swimming trunks were hanging on the towel rail. Carver looked at his watch; he could fit in a quick swim while Patrick was putting the piece together, then come back up and record his links. Chances were, Jean was down there. He could ask her about those painkillers she'd mentioned and say hi.

The air conditioning had dried the trunks too well; they were as stiff as cardboard. He struggled out of his trousers and Y-fronts and into the unyielding trunks. When he walked back into the bedroom, Patrick and Zahra exchanged a look but said nothing. Patrick had copied the audio from the Brotherhood's meeting on to the laptop and Carver pointed at the first jagged block of audio.

'The interview I need is at the beginning of that band.'

Patrick slipped his headphones on and listened. When the short interview had finished he glanced up at Carver. 'I don't see why this is so significant. He's just saying that people should use their own judgement, make their own decisions about whether to join the protest.'

Zahra shook her head. 'The men who were at this meeting will understand what it means.'

Carver agreed 'Egyptians learn to read between the lines before they learn to read. This is the Muslim Brotherhood giving their lot the green light to get out on the streets. It's bad news for the regime.'

Zahra smiled. 'And great news for the people.'

Carver shrugged. 'Maybe. I'm going to go do my lengths.'

There was no sign of Jean at the poolside bar. Carver swam a few grudging lengths then – still in his trunks – went and checked the main hotel bar, attracting interested looks along the way. There were several familiar faces in the bar but none of them belonged to Jean Fitzgerald. He bought a large whisky for himself, a bottle of beer for Patrick and some peanuts and took them back to the room.

Zahra had returned to work and Carver took her place on the bed, working on his script between sips of whisky and occasionally checking his phone.

Patrick noticed. 'Are you expecting a call?'

'Jean mentioned we might meet up. No big deal.'

Patrick took a glug of his beer. 'Have you tried calling her?'

'No. Like I say, it's not a big deal.'

Patrick shrugged. While William was finishing his script he scrolled through Twitter checking the latest news from Tahrir.

@tsquarelawan
> Heard police on radio 'eiwa ya basha'. The tear gas is coming.

@tsquarelawan
> Bring gloves. Throw the gas back when you can and keep the old canisters . . . EVIDENCE!

'It sounds like they're having quite a party down there.' He held the laptop out for Carver to read. 'Have a look.'

@tsquarelawan
> Come to the square to collect your new passport! It will read . . .

@tsquarelawan

> Name: citizen. Place of birth: Tahrir Square.
> Religion: Egyptian. Occupation: Revolutionary!

@tsquarelawan

> A couple will have their katb el ketab (marriage) in
> Tahrir Square tonight. All welcome!

Carver nodded. 'Sounds like it's hotting up again. Let's get this piece finished, then you can head back to Tahrir.'

'You're not coming?'

Carver shook his head. 'Nah, I reckon the newsgathering monkeys will have all that covered. But *you* should go take a look. Sounds like it's more for the likes of you and Zahra anyway. *Bliss to be young in that new dawn* and all that.'

Patrick smiled. 'Wordsworth. He's one of Rebecca's favourites.'

'She's got good taste.' He glanced at Patrick. 'In poets anyway. Chuck the duvet over me, I'll record my links and then you can bugger off.'

Carver recorded his script with the duvet draped over his head to dull any echo or buzz from the air conditioning. Patrick mixed the radio report and filed it.

'Are you sure you don't want me to stay?' He glanced at Carver's glass.

Carver shook his head. 'Yes I'm sure. An early night will do me good. And don't worry, I'm not going to drink any more, I'm done. I'll see you tomorrow.'

Walking to the lift, Patrick decided to call Rebecca. It was late but he hadn't spoken to her for almost twenty-four hours. She picked up on the second ring, her voice full of sleep.

'Hello, stranger.'

'Hello.'

'It's late, everything okay?'

Patrick reassured her that everything was fine, told her about his day and asked about hers. She enquired about William.

'He's fine, I just left him in the hotel room. He's mixing whisky and Wordsworth.'

'It's a good mix.'

'*Bliss to be young* or something like that.'

'Philistine. Let me remember: *Bliss was it in that dawn to be alive, but to be young was very heaven!* That's one of his French Revolution numbers. Does Cairo feel like a revolution?'

'It's starting to. It feels different from Tunisia. Wilder, more hopeful somehow.' He stopped at the lift. 'I'll get Carver to use a bit of Wordsworth in one of his reports.'

'He won't buy that, too flowery for William.'

'He might. Give me a bit more, will you?' Patrick loved Rebecca's voice.

'Okay: *Earth is all before me. With a heart joyous, nor scared at its own liberty.*'

'Brilliant. You're my muse.'

'Yeah? Well, I'm a tired muse who's got to get up at six and teach thirty-five ten-year-olds, so go away.'

'Okay.'

'I love you.'

Patrick heard the line click dead and then an automated voice in Arabic informing him that the other person had cleared. He pressed the lift button and watched as it made its way down from the top floor to his. As the doors slid open he saw panicked movement from the four men standing inside. One of them, an Egyptian man so huge that he had to stoop to avoid hitting his head, placed himself in the centre of the doorway blocking any attempt at access. The other two men surrounded the fourth who had turned away and was standing in the far corner of the lift, his nose against the gold-mirrored glass. Patrick's view was obstructed but he saw the back of the hidden man's head and in his hand, hanging loosely at his side – a thick cigar. The gorilla in front just stood, shaking his neckless head and Patrick wasn't going to argue. He took a half step backwards.

'I'll get the next one.'

The doors on the golden lift slid slowly shut. They weren't as soundproof as they looked; as they closed Patrick heard a voice, tight with fury.

'Which one are you?'

'I am Panya, sir.'

'Next time I tell you to get the pass-key for the lift, Panya – get the fucking pass-key. You understand?'

'Yes, sir.'

It was an English accent. The type of accent that Rebecca would describe as *proper posh*. Patrick watched the indicator above the door count down as the lift moved past the lobby and then the lower ground, coming to a halt at basement level.

PART TWO

@tsquarelawan

> We are acclimatised – tear gas is like fresh air,
> rubber bullets are like drops of rain, sticks are like
> Thai massage.

12 A Man. A Plan

DATELINE: Embankment, London SW1, January 28 2011

It was an old 1970s maroon-coloured Jag. As it pulled away from the kerb, Leslie Craig settled himself on his half of the back seat and sniffed. The upholstery reeked of cigar smoke; he leaned forward, away from the seat and tried to breathe through his mouth. The car crawled up the side of the Ministry of Defence and turned left on to Whitehall. He glanced at the man sitting next to him. Bellquist wore his blond hair slicked back, his eyes were blue, his eyelashes white. Craig studied his chalk-stripe suit: the tailor had done his best but there was no getting around the fact that Bellquist was an odd shape – thick and muscular in his top half but scrawny, almost underdeveloped, from the waist down.

'Do you mind if I look after your mobile phone, Leslie?' The question was rhetorical, Bellquist had his hand out.

The permanent secretary took his government-issue smartphone from his inside pocket and passed it over. 'It's switched off.'

Bellquist ignored this and, using a hair clip, swiftly removed the chip from inside Craig's phone and dropped it together with the handset into a compartment underneath the armrest.

'Lead lined.' He pushed the armrest back down and it closed with a reassuring click. 'Just because your phone's switched off, doesn't mean it's not tracking you.' He took an old model phone out of his pocket. 'I use this old Nokia when I'm out and about. When that's off – it's off. We don't want the Russians knowing our every movement, do we? Or the Chinese . . . or the wife.'

The civil servant waited for Bellquist to finish chortling at his own joke before he spoke. Craig didn't particularly like this man and wanted to keep the meeting as brief and businesslike as possible.

'Did your trip go well?'

'It was a bit of a curate's egg, truth be told.'

'Tell me about the good parts.'

Bellquist smiled. 'I was introduced to a young lady called Fatma, she was most hospitable.'

Craig shook his head. 'I don't have time for silly stories, Bellquist. You were there on business.'

Bellquist turned in his seat and met the civil servant's eye. 'I'd remind you, Mr Craig, that I am not your employee. You are not my master.'

Craig nodded. 'Of course' – Bellquist stayed silent – 'I apologise.'

'Apology accepted. So the good news is that our Egyptian friends are still willing to meet, to talk. They still like us – or *me* anyway, but they're confused. It was more like a marriage counselling session than a business meeting. They want to know why we don't love them anymore.'

The permanent secretary sighed. 'You've just been there, presumably you saw some of what's going on?'

'Some. As far as our mates are concerned, it's a little local difficulty. It'll blow over – like Bahrain, like Saudi.'

'It won't. Not in the short term anyway and maybe not ever

and no politician likes to end up on the wrong side of history, you know that.'

Bellquist shrugged. 'Who knows what the right side is? History's not finished yet.'

'Of course but—'

'But we're hedging our bets, I understand that.' Bellquist shuffled back into his seat, making himself more comfortable. 'So we can't cut them off entirely. That would hurt that famous Egyptian pride of theirs.'

'We haven't cut them off entirely. Several blind eyes have been turned.'

Bellquist smiled. 'And they're grateful.'

Craig shot Bellquist a look.

'I'm grateful too, but that's small beer. Our friend says the Russians and Chinese are already offering to step in and fill any gaps that your export bans leave. They're offering very favourable terms.'

Craig nodded. 'I'm sure. But they'd still rather deal with us?'

'For now, yes.'

'Good. I have a plan and the right man to carry it off, I think.'

Bellquist smiled. 'A man, a plan . . . does he have a canal in Panama?'

'I beg your pardon?'

'Palindromes, I love a good palindrome. Fair enough, despite all this hypocritical hand-wringing, they'd still rather deal with us. Do you know what our Egyptian friend told me about his last meeting with the Chinese?'

Craig shook his head.

'He said: *We know what the Chinese want to do with us Egyptians – with all of Africa. They want to fuck us with their billion tiny little dicks.*'

Craig winced. Bellquist's laughter was so loud that his driver turned to check his employer was okay.

Craig gave him time to recover then spoke quietly. 'So you will speak to him again, reassure him?'

'Of course. I can give you a progress report at the arms fair dinner. You are coming, aren't you?'

Craig gave a reluctant nod of the head. There was no avoiding the damn dinner now.

'One last thing, Permanent Secretary?' Bellquist was drumming his fingers on the hand rest.

'Yes?'

'Your boss is four-square behind this strategy, isn't he?'

'The new Secretary of State is absolutely on board.'

Bellquist laughed. 'Not the new minister. Of course he is, otherwise he wouldn't be the new minister. I mean the main man – the Prime Minister.'

Craig nodded gravely. 'This whole strategy is of the Prime Minister's making. I wouldn't be asking you otherwise. You won't hear him say that of course – not in private or in public.'

Bellquist smiled. 'Course not. He was a sneaky bugger at school and he's only got sneakier since.'

Craig glanced out of the window; they'd crossed the river twice and were back on Whitehall. He pointed at a bus stop, twenty yards up on the right. 'I'd be grateful if you drop me just there.'

The permanent secretary was keen to bring the conversation to a close. He had learned from bitter experience that once these men started talking about their ridiculous school it was almost impossible to stop them.

DATELINE: New Broadcasting House, Portland Place, London W1, January 28 2011

Rob Mariscal paced up and down the piazza working on his spiel. Not that the spiel needed much work. 'The Story of the Sodding

Ship' as he'd come to refer to it was more or less perfect. A powerful tale designed to appeal to the emotions, interests and prejudices of whoever heard it. He was in a nervous mood; returning to his former place of work always put him on edge and he went and smoked a quick cigarette round the back of All Souls Church before returning to the piazza.

Mariscal was always on the lookout for fresh evidence to support his belief that God – or whoever – had flung the gears of evolutionary progress into reverse. Most of this evidence arrived in human form but he was willing to consider it however it came and this morning it was bricks and mortar. Standing in the shadow of the new BBC extension, he wondered how a civilisation capable of building something as glorious as the Regency church at his rear had decided it would rather spend time and money making glass and steel monstrosities like the one in front of him.

'Un-fucking-believable.' The word *carbuncle* came to mind but Rob rejected it. To his eye, the News Centre was less carbuncle, more eight-storey glassy scar. 'Thank Christ I don't have to work in there anymore.' It was nearly 9 a.m. and a steady stream of people was arriving for work; some clocked Rob and recognised him but he avoided eye contact. He had no interest in renewing old acquaintances, he wanted to meet the person he'd arranged to meet and then put some distance between himself and his former employer.

There was *one* interesting-looking individual on the piazza – a bearded man, wearing some kind of safari suit with short trousers despite the cold, and heavy hiking boots. He'd appeared from nowhere while Rob was having a fag and looked even more out of place than Mariscal himself. The man was standing at the centre of the open space, very still, staring up into the sky. Rob moved closer and as he did, he noticed that the man wore a thick brown glove on his left hand. Standing on the glove, rigid and alert, was a bird. Rob's curiosity got the better of him. 'All right, chief? What's the bird for?'

The man pointed upwards with his unencumbered hand. 'Pigeons.'

'What about them? He kills them?'

'Bird's a she, not a he. Hers a Harris hawk – she don't kill them, just gives 'em a scare. Moves them on.' The man had a broad West Country accent.

'Why?'

'Health and hygiene. Pigeons are vermin, aren't they?'

Rob shrugged, he wasn't sure about that; he'd always had a soft spot for pigeons. There was something unflashy and honest about them.

'Yous can pet her if you like?'

Rob gave the bird's breast feathers a nervous stroke.

From somewhere high above there was a faint sound, a flutter of wings; the hawk cocked her head, waiting. Mariscal studied the bird: she had a small black leather hood covering her head, and a silver bell was tied to her clawed foot.

'So she just chases them off then? Never catches them? Eats them?'

The falconer glanced around the piazza; people strode by but no one was paying them much notice. 'Sometimes she'll get one. If she gets one, she'll 'ave it. But most of the time that's 'cos pigeon's poorly. Or old. She's mainly doin' what I said – scarin' 'em off, moving them on.'

'Right.' Rob paused. 'Is this your job then? They pay you for this?'

The falconer glanced at Mariscal. 'Course they pays me, what d'you think? I do it for the giggles?'

'No. I guess not.'

Rob moved away, curiosity satisfied. He took a table outside the coffee shop next to new Broadcasting House and waited. The woman he was meeting was late but there was no point getting het up about it; she was doing him a favour seeing him at all and he knew how hard it was to extricate yourself from those post-programme meetings.

Just then Rob's successor as *Today* programme editor appeared outside the revolving doors of New Broadcasting House and shaded her eyes against the sun. Rob raised his hand.

Naomi Holder was wearing flat shoes, a light blue sweater and black cigarette pants, a shapeless black bag hanging from her shoulder. Her make-up had been freshly applied and Mariscal wondered fleetingly whether this might be for *his* benefit before deciding that it probably wasn't. They had got along fine when Naomi first worked at *Today* – years back now – but she'd never shown any sign of having a romantic interest in Rob and that was when he was young-ish and powerful as opposed to fat-ish and vilified. Arriving at his table, Naomi bent low and brushed Rob's cheek with her lips. He was grateful for this and glanced around to see if anyone else might have noticed. Naomi smelled faintly of jasmine.

'I thought you were going to meet me inside?'

'I figured it was better meeting out here. I think I'm still *persona non grata*.'

'Is that Latin for *guy who everyone thinks is a dick*?'

Mariscal smiled. 'Yeah.'

'Speak a lot of Latin working in Whitehall, do you?'

'*Certe*. Is it *certe* or *valde*?'

Naomi shook her head. 'No idea. State school remember. What's the plan? Want to get a coffee and a croissant here?'

'No, not here, I've booked that place down the road, that fancy new Fitzrovia diner. I thought we'd have a proper breakfast?'

'*Breakfast!* I can't remember the last time I had breakfast.'

Mariscal nodded. 'That's what I figured. One of the worst things about being *Today* editor, you never get to eat the most important meal of the day; one of the reasons I quit.'

113

Naomi laughed. 'Come on, Rob. You jumped about thirty seconds before you were pushed. We've known each other long enough to be honest about stuff like that, haven't we?'

'I guess so.'

Inside the restaurant, they were given a window seat and a tight deadline. The young waiter seating them apologised that they'd need the table back at ten.

Rob nodded. 'You better serve us quick then, I'm an extremely slow eater. Have you got Winchester cutlets?'

The kid had a diagonal fringe that looked like it had been cut with the aid of a ruler. When he shook his head it looked like someone was drawing the curtains.

'No? How about broiled partridge? Reindeer tongues?'

The curtains closed again and Naomi intervened, taking the menu from the boy's hand. 'We'll have two full English. Eggs scrambled, everything well-done and black coffee.'

The waiter gave a grateful nod and withdrew.

'Nice ordering.'

'I remember you used to eat a full English whenever we went out for lunch. I assumed you wouldn't mind having it for breakfast too.' Naomi started the meal with her mobile phone sitting on the table next to her, but when she realised that its repeated buzzing was bugging Mariscal, she put it back in her bag.

Their time together at *Today* had lasted just six months but both remembered it fondly. Naomi was on a series of attachments to the flagship BBC news programmes and the *Today* programme was her penultimate placement. It was part of a scheme aimed at nurturing high flyers – an initiative that Mariscal hated in principle, but try as he might he could not hold this against Naomi, who was exceptional from the get-go. After the attachment was up, Rob tried to persuade her to stay but she insisted she should do her six months in telly before deciding whether to come back. She never came back, or not until she was offered the editor's job anyway.

'So I hear you've prettified my old office. Feminised the place?'

Naomi took a sip of her coffee and smiled. 'I took the pornography down off the walls, if that's what you mean?'

'Ah yes, that's a shame. It wasn't really porn – it was more arty. I don't suppose you—'

'No I didn't. I threw it away.'

'Fair enough.' Rob refilled their water glasses. 'What else have you changed? Do you still go for Monday night drinks?'

'Not *every* Monday but I do try and keep that one going. Smoking isn't as rigidly enforced as it used to be.'

'Really? I always thought the smoking was pretty good for *esprit de corps*?'

'Perhaps, but I think making people go outside with you for a cigarette is probably against the law now. You still puffing away?'

'Sure, nine quid a packet these days.'

'Then quit.'

'I'd like to, but it's so exciting.'

'What's exciting?'

'My life. It basically all boils down to a race between bankruptcy and lung cancer. I can't wait to see who wins.'

Naomi smiled at her old boss. The food arrived and she watched Mariscal over-salt everything on his plate before tucking in.

'I'm not sure I ever really thanked you for that placement, way back when.'

'No thanks necessary, you were good. Better than good.' Rob spoke through a mouthful of egg.

'Thanks, but I've always been grateful. My time with you made a difference, you were always very straightforward with me.'

Mariscal shrugged.

'There were a lot of people at the BBC who were nervous around me when I first arrived, bashful about even *describing* me. I'd been described as the lady with frizzy hair, the woman with very dark hair and hoop earrings. My first day at *Today*, someone from personnel came and asked you who I was – you pointed at me: *She's over there, the lanky black girl by the photocopier.* It was a relief. You made me welcome.'

'Yeah, well, that was before I knew that you'd climb over my dead body to get my job.'

'You're not dead yet, Rob.'

'How do you know?'

It took a while for Rob to get around to talking about the real reason he needed to see Naomi. Partly because he was enjoying her company and partly out of embarrassment.

Halfway down Rob's list of ways in which he might start selling the story of the ship was an idea that the permanent secretary particularly liked. Mariscal suggested inviting a *Today* programme presenter to spend a week on board an aircraft carrier, experiencing the day-to-day working of one of these giants and sending back regular dispatches – radio pieces of course but also films, digital diaries, photos, tweets, the works. His boss told Rob to move this plan up to the very top of the list, and so with the food finished and the waiter loitering, ready to reclaim the table, Mariscal made his pitch. Naomi listened carefully, a slight smile on her face. Rob wasn't sure he liked the look of this smile.

'What're you grinning about?'

'Do you remember what you used to tell us about embeds and MOD facilities?'

'Thankfully, no I don't.'

'You used to say they were as journalistically credible and appetising as a tablespoon of dog shit.'

'Right. Well, I changed my mind. It turns out that MOD facilities aren't dog shit, in fact they're a very good way to build trust between the government and the governed.'

Naomi raised her coffee cup in a toast then placed it back down.

Her brow furrowed as she considered Rob's offer. 'So, you're bringing me this because you're in a knife fight with the Treasury over the defence budget and the aircraft carriers are vulnerable.'

Mariscal smiled. 'On the record – that's a dreadfully cynical suggestion that has no basis in fact.'

'Off the record?'

'Off the record – sure.'

He watched as she weighed up the pros and cons of the MOD facility. He remembered Naomi telling him that she'd almost chosen law over journalism as a career and he had no doubt that she'd have excelled in that arena too. When they were working together, he delegated all the conversations with BBC lawyers to Naomi and, to Rob's amazement, she actually seemed to enjoy it. Her ability to analyse a story and cross-examine arguments was impressive, though Rob felt that it made her over-cautious. He remembered telling her how an editor sometimes has to just trust their gut and take a punt. Naomi wasn't that type.

'The MOD must be an interesting place to be right now.'

'What d'you mean?'

'If this whole Arab Spring thing turns out to be real, if there's genuine change across North Africa, across the Middle East, then that's more than half a dozen countries in flux – some of our biggest arms importers.'

'The Ministry of Defence's sole purpose is to defend the realm.'

'And facilitate arms sales.'

'I refer you to my previous *on the record* response.'

Naomi grinned. 'Come on, Rob, you've got at least a hundred and sixty people, working in the same building as you, whose job it is to help British arms companies flog their wares around the world.'

Mariscal shrugged. 'We live in a turbulent and challenging international environment. British firms can provide solutions to some of those challenges. We should be proud of that.'

Naomi shook her head. 'What a load of bullshit.'

'It's not. I genuinely believe that, or some of it anyway. But dog shit and bullshit aside, this is actually a pretty decent offer, Naomi. A week on a working aircraft carrier, completely exclusive, access all areas.'

'Have you offered this to anyone else?'

'You know I haven't but you also know that if I do, *Good Morning* wotsit or Sky would have my arm off.'

After breakfast they loitered at the door of the diner a while, making vague promises that they'd meet again soon; dinner was mentioned. Naomi was heading back in the direction of his old office, her new one, when Rob stopped her. 'I meant to ask, how's Carver? I mean I hear his pieces but we're not . . . you know . . . in touch.'

Naomi smiled. 'He's fine. Older, grumpier but he's doing okay. Patrick's keeping him on the straight and narrow and they've had a good Arab Spring. He called it early.'

'He does that.'

'I spoke to him briefly this morning. The world's press are arriving en masse. I think he finds that a little dispiriting.'

Rob smiled. 'Yeah. I bet he didn't put it quite like that. You should watch out for that one. When the whole world gets an appetite for a story, Carver tends to lose his.'

13 *Quod Erat Demonstrandum*

DATELINE: The Seti Hotel, Cairo, Egypt, January 28 2011

'What a goat fuck this is.'

Carver pointed a finger at the object of his displeasure – a lobby full of breathless hacks, half of them with phones clamped to their ears, talking themselves and each other into a frenzy. TV crews from a dozen different countries were gathering their kit together and arguing over taxicabs. Carver sat on the banquette outside the main hotel bar and stared at it all. He elbowed Patrick in the ribs. 'That guy over there, the one that looks like a used car salesman . . .'

Patrick nodded; a square-jawed American was talking into his laptop, giving his TV audience the news via Skype.

'He's been there since breakfast, he hasn't moved! Every fifteen minutes he starts yelling into his computer about how he's got *the latest information*. The rest of the time he's staring at his phone.'

Patrick shook his head. 'Not great.'

'Not great? As far as I'm concerned it's the end of bloody civilisation.'

Patrick stayed shtum. The American newsman's way of working

probably lay somewhere on a line between *not great* and *the end of civilisation* but arguing with William about where it lay on that line was pointless.

'Why are we here then? Why didn't you meet me back down at Tahrir?'

'You think I want to be stuck here? I promised Zahra I'd meet this mate of hers.' William owed Zahra several favours and that morning she'd finally called one in, asking him to hang around the hotel and meet with her. The girl had a story that she thought the British media might be interested in. 'Chances are it'll be a complete waste of time but I said I'd check it out.'

'Why do you need me?'

Carver shuffled in his seat. 'The way Zahra described this friend I thought she'd be more up your street than mine. She's a Twitter and Facebook kind of person apparently.'

'I see.'

'Zahra called her a *citizen journalist*.' Carver could not have sounded more disdainful if he'd tried.

Patrick smiled. 'Do you even know what *citizen journalist* means, William?'

'Yeah. It means not a real journalist.'

Once Zahra had finished dealing with the latest lot of new arrivals she strode over to where Carver and Patrick were sitting.

'Mr Akar is in his office, I cannot bring Nawal into the hotel. I will take you to meet her.'

'Where is she?'

'Outside. In the storeroom next to the pool.'

Carver hauled himself to his feet; the cartilage in his knee clicked loudly as he stood and he winced with pain, Patrick noticed.

'Did Jean get you those painkillers yet?'

'No, she disappeared on me. It's no big deal, I've got my own pills.'

They followed Zahra through the empty dining room and out

the French windows towards the swimming pool. The sun was high and the garden contained every possible shade of green, set off by splashes of bright red from large terracotta pots filled with geraniums. Zahra walked quickly – occasionally glancing back over her shoulder. They walked around the pool bar to a white-washed concrete building with thick metal doors where the sun umbrellas and other swimming pool paraphernalia were kept. It took a while for Carver's eyes to adjust to the gloom. When they did, he saw a stooped, dark-haired figure standing at the back of the storeroom, a black rucksack on her back.

'This is Nawal al-Moallem. Nawal, this is the William Carver that I told you about. And his assistant, Patrick.'

The young woman stepped forward and shook hands, pumping Carver's arm enthusiastically. She was wearing black jeans and a green bomber jacket over a dark grey hoodie; her build was slight, her hair cut short and combed. Carver looked at her; she looked more like a boy than a girl – wearing what she was wearing. He was used to seeing androgynous kids like this in the west but it was unusual in Arab countries. Patrick stared too; he was sure he'd seen Nawal before but was having trouble remembering where.

Zahra pushed four large plastic tubs of chlorine into the centre of the room with her foot and they sat in a square. Nawal smiled nervously at Carver. Her eyes were dark, set wide and she looked like she could use a good night's sleep.

'It is a pleasure to meet with you. I am sorry about my English, it is not good. Zahra helps me all of the time.'

Carver nodded and suggested that Zahra translate.

'Of course. But we should talk quickly, Nawal must not be long. I don't want anyone to see her here.'

Carver nodded. 'Sure, I'm busy too. So what's this all about?'

Zahra jutted her chin in the direction of her friend's rucksack. Nawal shuffled the bag from her back, reached into the bottom and brought out a parcel, wrapped in what looked like a ripped-up bed sheet and tied together with a yard of bright yellow climbing rope. Nawal stood and unrolled the contents of the parcel on to the top of the barrel she'd been sitting on.

Carver nodded. 'That's quite a collection.' Laid out in front of him were half a dozen tear gas canisters, a handful of rubber-coated bullets, some live ammunition and a police baton strikingly similar to one he'd seen before. 'I saw a boy killed with a baton like that – just the other day.' Carver racked his brain for the boy's name . . . *Adjo*, that was it.

He picked up the truncheon and studied it but there were no markings or serial numbers to be seen. Nawal watched him and when he put it back down alongside the rest of her collection she spoke in broken English.

'It is a new type. Other things here are new also.'

'Where'd you get all this stuff?'

The question was directed at Nawal but it was Zahra who answered.

'She collects some herself and other people bring it to her too. It is evidence.'

Carver nodded. 'Evidence of what?'

Zahra was about to speak when Nawal butted in with an indignant-sounding burst of Arabic. Zahra let her finish then translated.

'Human rights abuse, the breaking of international law. Nawal has researched this. She says it is against the law for British-made tear gas to be used here.'

Carver shook his head. 'No, it isn't. It's only against the law for a British company to sell the gas if they knew what it was being used for – *internal repression* they call it. Depends when they sold it too . . .' He picked up one of the canisters. 'If it was back when your President was our best mate then it's all completely kosher.' The metal canister was about ten centimetres long and coloured with red and white stripes. There was a serial number stamped in a typewriter face across the white part of the canister. It looked pretty much like every other CS gas canister Carver had ever seen. 'This looks like old stock to me.'

Zahra nodded. 'Yes, but a few days ago Nawal picked up some different canisters, a new type, bigger. They were so hot they burned through leather gloves.'

Nawal was nodding. 'Say about the police . . .'

Zahra held up a hand to silence her friend. 'The police were different at that demonstration too.'

'Different how?'

'Every time they fired the gas and people ran, police in gas masks came and swept the containers up, took them away.'

Carver felt his stomach shift. A familiar feeling, but not one he'd felt for a while. 'The cops went out into the crowd to collect the used canisters?'

Zahra nodded.

'That's a lot of work right in the middle of a riot. I wonder why they did that?'

Zahra did not give Carver much time to wonder. 'The old canisters were all made by a British company; this new type look the same. So we think maybe this is British too.'

'Has she got one here? One of this new type?'

'She only collected two but she has said you can have one.'

Nawal unzipped her jacket, revealing the silvery tops of two tear gas canisters poking from an inside pocket. She handed one to Carver, who examined it. It was almost identical to the others, with the same stripes of red and white paint but when you placed the two side by side you could see that the new canister was maybe two centimetres longer.

'I can keep this?'

Nawal nodded.

'What about the truncheon?' He pointed at the police baton and Zahra and Nawal consulted.

'No, she says she only has one of these. If someone brings her another then you can have it.'

'Fair enough.' Carver pointed at the row of shorter CS gas canisters. 'What makes her think those are Brit-made?'

'She doesn't think this, she knows it. She searched these numbers on the internet.'

Carver glanced at the scrawny-looking girl. She had initiative, he had to give her that. Zahra explained that every serial number on the old canisters had led Nawal to the same website.

'She could not understand very much that she read but she wrote down the details and the name of the company.' Zahra gestured at her friend who handed Carver a piece of paper, torn from a school exercise book. On it was a list of serial numbers and a name – written carefully once in upper and again in lower case: *Quadrel Engineering and Defence*. Zahra pointed at the canister in Carver's hand. 'There is no number on the new gas but maybe you can show it to someone who knows more about these, discover if it is the same company?'

'I'll check it out.'

Nawal spoke again, at length, and Carver waited somewhat impatiently for Zahra's summary.

'She says they were firing the gas *into* the people that day, not up in the air. There were children and women there. She says you can interview her now if you like and she will tell the story?'

Carver shook his head. The storeroom was baking; he could feel rivulets of sweat flowing from both armpits. 'No need to do that right now, I'll do my own checks first. Are we done?'

Zahra shook her head. 'I want your advice. I have told Nawal not to write too much about this on her Twitter or Facebook. You agree, don't you?'

Carver shrugged. It seemed he was being asked to adjudicate in some dispute between the two women and he didn't want to. 'I suppose there's a chance the police are reading that, although you'd have thought they had better things to do.'

'Certainly they read it, Nawal's work is important. Her Facebook page and Twitter tell people what is going on – where the next protest will be and what the police are doing. She is becoming famous.'

'Ha, of course.'

Patrick slapped his hand on his knee and made a sort of snorting sound. The penny had dropped. 'What's her Twitter handle, Zahra? Just between us.'

'Lawan. Tsquare Lawan.'

Patrick laughed. 'I knew it.'

The four exited the storeroom together. As Patrick watched the two young women say their goodbyes he wondered how Zahra planned to get Nawal back through the hotel unseen. The answer came soon enough. After giving his and Carver's hands another enthusiastic pump, Nawal took off, running full speed in the direction of the high garden wall. For a moment Patrick thought her self-belief was such that she planned to run straight through the bricks. Instead her right foot landed on one of the large terra-cotta pots and she launched herself into the air, landing cat-like on the thin wooden trellis before scampering up. She stood on top of the wall staring down, a broad smile on her face. She was staring at Zahra – this show was for her and no one else. Zahra sucked at her teeth in mock annoyance and waved her friend away. Nawal smiled, pulled her hoodie up, turned and jumped.

Walking back across the gardens, Carver took the gas canister from his pocket and studied it again. He lifted his glasses and took a closer look. Nawal was a smart kid, brave too. But she'd missed something.

The Way of Sorrows (i)

Asmara, Eritrea

The meeting that Gabriel organised for his grandsons had left them more confused than reassured. As far as Gebre could work out, all Mr Adam had given them was a piece of paper with their names on – spelled incorrectly – and a vague promise that they'd be picked up in a taxi two days from now. The big man had stood, straightened his red leather tie and ushered them from the room with a wave of his hand and a gaseous burp. 'Good luck little brothers. Not that you will need luck, you are in the hands of Mr Adam.'

Outside the breezeblock house, Solomon took the letter from its plastic envelope and studied it again. Each line contained the same message: once in Arabic, once in Tigrinya and once in English.

Mr Adam does guarantee good character and cost of transport for the two boys holding this paper: Gebra and Soloman Hassan.

Solomon sucked at his teeth.

'For this, grandfather pays two years' wages? I don't know who

126

is the bigger fool. Him, Adam or you and me.'

The brothers had only walked a little way down the street when they heard their names being shouted: they turned to see Mr Adam standing in the doorway of the borrowed house, waving them back.

'I almost forgot, these are also yours – more VIP service.' He gave them a crooked grin and handed each brother a black plastic sack.

Solomon looked inside and saw a bright orange lifejacket. 'We have to carry this all the way across the desert?'

Mr Adam nodded. 'This is the genuine item, do not lose it or let anyone swap it for another; others are not good.'

14 The Fear

DATELINE: The Seti Hotel, Cairo, Egypt, January 28 2011

Carver ate alone at a table just outside the hotel dining room. The meal was something that Zahra had managed to organise that looked and tasted vaguely like an omelette. He was unsure what part of a cow the meat inside the omelette had come from and he tried not to ponder it too hard. Zahra had also found him the nail file he'd asked for and as soon as he'd taken the edge off his appetite, he set to work on the tear gas canister. The thing that Carver had noticed, the detail that Nawal had missed, was that the stripe of white paint on the new canister was thicker than the red – thicker for a reason, he thought, or hoped. He unfolded a napkin and laid it out on the table, put the canister on top and started filing away at the strip of white paint.

His hunch was correct, although finding the paint-covered serial number and reading it were two different things. The paint had dried hard inside the indented stamp and as he filed the thing down Carver began to realise that he was erasing the number at the same time as filing away the paint.

He considered first white spirit, then a candle flame before a more sensible solution occurred to him, courtesy of his dead mother. Carver's mum had been an incorrigible hobbyist and brass rubbing was one of the many mind-numbing pursuits that a pint-sized William Carver had put up with. After a little confusion he managed to borrow a blunt pencil and some greaseproof paper from the kitchen. Rubbing the pencil sideways across the paper-covered canister brought back memories of cold churches and sore knees but after several attempts and some more work with the nail file, he had a nine-figure serial number. He scribbled it down on the same piece of paper where Nawal had written the details of the old, allegedly UK-made, tear gas and finished his food, washing the omelette down with regular swallows of coffee.

As he cleaned his plate, Carver weighed his options. Patrick had agreed to cover for him for a couple of hours so he could check out Nawal's story. It was supposed to be another big day in Tahrir Square with busloads of pro-democracy protesters arriving from all over Egypt. The calls for the President to step aside were getting louder. Carver checked his watch; he had an hour of his two free hours left, time enough to find an internet café and see if Nawal was on to something. He tucked the gas canister down into the bottom of his plastic bag, belched into his hand and stood.

Nawal had the feeling she was being followed from the moment she stepped off Seti Hotel property and was back on the street. The guy must have seen her scale the wall that separated the hotel car park from the gardens and waited there, assuming she'd leave by the same route. A lucky guess.

She wasn't worried, she'd been tailed before – by plain-clothed police and their goons – and she never had much trouble losing them. She let the guy follow her as far as Café Riche, then shifted her rucksack from her back to the front, quickened her pace and lost him with a couple of quick turns. Once she was sure she'd lost her tail, Nawal walked halfway down the residential street where she'd ended up before stopping and getting out her phone. Up ahead, in a narrow doorway, she saw an old woman using a broom to brush the dust from her dog. Seeing her, the woman hooked a finger through the dog's red collar and dragged it back inside, closing the heavy door firmly behind her; Nawal heard a key turn in the lock. If the revolution failed, it would be because of people like this, people scared of the young, scared of change. But the revolution would not fail. Nawal sat down on the pavement, her back against the warm brick wall and rucksack by her side. She hacked into some nearby Wi-Fi and set to work.

@tsquarelawan
Friday, January 28th will be the biggest day yet. A day that will live in history.

@tsquarelawan
Come! If the amazing scenes and emotion do not make you cry then the tear gas will!

@tsquarelawan
And speaking of tear gas. Journalists are asking who is selling the President the CS gas he fires at children?

@tsquarelawan
Before long the people will be in the palace and the President and his friends will be in prison!

She posted these then sent a direct message to Zahra asking her to check them for her and correct any mis-translations. She ended this message with a string of 'x's. Then deleted them. She tried a mix of 'x's and 'o's before deciding this looked childish and settling on a simple Nx as a sign-off. The sun was high and Nawal was typing away, concentrating. When a shadow suddenly fell across her, she jumped and almost dropped her phone. The stranger standing above her shaped his face into a smile.

'You are all right?'

It was the same man who had been following her, the tail she thought she'd lost.

'I am fine.'

'Good. I saw that you were on the floor. I feared for you.'

'No need.'

He spoke slowly and with a thick Cairo accent, similar to hers; he was local. He had a long face and close-cropped dark hair and Nawal guessed that they were of similar age although wear and tear and poverty had left this guy looking considerably older. He wore a purple shirt that was a size too small and needed washing, his jeans were loose fitting and worn low enough that she could see an inch or so of labelled underwear between belt and shirt.

'What are you doing?'

'Sitting, working; minding my own business.' She picked up her rucksack and stood, hoping that this might help even things up but the guy was tall, six foot two or bigger.

He eyed Nawal up and down then stepped closer. She tightened her grip on the rucksack – her unwanted observer noticed this and smiled. It was the rucksack and its contents that he had come for; anything else he could get was a bonus. Nawal found herself staring at the thick scar that ran down the left side of the man's face, from ear to jaw. Sensing her stare, the stranger raised his hand and cradled that side of his face in a considered manner.

'I almost lost you, little sister. You know the city well. Nearly as well as I know it.'

'I'm not your sister.'

Nawal tried to move away from the man, edging sideways down the street but the purple shirt moved with her, keeping her pinned close to the wall. His hand moved towards his belt

131

buckle and Nawal had her mouth half open to scream when his filthy, knuckle-scabbed hand shot out and muffled her mouth, gagging her. He grinned again.

'Shh, don't fear. That's not what I want. You are not my type anyway. Too ugly. Just empty your pockets, hand me your bag and we will be done.'

She shook her head. At her back she could hear the old lady's dog, sniffing inquisitively at the foot of the door. Nawal spoke, spitting the words through his scabby hand. 'Fuck you.'

The man shrugged, a look of resignation on his long face; he glanced left and right – there was no one else on the street. He took his hand from her mouth and reached again for the front of his jeans. She felt her stomach tighten. Nawal glanced up at the balcony opposite in time to see a pair of curtains being pulled shut and when she looked back, purple shirt was holding a knife. He jabbed it sharply in the direction of her face. Nawal jerked her head backwards, bashing it on the wooden door behind her.

'Bag and money, bitch.'

She glanced at the weapon. Not a knife but a scalpel, its handle reinforced with dirty brown gaffer tape but its blade silvery sharp. He reached again for the rucksack. Nawal's reaction was unplanned, instinctive: she raised her hands and shoved the man with all her strength. He staggered backwards, tripping on a broken kerbstone and ending up on his backside in the gutter. He'd dropped the blade and Nawal watched as he scrambled around on the ground looking for it. She knew that *now* was the time to run; she tried to lift a foot, willing her legs to move but they would not. Within seconds her attacker was back on his feet, scalpel in hand. He stared at the skinny girl, waiting for her next move. But Nawal didn't have one. For the first time in a long time – she was scared.

Jean ran into Carver as he was walking out of the dining room.

'Hey there, Billy.'

'Hello.'

'You're still walking a little stiff there, aren't you? Good thing I brought my medicine cabinet with me.' She had a large make-up bag in one hand and a laptop case in the other.

Carver shrugged. 'I thought we were supposed to do this yesterday?'

'I'm sorry, I got a little caught up with something.'

William wanted to ask for further details but he was aware how that might sound. 'It's not a problem, I was busy anyway.'

'Really? Some people said you were wandering around in your budgie smugglers looking for me.'

Carver felt his face redden. 'Rubbish.'

'If I'd known, then I certainly would have been here. Anyway, I'm sorry for blowing you out. You got a few minutes now?'

They found a quiet corner of the main hotel bar and Jean dug through her make-up bag until she found a strip of bright pink pills. 'Two with food or just after. You eaten?'

'An omelette.'

'Lucky you. What does that horse meat taste like?'

'Eh?'

'Rumour is that's what we're eating now. They've run out of cows. What's that you've got there?'

Jean was pointing at the canister, poking from Carver's jacket pocket.

'A story, possibly.'

'What kind of story?'

'Someone selling the Egyptians stuff they shouldn't.'

'Tear gas? British?'

Carver hesitated. 'Could be.'

Jean smiled. 'Don't worry. Like I said before, I'm not your competition, I'm no kind of newshound anymore.'

'What are you then?'

'I'm a house pet: features and interviews, shit like that. You *know* the kind of stuff I do these days, Carver.'

'So why'd they send you *here?*'

'I'm going to do some human interest stuff. Profile some of the protesters and maybe the other side too . . .' Fitzgerald paused; now they were getting to it. No one other than her editor knew the real reason she'd been sent to Cairo, but she didn't mind telling Carver, he was a good man with a secret. 'I interviewed him once.'

'Him? Who? The President?'

Jean nodded.

Purple shirt brushed the dust from his jeans and grinned. The fact that his victim had been too frightened to run obviously amused him. Nawal raised her hands in a placatory gesture; she was about to speak, to beg even. Before she could, the man took a fast step forward and punched her hard in the gut. The force of the blow folded Nawal in two. She gazed down at the pavement, swallowing for air, her mouth filled with a sour-tasting bile; she spat and dribbled and tried to draw breath. She could hear the old lady's dog, its low growl on the other side of the thick wooden door behind her. Her attacker heard it too and it seemed to unsettle him; he grabbed a handful of Nawal's hair and yanked it upwards. She lifted her head, straightening her body and stretching her neck against this new pain. The man pulled her higher, holding the scalpel close to Nawal's throat as he did so. When suddenly he let go of Nawal's sweat-wet hair and her head dropped, the blade drew blood.

Purple shirt kept the scalpel close to her neck while, using his free hand, he frisked her, reaching into Nawal's pockets and emptying them – keeping what he wanted and throwing the rest away. He had been hired to do a job but this girl had already been more trouble than he'd expected and he wanted to make it worth his while. Any money or valuables the girl had on her were his to keep. Once he'd taken what was worth taking from her pockets, he turned his attention to the rucksack. Nawal gripped the bag tight; she'd decided that she would not give up the rucksack and its contents, regardless of what this man did to her. He was trying pull it from her hand when there was a noise: a key turning in the lock.

Nawal felt movement at her back and someone pushing against her, forcing the door open, only a few inches, but enough – the dog squeezed through. Glancing down, Nawal saw the animal at her side, teeth bared and barking with a volume out of all proportion to his size. Her attacker panicked and dropped his knife; he grabbed again for the rucksack but still Nawal would not let go. He kicked at the dog but missed and the dog locked his jaws firmly around his flailing ankle. He swore, shook the dog loose then slammed Nawal's head hard against the door and ran, sprinting down the street, the dog chopping at his heels.

Nawal felt every ounce of strength leave her; she slid to the floor and out of consciousness, her hand still gripping the rucksack straps.

'I spent a few days with him – at the Presidential Palace and his place in Sharm El Sheikh. It was a while back, but my boss at the *Express* thought I might have a shot at a follow-up.'

Carver stared at Jean. 'I can't believe I never saw that. What was he like?'

Jean paused. 'Interesting, not the sharpest knife in the drawer but he had a good sense of humour, he liked to gossip about other world leaders; and he liked a drink – whisky. I remember it got a little out of hand after the whisky.'

Carver waited, he knew better than to rush Fitzgerald when she was working up a yarn.

'He chased me round the furniture for a while. Told me a few things he probably shouldn't have.'

'Did you get a news line?'

'I got more than that, I got a front page lead. Plus he offered my dad a dozen camels and a villa in Sharm.'

'For what?'

'For my hand in marriage, you idiot. What else? He said he wanted me for wife number three.'

'Tempted?'

'Sure I was, three's not bad. Marrying dictators is like buying Microsoft stock: you've got to get in early.'

'But you said no.'

'Yeah, though sometimes I wonder why. I could be living the life of Riley. Rather than the life of Fitzgerald, which I can tell you is no bloody picnic these days.' She saw him glance again at his watch. 'You need to be somewhere else?'

'I want to check this tear gas out 'fore I meet Patrick down at Tahrir.'

'Go. We'll do that proper catch-up later. I need to work anyway.' She patted the laptop computer. 'I have to message the President's man and tell him I'm here, hassle him some more.'

Carver stood and tucked his shirt-tails into his trousers. 'Who are you dealing with?'

Jean paused before answering. 'Abdul Balit.'

'You're kidding.'

'Nope. I got to know him a little too. He was never far from his boss's side. I try to keep all my old contacts warm: the odd email, a Christmas card. You know Balit too?'

Carver shook his head. 'Only by reputation, I'm not sure I want to know him any better than that.'

Colonel Balit was an enigmatic figure in Egyptian politics. The President's chief security adviser, fixer and right hand for many years, Balit was thought to wield a good deal more power and influence than politicians whose names were far better known internationally.

'What's he calling himself these days?'

Jean opened her laptop and looked at her emails. 'Colonel Abdul Balit. Head of Egyptian Security and Presidential Chief of Staff.'

Carver nodded. 'You know what most Egyptians call him these days, do you?'

She shook her head. 'They call him the *Torturer in Chief.*'

Jean nodded. 'I'll be careful.'

'Do.' He stood. 'You've got friends in high places, Fitzgerald, I'll give you that.'

'Some in high places, others in low places. That's how it always used to work. I know some things have changed but I don't suppose that has.'

When Nawal came to, her hands were empty, the rucksack gone. She panicked and tried to move but the pain and dizziness were immediate and extreme. She lay very still and gave the light fittings and floor a chance to stop spinning. She was lying on her side in what looked like a hallway; the wall in front of her was a textured wallpaper painted with a thick layer of brown lacquer. She turned her head and a long pink tongue swept across her face, Nawal grimaced and tried to focus. The dog was a dusty brown colour with a red collar. She'd seen the dog before. The details of what had happened came back piecemeal. The dog pushed his muzzle up towards Nawal's face; she felt his blunt whiskers on her neck, as he unfurled his tongue and gave her another long lick.

'Ow.' She winced and her hand went to her neck then stopped; she poked gently at the wound – an inch-long cut. Examining her fingers she saw congealed blood mixed with a viscous white antiseptic cream; as she considered the meaning of this, the dog took another lick. Nawal pushed him away. 'La!'

She worried briefly about the wound – about rabies and disease – before remembering her grandfather's absolute belief in the healing power of dog saliva. There was a thick rope of spit hanging from the corner of the dog's mouth. Nawal wondered whether

her granddad's rule applied to *all* dogs. She hoped so. The animal sensed Nawal's change of mood and leaned into her side, lifting his muzzle so she could return the favour and scratch his chin and bony chest. This done, he gave Nawal another lick and lay down in the crook of her arm. The dog had saved her, but not the dog alone. Nawal pushed herself up into a sitting position and took a proper look around – whoever had come to her rescue had managed to drag her off the street but only as far as the hall. The door to the ground-floor flat was closed but as she looked a strip of yellow light appeared at its base and she heard the rattling of keys; the dog left her and moved to greet his owner.

The old woman who opened the door wore a black jellabiya and headscarf; the sight of Nawal sitting up and staring at her startled the woman and she stopped. The dog sniffed at her slippers before taking up position at her side.

Nawal nodded. '*Hala.*'

The woman did not respond; if anything her brow became more furrowed. An informal *hi* was not the correct greeting and Nawal tried again, '*Marhaban.*' The woman nodded and encouraged by this Nawal put her hand to her chest and continued: '*Shukran, shukran Madaam.*'

The woman stepped back into her apartment then quickly re-appeared carrying a gold tray, and shuffled into the hallway and placed it on the floor a foot or so from her guest. On it, to Nawal's considerable relief, was her rucksack as well as her phone, some scraps of paper and coins and also the scalpel, with its dirty gaffer-taped handle. Nawal's hand went again to her neck.

As well as these things there was a cup of black coffee. '*Shukran.*' The old lady stood with her hands folded in front of her, twisting her wedding ring and waiting for the visitor to finish her drink, gather her things and go. Nawal took a sip of the sweet, bituminous coffee and felt immediately better. The brown dog wandered back to Nawal, sat at her side and allowed himself to be petted. The old woman smiled for the first time, a gentle smile that softened her features and changed her face. The dog's good opinion clearly counted for much.

'*Eghsilly wajhaki*.' The old lady lifted her hands to her face, miming a washing motion, stepped back into her apartment, held the front door open and ushered Nawal in.

The flat was cramped but impeccably clean; it smelled of bleach and rosewater. There were two of almost everything: two large lumpy armchairs, each with its own piecrust-top side table; two high-backed dining chairs either side of a dark wooden table; two sets of drawers, one with an old Bakelite telephone on top. On the walls, no paintings just a simple mirror and a gallery of framed photographs, all but two of them black and white. The faces that stared out from inside the silver frames were of varying ages but Nawal recognised the old woman in most, usually standing alongside a well-dressed man with a moustache. The dog cropped up in both of the colour pictures: in one he was a scrawny-looking puppy cradled in the woman's arms; in the other he was leaning hard against the man's leg.

The old lady returned from the kitchen with a basin of steaming hot water, a hand towel and a block of soap. She placed them down on the dining table and encouraged Nawal to sit and wash her wound. While she washed, turning the soapy water a pale pink as she did so, the old lady made herself busy moving around the flat, talking quietly to herself or to the dog.

She brought another cup of sweet coffee and put it next to the basin along with a tube of white cream – the same antiseptic that she had applied earlier – a small square of gauze and some tape. She muttered something, pointing at Nawal's neck before returning again to the kitchen. As she dressed the wound Nawal tried to recall as much detail of the attack and her attacker as she could and to work out what it meant. It had not been random, she knew that; the man had followed her from the hotel. It was not a straightforward robbery either – he wanted her rucksack more than he wanted her expensive phone or any money she had. He wanted the bag despite not knowing what was inside it. Or did he know? Or he'd been hired to steal the bag by someone else who knew what was in it? It was this explanation that rang most true and once Nawal knew this she also knew that she couldn't risk being back on the street, still carrying her collection of gas canisters, bullets and batons.

The old lady was still in the kitchen, muttering endearments to the dog. Nawal looked around the room; it was obvious which armchair the old woman sat in and which belonged to her dead husband. Nawal unzipped the rucksack.

The Way of Sorrows (ii)

Asmara, Eritrea

Gabriel was keen that the brothers meet with a couple of their fellow passengers before the day of departure. Strength in numbers was his explanation.

'The smugglers who will take you across the desert will try and divide you, so it is better if you have made a connection.'

Sitting across a table in the almost empty Taxi Café, Gebre had his doubts. He knew the two, at least by reputation: Titus and Dumac had been students at the same school as the brothers but they were a couple of years older than Solomon and had left the school as soon as they were allowed to. The pair had been trouble while at school and had remained troublesome ever since; both had served short prison sentences – not for political crimes but for pick-pocketing and theft. They were banned from most shops in Asmara and unemployable anywhere. It was no surprise that they wanted to leave the country. After some awkward introductions and a little small talk, the five men sat in silence around the table nursing their drinks; it was Titus who spoke first, directing his question at Solomon.

'The cycling did not work out for you then?'

Gebre felt his brother bristle slightly.

'Not as I hoped.'

'Shame. Still, you two have family connections here, your grand-father looks after you, why do you need to leave?'

'For the same reasons as you, I think: for a better life.'

Titus flicked a quick smile in the direction of his friend. 'Some people will never be happy, eh?'

The suggestion that he and his brother were a couple of poor little rich boys was too much for Gebre. 'What is your reason? You have stolen from every shop in Eritrea so now you have to find another country to steal from, is that it?'

The two older boys stood and squared up to Gebre but when Solomon got to his feet, they quickly backed down. Gabriel tried to patch things up but to no avail. When the pair picked up their half-finished bottles of beers and strode from the bar, Gabriel sent Solomon to apologise. Gebre had to endure his grandfather's angry silence and then a lecture.

'That was foolish.'

Gebre shrugged.

'You just fell a little in my estimation, grandson. Sol is the strong one – you are meant to be the smart one. What you just did was stupid. Where you are both going, there will be plenty of people ready to hate you without any reason – no need to give them an excuse.'

Gebre blushed. 'I'm sorry, Grandfather.'

15 Error 404

DATELINE: The Corniche, Cairo, Egypt, January 28 2011

Patrick had kept London at bay for as long as he could. His mobile rang again; he checked the caller ID and grudgingly answered it. The sequence of calls to his phone in the last few hours had offered a neat illustration of the BBC hierarchy: first programme producers called him, then senior producers, assistant editors, a deputy editor and now his boss, Naomi Holder.

'What the hell's going on?'

'William sent me a text about an hour ago saying he'd see me soon but he's not here yet. The traffic is crazy, almost every street is blocked, I'm sure he'll be here soon.'

'Don't make excuses for him. I can reach *you* on the mobile, why not him?'

'Well, quite a few of the networks are down . . .' Patrick heard the sound of an open hand hitting a computer keyboard.

'Shit, I really am going to kill him this time.'

Patrick waited. He listened as his boss attempted to slow her breathing.

'Okay, so listen, I already promised you'd file for radio bulletins and other programmes. You're going to have to take the material you've gathered and go beg newsgathering for a voice, any decent voice. If you do most of the work, they might say yes. If they don't, then I don't know what we do. Head down to the Corniche and see who you can find.'

'I'm already here.'

'Good boy, so go turn on the charm. And Patrick?'

'Yes, boss.'

Naomi paused; she was remembering now what Rob Mariscal had told her earlier, about Carver losing interest in stories after a certain point.

'You're quite sure William's just held up somewhere. He's not gone chasing after something else?'

'What? Sure he's just—'

'Because there is nothing else. I'm sitting in a newsroom with a hundred different TV screens on and Tahrir is on every single one. There *is* no other story – Tahrir Square is the only bloody story in the world right now and if I find out that you're covering for him, I'll fire the both of you.'

Carver remembered seeing an internet café not far from the hotel and in the same general direction as the city centre. If Patrick had waited this long, he could wait a little longer. He considered leaving the canister in the room, hiding it somewhere, before deciding he'd feel safer having it with him. He'd buried it at the bottom of his bag, underneath his notebooks and MiniDisc recorder. Walking away from the hotel he felt the warm sun on his back; the cafés were busy, with groups of elderly men sitting outside in plastic chairs playing chequers and dominos.

The internet café was easy enough to find but it was busy; walking up and down the rows of seats it seemed that every terminal was already in use. The café manager waved Carver over. The man was sitting on a high stool next to an old-fashioned cash register. He wore a white T-shirt and had heavily gelled, spiky black hair, which made him look like an oil-stricken seabird. He told Carver that it was ten American dollars for an hour; this was ten times the rate shown on the chalkboard behind him but Carver paid it.

'Come back to here in two minutes, you will have this machine.' He pointed at a kid in headphones who was soon to have his game of World of Warcraft cut short.

Carver stepped outside to wait. Standing on the pavement he heard a low rumbling noise and, looking up, saw an Egyptian army jet flying low across the city. Within moments the F16 was back, making a return pass and this time the plane flew so low and made such a mighty noise that a chorus of car alarms went off in its wake. Back inside the café, he nodded at the owner and made himself as comfortable as possible on the rickety wooden chair. He put his yellow carrier bag down at his feet and got out his notebook and the piece of paper where Nawal had written the list of serial numbers.

Carver looked at the computer and saw that it had a built-in camera just above the monitor. He took another look inside his bag and found the three-day-old chicken shawarma sandwich, its brown paper wrapping now almost black with grease. Carver glanced at the café owner, who was busy counting a pile of dirty green notes, then unwrapped the sandwich, tore a piece of pitta bread off, smeared it in tahini sauce and stuck it over the computer's shiny eye. He switched the hard disk on and waited for the thing to warm up.

He started from first principles, typing one of the serial numbers from the old gas canisters into the search engine, initially by itself, which yielded nothing and then with a few other key words: gas, CS, canister. The words *canister* and *public order* both took Carver to a list of entries that included the company Nawal had identified: QUADREL.CO.UK.

Carver glanced around the café. No one was paying him the

least bit of attention, every face glued hard to its own screen. He double-clicked on Quadrel.

The company's front page looked impressive: the main picture was of a huge aircraft carrier, bristling with weapons systems, planes and helicopters. The carrier was sailing into a rather beautiful sunset and it was about as pretty as a picture of a huge piece of military hardware could be. Above this photo, in good solid sans serif lettering, was the company name: *Quadrel Engineering & Defence* and its logo – a stag beetle. He clicked on the first link. The neatly written introduction told you very little beyond the fact that Quadrel provided *Defence equipment for national armies and navies worldwide. Everything necessary to meet a turbulent international security context head-on.* He clicked on a few more links, looking for some specifics and found commendations from the *World Defence Almanac, Naval Forces* magazine and other similar trade publications.

Several of the clickable boxes led to the same message: a polite request that he email Quadrel with details of his enquiry. He clicked on the link for press and publicity and got a different email address; this was for a well-known PR company situated near Pall Mall. Carver had dealt with them before, the boss was some New Labour numpty who had sold out in spades and he had no interest in contacting them. His eye kept wandering back to the search function at the top of Quadrel's homepage. He scratched at his chin and took another quick look around the café.

'*In for a penny . . .*'

Carver flicked through his notepad until he found the nine-figure serial number he'd discovered hidden under a layer of white paint on the gas canister that Nawal had given him. He carefully typed the number into the search box, paused, and then pressed ENTER.

Nothing happened for what seemed like a very long time; so long that Carver eventually got to his feet and glanced around to see if anyone else in the café was having trouble with their internet connection, but there was no sign of it. When he looked back there was an error message in the centre of the screen:

HTTP Error 404 – File not found.

'Fair enough.' He was about to delete the search and try again when the screen suddenly flashed bright white and then black. It stayed that way for a couple of seconds before another message appeared in the centre of the screen.

This website would like to use your current location
Do Not Allow / Allow

'Use it for what? Fuck off.' Carver clicked firmly on the box marked *Do Not Allow* but it remained unselected. He tried again. And again. Nothing. All of a sudden the box marked *Allow* selected itself and a grey-coloured egg-timer started to spin. Carver looked up and saw that a dull green light had appeared above his screen, shining through the thin layer of pitta bread and tahini – the computer's camera had switched itself on. He shoved his chair back, reached underneath the desk and switched off the hard drive but when he looked back up, the egg-timer was still spinning, the green light still lit. He scrambled back down on to the floor and pulled every plug he could lay his hands on. When he got back to his feet he saw that his machine and several others in his row were dark, and the entire café was staring at him.

Carver gave a sheepish smile and turned to the spiky-haired manager. 'Sorry about that – almost gave my credit card details to some German porn site.'

The man looked Carver up and down and went back to counting his money. William packed his stuff away and hurried out of the café and into the street; he could hear the blood pumping in his ears. Nawal was on to something, and now – so was he.

The BBC broadcast point Patrick was looking for was sandwiched in between CNN and a Spanish network halfway down a growing line of TV crews. The person in charge of the operation was Vivian

Fox, a calm-headed and competent producer who Patrick knew reasonably well. Vivian had worked as Carver's producer a few years back in Kabul but the partnership had ended early and with a good deal of acrimony – Carver had behaved badly and Vivian had refused to put up with it. Patrick had always rather admired her for this. He stood and watched his colleague brief her cameraman and presenter. She was wearing cargo pants and a blue linen shirt buttoned to the neck; her dark hair was pulled into a tidy ponytail and covered in a white headscarf, and in her hand she held a black clipboard. When she saw Patrick she smiled and strode over.

'Hey there, radio boy, come to see how the other half live?'

'Something like that.'

'Look at this . . .' Vivian waved her clipboard in the direction of the crowds of people making their way down the road in the direction of Tahrir Square. 'Exciting, huh? History in the making and all that?'

Patrick shrugged. 'I guess so.' He paused. 'Carver keeps reminding me that it's our job *not* to get excited.'

Vivian pulled a face. 'Ah, William. One of the most annoying things about him is that he's usually right. He's a walking rebuke to me, that man – the one who got away.'

Patrick shook his head. 'From what I hear, you did everything you could.' Patrick looked up and down the long row of live broadcast points, the smart-suited anchor-men and -women lit by bright arc lights. 'Maybe you'd fancy another shot? We could do a job swap?'

'You don't mean that, take a look at this . . .' Vivian handed Patrick the clipboard; the top page was a complicated-looking grid of times and broadcast commitments. 'That's just the next few hours, endless live two-ways and bulletin pieces. I can barely go for a pee, let alone walk around and find out what's going on.'

Patrick gave her a sympathetic look.

'Then there's Brandon.'

Just then a well-maintained man aged somewhere around sixty and wearing a cream-coloured linen suit walked up.

'Viv. A word?'

'Of course, John. You remember Patrick? William Carver's producer.'

John Brandon gave Patrick an incurious look. 'Course I do, yes.' He turned away. 'So, Viv, I'm going to mention these rumours about Egyptian soldiers deserting in my next two-way. That, and maybe this fuel shortage stuff too.'

Vivian stared at Brandon, who was pointing a thick finger at his phone. 'Where are you getting all this from?'

'@bigbeartahrir – he's got a load of followers.'

'Right, well I'd rather you—'

'Don't worry, I'll just say *reports*.'

'How about you say *unconfirmed reports*.' Vivian sighed and followed her presenter back towards his chair.

Brandon's presence was confirmation that BBC newsgathering believed some sort of major world news event was on the cards. A story that would require blanket coverage, including the icing on the cake: an outside broadcast from John Brandon, live into the *Ten O'Clock News*. Before long Vivian was back, an exasperated grimace on her face.

'I've got about ten minutes, shall we try to get a mint tea or something?'

Patrick shook his head. 'I'm afraid it's not really a social call, Viv, I'm here with my begging bowl.'

'I thought you might be, you and Carver don't talk to us TV types unless you have to. I believe *newsgathering monkeys* is what William calls us?'

'What? No, I've not heard him say that.'

Vivian gave him a disbelieving look. 'So what do you need?'

Patrick explained his predicament and made as convincing a case as he could. He showed Vivian the script he'd drafted and said that he'd be happy to record it with whoever she could spare and that they could do it right here. Vivian was consulting her clipboard to see whether there was a correspondent free when Patrick's phone rang. He checked the screen – it was Rebecca. He hesitated a moment then let it go to answerphone.

'Sorry.'

'No problem. London?'

'No, no, it was my girlfriend, Rebecca.'

'Course. Rebecca, the teacher. How is she?'

'She's good, yeah, great. Er, how do you . . .?'

'We met at one of those god-awful *Today* programme parties a year or so back.'

Patrick nodded; he had no memory of this.

'She's great, Rebecca, you're lucky to have someone like that. Someone normal.'

'Yeah, very lucky.' Patrick paused; he sensed that some sort of reciprocal enquiry was expected. 'How about you? Are you seeing someone?'

Vivian shuffled her feet. 'Well . . . actually I'm seeing Steven.'

'Steven?'

'Yeah, you know? Our Steven?'

'Steve? Security Steve?'

'Yes. He doesn't really like being called that, but yeah, Security Steve. He's actually all right and . . .'

Patrick noticed Vivian's face had reddened. 'And?'

'Well, you've seen what he looks like.' She was blushing now. 'Bet you're sorry you asked?'

Patrick shook his head in a way that must have looked more convincing than it felt because Vivian continued.

'I think that every woman deserves to experience someone like that. At least once in her romantic career. Don't you?'

'Er, I'm going to have to think about that one. I'm busy wondering whether Rebecca feels the same way. Hopefully not.'

Vivian laughed. 'I don't think you have to worry about Rebecca, I reckon she's only ever had time for the sensitive types – blokes like you.' Vivian gave Patrick a watchful look. 'You're still the sensitive type, aren't you, Patrick?'

'Sure.'

Carver was standing outside the internet café with his arm in the air for ten minutes before it became clear that any cab heading into the middle of Cairo was booked or busy. He set off walking and as he walked he took stock: it was obvious that Nawal's story was worthy of further investigation. First the Egyptian police didn't want people knowing they'd fired a particular type of tear gas and now a British company was being a bit shy about having manufactured it – that was a decent start. Carver had a familiar, premonitory feeling – one that down the years he had learned to trust. The problem was going to be pursuing this story at the same time as doing the day job.

At the first crossroads, he came upon a group of students, organising themselves before marching in to join the larger demonstration. At the centre of the group was a woman with a thick artist's brush and a jar of black ink, kneeling next to a pile of paper and recycled cardboard boxes. Some of the hand-painted placards she was making were written in English, others in Arabic. They made the familiar demands: disband the police force, end the regime. The largest of the banners, attached to broom handles and held aloft by two school-age kids, was more straightforward: it demanded *Bread & Freedom*.

When the group of students set off, Carver followed on behind, his tape machine in hand. No more than fifteen or twenty young people, walking down the street at an easy pace, clumped together in solidarity and at the front – riding on the shoulders of his friend – a boy barely out of his teens with his hands cupped around his mouth, shouting slogans that echoed the banners being carried.

They walked down narrow residential streets and main roads, passing cafés and juice shops overflowing with interested onlookers and as they walked the numbers grew. Now and again a marcher would peel off to buy some buttery sweetcorn or peanuts from a street-seller before running to catch up again with their friends. The streets were alive and for now, at least, the mood celebratory.

Carver had arranged to meet Patrick near the ever-growing line of live broadcast points. Patrick was up on the BBC gantry talking to a woman Carver recognised and was keen to avoid and so he decided to wait on the pavement below. While he waited, he counted the number of media organisations: twenty at least. While he was waiting he walked up and down the line and tuned his ear to a few of the live broadcasts. The same people he'd seen on TV screens in hotel rooms over the last few weeks saying that an Egyptian revolution was impossible, now seemed to believe it was inevitable. Patrick didn't take long.

'Hey, William.'

'Playing footsy with the newsgathering monkeys, are you?'

Patrick glanced back over his shoulder to see if Viv had heard this; a fractional lifting of her eyebrow told him that she had. She wasn't the only person who had noticed William; before Patrick could get them away, John Brandon was bouncing down the steps, bellowing Carver's name. Patrick leaned towards William. 'Play nicely, please? I need favours from these guys.'

Brandon put a ham-like hand on Carver's shoulder. 'I was hoping I'd see you, William. I was just telling your boy here how good I thought that Muslim Brotherhood interview you did was.'

Patrick looked at Brandon, he'd told him nothing of the sort.

'I wondered if you fancied doing a turn on the telly with me? Tell the great British public what you think it means?'

Carver smiled. 'I think it's too early to say.'

Brandon guffawed. 'Ha, yes. Bit like Mao on the French Revolution – or was it Nixon?'

'Neither, but you're close. I think I'll pass. Journalists talking to other journalists about journalism: that's not the kind of stuff we should be doing, is it?'

'Good point, couldn't agree more. Danger of us disappearing up our own whatsit sometimes, isn't there? Talking of scoops though, I've got a sit-down with the ambassador later on. Dinner first and then something on the record with our man in Cairo. I'm happy to let you have a listen if you like.'

'Thanks, John.'

Walking away from the BBC broadcast point, Patrick nudged Carver with his elbow. 'Cheers for that, you can be pretty diplomatic when you want to.'

Carver grunted.

'Do you want me to get hold of a copy of his interview with the ambo?'

'Fuck no. The man only moved here from Estonia a few weeks ago, he probably knows even less about Egypt than John Brandon. Have you spoken to London?'

'Yep. Naomi's pretty het up but I reckon a solid afternoon's work will calm her down.'

'What does she want? More blood, sweat and tear gas?'

'That's it. She's worried we're losing focus, told me to tell you that Tahrir is the only story in the world right now, there's no other story.'

'Yeah? Well, she's wrong.'

By 9 p.m. Carver was knackered. He could happily have fallen into bed and slept but he was determined to give some time and thought to Nawal's discovery. He took his laptop down to the hotel garden – empty now that the pool bar had closed for the night – and set himself up on a lounger at the end of the swimming pool furthest from the hotel. Carver connected to the hotel's internet, balanced the laptop on his belly and started reading. He looked at the current rules around exporting to Egypt, at international law regulating the sale of CS gas and definitions of internal repression. He sent emails to his contacts at *Jane's Defence* and Chatham House but kept the nature of his enquiries vague. The curious behaviour of his computer at the internet café had left him cautious, wary of putting too much information out there – at least for now.

He'd been at it for almost an hour when he heard footsteps, the ricochet of high heels on the hotel flagstones. Looking up he saw a tall figure at the other end of the pool. Carver squinted against the darkness; the woman was walking his way. Eventually the lanky shadow resolved itself into the distinctive shape of Jean Fitzgerald. When it did, Carver felt his heart lift.

Jean considered the limited seating options close to William before lowering herself on to the sunbed nearest to his.

'You might have to help me out of this thing.'

'Of course.'

'I thought I might find you out here, you antisocial old bastard.'

Carver pushed his laptop shut.

'Not that you're missing anything. John Brandon's holding court in the hotel bar so I thought I'd mooch about.'

William nodded; he'd noticed down the years that Jean and John Brandon gave each other a wide berth. He'd always assumed there must have been some kind of romantic falling out at some point, though he really hadn't given it much thought.

'You two don't get along.'

'No. You know the story of course?'

Carver shook his head.

'Really? I thought everyone knew the story. Brandon's got this line, a chat-up line he uses. Anyway, back in the day – the Balkans it was – he tried it on me.'

Jean explained how Brandon would begin by telling the object of his affection how lovely she was, how irresistible, how much he longed for her. 'He used to seal the deal by telling you his balls would explode if you didn't sleep with him.'

Carver stifled a laugh. 'He told *you* this?'

'Yeah.' Jean shrugged. 'It sounded like a pretty serious situation – volatile. I decided the best thing to do was perform a controlled explosion. Using my knee.'

Carver grinned.

'I might've overdone it. A friend told me it took him a while to find the second ball. Anyway, he's stayed pretty clear of me since then.'

'I bet.' Carver could feel the darkness thicken around them.

Fitzgerald put a hand to the front pocket of her loose trousers and pulled out a silver hip flask. 'I know you're doing all that *swimming, not smoking* thing but I assume you're still allowed a slug of brandy?'

'Sure.'

'Excellent, have a go at this . . .' She handed him the flask. 'It's cognac, the best that Auckland airport duty-free had to offer. That's *my* resolution. No more cheap booze, I'm too old for cheap booze.'

While they took turns with the flask, the pair chatted. Jean was no closer to getting an interview with the President but she'd started work on some feature articles. 'Hopefully that'll keep the editor happy until I land the big one.'

'What kind of thing are you doing?'

'Personality-led stuff. Kinda thing you hate.'

Carver shook his head.

'I'm gonna do something about this priest: Father Rumbek. You heard of him?'

'No.'

'He's interesting, a sort of international do-gooder. Pope's man in North Africa right now, bit of a hero for some. Think Mother Teresa with a schlong.'

'There's your first paragraph.'

'Yeah, the story should more or less write itself. He's a bit of a big-head but good company and you know I've always had a soft spot for a priest.'

'Did he hear your confession too?'

'Nah, we only had a few hours. Maybe next time, I'm seeing him again. How about you?'

Carver gave Jean the short version of his day, most of which had been spent in Tahrir watching the square steadily fill and filing regular updates.

Jean nodded. 'It doesn't sound like you're loving it, Billy.'

Carver shook his head. 'No. Now that the world and his wife have arrived I'm not sure what I can offer. Brandon and that lot are all over it. I'm just adding to the noise.'

'Not your kind of story anymore, huh?' She took the flask from his hand. 'Did you get a chance to check out that tear gas thing?'

Carver sat up a little straighter. 'Yeah. Looks like there might be something in that. I was just doing a little digging.' Carver explained that he needed to get the young woman who'd seen the gas being used on the record and find some other witnesses if there were any. 'Then I'll see if I can get someone on the Egyptian side to admit they were using something new, something that's found its way in since the export ban.'

Jean gave this some thought. 'If I get anywhere near Colonel Balit, maybe I can help? He could be pretty indiscreet, back in the day.'

Carver smiled. 'He had the hots for you too, huh?'

Jean shrugged. 'If you're a drunk or a sociopath – I'm irresistible.' She passed the booze back. 'It's only nice fellas never been interested.' Carver stuttered – reaching for some sort of reassurance – but Jean waved him away. 'Don't worry, I wasn't complaining. Maybe I should've said yes to the President, back when that offer was on the table.'

'A dozen camels and a villa, was it?'

'Yeah. My old dad never forgave me for turning that one down. That time Tony Blair was staying in the President's villa in Sharm, he phoned me up – he never phoned me up – gave me an earful.' Jean's accent thickened as she slipped into an impression of her beloved, sheep-farming father. '"*Jeanie, look what you've done. I could be drinking tea with the fucking British Prime Minister!*"'

Carver smiled. 'Is your dad still going?' It seemed unlikely.

Jean took the hip flask from William and drank the last of the cognac. 'He died Christmas before last. Ninety-nine years old.'

'I'm sorry.'

'Thank you. That one hurt like a bastard; burying him nearly killed me. But it was time, he was old and he was living all by himself way out in the wops, still working.'

'Still sheep?'

'No. No money left in sheep, he'd moved into dairy but he didn't really get along with them. He bought a load of Devons and then realised he couldn't find their teats in all that fur. He was bloody hilarious about it – hilarious and furious. The last time we talked about farming he said he was going to get into wine: "*I'm going to sell those furry fuckers and plant a vineyard, Jeanie.*"' Fitzgerald was smiling but her dark eyes brimmed with tears.

William's hand moved in her direction and Jean took and held it. Carver struggled in these situations but he knew he needed to say something. 'You introduced me to him once. He was a good man, your dad.'

Fitzgerald wiped a sleeve across her face. 'A stupid man, more like. A vineyard! I don't think he drank a glass of wine in his life, the ignorant Maori bastard. Beer was his drink.'

Carver knew how proud Fitzgerald was of her mongrel roots: part Maori, part Scots Irish and all Kiwi although she hadn't lived there since her father put her on a boat to England aged seventeen.

'I miss him so fucking much.'

16 Hospitality

DATELINE: Reception desk, Seti Hotel, Cairo, Egypt,
January 28 2011

@tsquarelawan
| The regime is a flea biten old hyena. We have it in
| the corner and so it lashes out. It means we are
| winning!

Zahra re-read Nawal's message – the first contact she'd had with
her since Nawal had waved goodbye from the top of the hotel
wall that morning. Ten hours. She took a moment to correct
Nawal's English and sent the tweet back, together with a message
of her own: *Where were u? I was worried and what does this tweet
mean? Are you ok?*

Nawal replied that she was fine, she'd been busy setting up a
new checkpoint near Tahrir and lost track of the time, that was
all. She asked if Zahra was free to talk. *Not now, boss is here. I'll
call u when he leaves. X*

Mr Akar was at his desk, studying the menu for the next day's
meals, a deep frown on his face. As far as he was concerned his

head chef was an idiot, an illiterate. The words he used to describe the dishes he planned to make made no sense in any language and the only person who could make head or tail of what he wrote was Zahra. She had translated his childish scribble into the English menu Mr Akar was reading aloud: '*Salmon, chicken quesadilla, vegetable frittata . . .*' He turned the page over. 'Where is the rest?' He stood, leaned across his desk and shouted: 'Zahra!'

She arrived with her phone still in hand. When her boss looked down at the menu she stuffed it hurriedly into her jacket pocket.

'Yes, Mr Akar?' She watched while her manager made a show of reading the menu again with look of great seriousness on his face. Akar was a small man with a preference for grey suits, a wide collection of bright ties and an unreliable hairpiece.

He waved the piece of paper in her direction. 'This menu is even worse than his usual. Where is the grilled beef fillet? The American burger?'

'We couldn't get the beef for the price you agreed to pay, sir. There is almost no beef in the market today.'

'Do not say *we*, Zahra. It is not your job to buy the meat; it is chef's job. How much did he say it cost?'

Zahra named a price that was almost three times what Mr Akar had been willing to countenance.

'Stupid, more than stupid – criminal. Who will buy beef at that price?'

'The Marriot.'

Akar sucked his teeth with contempt. 'Fine. Then the Marriot will go out of business and I will laugh. I let them have the beef, I do not want it.' He looked again at the menu. 'What about this?' He poked a finger at the paper. 'Frittata? What is frittata?'

'It is a thick omelette, it's Italian. We have lots of eggs so I spoke to the chef about making frittata to fill the gaps. They have frittata at the Marriot.'

Akar nodded. 'Yes, good, so I will approve this. And please will you tell chef that I want him to make some cheesecake tomorrow; we have not had this for a while.' Mr Akar had a sweet tooth.

'Of course, yes.'

'Puddings are the only thing that man is good for – the only thing.' Akar went to hand the menu back to Zahra then pulled it away. 'There was something else I meant to ask you . . . but now I forget. What was it?'

The young woman shook her head.

'I guess I will remember later.'

Zahra lowered her head. 'Yes, Mr Akar.' She was backing out of the open door and about to pull it shut when he shouted.

'I know what it was!'

'Sir?'

'What did Mr Carver want from you?'

Zahra felt the hairs rise on the nape of her neck but she met Akar's eye and held it. 'Mr Carver? The English journalist?'

'Yes, I have seen you talking together; more than once.'

She nodded.

'So what does he want?'

Zahra glanced down at the floor; she was not a good liar. Her manager walked around his desk and took her hand in his. His grip was soft, his hand clammy, almost wet.

'Come, Zahra. We are old friends you and I, old friends cannot have secrets. Was it help with his work, or' – the hotel manager's gaze fell, his eyes settling on Zahra's skirt, her bare legs – 'perhaps he was making inappropriate advances?'

Zahra looked at Akar's hungry eyes and decided to give him the story he was most ready to believe. 'Yes.'

Mr Akar sighed. 'I feared he was this type, he has the look.' Akar gestured in the direction of his office chair and encouraged Zahra to sit. The brown leather still carried the heat of its previous occupant and she shuffled herself towards the front of the chair. Her manager took up a position directly in front of her, leaning back casually against his desk. He saw her glance at the open drawer and pushed it shut but not before Zahra had seen Mr Akar's spare hairpiece, a set of pass-keys for every room in the hotel and a small collection of gold watches and pens: lost property that was thus far unclaimed. 'Yes, I am afraid that we will have this problem for as long as all these journalists are here. These people are not the same class of people that our hotel usually welcomes, you understand?' The question expected no answer. 'Just today I was thinking about gathering all the female members of staff together and asking you to dress more modestly.'

Zahra said nothing, although this advice contradicted guidance Mr Akar had given her in the past. On several occasions he had suggested that she consider wearing something that *made more of her figure*. He had even turned to religion to back up his argument.

'*Remember that Allah loves those who do what is beautiful.*'

'*Yes, but I am not sure this passage means that Allah wants me to wear a shorter skirt.*'

'*We can never be sure precisely what Allah means, Zahra, we can only interpret to the best of our ability.*'

She glanced up at her employer; he was still wondering out loud about how he might best protect his female staff.

Zahra had known Mr Akar since she was a child; he had worked as an apprentice to the doorman at the apartment block – one of Cairo's more salubrious – where her family lived, from her birth until she was a young teenager. However, Zahra's family had been forced to give up the place and find cheaper accommodation when her father lost his job, but Akar had stayed in touch. As her family's fortunes suffered, Mr Akar's went from strength to strength. Doorman work was one of the most coveted and simultaneously hated jobs that any ambitious young Egyptian could do. It involved fulfilling the residents' every need, around the clock, and, at the same time, monitoring their every movement and passing that information on to the secret police as and when they asked for it.

Akar discovered that he had a talent for the position and it taught him a range of skills that had served him well ever since. He had quickly risen from apprentice to assistant, eventually becoming the head doorman when the browsing history on his boss's computer was found to contain links to Muslim Brotherhood websites; the man was sacked and arrested. When Mr Akar took his place he made sure that his own laptop was always kept under lock and key.

When he heard that the Seti Hotel was looking for a manager he did not hesitate: a thousand Egyptian pounds in a manila envelope and a glowing reference from a senior figure in the Egyptian army were enough to win him the job. Zahra's father was one of the first people to hear the happy news; Mr Akar arrived at their door wearing a new suit, Italian shoes and with a fuller head of hair than anyone remembered seeing previously. He wanted to share his good fortune but also to let Zahra's father know that if ever his daughter decided that the *industry of hospitality* was for her then Akar would pay a fair wage and protect the family name. It was another couple of years before circumstance forced Zahra to take him up on the offer.

For the first week Mr Akar did nothing more than watch Zahra; it was unsettling but not unusual. It wasn't until the end of her second week at the hotel that Mr Akar asked if she would mind staying behind that evening and helping him make a full inventory of the storeroom. She agreed and then quickly sought information from one of the more seasoned members of staff. Before Zahra arrived, his favourite had been a woman called Fatma.

'*He does not do much, mainly just touching. Sometimes you will have to wash your skirt.*'

Fatma told Zahra that the abuse was unpleasant but predictable and that after it was over, Mr Akar would press an Egyptian ten-pound note into the woman's hand and make her a gift of whatever storeroom item came most readily to hand. The woman would return to her work with the money and a couple of sixty-watt bulbs, some Lifebuoy soap or a few small bottles of shampoo. Fatma's advice to Zahra was that she should close her eyes until he was finished doing what he was doing and always take the gift.

Zahra was working in the restaurant, serving coffee to the last few tables when Akar came to find her, a ledger in his hand.

'*Miss Moussa, would you mind assisting me with the inventory when you are finished?*' His polite tone was for the benefit of the guests, a couple of whom nodded approvingly.

'*Of course, Mr Akar.*'

Zahra found her employer in the corner of the storeroom counting tins of instant coffee.

'*Twenty-eight cans of Nescafé we have. Zahra, you take this and take down the numbers as I say them.*' He handed her the book. They walked up and down the rows of metal shelves, counting things that did not need to be counted. The storeroom was dank; the white paint on the walls was flaking and falling away. Zahra followed, writing down the numbers he called out and waiting; the wait was so long that she began to wonder whether her suspicions were unfounded; perhaps Mr Akar's intentions were harmless. Then they arrived at a dead-end, a narrow, inky alley where the blankets and bed linen were stored. Akar sighed deeply, as though suddenly overwhelmed by passion and moved towards her. Pushing her gently back against a pile of starched sheets, he touched her cheek with the tips of his fingers. '*Ah . . . Zahra.*' His other hand headed south, searching for the hem of her skirt but Zahra shielded herself with the book.

'*Mr Akar, please, sir! Stop a moment.*'

He stopped.

'*I can see that you have feelings for me*' – Akar nodded coyly – '*and I am flattered.*'

His right hand started to twitch again but the book held firm.

'*I am fond of you too, but not in this way. You have known me since I was a girl, a baby – before I could walk I think?*'

Akar gave a reluctant nod of the head and took half a step back.

'*You are like an uncle to me, Mr Akar.*'

Her manager sighed again, this time with genuine frustration rather than manufactured passion. '*Yes, I see. But I think, Zahra, maybe even uncles sometimes . . .*' He left this line of argument incomplete.

'*I know you would not do anything that could damage my reputation or my family's name?*'

Before Akar knew it, he was holding the ledger of pointless numbers and Zahra was gone.

Fatma had stayed behind to wait for her colleague at reception – a combination of solidarity and curiosity. She watched Zahra closely as she walked towards her across the lobby; her colleague was empty-handed.

'*Are you okay? He did not give you a gift?*'

Zahra shook her head. '*I gave nothing, so I got nothing.*'

'*You gave nothing. He did not touch you? How?*' The look on Fatma's face suggested she'd witnessed some small act of magic.

'*I told him that I could not, that it would be wrong, given we have known each other so long. I called him uncle.*'

Fatma grinned. '*You are the cleverest person.*'

Mr Akar let Zahra alone for a week before trying again: cornering his employee behind the pool bar and pressing his case. But again the word *uncle* halted his advance and cooled his ardour. Zahra was reminded of an advert she had seen on television. The product was a dog collar, an American invention, which would squirt water up into the dog's face if the animal became dangerous or threatening. The word *uncle* had a similar effect on Mr Akar.

The touch of the hotel manager's hand on her hair brought Zahra back to the present and she realised he was still talking.

'So there are some things we can do, but you see that these unwanted attentions are in many ways a hazard of our occupation.'

Zahra gave an understanding nod.

'Perhaps you would like for me to talk to Mr Carver?'

Zahra decided to call her manager's bluff. 'I *would* like that, Mr Akar, if you don't mind?'

Akar's hand went to the knot of his tie. 'Yes, well, of course I don't mind – my first duty is to my staff. Especially you, Zahra.'

She got to her feet and edged past Mr Akar in the direction of the door.

'Especially you. I only want what is best for you. To look after you.'

She opened the door. 'Thank you, *uncle*.'

Mr Akar gave Zahra a doleful look. 'You're welcome.'

@tsquarelawan

> This regime is like a flea-bitten old hyena. We have
> it cornered and so it lashes out! But all this means
> is we are winning.

Patrick smiled. Tsquare Lawan had gone AWOL for a large part of the day and it was good to see her back. Now that he knew that the messages were a joint enterprise between Zahra and her slightly scary, skinny friend he had a feeling he could hear Zahra's voice as he read them. He sat down on the edge of his bed and as he did so, his phoned pinged.

> Hey, Radio Boy, are you at the Royal View? A few of us telly
> types are heading your way (nearest open bar); come down
> and join? All fun people – promise. Viv

Patrick chucked the phone to one side. He'd been planning to call Rebecca but it was probably too late to do that now. He was tired but maybe not so tired that he couldn't have *one* drink. It'd be the polite thing to do too, especially since Vivian had been kind enough to help him and William out earlier.

Carver and Jean had said their goodnights in the hotel lobby; he'd given his teeth a quick brush and was in bed when there was a knock on the door. He opened it to see Jean holding a bottle of red wine in one hand and two plastic glasses in the other.

'I got to thinking . . . it's not that late, maybe you'd be up for a nightcap?'

Carver stared at Jean. 'Are we talking sex?'

'Yes.'

'I should warn you, there's no guarantee I'll be able to get it up.'

'Don't worry. I'll probably change my mind before we get anywhere near the bed.'

Carver smiled at Jean and opened the door wide. 'Fair enough.'

The Way of Sorrows (iii)

Mr Adam was as good as his word in one respect at least. Two days after having met Gebre and Solomon, their grandfather received a call from a nameless man saying that his boys should be waiting outside the derelict cement plant on the edge of Godaif district at six o'clock the following morning.

'One bag only.'

'One bag each?'

'One bag in total. No exception.'

For this reason the brothers spent their last night repacking: making the already modest pile of clothes and worldly possessions that they had in their individual suitcases smaller still and packing these into a single case. The boys had their travel documents in a waterproof envelope along with their phones and chargers, a small torch, Gebre's educational certificates and a handful of photographs including one of them as children, dressed in their best clothes, sitting in between their parents at a restaurant table. The other piece of paper the boys' grandfather insisted they take with them was the name and contact details for a man Gabriel used to know:

'A young theology student from Sudan – quite a character. He is a priest now. I helped him once, a long time ago, but perhaps he will remember.'

They took three shirts, two sweatshirts and one extra pair of trousers and trainers each. On their grandfather's advice they took several packs of Marlboro cigarettes: not to smoke but to use as currency. They stuffed a roll of notes – around two thousand nakfa – down the side of the case.

'It is the first place a thief will look, but it is an amount that you can afford to lose and also just enough that they might think it is all you have.'

The extra money that Gabriel had given them – five hundred American dollars and the same in euros – was split into two equal shares and sewn into the lining of the jackets they were travelling in. Once all of this was packed, together with a tin of biscuits and a few lemons that their mother insisted they take to combat Gebre's travel sickness – the case was full.

They rose at five and dressed quickly; both boys had said goodbye to their mother the night before and although they could hear her moving around in her bedroom she did not appear and Gebre thought it best not to disturb her. They pulled the front door closed behind them and Solomon hesitated before deciding that he would keep the key with him. They took one last look at the only home they'd ever known and left, walking the couple of kilometres to the cement factory at a good pace. Their grandfather was already waiting for them when they arrived, standing outside the padlocked factory gate. He had already spoken to the nervous-looking taxi driver, who was sitting on his haunches some distance away, chain-smoking cheap Turkish cigarettes. Gabriel told the boys that this first leg of the trip would only take an hour or two, that this yellow cab would transport them, together with Titus and Dumac, to a pick-up point – a service station the cabbie said – eighty kilometres outside Asmara where the real journey would begin.

Solomon pushed their case into the boot and the brothers were about to climb into the car when Gebre saw something and stopped. There, at the far end of the street, was a woman, a tiny figure. His mother took a few steps in his direction but then changed her mind and stopped. Gebre could see that she was speaking to herself. He watched her now with tears welling in his eyes, knowing that it was some kind of prayer or promise that his mother was making. He saw her pull her tattered shawl tighter across her chest.

She raised a hand and held it there – hanging in the air – and the boys waved back. Then she lowered her arm, turned and walked away. Half a dozen small steps took her to the corner and then she was gone. Gebre felt a stabbing pain in his heart as he climbed into the back of the car.

17 Arms and the Men

DATELINE: Old Kent Road, London SE11, January 30 2011

Rob could have kicked himself for ever mentioning the dinner to Lindy.

'It's not really a party.'

'That's what you called it last night. I don't understand why you don't want me to come.'

'It'll be a bunch of arms dealers, dealing arms and drinking brandy. You can't drink in your condition, so unless you're looking to buy a surface-to-air missile I really don't see the point.'

Lindy liked attention and she wasn't overly concerned about the direction that it came from. She also liked an occasion. 'I've always wanted to see inside the Tower of London – I've never been.'

'We'll go another time, when it's not packed full of the most reprehensible people on the planet.'

'And you.'

'Yeah, and me.'

'So why *are* you going?'

'You know why I'm going, Lindy, it's my bloody job. My boss wants me to go, so I'm going.'

The truth was that Mariscal wasn't sure why the permanent secretary wanted him there. The dinner at the Tower marked the end of the London Arms Fair, a trade show that according to press reports had been the most successful in years. Rob knew that the Ministry of Defence needed to be represented: the new Secretary of State, perhaps another junior minister and a couple of senior civil servants but he didn't see why the press guy would need to be there. The reason was made slightly clearer by the permanent secretary himself as they were driving east down Embankment from Whitehall in a ministerial Rover.

'I don't enjoy these occasions, Robert. I invited you along for moral support.'

Mariscal nodded. 'Of course.'

If it was moral support he was after then Rob couldn't help thinking he'd chosen the wrong man. He wasn't sure he believed this explanation anyway.

The government car dropped them at the main entrance to the Tower. Usually this whole area would be thronging with tourists but the Tower had closed early in order to host the event. Craig and Rob strolled round the ramparts looking down at thousands of bright ceramic poppies on display in the old moat below – a piece of public art that was travelling the country ahead of the anniversary of the First World War and had been widely lauded.

As they approached the welcoming desk for the arms fair dinner, Mariscal mumbled under his breath. 'There's another kick in the bollocks for satire.'

'What was that?'

'Nothing.'

Rob took his name badge and followed Craig up the gravelled path to the White Tower. No expense had been spared; there was even a ceremonial guard to greet the guests – four straight-backed Scots Guardsmen standing either side of the path in all their red splendour. Several people had stopped to take selfies on their phones. Inside the high-ceilinged dining hall, Rob was handed a champagne flute and ushered through. A skinny young man in a blue velvet suit and bow tie was having a good go at one of Bach's cello suites; Rob couldn't remember which – not the famous one.

Craig turned to Rob. 'You go on ahead. I have to introduce the Secretary of State to a few people, I'll catch you up.'

Mariscal made his way to the far corner of the room, stood in a corner and looked around. He was aware of the revolving door that operated between government departments and the private sector and he knew that the door between the Ministry of Defence and business span faster than most – well-oiled by the amounts of money involved. Nevertheless the number of familiar political faces in this room surprised even him: former ministers, political advisers and senior military figures who were now employed by defence companies, risk assessors and countries who felt like they needed defending. Mariscal counted a dozen political retreads without having to try very hard at all. He mentioned this to Craig when he returned.

'That's the world we live in, Robert – the bad old world we live in. There's a fair few civil servants here too, faces you might not know so well but senior people. Breathtaking in their mediocrity – most of them. Come, I suppose we better go and sit down, we're on one of the corporate tables.'

The gold-framed card in the centre of table ten read *Quadrel Engineering & Defence* in bold copperplate. Sitting at the end closest to the wall and just in front of a fine-looking medieval tapestry was a broad-shouldered man in dinner jacket and black tie, holding an unlit cigar in his hand. Bellquist's blond hair was freshly cut and gelled back, his eyes pale blue. He was holding court and although he glanced briefly at Rob as he took his seat he made no attempt to acknowledge him, preferring to continue with his story, which seemed to have the table rapt.

'Perception matters. Take young Paul here . . .' He waved the cigar in the direction of a proud-looking fellow in a dinner suit and stud dress shirt identical to that of his boss. 'I hired him to do our press work because of the sterling job he did with Formula One. He put that piece of research together that helped persuade people that motor racing brings in over a billion pounds a year for the UK economy, that it employs tens of thousands of people.' He grinned. 'It's piffle of course . . .'

Paul cleared his throat. 'Well, it's not—'

'True or not, it doesn't matter. What matters is it worked, those numbers got traction. So now he's doing something like that for us – although it's taking a little while, isn't it, Paul?'

Paul's smile didn't quite reach the eyes.

For the most part, Mariscal let the dinner conversation flow around him; he only spoke when asked a question or in order to show that he was broadly in agreement with everyone else. He had expected to feel intimidated and rather out of his depth but he felt neither – most of the people at the table were spouting opinions based on the same *Economist* articles he'd read. Nevertheless it seemed wise to keep a low profile and go easy on the red wine. This was difficult because it was Château Musar and very good. When the waitress arrived to fill his glass he smiled up at her with a look that he hoped might communicate the fact that he was not really with these people, or rather that he was with them but not one of them. He was an outsider, an observer – like her. The young woman filled his glass and moved on; as far as she was concerned, he looked exactly the same as all the others.

During the starter course the conversation revolved around what Mariscal began to think of as *geopolitics for dummies*. When these arms dealers and buyers actually got around to talking about arms and weapons – over the main course – the conversation became allusive and acronym-heavy. Several different countries were

173

represented at Quadrel's table: Arab thawb sat next to black tie next to Indian jodhpuri but there were only two women and not a single representative from the world's *next* great superpower. It was an absence that clearly irked their host.

'I wanted to invite one or two of our Chinese friends but the good people from the Ministry of Defence are reluctant to sit at the same table . . .' He was looking directly at Craig as he said this. 'Isn't that right?'

'I prefer not to.'

'Why? You could have brought your long spoon, Permanent Secretary . . . supped with that.' Bellquist was grinning.

'I'm already using that particular spoon, Mr Bellquist.'

Their host laughed. 'For most of us here, the good old yellow peril isn't a peril at all – it's just a different kind of opportunity. Of course China's rise is unsettling, change is always unsettling, but as far as I'm concerned – it's all good for trade. Like failed states and Arab Springs and whatever else . . .'

The table laughed nervously and as Bellquist raised his glass for a refill his press man Paul cleared his throat. 'What I think Mr Bellquist means is that . . .'

His boss raised a hand to silence him. 'Don't do that.'

'I'm sorry?'

'Don't contradict me.'

'I wasn't, I was just—' His voice had risen an octave.

'Spinning, I know. Well don't.' He studied his cigar. It had a fine-looking Cuban band on it and was as thick as his thumb. It was clear that Bellquist was keen to smoke it but he was sitting underneath the tapestry and alongside a *no smoking* sign – the warning written in a rich gothic script that Rob guessed was meant to make it blend with the room. Bellquist took a box of matches from his pocket and lit up anyway. The head waiter was at their table within seconds, his face an interesting mix of obsequiousness and panic.

'I'm so sorry, sir, but you really can't smoke in here.' He gestured at the tapestry.

'Of course, I understand.' Bellquist continued to pull and puff on the cigar; the match had burned down to a point where the flame was almost at his fingers.

'I have to ask you to put that out, sir. Or take it outside?'

Bellquist removed the cigar from his mouth; the end was wet with spit, the tobacco dark.

'You're a waiter, aren't you?'

'Yes, sir.'

'So . . . wait. I need to concentrate on this bit, get a nice even burn. As soon as I have, I'll step outside. Mr Craig and I will continue our conversation in the fresh air.'

Around the corner from the entrance to the White Tower was a smoking area, empty apart from them. Bellquist pulled two cast-iron garden chairs together and they sat.

'So, shall I update you on that charm offensive of ours?'

Bellquist took a long draw on the cigar, deep enough that the ash burned bright and lit his face yellow in the gloom.

'Since that's why I'm here, I suppose you should.'

Bellquist's summary was a sunny one. His friends in the Egyptian military were willing to bide their time. They had been approached by other countries offering to fill the gaps left by the UK's decision to clamp down on exports but had resisted those advances on the understanding that the tap wasn't to be turned off entirely.

'I agreed to that on your behalf. I hope that's acceptable.'

'Provided it's carefully done. How will the shipments get to where they're going?'

'I assumed you wouldn't want to know.'

Craig nodded. Bellquist was right – he didn't want to know.

'I thought not. But don't worry about that one. The bottom line is the stuff's not going to show up on any cargo manifest or FedEx docket.'

'No paper trail?'

'None whatsoever. That's not the issue.' Bellquist leaned down and tapped his cigar on the leg of Craig's chair; a centimetre of ash fell to the ground next to his polished shoe. 'The issue is who's going to pay the bill? Thanks to your sanctions our Cairo friends don't have two Egyptian quid to rub together. We're going to need a line of credit or something like that.'

Craig glanced backwards over his shoulder then spoke. 'The ministry will take care of that for the time being.'

'Bankroll it and keep it off the books?'

Craig shook his gargoyle's head slowly. 'That would be illegal. On the books but hard to find is what I have in mind. *You* don't need to know the details of that.' He sighed and stood. 'Is that everything?'

'Not quite.' Bellquist was staring at his cigar with a look that suggested he'd lost the taste for it. 'There's one little wrinkle.'

Craig sat back down. He was cold, he regretted not bringing his coat. He regretted a lot of things. 'Tell me.'

Bellquist told him that Quadrel had sent a small consignment to Cairo a few weeks previously. 'A belated Christmas present or early Ramadan or whatever.'

Bellquist grinned and glanced at Craig, who remained unsmiling. 'A few boxes of kit, that's all. Just some anti-insurgency stuff.'

'Anti-insurgency when the government's position is *pro*.'

'Yes, well.' He explained that some of the kit had gone missing, ending up in what Bellquist called *the wrong hands*.

Craig shook his head. 'Why are you telling me this? What do you expect the ministry to do about it?'

'For now – nothing. The chances are that our Egyptian friend will sort it out all by himself.' Bellquist took one more puff of his cigar before letting it drop and grinding it into the grass with his shoe. 'And I've put him in touch with a contact of ours who might be able to help. But in the spirit of belt and braces, I thought you could check how well your pal Mariscal gets along with his old BBC mates these days?'

'Why?'

'It's one of those fellows who's got a sniff of it. We might need Mariscal to weigh in on our side.'

Craig turned and stared at Bellquist's profile. His slicked-back hair, his thick neck. 'I feel it might be worth reminding you of something, Mr Bellquist.'

'What's that, Mr Craig?'

'Your contacts mean that right now, you're holding a pretty good hand.'

'I know that.'

'But you should remember that it's possible to overplay, even a strong hand.'

Bellquist laughed. 'Consider me warned.' He stood up. 'Now if you'll excuse me, I'm neglecting my duties as host.'

Craig didn't look up. 'You go on ahead.'

By the time the permanent secretary arrived back inside the White Tower, the cello player had been replaced by a red-haired harpist, playing 'Norwegian Wood'. Craig had had enough and was keen to find Rob, retrieve his coat and leave. Back at their table, Bellquist was gathering a group together for a private tour of the Crown Jewels and cracking jokes. He was standing behind one of his Saudi guests, hands on his shoulders and a broad smile on his face.

'Do you know how much the Saudis spent on UK-made kit last year?' Heads shook. 'One point eight billion! Pounds not euros and you know what they say? With friends like that – who needs Yemenis?'

The table laughed obligingly.

Craig and Mariscal made their way back across the ramparts and away from the Tower in silence. Rob saw a raven hopping about on the grass, close to the gravelled path. The bird was pulling a coil of gut from something dead, a cat or rat. He didn't have the stomach to stop and work out which.

His boss mumbled something: 'A clean corner.'

'I beg your pardon?' Rob glanced at Craig, bundled up against the cold in his thick overcoat and scarf.

'That was my only ambition: to keep my corner clean – like the man said.'

'I see.'

'And I have tried, as God is my witness I have.'

Rob nodded. 'I'm sure.'

'But it isn't easy.'

18 Lions

DATELINE: The Seti Hotel, Cairo, Egypt, January 30 2011

Carver had agreed to meet Patrick at the lion statues at Kasr Al Nil bridge and do some interviews there, talking to a few of the middle-class Cairenes who were making their way to Tahrir for the first time. This was Patrick's idea but William was happy to go along with it – he owed his colleague one. Patrick had covered for Carver for the whole of yesterday, while William was confined to his room with a nasty-sounding stomach bug. Patrick had offered to call in at a chemist and get them to recommend some kind of treatment but William refused the offer. Apparently Jean had something that appeared to be working.

After he'd finished with Patrick and London got off his back, Carver planned to try and meet up with Nawal so he could record her version of how she came across the Brit-made tear gas canisters. He'd feel better once he had that in the can. Carver checked his plastic bag and decided to chuck in another box of batteries alongside the MiniDisc recorder, his notebook and pens. He dug around in the bottom of the bag in a fruitless hunt for an inhaler and took another five minutes searching various jacket and trouser pockets before he found one buried at the bottom of his suitcase. He was sure he had two or even three but there was only one left. Carver gave the blue device a shake and got a half-full-sounding rattle in return – good enough. He dropped it in the plastic bag, took one more look around and left the room.

Steve clocked Carver the moment the lift doors opened and kept a close eye on him as he walked across the lobby.

'Tahrir Square today, is it, Billy?'

This nickname was both unwelcome and unconvincing – the former Special Forces man's tone was less than friendly.

'Possibly.'

'Right, well then, you're going to need the flak jacket for starters.'

Carver waited while Steve selected the right size for him from a leaning tower of Kevlar jackets he'd constructed next to the stone sphinx. He pulled the blue vest on over his shirt; it was heavy but not nearly as bad as the old jackets used to be. He pulled the front flap down over his groin and then waited while Steve studied his clipboard.

'I need to ask whether you want to take the respirator?'

'No.'

'I thought that's what you'd say. You've got your inhaler though?'

Carver nodded.

'Plenty of Salbutamol in there, is there? Mind if I take a look?'

William handed the giant his plastic bag and waited while Steve found the inhaler and gave it a shake.

'Looks like you're good to go then, Billy-boy.' Steve stuffed the inhaler back in the plastic bag and handed it over. 'Take care.'

There was a long queue of people waiting for taxis outside and not a cab in sight. Carver decided it would be quicker to walk than to wait. He took it slow, but the flak jacket – which had felt light to begin with – became increasingly burdensome. It took him over an hour to reach the bridge and the walk had taken its toll; looking down he saw a sweaty tide mark under each arm. Carver realised that he hadn't agreed with Patrick which end of the bridge to meet at. He moved into the shade of one of the huge lions and tried his phone but there was no signal. Either the government had pulled the plug again or the network was just overloaded.

Looking to his left he saw that the next bridge along was where the real action was. Several lines of police were massed at one end of the October Sixth Bridge, facing an angry-looking crowd at the other. The police were trying to block any more people from reaching Tahrir Square and missiles were being thrown. Carver was considering whether the crowd noise he could hear from his position was worth recording when he felt someone at his back and turned. A homeless man, with fleshy stumps where his hands should be, was struggling with a slab of stinking foam – attempting to wrestle the makeshift mattress he'd slept on last night back into a black plastic sack. Carver wondered where the man had been sleeping; underneath the bridge he guessed. He put his bag down, found some money and after an awkward exchange during which he realised the man had no obvious way of accepting the notes, pressed the cash into the man's filthy jeans pocket. The man dropped the foam mattress to the floor, covered his heart with one stump and bowed.

'*Shukraan.*'

Carver nodded. The crowd around him was growing now; demonstrators frustrated by the blockade on the neighbouring bridge were attempting to reach Tahrir Square using this route. But there was still no sign of Patrick; either he was late or he was at the other end of Kasr Al Nil. Carver set off across the bridge, trying to stay as close to the side as possible and away from the crowd. He heard a familiar *popping* sound and looking over at October Sixth saw that police in riot gear had arrived and were firing tear gas. A light wind carried the gas in Carver's direction

– down on the river he could see smoke from the canisters drifting towards him across the water.

He concentrated on his breathing: in through the nose, out through the mouth but he could feel his throat starting to tighten. He glanced down at his bag but kept walking – best to save the inhaler for when he really needed it. He caught sight of an old woman who was moving among the crowd handing out halved onions to protect against the gas; Carver took one of these and gave it a sniff. It delivered a jolt of something – a sharp hot stink like smelling salts, but the relief was temporary. He pulled away the brown papery skin and tried again, pressing the onion hard against his nose and mouth, inhaling deeply. It wasn't helping and the gas had reached him now.

William felt like he was being strangled, his windpipe slowly crushed; the panic that came with that feeling was hastening the process.

'*Fuck it.*'

He reached into his bag for the inhaler, his hand scrambling around among his stuff trying to find it. But it wasn't there. He patted at his pockets, although he was sure the thing had been in his bag. He crouched down and checked the contents of the plastic carrier. He saw boxes of batteries, his MiniDisc recorder, note-books and pens and a sandwich he should have thrown away days ago, but no inhaler. He struggled to his feet, coughing violently as he did so. William felt like someone was standing on his chest. He stood and patted at his pockets again but found nothing. People moved past him and pushed into him, carrying him forward against his will. Carver was too far in to go back. And he was suffocating.

The Way of Sorrows (iv)

The yellow taxi pulled into the petrol station forecourt, slowed and stopped. The station attendant was sitting on a wooden folding chair outside his office. The taxi was the only vehicle he'd seen in several hours and he observed it with interest. The cabbie jumped from his seat – leaving the engine running – and started dragging his passengers' luggage from the boot and dropping it on the ground. The attendant walked over, clearly hoping to sell some fuel or at least give the windscreen a clean in return for a few coins but the driver waved him away. Gebre was standing and stretching out his back when he realised that the cabbie was back behind the wheel and ready to drive off without a word.

'Hey, what do we do now?'

'Wait.'

'For how long?'

The man shrugged, pushed the car into first gear and was gone.

The four young men wandered around for a while before settling in a thin strip of shade at the back of the garage, backs against the whitewashed wall. Solomon passed the time playing cards with Titus and Dumac while Gebre dozed. The stench of cigarette smoke and the sweat of his fellow passengers had made sleep impossible during the journey from Asmara but he slept now, slept and dreamed.

In his dream, he and Solomon were standing on top of a tall building; it was early morning with a ribbon of red sun on the horizon and they were staring northwards. As Gebre watched, his brother grew wings – not feathered or fleshy but good solid, steel wings which Solomon could move as easily as he would move his arms but which were twice as long. Solomon took a few steps back from the edge of the building and encouraged Gebre to climb on to his back and lock his hands around his neck. Once he was sure that Gebre was holding tight, Solomon ran and launched himself into the air. They fell and they fell – and then they flew. When Gebre woke, he told his brother about his dream.

'Even in dreams I have to do all the work, flapping away while you do the sightseeing.'

After two hours of waiting, a white Toyota flatbed truck pulled up at the front of the service station. The car had no licence plates and what appeared to be a full load of passengers. Gebre counted eight men and three women crushed into the back of the vehicle, all either sitting on or clinging to their suitcases and bags. The driver was a round-faced Sudanese man with a short temper. After noisily relieving himself against the garage wall, he climbed up on to the riser at the back of the Toyota and started shouting and manhandling his cargo so enough room could be found for his final four passengers. Gebre was the last to climb in, passing their suitcase up to Solomon who was standing looking around for somewhere to put it; there was nowhere. The Sudanese driver grew impatient at this further delay and, jumping back up, grabbed the case and thrust it on to the lap of an old man who was sitting squashed in the corner. The man put up no fight, folding his arms across the boys' bag and giving Gebre a nod of reassurance.

'I have it, friend.'

'Thank you.'

The driver performed a quick head count, pulling a scrap of paper from his pocket to check the number tallied. Solomon was sitting closest to him.

'Where do you drive us to now, brother?'

'Omdurman.'

Solomon shook his head. 'We were told you would take us to Khartoum.'

The driver laughed loudly and walked away.

Once out of earshot, the old man tapped Gebre on the shoulder. 'It is okay. Omdurman is close to Khartoum, just across the Nile River. He is taking us to the right place.'

'Thank you.' Gebre remembered his grandfather's advice about making connections. 'I am Gebre, this is my brother, Solomon.'

'An honour. I am Simon.'

Their grandfather had warned the brothers that this leg of their trip would involve at least twelve hours of near continuous driving and their fellow passengers confirmed this. The Toyota had to get them across the Eritrean border at an unguarded point and then through eastern Sudan to within striking distance of the capital Khartoum.

Simon had made the journey before: 'You have to remove the word *dignity* from your dictionary, my friend.'

Gebre amused himself for a while by thinking of all the other words he would have to remove: *privacy, comfort, space* . . . the list was long. Solomon was less sanguine about the situation; he had folded his large frame into as small a space as possible and it was not long before his muscles started to cramp. More upsetting than his own discomfort was the distress he was causing the woman next to him. Every sharp brake or jolt the truck made pushed him hard against her. She was uncomplaining but that only made Solomon feel worse.

After four hours of driving, the Sudanese man slowed the truck and stopped. His passengers watched him climb from the car with a jerry can of petrol and walk round to fill the tank. A couple of men, Titus among them, pleaded with the man for a few minutes outside the car so they could stretch their legs and relieve themselves.

'One minute.'

Solomon saw his opportunity; he'd noticed that the passenger seat in the Toyota was empty save for the Sudanese man's lunch, a couple of mobile phones and a crumpled map. While other passengers stretched their legs, Solomon took the travel documents Mr Adam had given them from the suitcase and approached the driver.

'Sir, may I ask a question?'

The driver grunted his consent.

'We have paid for the VIP journey . . .' He showed the driver the piece of paper. 'I do not ask for special treatment for myself but I wonder if you could carry the woman I am sitting next to in the front of your car – for her greater comfort?' Solomon smiled hopefully.

'Let me see this.' The driver took the piece of paper from its plastic wallet and studied it. 'VIP journey you paid for?'

Solomon nodded.

'I did not realise. Now I understand.' He turned and walked a few paces, seemingly reading the letter as he went.

Solomon and Gebre watched and Gebre suspected that the man was having trouble understanding the words, barely literate in any language.

The man turned back and faced the group; he had the letter in his left hand and with his right he unbuckled his belt and dropped his trousers and boxer shorts, then – crouching in the sand – he defecated noisily before using Solomon's letter to wipe his backside. He stood and held the shit-covered piece of paper out for all to see before pressing it down into the sand and giving the group a broad, gap-toothed smile. 'This is what your VIP letter is worth here.'

19 Close Calls

DATELINE: Tahrir Square, Cairo, Egypt, January 30 2011

It was blind luck that brought Carver and Patrick together; they almost walked into each other as several streams of protesters merged into one at the Tahrir Square end of the bridge. Carver spotted Patrick and elbowed his way through a group of men in white robes to reach him, grabbing him by the arm.

It took Patrick a second to recognise the grey-faced Carver; he looked dreadful. 'Jesus, William, are you all right?'

Carver shook his head; he was reluctant to use his last breath to explain that he couldn't bloody breathe.

'Asthma?'

He nodded at his colleague. Patrick turned away and for a moment Carver feared he was about to leave him; he gripped his arm tighter.

'Don't worry, I'm just gonna . . .' Patrick untangled his rucksack from his Kevlar vest and groping around at the bottom of the bag found a blue inhaler. Carver grabbed it from him and shook it; it was full. He put it to his mouth and fired a puff of Salbutamol as far back into his throat as he could, holding his breath. He took two more long puffs and then stood still, eyes closed, holding hard to Patrick's arm. After a minute or so the colour had returned to his face and Carver was able to speak.

'What the hell are you doing with my inhaler?'

'You asked me to look after it.'

'Did I?' William tried to remember. 'I did, I gave you my spare.'

'That's right.' Patrick pointed in the direction of the Royal View on the far side of the square. 'How about you go have a lie down in my room? Take it easy for a while?' He offered to walk over with him if William wanted.

Carver let go of Patrick's arm and pushed him gently away. 'I don't need a bloody lie down. I need to think.'

They headed instead for the nearest café and Carver took a seat at one of the outdoor tables. He ordered a strong coffee and a piece of syrupy cake and ate these while Patrick went and worked, collecting the interviews with new arrivals in Tahrir. Carver had another look through his plastic bag and trouser pockets to confirm that the only inhaler he had with him now was the one Patrick was looking after. He stirred some sugar into his coffee and tried to replay the last couple of hours in his mind.

The streets had been busy, the bridge more than busy . . . teeming. Any number of people could have dipped a hand into his bag and taken the inhaler. It was completely plausible. The trouble was, Carver didn't buy it. Not for a second.

Carver found Security Steve where they'd parted – standing next to a stack of Kevlar jackets just inside the entrance to the hotel. He strode up to him, his voice raised. 'You never put that inhaler back in my bag, Steve, did you? You pretended to, but you didn't.'

Steve shook his head slowly; he reached into his camo jacket pocket and brought out William's grey inhaler.

'It fell on the floor, Billy. I went after you, but you'd gone.'

'You're a bloody liar. Who asked you to do that? Who are you working for?'

Steve smiled at William. 'You've had an asthma attack, Billy, you're still short on oxygen. You're not thinking straight.'

'Bollocks.'

Steve moved his head closer to Carver's and lowered his voice. 'You dropped your inhaler, William. You need to be more careful, you need to be more careful about all sorts of things from what I hear. Or you might get hurt. Properly hurt.'

Carver studied Steve; every part of him appeared hard and impenetrable. The only thing about him that looked soft was his big doughy face. So Carver hit him there, smack on the nose. It was such an unexpected development that Steve made no attempt to move – either to block the blow or to avoid it. He took the punch, which wasn't a bad one, then lifted his fingers to his face and saw that he was bleeding.

Carver stood and watched. His heart was pumping furiously; adrenalin flowed like mercury through every vein. He felt exhilarated. Then he felt guilty and then he felt nothing because Steve had punched him into the middle of next week.

The Way of Sorrows (v)

Omdurman, Khartoum State, Sudan

Gebre was woken by the sound of the driver wrenching open the back of the pick-up and urgently ordering his passengers out. Simon put his bony hand on Gebre's arm and explained.

'It is still the early hours, brother, but we are here. We will wait inside this warehouse; can you help me with your case? My legs are still asleep.'

There were already three or four Toyota truckloads of people waiting inside the warehouse, lying exhausted underneath blankets, tarpaulins or whatever else they could find for bedding. The three men found a space on the floor and lay down in the hope of getting some more sleep; Gebre used their suitcase as a pillow. Just the feeling of stretching out on the ground was sweet relief for Solomon after hours in the back of the pick-up.

The next leg of the journey began sooner than the boys had dared hope; the lorry that would take them across Sudan's northern desert and over the Libyan border arrived later the same day. No one, including the usually well-informed Simon, was prepared and the scramble that began when the burly looking lorry driver arrived and told people he was leaving in twenty minutes was chaotic and cruel. Eritreans, Ethiopians and Sudanese climbed over each other as they tried to gather their belongings, other family members and in some cases small children and board the lorry. A few fights broke out. This unruly loading was overseen by the driver's associates; two light-skinned Sudanese men with revolvers sticking from their belts.

Simon explained that this part of the drive could take anywhere between three and five days. He said it was not just the longest but also the most hazardous leg of the journey: 'If you fall from the truck they will not stop – dehydration will kill you in a few days. If the sand storms come then they can bury a truck in a few hours and everyone will die. Then there are the bandits, the militia, border police.'

Gebre stared at Simon. 'You have made this journey before?'

'Yes.'

'What happened?'

Simon told Gebre that the traffickers he'd paid to take him to Libya had sold him to a militia who had tortured him until his family agreed to pay for his release. He undid the top few buttons on his shirt and pulled it down to reveal his chest – burned black and scarred.

'They telephoned my wife and make her listen while they poured burning plastic on me. Over my chest and my back, my legs . . . everywhere.'

'But you are trying again?'

'I have no choice. I will go to Europe and work all day and all night and send this money back for my wife. This is the only useful thing I can do for her now – the only way I can be a man.' He rebuttoned his shirt.

It soon became clear that any stops during this part of the journey would be few and far between; the hundred or so passengers learned to urinate in bottles which were then passed to the back of the truck to be poured over the side. Occasionally the driver or one of his colleagues would need to stop and then the people would pile from the back of the vehicle, running back when the horn was sounded. The only other breaks were ones that were forced on the Sudanese traffickers: several times the wheels of the overloaded truck got stuck in the desert sand and the men would enlist passengers to help them dig the wheels free and wedge planks of wood underneath for purchase.

It was halfway through the first day's driving, while helping dig the truck out of the sand, that Solomon saw what looked from a distance like a pile of discarded clothes at the foot of a nearby dune. When he'd finished digging and others were placing the wood under the wheels, Solomon found his brother and together they walked over to take a closer look. Gebre was just a few feet from the bundle when he realised that the clothes contained a corpse – a girl, younger than them.

Death and the sun had withered the girl's body to such an extent that she appeared too small for the clothes she was wearing. Around her neck was a Christ-less cross and in her outstretched right hand some kind of parcel. Solomon took the package and unwrapped it – realising as he did so that the girl had used her hijab as wrapping. He handed the contents – a thin blue notebook – to Gebre who recognised the book straight away. It was the same sort of lined exercise book that he and most other Eritrean schoolchildren were given to do their homework in. Gebre flicked through the pages, each carefully numbered and dated – the dead girl's diary. He stopped at the last page that had writing on it; the date at the top of the page was just over a month ago. He read the short entry, written in a blunt pencil and in large script:

My name is Veronica Redda of Akordat. [Gebre knew the town; it was only a few hours' drive from his own home in Asmara.] *I listened to something I should not have listened to and the men pushed me from the truck. I chased a while but the driver would not stop. I have no water, only thirst. I will die soon.*

If you find my message and it is possible, I beg you please take my body back home to Eritrea or onwards to Libya. Please put me in the earth and pour a cup of water on my grave so I may drink.

He handed it to Solomon to read.

'We should do this.'

Gebre shook his head. 'We can't. You know we can't.'

'We must do something.'

The brothers used their hands and feet to dig as deep a grave as they could manage in the little time they had. Solomon lifted the girl – she weighed almost nothing – and placed her gently down. He covered the thin body with sand while Gebre muttered a few words of prayer. When Solomon had finished burying the girl and he turned around, Gebre was dismayed to see that his brother's eyes were wet with tears. Looking back towards the truck he saw that the other passengers were getting ready to leave.

'Sol, we need to go.'

'Give me the water.'

'What? No, Sol, this is useless.'

'Please.'

They had just over half a litre of clean water left and no more in the truck but Gebre handed the bottle to his brother who poured its contents slowly into the sand where the girl's head was buried. Once it was done he handed the bottle back to Gebre.

'Thank you.'

Gebre nodded and led them back towards the lorry. One of the armed Sudanese smugglers was waiting for them; he had watched the whole performance and was wearing a snide-looking smile.

'So you brothers are grave diggers now? This is very good; there will be lots more work for you between here and our destination I think. I wonder which one of you will end up burying the other?'

As Solomon brushed past the man and jumped into the truck he spat a few words in Tigrinya: 'Maybe we will bury you first.'

The Sudanese grabbed at Gebre's sleeve. 'What did he say?'

'He said blessings on you, sir – for waiting for us.'

Once they were under way Solomon reached again for the dead girl's blue notebook. The pages that followed her dying wish were blank – right up until the last page where there was one more sentence.

They take the people north but I heard them say that the real money they make is by bringing the boxes south.

Solomon handed it to Gebre. 'What do you think it means?'

His brother shook his head. 'Who knows? She was dying, nearly dead. Probably it means nothing.'

20 Good Riddance

DATELINE: The Seti Hotel, Cairo, Egypt, January 31 2011

'I need some painkillers.' Carver lifted himself up on to one elbow and looked around the room. 'Patrick?' A pile of blankets and sheets heaped against the far wall started to move and before long resolved themselves into his producer. 'How come you're kipping down there?'

'I've been here all night. I've been looking after you.' He rubbed at his eyes. 'Jean and me. But mainly Jean.'

'Where is she?'

'She was here most of the night too, she had to go meet someone.'

'Who?'

Patrick shrugged. 'I don't know, some bloke. How're you feeling?'

'Sore head. How long have I been out?'

Patrick looked at his watch. 'He decked you around six last night, so . . .' He counted three hands worth of fingers. 'About fourteen hours. Jean had a doctor come check you out; no serious damage apparently.'

'I need to piss.'

Patrick helped Carver to the toilet. After emptying his bladder he took a tentative look in the mirror – it wasn't great. His left eye was swollen and bruised an interesting shade of purple. He had a long cut above the eyebrow that had been butterfly stitched, the whole of the left side of his face looked yellow and significantly larger than the right side. 'I look like the bloody Elephant Man. Or half the Elephant Man anyway.'

Patrick nodded. 'You should see the other guy.'

Carver turned sharply. 'Yeah? Was it bad?'

'No, not a scratch on him. He's gone, though, Zahra said he cleared his room and checked out about an hour after he decked you.'

'Good riddance – mercenary toerag or whatever the hell he is.'

'You think Steve took your inhaler on purpose?'

'I know he did. I know a few things now that I wasn't sure about before. That ox knocked some sense into me. Can you go and see if Zahra can come up here for a few minutes?'

While Patrick was gone, William tried to clean up his face a little with some damp toilet roll. He was annoyed that Jean had had to see him looking like this. He went and set his laptop up and checked his emails; he'd got a response from his contact at *Jane's Defence*. The person had emailed from an anonymous-sounding Gmail account and titled the email *PPI Latest*. Carver opened it and read.

Hard to say without seeing it but the company in question has a new product in that area, stronger dose of gas and longer to accommodate a gyro in the nose to make it hop about – harder for the rabble to pick up or chuck back.

Carver's mind turned to Nawal – harder but not impossible. He got up from the desk and starting rifling through his bag, then the cupboard drawers and finally his suitcase. He was on his hands and knees next to his case chucking the contents around the room when Patrick returned with Zahra at his side.

'What're you doing?'

'Gas canister's gone.'

Patrick shook his head. 'Jean's got it.'

'What? Why?'

'She said you were mumbling about how important it was, so she took it. For safe-keeping.'

Carver pulled himself to his feet using the side of the bed for leverage. 'Good, fine. So, Zahra, listen . . .'

Carver told her about his visit to the internet café, leaving out the part where the computer started to behave a little strangely. He told her that Nawal had been right, that she was on to something. Something important.

'I need to talk to her and record that interview. Can you get her to come to the hotel? Soon as possible, how about . . .'

Zahra was shaking her head. 'I will make a meeting, but not here. Someone followed her when she left the hotel last time. She was able to lose him with no problem but I don't want her to risk this again.'

Carver agreed. 'Fine, not here but somewhere nearby and soon.'

'There is something else . . .'

'Yeah?'

'Mr Akar wants to meet with you.'

'Is this about the fight? Just tell him—'

Zahra interrupted. 'It is not about the fight. Not just that anyway. He wants you to be his guest, later today, for a drink upstairs in the Garden Suite.'

Carver could tell from Zahra's tone that this unwanted invitation was bad news.

She answered his question before he was able to ask it. 'He will not take no for an answer.'

The Way of Sorrows (vi)

Near Dongola, Sudan

The truck did not stop again until one in the morning when the driver pulled his rig and restless load to a halt and announced that they would stop and sleep for a few hours. Some passengers stayed in the back of the truck, which was cramped but warm, while others tried to make themselves more comfortable away from the lorry. Both brothers chose the latter and together with a dozen or so men made camp a few yards from the truck. Simon stayed with them and Gebre opened the suitcase and shared out the clothes so all three could wear as many layers as possible to protect them against the cold desert night. In return Simon handed round a paper bag of figs and some water. The three ate and drank then lay down, side by side, to sleep.

Gebre was woken by an urgent need to defecate; he stumbled away from the group of swaddled and snoring men to find somewhere to relieve himself. The moon was full and bright enough to see by and Gebre found a patch of scrub and crouched and shat then did his best to clean himself with handfuls of rough grass and sand. When he stood, he saw a shape – a vehicle – half buried in the sand. He moved closer and saw that it was a pick-up truck, a Toyota similar to the ones the smugglers used. The car was facing south, back the way they'd come. Gebre was wondering why the truck had been left and worrying that he might stumble across another dead body, when he saw that although the outline of the vehicle was intact, there was a huge blackened hole where the back of the truck should be. He moved nearer and saw a mess of twisted metal; the base of the truck had been blown down in the sand and lying on top was a long black metal box the size and shape of a coffin. Its lid was gone, sides distended and the thick clips at each end twisted into corkscrew shapes.

Gebre turned and walked away but after a minute's walking he started to worry that he was moving away from his camp instead of towards it. He was on the point of turning and trying another direction when his right foot found a hole of some sort and he fell. The sand that he landed face down in was as fine as flour and Gebre was thankful for that; he sat up gingerly and massaged his foot and ankle for a while.

From a nearby sand dune, Gebre sensed movement; he stayed very still and stared at the base of the dune. In the dark crease between the flat of the desert and the rising dune he could just make out a face and most clearly a pair of bright black eyes staring back at him. A dog? The animal climbed from what he guessed must be its burrow and moved closer. It was no more than a foot long and thin in the body but with a large head and bushy tail. It had thick cream-coloured fur. It was bold to come this close; perhaps it sensed the possibility of food, perhaps the animal was as desperate as they were?

Gebre heard a shuffling noise from behind him and the animal heard it too and took a few paces backwards, cautious but not fearful. Perhaps these creatures saw so few men that they had not yet learned to be scared. It lifted its ears to hear better and Gebre could not help but smile; the creature reminded him of cartoon characters he and Solomon used to watch on TV, with huge ears, nearly as long as its body, or so it seemed from where he was lying. The person he'd heard crawling from behind him, snaking through the sand, now drew level. Gebre glanced sideways and saw it was one of the Sudanese smugglers; he had his revolver in his hand. He jogged Gebre with his arm.

'You see it?'

'Yes, a dog?'

'Not dog, *fanak*. A fox.'

Gebre looked again, he could see that now, the sharp muzzle and long tail.

'I will not hit it with this . . .' The smuggler lifted the handgun. 'Stay quiet and watch it, I will get my rifle.'

'Why? For food?'

The man shook his head. 'Not food, *fanak* meat is sour. We kill them for the fur; the Tuareg will pay us for the skin.'

Gebre shrugged and the man shuffled backwards through the sand.

In his absence the fox moved closer, eyes fixed on Gebre. Seconds passed and from behind the *fanak* there was more movement. Gebre strained his eyes and saw two smaller heads peering from the burrow – cubs watching out for their mother. Gebre reached into his pocket and found one of the figs Simon had given him. He threw it with as little motion as he could manage and the fruit flew over the animal's head and landed close to the cubs who ducked back into their burrow. The adult fox turned tail and ran to the food, sniffed it once, grabbed it in its mouth and disappeared back into the sand. Moments later the smuggler was back, snaking through the sand on his belly, rifle in hand. He stared at the sand dune and sucked his teeth in frustration.

'*Matha hadath*? What happened?'

'The fox run when it heard you.'

Gebre stood and stretched, putting weight carefully on his right ankle. It seemed to him that the fox had more right to be in this place than they did; the fact that any living thing could survive here was some kind of miracle. He looked down at the smuggler. 'Sir? The Toyota back there in the sand, what happened to it?'

'It was shot at. Blown up.'

'Bullets do not do that.'

The smuggler grinned. 'They do if they hit the wrong thing.'

'What did they hit?'

The man waved Gebre away. 'Enough. You are cargo. Cargo does not ask questions.'

He lay back flat on the ground, his rifle aimed at the sand dune. Gebre hoped the fig would keep the animal occupied until the smuggler either grew bored or fell asleep. There was enough death already in this desert without this man adding his quota.

21 Patron Saints and Pictures

DATELINE: Tahrir Square, Cairo, Egypt, January 31 2011

@tsquarelawan

| No more votes for the Titanic movie! We want inspiring
| films. About people like us! With happy endings!

Nawal bought herself some breakfast – an ear of buttered corn – and made her way across Tahrir Square. The occupation was growing every day: organic but somehow also organised, and for the first time in her life Nawal felt at home. It was not a utopia – it was too real for that and too dirty although people did their best to keep it clean. She had helped draw up a litter-picking rota and several of the many colourful posters displayed around the place urged people to tidy up: *Cleanliness is half of faith*.

She walked past a group of Nasserite Arab nationalists and some Azhari preachers in their turbans and cloaks sitting on a carpet of cardboard boxes and also eating breakfast. She was heading for the younger and more anarchic side of Tahrir. In the distance she saw a boy in a red football shirt, who'd climbed halfway up a lamp post and had a white sheet clamped between his teeth. The to-do list she'd made on her phone was a long one and her first job was to help set up the Tahrir Square Cinema. They'd made a screen from stitched-together bed sheets and by the looks of it that was almost in place. The plan was to run the projector on electricity stolen from a nearby streetlight and Nawal had asked her followers to suggest films. Now she had to source the most popular movies and organise a programme.

Once that was done, the plan was to establish a University of Tahrir next to the cinema, with an open mic some of the time and invited lecturers as well. Nawal read through the rest of her to-do list. She smiled when she remembered that Zahra was coming down later, together with William Carver so he could record an interview with her. Nawal had meant to try and write down an English translation of everything she'd seen on the day she found the gas canisters but there hadn't been time. It wouldn't be a problem, Zahra would help. She'd also planned to go and retrieve her collection of other canisters, bullets and batons from the old lady's flat but there had been no time for that either – at least not during daylight and while she had almost convinced herself that the attack had had no effect on her, the truth was Nawal didn't want to walk the back streets at night. Perhaps Zahra and she could go and do that together too? Her hand went to her neck; she was wearing a green silk scarf, which hid the knife wound, and she hoped might also appear a little elegant.

The boy at the top of the lamp post was shouting down at her. 'How does it look?'

Nawal tilted her head. 'Not bad.'

'Cool. Have you got that copy of *Titanic* yet?'

Nawal laughed. 'No! And I'm not going to, Tarek. So you may as well stop voting for it.'

Carver was looking for Jean. He wanted to thank her, to apologise for being so much trouble. He also wanted to find out what she'd done with the tear gas canister. Her phone was off and she wasn't in her room. He searched the hotel with Patrick's sunglasses perched on top of his own regular spectacles. This hid the most obvious bruising but he wasn't sure it made him look much less conspicuous; certainly it seemed like he was getting more than his fair share of strange looks as he checked the bar and lobby. There was no sign of Jean in either place and so he decided to try the garden, via the dining room.

At first he mistook the skinny black man waving at him from the other side of the dining room for a waiter. As he moved closer, he realised it was the Good Samaritan who'd come to his rescue at the mosque.

'Mr Carver! I had a feeling we would meet again. A wish, I should say.'

The man's accent intrigued him: East African, he was certain, but with an interesting Italian twang to it.

'Hello, it's good to see you again.'

'And you, and you. Have you time to drink a coffee with me?'

Carver looked around; there was no sign of Jean. 'Of course.' He sat down at the table. 'I looked for you after I finished that interview with the Muslim Brotherhood man.'

'Mr Shalaby.'

'Mr Shalaby, yes. I wanted to thank you.'

'No thanks necessary. I planned to wait and introduce myself properly as well but it became clear that I had outstayed my welcome.' He smiled. 'I suspect that both of us are used to the *cold coming* as the poet said? Doing the work that we do?'

Carver was doubly confused. Unsure both of the poet in question and also why this man's work would make him less than welcome. 'What is it you do?'

'You cannot guess?'

Carver looked at the man's suit, his briefcase and shoes: the usual clues, and took a guess. 'A diplomat?'

'Diplomat?' The man laughed, put a finger to his collar then looked down at his shirt and laughed again, louder. 'Ah, I forget – I am not wearing my uniform!' He grinned at Carver who remained confused. 'I am a priest, I am Father Rumbek.'

'Father Rumbek, of course. Then you're here to see Jean?'

'Yes, we are making an interview. She has gone to get some more batteries for her little tape recorder.' He offered his hand, which William shook; the priest had a good hold. 'I did not mean to be mysterious, I assumed you would guess from my *collarino ecclesiastico* but it is not there to be guessed at.'

Carver nodded. 'Dog collar.'

'Yes. I like your English word better than my Italian. Although' – the priest reached for his briefcase – 'we Italians have another word too, a better one I think.' He opened the briefcase, and buried beneath a sheath of papers he found a folded black shirt and stiff white collar; he removed the plastic collar and held it up for Carver to see. 'We also call it *strozzapreti* – like the pasta?' He twisted the strip of plastic and smiled. 'You name them after dogs, we name them after pasta – both things our countrymen love. It is encouraging I think.'

Carver suspected that Father Rumbek found encouragement easier to come by than most.

Jean returned with her old Dictaphone in one hand and a pack of batteries in the other. 'How lucky am I? I've got two fellas at my table now.'

On seeing Jean, Carver's hand went to his swollen face.

'It's looking better already, Billy.' She turned to Father Rumbek. 'William had an altercation with a colleague – no big deal.'

The priest nodded. 'Sometimes it is better to turn the other cheek.'

Jean laughed. 'Yeah, I think that's what he did. Anyway, I'm glad you two met, I was going to introduce you anyway. You remember I mentioned Father Rumbek?'

Carver nodded. 'I remember very well. Jean compared you to Mother Teresa, Father. Mother Teresa with' – he glanced at Jean – 'a similar moral compass.'

Rumbek shook his head. 'That is much too much. I am God's servant, like St Teresa of Calcutta, but I think that is all we have in common.'

Jean put her hand over the priest's. 'You're being modest.'

Jean explained that Father Rumbek was in Cairo at the behest of Rome, to check in with the Catholic congregation, with Coptic Christians and others and find out what the Arab uprising might mean for them.

Carver nodded. 'You're worried about sectarianism?'

'Rome is worried, I am more hopeful. I like to think of what is happening here now as a shaking of the kaleidoscope; if we are lucky then perhaps we can make the various pieces fit together better afterwards than they did before. I have already had meetings with my fellow Christians and with senior imams and I was encouraged.'

Carver nodded.

'I have even been asked to hold a small mass in Tahrir Square – a great honour.'

'Encouraging.'

'Exactly.'

Jean chipped in. 'It's important work.'

The priest waved a modest hand.

'But I also want to talk to you about the migrant stuff, Father. The work you do with refugees?'

It transpired that Father Rumbek had become a point of contact for his fellow Sudanese and other refugees trying to make their way up through Africa and across the Mediterranean.

'Of course, we can talk about this, but others do much more than me.'

At that moment, the priest's mobile phone began to ring. Carver recognised the ringtone: it was the singsong sound his first mobile phone had made. Father Rumbek answered, first in Arabic then English and French and at least two or three other languages that Carver did not recognise. Then the priest waited, the phone pressed hard against his ear. After a few more multilingual hellos and invitations to speak he put the phone back in his pocket.

'This happens more and more. People call me from somewhere, from only God knows where. The phone connects, but I cannot hear them and I have no idea if they hear me.'

Carver nodded. 'Where might they be calling from?'

'That call? The desert, I think. Once they reach the sea they have satellite phones and those work better. I think these calls come from somewhere in the Sahara and my writ does not run there. Who knows the horrors they endure? Even if they reach me, there is no coastguard I can call. I fear that as many people are dying in the sand as are dying in the sea. It breaks my heart.'

'Wait, wait . . .' Jean held up a hand. 'I need to be getting some of this on tape.' She started fiddling with her machine, removing the old batteries with her painted fingernails and inserting new ones. 'What's your plan, Billy? Do you want to stay and listen?'

Carver shook his head. 'I'd like to but I can't. The hotel manager wants a chat and then I'm heading down to the square with Zahra.'

Jean glanced at Carver's swollen face. 'You're feeling up to that?'

'I need to get her friend Nawal on tape. Soon as possible.' He looked over at Father Rumbek who was busy on his phone. 'I'm sorry, Father.'

'Do not worry, I have plenty to occupy me.'

Carver turned to Jean, his voice lowered. 'I wanted to ask you 'bout some other stuff.' He hesitated. 'And to thank you. For . . . you know, looking after me.'

Jean put a hand on his arm. 'Let's catch up later.' Jean glanced at the priest. 'Father. William has to make a move.'

'Goodbye, Mr Carver, good to see you again. I wish that you

could stay. I am concerned that Miss Fitzgerald might exaggerate my modest contribution.'

Carver nodded, but thought the priest didn't look too concerned.

Jean switched her machine on. 'Father, by the time I'm done you'll be in the running for Humanitarian of the Year and I'll have won a Pulitzer.'

The Way of Sorrows (vii)

Near El 'Atrun, Sudan

Objects that Gebre knew to be fixed in place, moved in the heat. The minaret, the dozen clay-built homes, the truck that had carried them hundreds of miles already and would carry them hundreds more – all wavered in the haze. They had been stuck in the small desert town for half a day already, waiting for a delivery of fuel. It was too hot for anyone to stay in the truck and so they found what comfort they could, moving from one shaded spot to the next as the sun moved across the sky.

Growing up in Asmara, Solomon and Gebre were used to the heat, but they had never experienced a sandstorm. The first indication of its approach came in the form of a welcome breeze, sweeping through the town, south to north. Gebre noticed that an old castellated fort that they'd driven past on their way into the town had suddenly disappeared from view.

The brothers were unaware of what was coming, but others were not. The Sudanese driver and his men climbed back into the cab of the truck and wound the windows up. A woman called Salim who the other women in their group seemed to respect and defer to, encouraged those around her to gather their children close and pull their scarves down over their faces. Before either brother could do much in the way of preparation, cloud after cloud of sand came sweeping towards them. The small clay houses that had been visible just moments ago were gone; it was as though a sand-coloured shawl had been thrown over the town. Gebre and Solomon pulled their shirts over their heads and screwed their eyes shut; the rush and roar of the sand was like nothing they'd heard before.

The dust storm travelled through the place in minutes, unroofing several of the small huts and leaving piles of sand banked high against every building, vehicle and unmoving object – including the huddles of people. After the storm had gone, Solomon stood and shook himself clean. The movement reminded Gebre of watching a wet dog shake itself dry – he grinned at his brother and climbed to his feet, fine sand cascading from his clothes.

The petrol tanker they'd been waiting for arrived soon after the dust storm left – as though it had been chasing the storm north. The traffickers filled the tank and another half-dozen plastic jerry cans and ordered their passengers back on board. The brothers now found themselves sitting close to a group of women and their children and Solomon did his best to tuck his legs and elbows close to his body and move as little as possible.

It was an uncomfortable situation and so he was grateful when, at around dusk, the truck rolled to a halt and the driver and his men climbed from the cab to relieve themselves. Solomon stood and stretched and was about to jump down from the back of the truck when one of the light-skinned Sudanese, the uglier of the two, climbed up on to the riser and stared in. His eyes settled on a young girl, sitting just a couple of places down from where the brothers were. It was Salim's daughter he was staring at. Her mother was sitting close by and as Gebre watched, she leaned forward in an attempt to block the smuggler's view of the girl. It should have worked, since from where he stood he could only have been able to see her trainers and trouser-covered legs. Gebre guessed that the girl must have caught the man's eye earlier in the journey; he pointed a finger.

'Auntie, I need your girl to help me with something; send her down.'

Salim did not look at the man; she stayed silent, slowly shaking her head.

He lifted himself on to tiptoes. 'It will not take very long, I will bring her back.'

Gebre felt his brother's hand on his shoulder pushing himself up. Solomon stood, moving the truck with his weight.

'I can help you.'

The man laughed. 'Not you, big man. You are not what I need for this job.' He pointed again. 'Woman, do you hear me? If you make me wait, it will be worse.' He took his gun from between belt and trousers and waved it at Solomon. 'Get that little one down for me.'

'No. Leave her alone.'

'What did you say?'

'I said—'

Gebre got to his feet and placed himself in between the man's gun and his brother.

'Sir, look at the girl.'

The man looked, he had a clearer view now.

'She is very young, just a child. Perhaps she is your daughter's age or younger?' Gebre studied the smuggler's face.

He shook his head, shaking any shame or second thoughts that Gebre had planted in his mind away. He raised the gun again but before he could make his next move, Salim was on her feet, picking her way past the other women and heading in the smuggler's direction. As she moved, she pulled her blue headscarf down, freeing her hair. She stopped next to Gebre and addressed the man in a low voice.

'I can you help with this. Not my daughter – me.'

The smuggler gave a grudging nod and jumped down with Salim following.

She returned twenty minutes later, walking slowly from behind a line of sand dunes, brushing dirt from her trousers and smoothing her long shirt down. Halfway back to the truck she seemed to stumble, then stood straight, reached into her pocket and found her headscarf. Gebre watched her tie the hijab and carefully tuck every strand of hair back beneath it. The hands of several fellow passengers helped her into the truck and back to her place, next to her daughter who was watching her keenly. As she drew closer, Salim's daughter opened her arms and her mother lowered herself into the embrace and buried her face in her daughter's neck, breathing deeply. The girl held her mother's hand, stroking it with her own and whispering words of comfort. The daughter mothered the mother and the two women cried and Gebre and the other passengers looked away; out of respect and shame and despair.

22 Appetite

DATELINE: The Garden Suite, Seti Hotel, Cairo, Egypt,
January 31 2011

Mr Akar had requisitioned the best suite in the Seti for his meeting
with Carver: an over-decorated room on the fourth floor with a
terrace facing the swimming pool and gardens. Glancing around,
it seemed to Carver that the room contained too many of
everything. Three sofas, four small occasional tables, the same
number of gold-framed mirrors and an entirely unnecessary white
marble fireplace with a pair of highly polished golden sphinxes in
the place where an Englishman of a certain generation might
expect to see two china dogs. There was even a walnut wood
grandfather clock standing against one wall, though the hands on
the clock face appeared to be stuck somewhere around half past
eleven. Mr Akar handed Carver the whisky and water he'd asked
for and encouraged him to pick a sofa. Carver sat and took a sip
of his drink; Akar smiled and gestured at his guest's face.

'The whisky will help the pain.'

Carver nodded.

'Do you enjoy this room?'

He looked around. 'Not particularly.'

'It is bigger than your room.'

Perhaps that was what this meeting was about. Akar was going to try and sell him an upgrade. If so, he was out of luck. 'I prefer mine.'

Akar looked around. 'Yes, this room is too big for you. It has too many excellent things; *you* like simple things. A good drink, good food . . .'

Carver gave a non-committal shrug. He wanted to get this unwelcome meeting over and done with as swiftly as possible.

'But there is one thing about this room which I think you will enjoy.'

'What's that?'

'Come, please.'

Carver studied his host: the hair an unconvincing shade of black, shiny grey suit and colourful tie – he looked like an old-fashioned spiv.

Akar strode over to the French windows and pulled them wide. 'The balcony . . .' The yellow curtains billowed and he ushered his guest through. 'The balcony is very good.'

The wide, paved balcony was dappled with afternoon sun. At the front, next to the stone balustrade, was a set of cast-iron garden furniture, painted a glossy white – a round table and two chairs with plump cushions in the same bright yellow material as the curtains. 'I sit here very much, it is the best place for my hobby.'

'Your hobby?'

'Yes, this is the correct word?'

'A hobby, a pursuit.'

'Yes, something for pleasure. An Englishman like you gave me this word – he gave me his hobby: I watch the birds.' Akar pointed at the table, on which sat a pair of binoculars in a battered brown leather case and a copy of the *Collins Field Guide to the Birds of Britain and Europe*.

Carver recognised the book; its blue cover was familiar, and he had a vague memory of his mother owning the same edition.

Mr Akar picked up the book and handed it to him. 'I write all the birds I see.'

Flicking through the pages Carver saw that Akar had ringed many of the neat little illustrations: egret, Egyptian nightjar. 'Many different birds fly here and stop, beautiful things you can see. The Egyptian people believe that the gods appear to us as birds. I believe this.'

Mr Akar was interrupted by a tentative knocking at the window behind him. Carver turned to see a large man in chef's whites standing in the doorway holding a silver tray. The man pulled the door open with his free hand and glanced around nervously before addressing his boss.

'Sir, you tell me to bring the Tutankhamun here?'

The hotel manager nodded. 'That is correct, chef, put it here . . .'

He moved the binoculars and the big man set the tray down gently and stepped back so that his boss and his guest could admire his creation. There on the tray, on a bright white serving plate, stood a golden pyramid, constructed entirely from spun sugar. Inside the pyramid was a coffin-shaped object, a miniature version of Tutankhamun's tomb made from dark chocolate, milk chocolate mousse and gold leaf. Carver bent down for a closer look. The detail was meticulous, the overall effect impressive.

William had heard about the Tutankhamun dessert but he'd never seen it himself. The Seti Hotel had invented the dish back in the 1970s and it was mentioned in guidebooks. The Tutankhamun was obviously a novelty rather than a significant culinary breakthrough but it had helped put the hotel on the map and made it a lot of money down the years.

'Thank you, chef, you can go.'

The chef's shoulders slumped at this lukewarm reception but

he left without complaint. Once its creator was out of earshot, Mr Akar felt free to lavish it with praise.

'It is a special thing, is it not? I have not served this dish for some time, but I wanted to see if the chef was still capable and I thought that you would appreciate it.'

'Thank you.'

'You must eat.' Akar encouraged William to sit. 'We will test it together.'

'Test it?'

'Yes, I am expecting an important guest, a friend to me and this hotel who I think will visit soon. When he comes, he will want the Tutankhamun.' Mr Akar sat and unbuttoned his suit jacket; he lifted his tie and draped it back over his shoulder. There were two forks on the tray and he handed one to Carver and took the other. The hotel manager broke a careful hole in the sugary pyramid and excavated a forkful of chocolate.

Carver followed suit on his side of the pudding with more serious consequences both for the pyramid and the crypt. He shovelled a mix of dark chocolate and gold leaf into his mouth and washed it down with a swallow of whisky.

Akar watched him. 'It is good?'

He nodded. 'It is.' It was delicious.

'Yes, my chef can still make this dish well. We should celebrate this.' Akar left Carver eating and went inside to get his glass and the bottle; on his return he poured them both a generous double. 'You appreciate good whisky and you appreciate good food, you are a man of appetites. We are similar I think . . .'

Carver ignored this, concentrating instead on what was left of the tomb; if he had one complaint, it might be that the coffin was a little on the small side.

'And we both appreciate beauty too.' Akar retrieved the binoculars and handed them over. 'Look, please . . .'

Carver put his fork down somewhat reluctantly and took the

glasses. He trained them on the highest of the tall pine trees that flanked the pool and adjusted the focus. The magnification and clarity were impressive but he saw no birds.

'Some evening I will see the African swallows, sparrows, jays. I can see all of those.'

'Not much around right now.'

'No, no. But even without birds there are things to see.' He paused. '*You* and Zahra for instance.' He laughed – an unconvincing sound.

'I beg your pardon?'

'Please, do not be embarrassed. Zahra is a very pretty girl.' He licked his lips. 'But she is not the right girl for you. If you are looking for a younger girl then I can—'

Carver had heard enough. 'I have no interest in Zahra, not in that way. She helped with some translation, a little local knowledge, that's all.'

Akar fell silent and stared at the table. Carver waited while he absorbed this information.

'I see. I was mistaken. Misled, I should say. I suspected as much but I wanted to give her the benefit of the doubt. I apologise.'

Carver waved his apology away. 'Zahra's smart, hardworking, you are lucky to have her.'

Akar nodded. 'She is the best employee I have – *a woman of all work* I used to say. I have known her since she was a little girl. I know her family well, her father and mother. When one thousand people want a job, I give it to her.'

Carver nodded. 'Good choice.'

'Yes, I made the good choice, I did a good deed. I do many good deeds for Zahra and her family but she is not so grateful. Not anymore anyway.'

'She works hard. Isn't that enough?'

The hotel manager shook his head. 'We all have to be grateful – grateful to the people who help us. That is how the world works.'

Carver studied Mr Akar. Until now he'd considered the hotel manager to be a simple crook – a crook and a creep. He was beginning to think that he might have underestimated him.

'I have looked after Zahra for a long time, I have kept her safe. But I cannot do it for ever. She needs to be careful.'

'Careful of what?'

'Careful with the company she keeps, careful what she does when she is not here – under my protection.' Akar took a swallow of whisky; his face twitched at the strength of the drink. 'Would you like me to tell you what is going to happen here in Egypt, Mr Carver? Isn't that what you and all the other news people want to know?'

'I guess.'

Akar poured another inch of whisky into both glasses. 'The President will wait until you all get bored of Egypt, until you've packed up and gone home and then he will teach the demonstrators their lesson. In a few weeks, all these young people you see on the streets will be in jail or in hospital. Or dead.' Akar delivered his prediction in a very matter-of-fact way.

Carver shrugged. He did not want to debate with this man. 'Perhaps. You could be right.'

'I am right.' Akar finished his drink and placed his glass down a little sharply on the cast-iron table. 'You say that Zahra does these things for you. Translation and information and so on. What does she receive in return?' Akar tried his best to make this sound like a casual enquiry but his face betrayed him.

'She receives money. I pay her, like you.'

'Is that so? She hasn't asked you to help one of her troublesome friends? Or look after something for her?'

Carver shook his head. The hotel manager had tipped his hand and both men knew it.

'Who's asking, Mr Akar? Not you, I think.'

'Of course me. I ask you so I can help Zahra.' He pointed a

shaky finger at Carver. The last whisky had been one too many – he was drunk. 'I care for her, not like you. If all you people would go away then I could keep her safe. I could . . .' He shook his head. 'It doesn't matter.' Akar looked at his watch. 'What is done is done.'

Carver rushed back to his room. Whoever had searched it in his absence had been thorough. From what he could see, every drawer and cupboard, bag and pocket had been checked. He switched his mobile phone back on and called Zahra.

Carver lay back on the bed with a cold, damp flannel over the left side of his face. He had a hard headache behind that eye. The tap on his bedroom door was so light that at first he didn't hear it; the second knock was firmer and Carver walked over in stocking feet and put his good eye to the peephole. His encounter with Mr Akar and the knowledge that his room had been searched had unnerved him. He saw a round-faced version of Zahra on the other side and opened the door. She strode in.

'What did Akar want?'

Carver noted that she had dropped the honorific. No longer Mr Akar, just a surname. He decided on a straightforward chronological telling: he told Zahra about her boss's fondness for bird-watching: '*birds and whatever else he can see from that terrace . . .*' He told her that Akar had seen the two of them talking and assumed that Carver was propositioning her. 'Ridiculous of course, insulting in fact.'

Zahra didn't seem surprised, nor particularly interested – not in Carver's reputation nor her own. 'Could he have seen Nawal from where you stood? When she came to meet you? Is there a clear view of the storeroom?'

William tried to remember. 'You can see the pool and the bar. But not the storeroom, I don't think so anyway. If I were you, Zahra, I'd be worrying less about Nawal and more about yourself.'

The flannel felt warm now, the same temperature as his swollen face. He dropped it on the floor. 'Akar obviously has some idea of what you're up to – you *and* Nawal. He told me you need to be careful.'

Zahra had remained standing and now started to pace between bed and bathroom. 'Careful. Careful, *hadhdar* . . . I have heard this word all my life, ever since I was a small girl. First I learned to say *mother*, then *father* and then they taught me *careful*.' She stopped pacing. 'Nawal says that the time for being careful is over. It is time to be brave.' She stared at Carver, daring him to contradict her.

'You can be brave and still be careful.' Carver wasn't sure he believed this, but it felt like the right thing to say anyway. He told Zahra about Mr Akar's ham-fisted attempt to find out if she'd given him anything to look after. 'I don't think Akar knew what he was asking for, it felt like a fishing exercise.'

Zahra nodded.

'And then when I got back here afterwards, my bloody room had been searched.'

He waited for the gravity of this news, the seriousness of the situation to impact on Zahra but she simply stood and processed the information.

'Did they find the gas canister Nawal gave you?'

'No. Jean has it.'

'That's good. None of this will have been Akar's idea, he will have been following orders.'

'Whose orders? Who do you think is doing the ordering?'

Zahra paused. Before she'd arrived, Carver had been worried that telling her about the meeting with Akar, his veiled threats against her and the searching of his room might frighten her. In fact, she'd shown no trace of fear – none until now.

'Colonel Balit.'

'You're joking?'

Zahra shook her head. 'It does not worry us. Soon it will not matter. Akar and Abdul Balit and all the others will be gone – swept away with the change; everything will change.'

Carver felt the way he always did when confronted with absolute conviction: both impressed and at the same time completely unconvinced. 'Perhaps.'

Zahra shook her head. 'Not perhaps – certainly. You haven't heard what has happened this evening. Tahrir is full; the police had no choice but to withdraw. The square is ours. Only the army are there and they are with the people, they will side with us against the President. Look . . .' Zahra handed Carver her phone.

On it Tsquare Lawan's Twitter feed – written by Nawal, translated by Zahra and read now by nearly two hundred thousand people. Carver scrolled through a few of the most recent postings. The tweets they believed heralded a great change.

@tsquarelawan
> News just in: the laundry workers have joined the protests! And the Tora cement factory workers!

@tsquarelawan
> No plan to march on presidential palace, embassies, ministries, state TV. Not yet! Just pack Tahrir.

@tsquarelawan
> These past few days we have won battles. This evening we will win a war!

William skim-read the tweets and handed the phone back – he got the idea.

Zahra looked at him. 'What do you think?'

'I think you should use the exclamation mark more sparingly' – Zahra glanced at her phone – 'and I think you should dial down the excitement. It's still too early to know what's going to happen here. Much too early'

She nodded. 'Nawal says exactly the same. She says revolutions take weeks or months – not days.'

'And the rest. Where are we meeting Nawal by the way? I need to tape that interview soon as.' His encounter with Mr Akar and the searching of his hotel room made recording Nawal's story seem all the more urgent.

'It is all arranged. My shift finishes in a couple of hours and then we will go.'

23 Traitors and Heroes

DATELINE: Ministry of Defence, Whitehall, London SW1, January 31 2011

'Walk with me, will you, Robert?'

The permanent secretary had arrived unexpectedly at Mariscal's desk, causing a hush to fall across the open-plan office.

'Of course.'

While Rob struggled into his suit jacket, Craig surveyed the mess that was Mariscal's desk. Rob was reaching for his overcoat, which was hanging on a nearby stand, when his boss stopped him.

'You won't be needing that, we're staying inside.' Craig was aware that his deputy and Rob's line manager, Mr Fielding, was watching them from his cubicle across the aisle.

Eventually he plucked up the courage to speak. 'Perhaps there's something that *I* can help you with, Permanent Secretary?'

'No thank you, Mr Fielding.'

'I see. You seem to be taking a strong interest in our communications strategy these days. Judging by the amount of time you're spending with Mr Mariscal.'

Craig shot his deputy a warning glance. A warning that Fielding chose to ignore.

'Perhaps I should remind you, Mr Craig, that *I* am Rob's immediate superior.'

By this time any low-level chatter in the open-plan office had ceased. Craig stared hard at his deputy.

'*Immediate and superior.*' He paused. 'I must say that when I think of you, Mr Fielding, neither of those words come to mind.'

If a collective intake of breath can be loud then this one was.

'Are you ready, Robert?'

They took the lift to the top floor of the ministry and then walked to the far end of the building where some renovation work was being done. Craig strode across the building site, pulling clear plastic curtains aside as he went. They ended up at a dust-covered window overlooking Whitehall.

'They've ripped out pretty much everything on this floor, I believe. Including the bugs . . .' He looked around. 'Or we must hope so anyway.' He smiled at Rob. 'So I need to ask you something.'

'Of course.'

'A hypothetical.'

'Sure.'

Craig asked Rob to imagine that a British arms company had sold some equipment they shouldn't to a country that was currently subject to export restrictions

Rob took a punt. 'A country like Egypt? Hypothetically speaking?'

'Yes.'

'Great. So dob them in.'

'I beg your pardon?'

'Throw the book at them. The timing's perfect – we make a big song and dance of it and people see the MOD doing the right thing. It'll lend weight to our case against the budget cuts.'

Rob waited for Craig to acknowledge this stroke of genius but his boss seemed unimpressed.

'That won't do.' The civil servant lifted his finger and drew a line down the dusty window. 'This company, their interests and ours . . . overlap.' He looked at Rob, who was staring back, eyebrows raised. Craig tutted. 'I wish you didn't get that lupine look to you every time I tell you something vaguely confidential, Robert.'

'Sorry.'

'This isn't some silky conspiracy we're talking about. It's simply how things are – for now at least. So *dobbing them in*, as you put it, won't work. I'd like you to try and think of something else.' He examined his finger, took a handkerchief from his breast pocket and wiped it clean. 'How often do you see your old colleague William Carver these days?'

Craig's tone suggested that this was an innocent enquiry but Rob knew better. The permanent secretary didn't deal in non-sequiturs.

'Not very often.'

'But now and again?'

Craig was pushing at one of Rob Mariscal's few sore points. 'As far as William's concerned I betrayed *him*, our profession and every principle he holds dear. So, no, we don't speak *now and again*. We don't speak at all.'

Craig nodded. 'Right, well we might have to revisit that.'

'I take it that it's Carver who's got wind of this story then?'

'It looks like it, an element of it anyway.'

'Then I hope your hypothetical friend is ready for the fight of his life.'

Craig met Mariscal's eye. 'I fear he is.' The civil servant looked at his watch. 'Remind me of the name of the young woman who replaced you at the *Today* programme – the coloured lady? Holder is it?'

Rob stared at his shoes. 'Naomi. Naomi Holder.'

Nawal had asked her followers to pack Tahrir and packed it was. How many? A hundred thousand? Maybe more. She'd heard Al Jazeera reporting over a million but that was just TV people getting over-excited. There were reports of soldiers deserting and government ministers tendering their resignations but she didn't re-tweet any of that – not until she was sure of her facts.

@tsquarelawan
| Let state TV tell the lies. We will tell the Truth.

Nawal was working on a rota for the new school – or a school of sorts anyway. A tarpaulined space where local street children were given free food and drink and then encouraged to stay for lessons in reading and writing or just to listen to stories. Half a dozen middle-aged women – mothers who'd come to Tahrir to find out where their children had got to – had offered to staff the new school and Nawal was sorting out a rota and filling in the names. She'd almost finished when Tarek ran in, his red Egyptian team shirt sticking to him with sweat.

'It has started again near the museum. Some *baltagi* broke through the checkpoint.'

They set off together, gathering reinforcements as they moved across the square.

@tsquarelawan
| Pro-president *baltagi* throwing Molotovs and slabs of
| rock from rooftops on to protesters near museum.
| Take care!

@tsquarelawan

Fighting on the Egyptian museum side – people
injured, they need help!

Nawal was supposed to meet Zahra and William Carver an hour
from now but this would not take long. She messaged Zahra,
telling her that she was helping out at the museum.

She was holding one end of a stretcher, moving a boy who'd
been hit in the head with a slab of rock from the street to a nearby
ambulance when an army sergeant asked for assistance. He told
Nawal there were more injured people in the gardens next to the
museum. He took her and a young paramedic through the main
museum gates, garlanded with razor wire, and into a wooden hut
that was being used as a security checkpoint. They were greeted
warmly by an army captain who said he would take them to the
injured.

'There are not too many and it will not take long.' He looked
at the paramedic. 'Thank you for your help, sir.' And at Nawal:
'And for yours, Miss al-Moallem.'

They were inside the pink-coloured museum and heading for
the back of the building before a nagging worry in Nawal's mind
took shape. She was trying to remember when she'd told the
sergeant or any of his soldiers her name. And then she realised
that she hadn't.

24 How to Spike a Story

DATELINE: Cavendish Square, London W1, February 2 2011

Rob suggested they meet around the corner from Broadcasting House, in Cavendish Square – less chance of an awkward encounter with old colleagues and he only needed a few minutes. The shorter this meeting was, the better.

He walked around the square twice before he found a free bench; the place was busier than he'd expected, local shop and office workers making the most of the bright winter sunshine to eat their lunch alfresco. Fat London pigeons strode around, demanding bread with menaces and a group of students from the nearby fashion college were playing table tennis and smoking spliffs. Not far from Rob's bench, half a dozen homeless blokes were sleeping off old hangovers or working on new ones with the help of strong Polish lager. The youngest member of the group, a kid with a blond mullet, was trying to persuade his Alsatian to take a sip from the can.

Rob glanced over at the park noticeboard, which gave a brief history of the square and a list of park rules; it seemed to Mariscal that the only rule not currently being broken was the one prohibiting roller-blading. He stood and glanced around – there was no sign of Naomi. Rob took out his phone and checked the messages: nothing. Perhaps she wouldn't come? Part of him hoped that she wouldn't.

Despite these reservations, Rob's dark mood lifted when he spotted Naomi Holder, crossing at the traffic lights near the back of the Langham Hotel. It then swiftly fell when he saw that there was a middle-aged man in red trousers, white shirt and blue blazer walking in lockstep next to her, a big grin on his face. He was regaling her with what he clearly believed was a very funny story. Naomi spotted Rob and headed for the bench with her companion one step behind.

'Hey, Rob.' She gave Mariscal a friendly peck on the cheek. 'You remember Lawrence?'

'Yep.'

The grin slipped from Lawrence Bew's face as he recognised Rob. The newest member of Naomi's team of presenters held out his hand and Mariscal gave it a half-hearted shake. The feeling was mutual.

Rob had spent years refusing the BBC bosses' suggestion that Bew be made a regular presenter. Every few months one big cheese or another would suggest that Bew – a long-standing Westminster correspondent – would be a good addition to the team and every time Rob would tell them to go whistle. The man's ego was too big, his ambition too obvious. Lawrence glared at Rob who glared back and nobody said anything until Naomi broke the silence.

'We were just talking about the seven thirty lead – the Home Secretary interview. Did you catch it, Rob?'

He nodded.

'What did you think?'

'I thought it was soft.'

Bew turned on Rob. 'Cheers, Rob, luckily no one gives a toss what you think anymore.'

'Naomi asked for my opinion – that's my opinion. You should've gone in harder, especially on prisons.'

Bew pulled his shoulders back. 'There's more than *one* way to remove a gentleman's overcoat, Robert. Sometimes a stiff wind is the thing – other times a nice warm breeze will do the job.'

Mariscal shook his head; he'd forgotten just how pompous Bew could be. 'I see. I didn't realise you were trying to undress the Home Secretary, Lawrence, I thought you were trying to hold him to account.'

Bew huffed and puffed and Rob waited while Naomi calmed him down and sent him on his way. Lawrence left without any kind of goodbye for Rob, which suited him just fine. Once he'd gone, Rob shuffled up the bench, making room for Naomi to sit down. She crossed her legs and turned to face him.

'I thought the new job involved making friends and influencing people.'

'Yeah, but I draw the line at Lawrence Bew. I don't understand why you had to go and give him a permanent presenter slot.'

Naomi shrugged. 'He's well connected.'

'He's well annoying.'

She smiled; Naomi was wearing a dark denim skirt with woollen tights and a bright yellow jumper. Rob wondered whether she might have time for breakfast, then remembered that the plan was to keep this meeting as brief and businesslike as possible.

They talked shop for a while. Naomi was interested to know what Rob thought of a few changes she'd made, most but not all of which he approved of. She told him her next idea was to shunt the regular 'Thought for the Day' slot back an hour.

Mariscal nodded. 'I think pretty much every editor in the last twenty years has had the same idea.'

'But they didn't do it.'

'There are reasons. I think it's great that you're moving some of the furniture around. Absolutely right you want to make a mark.'

'But . . .'

'But I'm just not sure that picking a fight with every faith leader in Britain is the best way to do it – picking a fight with God.'

Naomi smiled. 'I don't think God listens to "Thought for the Day" anymore.'

'No, you're right about that. Just the *Shipping Forecast* – he's a vain old bastard.'

As they spoke, Naomi's phone vibrated silently in her skirt pocket.

'So, I'm guessing this is about the aircraft carrier send? Are you about to tell me all that exclusivity and access all areas stuff doesn't apply anymore?'

Rob shook his head. 'No, no, it's all good. I've had to piss off a dozen other angry broadcasters to make sure it's just you – but it's just you.'

'We're grateful.'

'Good, who're you going to send?'

'Well, I assumed you wouldn't want Lawrence?'

Rob pulled a face. 'Not unless we're allowed to cram the fat bastard in a torpedo tube and fire him at North Korea – no.'

Naomi suggested one of her two female presenters and they discussed dates. Everything they'd spoken about so far could have been handled over the phone. Everything up until Rob's next casual-sounding conversational gambit. 'How's William by the way?'

Naomi had her phone out and was checking messages. She threw Mariscal a sideways look. 'You two should try talking to each other – save you having to ask me about him every time we meet.'

Mariscal smiled. 'Yeah, I guess. Does he ask about me as well then?'

'No.' She put her phone away. 'How is Carver? He's okay, not as focused as I'd like him but you warned me about that, didn't you?'

Rob nodded. 'I thought the last couple of pieces sounded a little off the pace, like his mind's on other things.'

'Yeah, I hear that too.'

Rob's brow furrowed. 'As it happens, I have an idea what this other thing might be.'

'Really?'

Mariscal told Naomi about a batch of British-made tear gas, old stock, that had somehow ended up in Egypt together with some other bits and pieces. 'Body armour, batons, that kind of thing. Complete accident on the company's part; the Egyptians probably bought it through a third party. Believe it or not, there are some dodgy characters involved in the arms business.'

Naomi smiled.

'Not that this is arms; more public order.'

'And William's working on this?'

'He's been making enquiries.'

Rob didn't like lying to Naomi but this was so close to the truth as to make no difference.

She shrugged. 'The way you describe it, it doesn't sound like much of a story.'

'It isn't – it's a *Guardian* page four, *Times* news-in-brief kind of thing at best, I reckon. But you know what he's like when he gets his teeth into something. He gets a bit obsessive, goes a bit mad.'

Naomi weighed up what she was being told; her phone still buzzed but she wasn't interested. 'Where do you fit in here, Rob? Why is what Carver's up to any business of the head of comms at the MOD?'

Mariscal had expected this question, it was the right one. 'The world I work in now is pretty small. I hear a lot of things and in answer to your question – I made this my business.' He shuffled an inch closer to Naomi and lowered his voice to little more than a whisper. 'The company that made this stuff, they're seriously litigious and from what I hear, their lawyers are licking their lips over this one. That's another thing no new editor wants – a big legal row, just when you're starting to make your mark.' Mariscal grinned. 'I speak from experience.'

'So you're warning me off the story?'

He shook his head. 'Not at all. I can't do that. And I wouldn't. I'm just saying keep an eye on him. Sometimes when Carver goes after something, all hell for leather, he gets reckless. You know what I mean.'

Naomi nodded; she retrieved her phone and tutted. 'I gotta go.' She leaned over and gave Mariscal a peck on the cheek. 'Thanks, Rob, I appreciate it.'

He watched as she strode away. He liked Naomi, he always had. He couldn't ask her to spike a story and he wouldn't, even if he could. But he could plant a seed of doubt in her mind and, most of the time, that's all it took.

The Way of Sorrows (viii)

The Sudanese-Libyan border

The brothers lay on their backs, staring up at the blue sky. Gebre could see a long, cigar-shaped cloud, but it was too compact and moving too fast; it had no intention of watering this land. He wondered when this desert had last seen rain. Not in months certainly, maybe years? He was aware that his brother was watching him.

After nearly three days of driving, the Sudanese traffickers had unloaded the truck and left their passengers at a deserted security post on the Libyan border. They'd told them that the men who would transport them from there to Ajdabiya in north-east Libya were late and that they could not wait for them. When Solomon asked for some extra water and food, in case the wait was long, the men laughed.

Gebre was hungry and weak and Solomon was worried. He tried to shade his brother as best he could and to distract him wherever possible.

'Do you see that, brother?' Solomon was pointing at a thin contrail, high in the blue sky.

Gebre lifted his head an inch. 'London?'

'No. No, that one is going to Germany, it has a string of sausages hanging from the wing, don't you see?'

Gebre smiled. 'I do not know what I want more right now, to be on that plane or to be eating a plate of sausages.'

Solomon shook his head. 'The plane ride, you must always choose the plane ride. When you're on the plane they give you a plastic tray, filled with food, all in different sections – my idiot cycling coach told me about this. The plane people place it on your knee: a little box of green salad, a box of chicken and carrots, a chocolate pudding and as much tea or coffee as you like.'

It was another night and the best part of the following day before the Libyan traffickers arrived in four pick-up trucks.

'Tourist luxury!' The man who acted as the trafficker's translator pointed at the vehicles. 'But of course we have to ask you to pay for this luxury.'

Reasoned explanations and desperate pleas from the people that they had already paid for the journey fell on deaf ears and the shakedown commenced. The smugglers went from person to person collecting money and valuables; if they received what they thought was enough, the individual was invited to take their bag and find a space in the back of one of the trucks. It was Gebre who noticed that they were demanding more of the older and frailer passengers.

'Sol, we have to look useful . . . strong.'

Solomon nodded and the pair got to their feet. Just as the traffickers were dealing with the group of women ahead of them in the line Gebre felt his legs go and he fell against his brother who caught him, propping him up against his own solid frame. The brothers had their suitcase open in front of them, ready for the traffickers to take from at will. While they were doing this, Solomon held his brother up, his hand gripping the belt at the back of Gebre's trousers. After he'd found the half-hidden money and taken a couple of shirts, the translator stood and stared at the brothers.

'It is not much.'

Solomon met his eye. 'It is what we have. But also we can help when the vehicle is trapped in sand. I know this work well.'

The man jutted his chin in the direction of the truck and the looting party moved on. Gebre was too weak to take much notice of who was allowed to board the pick-ups and who was left behind; the gang crammed about thirty people into the three lead cars while the fourth was loaded with supplies: hundreds of litres of water, tinned food and fuel. The space left in the back of this last truck was reserved for a few of the younger women and once they had been chosen the cars set off in convoy.

Some people died from dehydration, others fell from the back or sides of the pick-ups and were left behind. On the second day, the convoy was chased and shot at by bandits; the traffickers returned fire and they escaped but three men and one woman died from gunshot wounds. The last of the four to die was Simon, but they were not allowed to stop and bury him or any of the others. The dead were simply lifted and dropped from the sides of the moving vehicles. During this part of the journey, Gebre drifted in and out of consciousness. At night, when the convoy stopped for a few hours and they slept, Solomon kept Gebre warm against the cold. Cradling his younger brother in his arms he stared up into the star-filled sky and wondered how much suffering one group of people could take before they submit. As usual they used their suitcase as a pillow and one of the nights, when he was sure everyone else was sleeping, Solomon opened it and dug around until he found the waterproof envelope containing their phones, photographs and documents. It was the piece of paper their grand-father pressed upon them that he was looking for, the one with the name and telephone number for the old priest. Solomon punched the numbers into his phone and pocketed it.

When his phone sprang briefly into life the next day Solomon buried his face in his brother's chest to muffle any sound and made a call. It rang for what seemed like an eternity and then connected – he heard a voice speaking many different languages before pausing. Solomon whispered into the phone, a frantic stream of information spoken as quickly as he could manage in case the line failed. When he stopped there was silence and then a reassuring voice.

'Of course I remember and of course I will help. As it happens, your timing is very good.'

On the morning of the fourth day Solomon shook his half-conscious brother awake and whispered into his ear: 'I can smell the sea.'

25 Missing

DATELINE: The Seti Hotel, Cairo, Egypt, February 2 2011

It had been two days and Zahra had heard nothing. She had retraced her friend's last known movements several times and distributed a photocopied picture of Nawal all around Tahrir Square. There had been a couple of possible sightings but these had come to nothing. Zahra had a reasonably clear idea of what had happened right up until the moment she'd disappeared: friends had seen her close to the museum entrance, helping move the injured to nearby ambulances. They'd seen a soldier ask Nawal and a paramedic she was working with to accompany him into the museum. Neither of them came back out.

Zahra had asked the soldiers at the checkpoint if they remembered seeing the pair. They insisted that no civilians had been let through on that day or any other; that only army personnel were allowed inside the museum. They said she'd been misinformed and when Zahra kept going back and asking the same questions each time the shift changed and different soldiers were on duty, they threatened to arrest her.

*

Carver didn't wake until gone eleven. He'd stayed up late again, trying to persuade some dullard of a duty press officer at the British Embassy in Cairo to pull his finger out and make some phone calls that might help find Nawal. In retrospect, Carver wondered whether he could have been more diplomatic with the guy but he doubted whether the idiot would have made much headway regardless of how nicely he had asked. He'd also tried calling his own Egyptian army and police contacts again as well as phoning the museum direct – he'd left a lot of messages in a lot of different places but so far he'd got nowhere. Carver had missed breakfast and, after leaving phone messages for Jean and Patrick, he decided he might as well go and do his lengths.

Carver swam up and down a couple of times then stopped and floated belly-up in the deep end, staring at the palm trees and pale blue sky above. His presence there was a significant obstruction for the several hotel guests attempting to do a few lengths before lunch, but he didn't give a toss – he was thinking.

He was worried about Nawal but he was also increasingly angry with himself for not recording an interview with her when he'd had the chance. Even with a good eyewitness account from Nawal the gas canister story was going to be a hard sell. Without her testimony all he had was the canister – which they'd decided was safest kept hidden in Jean's room – and a second-hand story. It was a dead duck. He was interrupted by a poke in the midriff from a fellow swimmer alerting him to the fact that Jean Fitzgerald was standing poolside and trying to get his attention. He swam over and trod water in the deep end while Jean lowered herself on to her haunches – a feat that impressed Carver more than somewhat. She was holding a piece of Seti Hotel headed notepaper.

'Guess who's coming to dinner?'

'Sidney Poitier?'

'Tragically not. We'll have to make do with Abdul Balit.'

'Today? I mean tonight?'

Jean nodded. 'I s'pose no notice means more secure as far as he's concerned? Though judging by the amount of activity in the hotel kitchen, I think we're just about the last people to know.'

Carver put a hand on the side of the pool to rest. 'And you still want me in on this?'

'I've got no choice.' Jean pointed at the letter. 'According to this, the colonel is expecting to see you and me both.'

'How come?'

'No idea, but worst-case scenario we get something to eat that isn't frittata. Have you got something to wear?'

Carver shrugged. 'I'll find something. How about we get a drink beforehand? Just you and me. For Dutch courage?'

Jean shook her head. 'I'd love to, but Father Rumbek just told me he'll come and finish the interview off early evening. After I've done with him I'll need every spare second to fancy myself up.'

Carver swam a couple of slow lengths but his mind was racing. He lumbered from the shallow end, dressed and was making his way back through the dining room towards the lift when the combination of noise and smell drifting from the direction of the hotel kitchen distracted him.

He walked over and poked his head over the swing doors. Mr Akar had borrowed cooks from hotels and restaurant kitchens across Cairo to ensure that Colonel Balit's visit went to plan. Nearest to where he was standing Carver saw two men in chef's whites shucking oysters and pulling them from their moorings; next to them, another pair were scrubbing and de-bearding mussels; and all this seafood was being dropped into a huge copper pot that was bubbling away on the largest hob the Seti kitchen had. Carver lifted himself on to tiptoes and saw inside a rich red bouillabaisse. The chef on the other side of the pot was chopping a bony-looking fish into large-sized pieces and dropping these in too. Beyond him, Carver recognised the Seti's regular chef, the big man he'd met before, who was busy skinning rabbits, a task which in his huge hands looked as simple as a person shuffling off a fur coat. There was no sign yet of the chef's speciality: the Tutankhamun pudding, but Carver was sure that would make an appearance later.

He decided he would try and enjoy the dinner – if not the company of the man he was dining with. He wiped his wet mouth dry against his sleeve and moved away from the doors and in the direction of the lifts.

Zahra caught up with Carver just outside his bedroom and almost shoved him inside. She pushed the door shut and spoke quickly, her voice a nervous whisper. 'Have you heard anything about Nawal?'

Carver shook his head. 'Nothing, I'm sorry. But I've got calls in to—'

'I have been thinking about it. You must ask Colonel Balit.'

'What?'

'It was the army that took her; if anyone can find out where she has gone, it is him.'

Carver shook his head slowly. 'I'm not sure that's such a good idea.'

'Please? We have no other choices. Look at these . . .' She got her phone out and scrolled through screen after screen of messages, all sent to Tsquare Lawan and all asking where they had gone. 'It is not just me; others need her – thousands of others.'

'Let me think about it.'

Zahra sat down on Carver's bed and started twisting the thin silver ring she wore on her middle finger, round and round.

'Nawal always says that I have a lion's heart.' Zahra smiled but when she spoke there was a catch in her voice. 'She taught me to be brave, so I am trying to be brave – but I am scared.'

The Way of Sorrows (ix)

Near Zuwara, northern Libya

Of the one hundred and four people who had climbed into the pick-up trucks on the Sudanese border, eighty-one arrived at the ocean. Neither Titus, Dumac, nor Salim or her daughter were among the eighty-one. The traffickers deposited their cargo in a half-finished tourist development on the Libyan coast. Among the buildings the smugglers had requisitioned were a breezeblock warehouse and, for people who had paid more, a couple of half-built villas facing the sea.

The villas were part of a government initiative, aimed at attracting what one senior Libyan politician described as *pink gold*: European tourists who had tired of Portugal, Spain, Morocco and the rest and might try this stretch of Libya's coastline instead. Gebre and Solomon were given space in the warehouse along with well over a hundred other men, women and children, most of them also from the south: Eritrea, Ethiopia, Somalia. The Libyan gang who ran this part of the operation provided sleeping bags, inflatable mattresses and a limited amount of food; they also warned their guests against leaving the development unless they were willing to risk being picked up by the police or a rival gang. Beyond delivering this warning, the smugglers made little attempt to guard the group. The only part of the development that was under regular guard was a long shed, newly built and painted black. The shed was surrounded by thick curls of barbed wire and windowless. The rumour among the people who'd been there longer than Gebre and Solomon was that it was used to store coffins.

Within a few days Gebre had regained his strength and was turning his mind to the next leg of their journey – the sea crossing. Every day he'd ask when they might travel and different members of the smugglers' gang would shrug and provide different reasons for the delay: they were waiting for the right weather; or for the boats that would take them to Europe to be fully fitted out; the tides were not right yet but would be before long and so on. Gebre wanted to believe these might be the reasons but instinct told him otherwise and as the numbers of desperate travellers being housed both in their breezeblock warehouse and the other buildings grew he became more sure of what was happening.

'It is the economies of scale, Sol. Do you remember they taught us about this at school?'

Solomon shook his head.

'The more people they move in one go, the more money they make. If they move us all at once then they only have to pay one night of wages to the men they will need to move us, one bribe to the police and the coastguard and whoever else they need to look the other way. I am sure.'

Gebre tried to spend the endless hours of waiting as usefully as possible; he was determined to understand everything he could about what the sea crossing would involve – giving him and Solomon the best chance of surviving it. With this in mind he befriended the youngest and most biddable member of the smuggling gang, an overweight teenager who was related in some way to the gang's leader and who Solomon insisted on calling Jabba but whose name was Wanis. Wanis responded to Gebre's invitations to friendship, partly because he was as bored with the waiting as anybody else but also because he'd discovered he had a taste for Marlboro cigarettes and Gebre was generous.

The best place to smoke out of sight of the rest of his group was on the roof of one of the unfinished villas and this was where the pair would go. Gebre taught Wanis some words of English and doled out the cigarettes and Wanis would reciprocate, answering Gebre's questions honestly.

'This wait is so long, perhaps we will not go at all?'

Wanis shook his head and choked on his attempt at a smoke-ring. 'Don't worry, you will go.'

'How do you know?'

'Because Gaddafi wishes it. He wants to send a message to Europe and you are the message; he wants Europe to see that if they get rid of him, boatloads of blacks like you will start arriving every week.' Wanis was smiling; there was no malice in the answer.

'Will you travel with us when we go to Europe?'

The boy shook his head. 'No way, I will not take a boat. I am saving my money for a passport and a plane ticket.'

Gebre had heard that this was possible, that there were people who would produce fake Bulgarian or Italian passports, which, in theory, could allow you to fly to Europe. But the sums of money involved in securing such things were huge, not thousands but tens of thousands.

'I will fly. It is more expensive but I have seen what the sea can do.'

Gebre gave him a questioning look.

'Your trip will not be the first trip we do. I was here last time, and it was bad.'

'The boats didn't make it?'

'Some did, one didn't; the people panicked and the biggest boat went down. Not far from here.'

'Tell me what happened.'

'The sea brought the bodies back.'

'How many?'

'On the beach? Twenty-three people. At the bottom of the sea we think two hundred or more. I will show you the pictures from the beach if you want? I am not supposed to but I will.'

Gebre passed Wanis another cigarette, which he pocketed, and in return received his mobile phone. The pictures were of women, men and children, all lying face up on the sand and shingle and all dead. Their limbs appeared swollen and blue; in some pictures the skin was split with bones visible – like boiled meat, Gebre thought. Some of the dead children had enormous stomachs like famine babies, puffed thighs, rounded arms. Where the limbs had been cut by rocks or who knew what, the photographs showed a frothy fluid seeping from these cuts – like burst sofa cushions. The worst picture of all showed a baby girl in a dress, her face bloated and a bloody plume of froth at her mouth and nose. Gebre forced himself to look – he looked at every picture and when he'd finished, he handed the phone back.

'Why do you keep these?'

Wanis shook his head. 'I don't know, I never look at them. But I can't delete them.'

Gebre nodded and then fell silent as he tried to process this information, these numbers. Two hundred and twenty-three people. Gebre decided that he needed to know more about the accident, he needed to know everything.

'What happened to the bodies?'

'We moved them, buried them together in a hole.'

'You didn't use the coffins.'

'What coffins?'

'The coffins in the long shed, the coffins that people talk about.'

Wanis seemed suddenly very nervous. 'You're talking shit. I should go.'

Gebre put his hand on the young man's arm. 'Sorry, don't go, please. Like you say it's probably just people talking shit. I guess it's just good that they were buried, you did the right thing.'

Wanis shrugged. 'Bodies on the beach are bad for business, that is what my uncle says, that is the reason he told us to bury them. Are you travelling alone?'

Gebre shook his head. 'No, my brother will be with me, we've been together for this whole journey.'

Wanis nodded.

'Okay, at least he is young. Strong. Travelling with parents or little children is bad. Alone is good. You must think only about yourself, that's how to survive. You can be a good person again, but later, when all this is over, do you understand?' The young Libyan was looking at Gebre as he said this but his voice was so low that he might almost have been talking to himself.

Gebre shook a couple more cigarettes from the packet and was lighting them when something occurred to him. 'Solomon doesn't swim.'

Wanis shook his head. 'Then he must learn. You are going to sea; it is foolish to think you will not have to swim. God willing it will only be a few metres, a little swim from your boat to the land in Italy or somewhere, but it could be more than that. Things go wrong. My uncle says that what kills people is the panic; they are so full of fear they wave their arms and shout and swallow water . . . and then they drown. Your brother needs to know the water.'

26 Fakes and Pharaohs

DATELINE: The Seti Hotel, Cairo, Egypt, February 2 2011

Father Rumbek spotted Carver the moment he walked into the hotel bar. He began gesticulating with such an extravagant display of arm waving that he looked like he was signalling an aeroplane on to its stand. Carver complied and wandered over.

'Mr Carver, I thought that was you, I hoped it was.' Father Rumbek smiled. 'You see I am in my uniform now – you cannot mistake me for what I am not!' The priest waved a finger in the direction of his dog collar and grinned. 'Can I buy you a coffee? Or perhaps something stronger? The Holy Roman Church will pay.'

'In that case, sure. Is Jean—'

'You have just missed her. We were finishing my interview.'

Carver nodded. 'How did it go?'

'Very good. Miss Fitzgerald says I have the storyteller's gift.'

'I'm sure.'

A waiter took their order: one black coffee and one bottle of the local beer – Carver wanted to keep his wits about him with Colonel Balit but one beer wouldn't hurt.

247

'My only problem is that I speak too quickly and when that happens my accent can make it difficult.'

'I wanted to ask about your accent. Italian, but before that . . . Eritrea?'

'You are close – Sudan. I have worked in Eritrea too. And Ethiopia. God's work has taken me to many places.'

Father Rumbek had been talking about himself for a couple of hours already, probably filling up several of Jean's miniature cassette tapes. Still, he seemed more than happy to start again for this new audience. He told Carver the story of a young Sudanese theology student, serving his apprenticeship in Asmara, Addis and Khartoum back in the 1970s before Rome came calling.

'It must have been a difficult decision.'

'In what way?'

'Leaving your family behind, your friends?'

Father Rumbek dismissed the question with a shake of the head. 'It was God's plan and we cannot argue with that. I did not have too much family to speak of and one can always make new friends.'

Carver shrugged. 'I suppose so.' He drained his beer. 'I'll look forward to reading the whole story when Jean's finished writing it.'

The priest was nodding enthusiastically. 'I hope that people will find some interest in my work. Maybe Rome will read it and provide me with an assistant? There is so much to be done here in North Africa but it seems I am the only person they have available to do it. I have become a *tuttofare*. Do you have a word like this? Someone who has to do all the work?'

'A dogsbody?'

Father Rumbek clapped his hands together. 'Dogsbody! Of course, perfect. Our conversation always finds its way back to dogs, Mr Carver. I am a dogsbody – but you will never hear me complain.' At that moment his phone began to ring, the old-fashioned ringtone Carver had heard before. Father Rumbek glanced at the screen. 'Ah, forgive me, but I will need to take this.' William watched him gather up his papers and briefcase under one arm and hurry from the bar, the phone pressed against his ear.

Carver checked his watch. He decided to call on Jean; they could walk to dinner together. He took the lift, straightening his tie in the mirrored glass on the way up. He strode up the long carpeted corridor and knocked.

'Hello?'

'It's me, William.'

Jean opened the door. Her hair was tied up and she was wearing a long black dress and silver earrings.

'You look . . . you look nice.'

Jean looked at Carver. 'Thank you, Billy. So do you, very handsome.' She pulled the door wide and encouraged him in.

Carver sat on the bed and waited while Jean put on a little lipstick.

'You know I was just thinking, sitting at the mirror, in most lives, you only get a few brushes at happiness.'

Carver nodded; this was the sort of conversation he preferred to avoid. 'Right.'

'And that for me, almost all those brushes at happiness have involved you. Either in a supporting or a starring role. I wonder what I should make of that?'

'Um.'

'Don't worry, Billy. That was rhetorical.'

Carver glanced around the room; the Garden Suite had been emptied of its surplus furniture and its more gaudy pieces of art. What remained was an oblong dining table, covered in a pristine white cloth and set for three – one setting on each of the longer sides and one at the head of the table, facing the garden. The French windows had been left open and the yellow curtains were pulled back. Mr Akar had removed all but two sofas and one occasional table. All the gold-framed mirrors were gone. The fireplace was set but not lit and the golden sphinxes had been so well polished that the shine on them hurt the eye. The walnut grandfather clock had been brought back from the dead and tocked loudly with every slow second that passed.

Colonel Balit walked into the room at seven o'clock precisely; he kissed Jean's hand, shook Carver's and without any hesitation took his place at the head of the table. He was a bald-headed, large-bellied man in an ill-fitting but impressively decorated army tunic – the shoulder boards several-starred. The colonel shifted his weight back into his chair. He looked around at the room and then at the table, which was already heavy with food – small plates of various cold and hot dishes, breads and olives. He gave a satisfied sigh.

'I used to like to eat at the Marriot but these days there is nothing decent there for a man to close his jaws upon. The last time I visited with them, I was given an empanada. It tasted like an English shoe.'

Mr Akar led a short chorus of laughter from the handful of staff who had arrived in the room. Carver glanced around; Zahra was not among them and he was grateful for that.

'Some say that the Hilton has better food than here but I have always preferred the Seti. You know how to run your kitchen, Mr Akar.'

The hotel manager blushed and practically folded himself in two with the bow he performed. Carver watched. It was obvious that Akar was Colonel Balit's creature. His lapdog.

'Thank you, sir.'

'You still serve the special dessert, I hope?'

Mr Akar lifted his head just high enough to speak and be heard. 'Not for some time, but this evening, of course.'

Balit gave a nod and glanced meaningfully at his empty shot glass. Akar hurried to the colonel's side, filling the glass with slow-flowing icy vodka. Balit tossed the glass down in one. Carver saw a shiver of pleasure move his shoulders; he caught Akar's eye and glanced at his own glass but Akar ignored him. It seemed that the frozen Stolichnaya was for the colonel only.

The guest of honour turned to Jean. 'I am sorry it has taken a little while to arrange this meeting, Miss Fitzgerald. I've been rather busy. I'm sure you understand?'

'Of course.'

'I've been looking forward to seeing you again.' He eyed his guest from her waist up and down again, settling on her cleavage. 'I see that time has been kind.'

Jean responded with a smile that Carver thought could have taught the sphinx on the mantelpiece a thing or two.

After supervising the initial filling of his plate, Balit reached into his tunic pocket and took out two mobile phones, placing them next to his collection of wine and water glasses. Occasionally the larger of the two phones would emit a low hum and Balit would glance at the screen and then ignore it.

The first dish to take the colonel's fancy was a sticky couscous with raisins that he started to eat with a fork but when that wouldn't transport the food in the quantities and at the speed required, switched to using his fingers. 'What are we to talk about then? The weather perhaps?' He lifted a pair of bushy grey eyebrows in Jean's direction while pushing handfuls of the couscous into his greedy maw.

'Well, Colonel Balit, perhaps we should start with the political situation.'

Balit tutted. 'How unimaginative – the weather would be more interesting.' Balit glanced at Akar who laughed again, lapdog and loyal audience.

Jean persevered: 'The protests are getting bigger every day. Tahrir is full to overflowing. How do you reckon the President will respond?'

Balit kept eating. 'To what?'

'To the demands of the people, Colonel.'

Balit shook his head. 'The demands of *some* people, not *the* people.'

Jean shrugged.

'You need to remember that Egypt is engaged in an existential battle – with radical Islam and other enemies.' The colonel made a list of these enemies: the Muslim Brotherhood, the Iranians, Hamas, the Israelis and other unnamed foreign forces and infiltrators.

As Carver listened he wondered how much of this Balit actually believed and how much was simply well-learned lines he felt obliged to repeat, regardless of the audience. Carver had done his research: Colonel Balit was not just the President's right hand and his enforcer, he was also the man who made sure that the one and a half billion dollars that America paid to Egypt every year arrived safely. It was the colonel whom the President trusted to do the quiet deals with Israel too. Yet here he was warning about the influence of foreign forces. When Balit finished listing the many forces ranged against Egypt, Carver cleared his throat.

'Those are your enemies, Colonel, but isn't the real problem now your friends? Are the Americans still taking your telephone calls these days? Are you worried that they might be about to choose democracy over stability?'

Balit smiled. 'An interesting question.' He pointed a greasy finger at Carver. 'That is an interesting question.' He took his napkin from its ring and wiped his hands. 'It seems to me that the Americans, you English, all of Europe – you are hypnotised by this Arab Spring. You are in love with it. In love like a teenager is in love . . . with no limit and no intelligence.' The colonel lifted his plate, which Akar duly filled with lamb. 'What else am I to think when I read that the American President would like some boy who works for Google to be the leader of Egypt? The

American President says this!' He shook his head. 'You said it yourself, Mr Carver, some have decided to place democracy before stability. Fortunately not everyone, but some.'

Carver would have liked to have pursued this point but he was struggling with a particularly stubborn lump of gristle.

'They believe we have outstayed our welcome.' Balit paused. 'And perhaps a few of us have.'

Carver swallowed the chunk of half-chewed meat. 'The President?'

Balit pushed his plate to one side and pointed at his bowl. Akar arrived with the bouillabaisse and filled it to the brim with the rich, red dish. The smell of fish and spice filled the room.

'The President might decide that he has no option but to step aside. This *might* happen.'

There was silence for a time, Jean and Carver weighing the colonel's words.

'Then you would have to go as well.'

Balit shrugged. 'Not necessarily. The people that you talk about – the young people cluttering up Tahrir Square – they hate the politicians, they hate the police but they do not hate the army. Egyptians love the army and even when they do not love it, they know they need it. Myself, I have always been more a soldier than a politician.' Balit pointed at his vodka glass and Akar filled it. 'Thank you, Mr Akar.'

'You are welcome, my Colonel.'

Mr Akar moved away and back to his position alongside the grandfather clock. Carver had noticed that the clock was gaining time and in between his other duties, Akar occasionally had to push the minute hand backwards.

'Take this uniform that I am wearing.' Balit pointed a thumb in the direction of his army tunic. 'The jacket was my father's jacket. These uniforms last for ever – even when the men who wear them crease or fray or die, the uniform does not. You understand? The army endures and whatever happens next here in Egypt, the people will need to be led.'

Balit sipped at his vodka. 'We Egyptians have had a Pharaoh or a man much like a Pharaoh for five thousand years and that is not an accident. The President is old, maybe he will step aside. But if that happens, we will simply replace him with a new President, a new Pharaoh. It is what Egypt wants – it is what we need.'

Carver was shaking his head. 'If the protesters get their way then there will be elections.'

'I do not fear an election.'

William stifled a laugh, the penny had dropped. '*You* would stand?'

'If called upon.'

'And you think people would vote for you?'

'Why not?'

'Well, I think you may have tortured a few too many of your fellow citizens to win a popular vote.'

Balit slammed his vodka glass down on to his empty plate, breaking it cleanly in half. Jean saw the cabling in Balit's neck harden and watched him wrestle with his temper. At that moment, the smaller phone rang – a loud and urgent sound. Colonel Balit grabbed the phone, picked up the vodka bottle and strode out on to the terrace with Mr Akar scuttling after him. The hotel manager returned a few moments later and glared at Carver.

'It is a great honour to sit down with the colonel, you need to show respect.'

William looked at the hotel manager; his beady eyes shone. The man was a mongrel – part lapdog, part attack dog.

When the colonel returned from the terrace, the vodka bottle was empty; he thrust it back into its ice bucket and called for a glass of wine. He drank this at the mantelpiece, staring at the wall.

Carver looked at Balit's broad back and listened to the clock tick. Eventually the colonel turned and took his seat.

'I think it is time for the dessert.'

Akar left the room and returned moments later, carrying a huge silver platter and, on it, the Tutankhamun. He placed it in front of the colonel and turned the silver plate, then moved some candles around until he was happy. The sight of the Tutankhamun had a calming effect on Abdul Balit; he took a sip of wine and stared at the spun sugar and gold leaf, glinting in the soft light of the candles.

'I grew up in a mud-brick house on the bank of the Nile.' He addressed these remarks to no one in particular, as though he were reminding himself. 'The meal I ate most often was porridge made from camel milk and flour.' Balit tapped gently at the spun sugar pyramid with his spoon. 'I have eaten this dessert many times now. I ate it once – right here in this room – with the American Secretary of State.' Balit looked at Jean. 'Henry Kissinger.'

She nodded.

'Secretary Kissinger thought it was very amusing. I remember he ate *very* slowly: first the sugar, then the gold, then the casket. He eats carefully, Mr Kissinger. I felt like an animal by comparison. I apologised many times but he would not have it, he said that a healthy appetite was good. He said that he wished that *he* could eat like *I* eat.' Balit ate a heaped spoonful of the chocolate mousse and washed it down with more wine. 'In those times, if America was going to fuck you, then at least you would understand why. The strategy would be clear; sometimes Kissinger would call me himself. Now – nothing. This generation of politicians do not tell you what they are doing, because they do not know what they are doing.' Balit reached for the wine bottle, getting there before Akar and refilling his own glass. 'That was one reason I agreed to meet with you, Miss Fitzgerald. I thought it might be worth trying to remind your readers and your pygmy politicians of something.'

Balit looked up from his plate and smiled at Jean, his grey eyebrows raised.

'What's that, Colonel?'

Balit ran a thick thumb round his chocolate-covered plate and licked it clean. 'You need men like me. We have been useful in the past and we will be even more useful in the future.'

Jean shook her head. 'What do you mean?'

'We are the guards at your gate. Egypt, Syria, Libya: these regimes you no longer seem to like, it is us who stand between Africa and you. What happens if we open the gate? Let Africa come, let Islam come too? How will you feel about this? Ask your readers and your politicians that for me, Miss Fitzgerald?'

Jean nodded.

'Thank you. I have another meeting that I must attend but I need a moment of Mr Carver's time first. Will you excuse us?'

The Way of Sorrows (x)

Persuading Solomon to accompany Gebre down to the shore with a spare pair of boxer shorts and an old towel was not easy.

'I have the lifejacket.'

'It isn't enough, you need to be able to move from here to there' – Gebre mimed a swimming stroke – 'from the boat to the land or our boat to a rescue ship. You have to be able to move, not just bob around like a cork from a bottle.' This argument seemed to be carrying some weight but Solomon was still unconvinced.

'You can drag me to the right place, pull me by my jacket.'

'And I will, if we are together, but what if we get separated?'

'We will not be separated, I will make sure of that.'

Gebre gave his brother a look of exasperation. 'Remember what Grandfather said, Sol: the clever ones survive. We have to survive and the clever thing to do is practise some swimming. Ten minutes, that's all.'

In fact they were in the water for more than an hour, a lot of it spent with Gebre coaxing his brother out of the shallows into the darker water that he knew was more representative of what

257

they would meet with when the day of the crossing came. If there had to be a swimming lesson then this was the perfect day for it. Although the sea was choppy close to shore, with some decent-sized waves, further out it was smooth with a gentle swell. The brothers stripped down to their underwear, hid their clothes under a pile of stones and waded out – Solomon wearing his bright orange lifejacket. It didn't take long for Gebre to realise that his older brother wasn't just uncomfortable in water, he was terrified of it.

'Be calm.'

'I am calm.'

'Be more calm. I am holding you, and the jacket will hold you too.' Gebre showed Solomon how to do a basic breaststroke, which he mastered without much trouble when it came to the arms but try as he might could not get his legs right. 'It's easy, Sol, move your legs like a frog.'

'Why a frog?'

'Because that is how the stroke works.'

'This is stupid. A frog? A frog does not even swim so good.'

'It swims better than you.'

Solomon sucked at his teeth; he stopped and looked down through the blue water at his thick muscled legs.

'I have a better idea.' He started pedalling his legs and to his delight, this worked. He moved forward a few feet. 'I will do my legs like this – the same as when I cycle.' Solomon pedalled faster, his arms joined in with their beginner's breaststroke and he was swimming. 'Forget your stupid frog, I am cycling to Europe. Look!'

Gebre looked, his face a broad smile.

After the lesson they shuffled out of their pants, set them on a rock to dry and put their spare boxer shorts on. The brothers sat together, staring out at the now slightly less intimidating expanse of sea. Solomon raised his hand in what looked like a loose salute, shielding his eyes against the white sun. Using his thumb and forefinger he measured the thin strip of blue sea between this edge of land and the horizon.

'Half a centimetre.'

Gebre looked at his brother. 'Eh?'

'That's all it is, between here and there. Half a centimetre of sea, that is all we have to cross.' He showed Gebre his hand, the long fingers all but touching.

'Right. Half a centimetre of sea straight ahead, a thousand miles of sea if we go east or west, enough sea to get lost in for ever.'

It was an unspoken agreement, one that they'd kept to throughout the long journey: if one brother were being pessimistic the other would be positive and vice versa. It was Solomon's turn to be the optimist.

'One of the gang told me that the crossing can take just three hours, sometimes closer to two' – he looked at his brother – 'if the boat is good.'

On the horizon, the starboard side of a long, expensive-looking yacht flashed in the sun, a dozen silver portholes winking like eyes. Solomon pointed at it. 'Perhaps we will travel on something like that?'

Gebre nodded. 'Perhaps.'

27 The Offer

DATELINE: The Seti Hotel, Cairo, Egypt, February 2 2011

The look that Jean gave William as she left the room was unambiguous: it warned him to be careful.

Balit noticed. 'Miss Fitzgerald worries about leaving you alone with me.' He grinned. 'Touching.'

Carver said nothing.

'My instinct tells me you are more than simply work colleagues?'

Carver shook his head. 'Your instinct is wrong, we haven't seen each other in years. What is it you want, Colonel?'

Balit sat back down at the head of the table and pointed a finger at his guest's empty wine glass. Mr Akar grudgingly filled it.

'You believe you know me, don't you, Mr Carver?'

Carver shrugged. 'I know your type. I've met plenty like you, in other dark corners of the world.'

Balit nodded. 'I suppose that makes us even. I know your type too – arrogant Western journalists. You travel to places you don't understand and pretend that you do. You raise people's hopes, whip them up and then, when it gets difficult, when they get hurt, you cry a few crocodile tears and run away.' Balit stared at the table, a mess of plates and half-eaten food. 'Mr Akar, will you clear this table for me, it upsets my eye.'

The hotel manager nodded and left the room, returning moments later with Zahra at his side. He muttered something and Zahra set about removing the plates, serving bowls and dirty cutlery, keeping as much distance between herself and Abdul Balit as possible. As she moved around the table, the colonel watched her and when she left the room carrying an armful of plates he spoke.

'It's funny.'

'What is?'

'Usually, towards the end, when the spirit is almost broken, when the pain is too much, they call out for their mothers. Always the mother.'

Carver looked away.

'But not Nawal al-Moallem. She called out for this one.' Balit pointed a finger at the door.

Carver felt the hairs on the back of his neck rise. 'Zahra?'

'Yes. She asked for Zahra. Why do you think that is?'

Carver looked down at his hands.

'We both know. I have advised Akar to give up on her but he will not. He has been looking after this girl for years. She is never allowed to attend my special parties' – he smiled at Carver – 'although my guests often ask for her.'

William pushed the glass away. 'I think I've heard enough.'

'No you haven't. Not yet.'

'What do you want?'

'We both have something that the other wants. I want you to give up on this silly story you are pursuing and return the items that were taken. If you agree to that, then Nawal al-Moallem will go free.'

Carver shook his head. 'All you've managed to do here, Colonel, is confirm that the story I'm working on is an important one.'

Balit remained silent.

'I won't make a deal like that. I can't.'

Still Balit said nothing.

'Apart from anything else, Nawal would not want me to.'

The colonel smiled. 'Are you sure? How do you know? I believe I have seen her more recently than you. She was not looking as resolute as you suggest.' He finished his wine. 'I instruct my men to use softer measures when they are dealing with women but sometimes they get carried away.' He looked around the room. 'I think our evening is over.' He called out for Mr Akar who appeared almost immediately. Balit stood and stretched his back, readying himself to leave. 'Think about my offer. You have until midday tomorrow. You can tell Mr Akar here what you decide.'

Carver stood. 'I have a story. With or without Nawal. I have other evidence.'

Balit glanced at the hotel manager, who shook his head.

'No you don't.' The colonel smiled. 'I think this makes my offer even more generous.'

Jean opened the bedroom door and stood to one side. Her room had been turned upside down. Carver went straight to the side of the bed and knelt down on the floor. He reached beneath the frame and groped around for a minute or more although he knew in his heart that the canister was gone.

William woke the next morning drenched in sweat, nightmares clawing at the edges of his sleep. He ate breakfast alone and when Jean found him and asked if she could join him for coffee his response was a shrug. She attempted a few conversational gambits but Carver wasn't interested.

When Mr Akar arrived, he pretended that he had happened upon the pair by accident. He exchanged a few banal remarks with Jean before asking the question he needed to ask.

'So, I am following up on that offer, Mr Carver. I am afraid I need an answer now.'

William nodded. 'The answer's no.'

Akar paused. He stared at Carver. 'I see. You're sure?'

'I'm sure.'

Jean waited until Akar was well out of earshot before allowing curiosity to get the better of her. 'What was that all about, Billy?'

William paused, preparing the lie. 'Akar offered me another fortnight here – at a reduced rate if I said yes straight away.'

'I see.'

'But I decided to say no.'

'I heard.'

'I said no.'

Zahra had been dialling Nawal's number at least once an hour ever since she'd gone missing. Just after three that afternoon, she dialled it again and after half a dozen rings, someone picked up.

'Nawal?'

'*Mn hdha?*'

The man who answered told Zahra he'd found the phone along with a lot of other handsets and sim cards at a rubbish dump near Hykestep military base. He said he'd kept this one because it was the most modern. Zahra knew Hykestep; there was a prison there as well as a military base.

She was trying to arrange cover for her shifts at the hotel, so she could catch the bus to Hykestep, when she received a phone call from the El Borg Hospital. A body had been found by the roadside, on the outskirts of Cairo, and a private ambulance had dropped it off at the hospital morgue. Zahra's phone number had been found among the deceased's personal effects. The driver of the ambulance wanted to know who was going to pay him for his trouble. Zahra said that she would come and she would pay. She was perfectly calm. She called Carver and asked him if he'd accompany her to the hospital.

28 Personal Effects

DATELINE: The El Borg Hospital, Cairo, Egypt, February 3 2011

The morgue was two floors down from reception in the basement of the hospital; it was a low-ceilinged room with white tiled walls and half a dozen caged neon lights that buzzed and flickered and generally messed with your head. The attendant met them at the door; he was an anxious-looking young man with shaving rash and a facial twitch that appeared to mimic the flickering strip lighting. Zahra's presence in his place of work made him even more nervous than usual. He took the piece of paper the hospital receptionist had given Zahra and read it through twice before walking her and Carver to the far end of the room. Here there were two steel tables, bolted to the cement floor; one was empty, on the other lay Nawal, naked apart from a bright white sheet, which covered her thin frame from thigh to chest. Zahra glanced briefly at her face.

'Her mouth. Why does her mouth look like that?'

The lower half of Nawal's face appeared sunken.

The morgue attendant nodded. 'Her teeth were broken, snapped. Some have been removed. She was also—'

Carver coughed loudly. 'Are all these details in your report?'

The young man nodded.

'Then we can read that if we want to know more. We don't need—'

Zahra turned away, heading for the door, and the young man hurried after her.

'Miss, your friend's belongings, my report, you need to take all these.' He went to his desk and returned with a white A4 envelope and a plastic zip lock bag.

Nawal al-Moallem had few personal effects: a wallet that the ambulance driver said was empty when he found it, a set of keys and a little black notebook that Zahra had given her for her birthday. The book had Zahra's name and number listed under emergency contacts and tucked inside the pocket at the back of the book were two photos. Zahra glanced at the pictures then handed them to William. One was a formal studio shot – a photograph of a young Nawal sitting alongside a woman.

'Her mother?'

Zahra nodded 'She died when Nawal was twelve.'

'No dad?'

Zahra shook her head.

Carver looked at the other photo; there was something familiar about it, and he took a closer look. It was a photograph of Zahra, both hands held open in front of her – feeding pigeons. She had a broad smile on her face, the air around her a blur of wings. In the background was the immense head and mane of a lion.

'Trafalgar Square?'

'I went there for one day when I was studying in England. I don't know why she even has this picture, it is so stupid. I look bad and the picture is blurred. She didn't even ask me if she could take it . . .' And then she broke down, her legs buckling beneath her. Zahra fell to the concrete floor and wept.

Carver had no appetite; he skipped breakfast and headed instead for the hotel garden. Perhaps some air would help. The tables around the pool bar were empty; he sat at one of these and took out his notebook from his plastic bag. His tape recorder was in there too – he'd told Patrick that he'd meet him later. Carver sat and leafed through his notes, his spidery black shorthand scrawled across page after page. The only distraction was the little Russian girl who was doggy-paddling about in the deep end. She'd outgrown her armbands in the space of a few days. Carver wondered when he'd last learned something useful in that space of time.

'I brought you some coffee.'

Zahra was in her work uniform, black hair piled unevenly on top of her head.

'Thanks.' Carver sighed. 'I thought Akar had given you a few days off?' If he'd known there was any chance of running into Zahra then he would surely have stayed in his room.

'He did, but being at home was no good. And I needed to talk to you.' Zahra sat down opposite him. She looked like she'd had even less sleep than he had – her eyes were swollen and red, her skin grey. 'I have had an idea.'

'Okay.' Carver took his glasses off and rubbed at his face.

'We can still make Nawal's story work.' She pulled her chair closer. 'I thought about it all last night. I can say that *I* was at that demonstration, *I* found the canister. I saw what Nawal saw. You can record the interview with me instead of her.'

Carver stared at Zahra. 'That would be a lie.'

'I don't mind.'

'I mind.'

Her chair scraped noisily on the stone as she pushed herself back from the table and stood.

'That's a better idea, Zahra. Leave me alone.'

She turned to go then changed her mind. She stopped and stared down at the man. 'I know that you're upset, William. I am upset, I am . . . empty. But you did everything that you could.'

Carver looked up at her. 'You have no idea what I did.'

She shook her head. 'You took Nawal's story seriously, you are investigating it, you—'

Carver stood. 'Please, I'm begging you, Zahra, just fucking leave me alone.'

He went to his bedroom and hid there. He texted Patrick telling him that he'd have to find someone else to help him out. He unplugged the room phone and switched off his mobile. Carver bought a single ticket for the early morning flight from Cairo to London and then he took a couple of sleeping pills.

DATELINE: The Seti Hotel, Cairo, Egypt, February 5 2011

A security guard was manning the reception when Carver left the hotel at five thirty the next morning; there was no sign of Zahra. His relief at this small mercy was short-lived. Jean was sitting in an armchair next to one of the white sphinx statues, waiting for him.

'You pulled a moonlit flit on me once before, I seem to remember.'

'This is different.'

'Sit for a minute.'

Carver looked at his watch.

'You've got time, you're early – like always.'

William sat but said nothing.

Jean studied him for a time. 'I don't know what it is you think you've done' – she held up a hand to stop his interruption – 'and I don't need you to tell me. But whatever it is, Billy, I know you did it for the right reasons.'

Carver shook his head slowly. 'I'm not sure that's true. And even if it is – it's not enough. Not this time.'

They sat in silence for a while. On the other side of the glass doors Carver could see a couple of waiting taxis; he wanted to be in one of them but Jean hadn't finished with him.

'Zahra came to see me, she thinks she's done something to upset you.'

Carver shuffled in his seat.

'She's worried that you might give up on Nawal's story – because of her. I told her you wouldn't. That isn't a lie, is it, Billy?'

'I don't think so.' Carver looked at Jean. 'I need to go. She'll be safer without me here.'

He told Jean that he'd speak to his London contacts, follow the story upstream and hassle the company that manufactured the gas. He thought he made a pretty convincing case.

'Sounds good, Billy.'

Carver attempted a smile. 'Why don't you come too?'

'Eh?'

'Back to London, we could travel back together?'

Jean shook her head. 'I can't. Not yet.' She put a hand on his arm. 'But that's the most tempting offer I've had in a long, long time, Billy. How about you hold it open for me?'

On the plane, he begged a bottle of red wine for pretend pre-flight nerves and drank it like medicine. When a lanky British backpacker took the seat in front and started playing with the recline button, Carver tapped him on the shoulder.

'I'll give you a tenner if you leave your seat like it is.'

The guy turned and sized him up. 'Twenty.'

'Fine.'

The plane took off half an hour late. Carver drank one more bottle of wine, pushed his seat as far back as it would go and let the turbulence rock him to sleep.

PART THREE

@tsquarelawan

29 A Man's Word

DATELINE: The Taxi Café, Asmara, Eritrea, February 5 2011

Gabriel stirred another spoon of sugar into his dark beer and stared down the Dekemhare road. He had agreed to meet Adam Adonay without hesitation, assuming that the smuggler had news of his grandsons and confident that this news would be good. Now that Adam was sitting in front of him, fanning himself with a Taxi Café menu and sweating from every visible pore, Gabriel wasn't so sure.

'Perhaps you'd be more comfortable without your jacket?'

Adam was wearing his usual uniform of electric-blue business suit, white shirt and red leather tie.

'No, no. I am quite comfortable' – he looked at his watch – 'and I cannot talk for long.'

Gabriel pointed at the Tag Heuer. 'The watch works well?'

Adam nodded. 'Excellent, yes. It has not dropped a second.' He paused. 'Thank you.'

Gabriel gave a gracious nod and topped up Adam's glass with the last of the beer. 'So I am assuming that this is about Gebre and Sol? How are they? Either their phones ring out or else they don't connect at all. I haven't been able to reach them.'

Adam nodded. 'That is to be expected, where they are – the signal comes and goes. Mainly it goes.' He smiled and his gold tooth winked at Gabriel. 'They are well of course, very well, just as I promised. So far, so good as the saying goes.' The tooth winked again. 'They are with my colleagues on the Libyan coast, staying in luxury's lap.'

Gabriel raised his old eyebrows. 'They have reached the sea?'

Adam nodded.

'Then they are nearly there. What sort of crossing have you arranged?'

'Well, yes, this is as yet . . . undecided.'

Gabriel stared at the sweating man. 'Undecided? What do you mean? I paid the total sum up front. I paid for the *VIP crossing* as you call it. So put them in the best boat you have.'

Adam folded his hands across his stomach. 'If only life was so simple. This is why I wanted to meet. It turns out that the nature of your grandsons' crossing is rather up to you.'

Gabriel sucked as his teeth in disgust and reached for his wallet. 'More money! Of course. A man's word is worth nothing in these times.'

Adam shaped his face into a look of great shock. 'No, no! This is not about money, old Gabriel. This is about friends doing other friends favours. Do you understand?'

Gabriel shook his head. 'No, I don't understand. No one involved in this undertaking is any friend of mine.'

Mr Adam lifted his thin black briefcase on to the table and clicked it open. He removed a single sheet of paper and handed it to Gabriel. 'This is what my colleagues are asking for. It is not very much. A small favour only.'

The old man ran his eye down the piece of paper. 'Impossible. You know what I move and what I don't.'

'But surely one box is much like another, one lorry looks much like the next. If it's a question of paying your contacts a little more then that is no problem.'

'No. I won't do it. I don't need you or your friends to help my grandsons, there are other people I can turn to.'

Mr Adam shrugged. 'So be it.' He closed his case and stood. 'But if you are thinking about some sort of divine intervention, Gabriel, then I would advise you to think again. Read the proposal properly, old man, take your time. I will call you later.'

Gabriel watched Mr Adam chatting and laughing with the taxi drivers outside before climbing into the back of one of their cabs and driving off. He could see why, to a man like Adam, it might seem like a small request but for Gabriel it broke every promise he'd made to himself when he first went into business. His pride told him to rip the sheet of paper into a hundred pieces and throw it away. But he could not afford to be proud. He folded the paper neatly and tucked it inside his wallet. He called out for another beer and his spirits lifted a little when he saw that the waiter who brought it was the café's newest employee. The boy to whom he'd promised the story of the world-famous Fiat Tagliero garage.

'Sit with me a moment, I owe you that story.'

The boy cast a nervous look back over his shoulder.

'Don't worry, your boss will not mind.'

Most people, who thought they knew the history of the garage and its gravity-defying concrete wings, got one key detail wrong. Gabriel delighted in putting them right. 'I am walking history. Soon I will be history in a wheelchair and then history in a wooden box, buried in the ground. I have to tell as many people the *true* story as I can, before I'm dead and gone.'

When the first wave of Italian architects arrived in Asmara most locals shunned them. 'My parents hated them, most people hated them. They were colonialists, racists, fascists – ugly people, that's what everyone said. But these ugly people were making beautiful things. Beautiful buildings. Not everyone could see it, but I could.'

Gabriel was only ten years old but he had initiative and no fear. He attached himself to one architect in particular: Giuseppe Pettazzi, making himself first useful, then employable and, eventually, indispensable to the Italian. Gabriel was a sponge, learning both Pettazzi's mother tongue and then the language of architecture very quickly. 'Giuseppe was not a tall man, he was small but he made monumental buildings. *Divine geometry* he called it. Pettazzi did not want to build *La Piccola Roma* or any kind of *Little* anything.'

Gabriel worked for the Italian on several projects before Pettazzi attempted his masterpiece: the Fiat garage that he wanted to build both as a celebration of the modern and a monument to air travel.

The building that Pettazzi and young Gabriel were sure would become the most iconic building in all Africa was to have cantilevered wings, stretching out a full fifteen metres on either side without the support of pillars. 'I remember when he was working on the drawings, the sums he did, all the mathematical equations written on scraps of paper all over his study. He said that he had discovered a *loophole in the law of gravity*.'

The official version of the story was that both his fellow architects and the local authority deemed Pettazzi's plan structurally unsound. When the huge plane-shaped building was all but finished, a team of inspectors turned up at the construction site and refused him permission to remove the temporary supports that held the long concrete wings in place. There was a standoff and Pettazzi pulled a gun, an Italian revolver, from inside his jacket pocket.

'People say that he put the gun to the foreman's head and threatened to shoot him if the supporting pillars weren't pulled down. But this is a lie. I was there.' Gabriel paused and gazed across the road at the Tagliero garage. 'It is nearly eighty years ago now and I remember it as though it was yesterday. He jumped up on to that wing . . .' He pointed at the wing furthest from the window. 'He stood there and put the gun to his *own* head. Pettazzi said he would kill himself if they didn't remove the pillars. His builders pulled the supports away and the wings stayed solid – just the same then as they are today. *Divine geometry.*'

Gabriel paused to let the boy absorb this key detail for a moment before finishing his story. 'I had a drink of champagne, sitting next to Pettazzi, on top of the Fiat Tagliero. It was the first and only plane I have ever been on.'

His story finished, Gabriel turned back to the young waiter, eyes shining. 'I'm sorry. I have tired the sun with my talking, sent him down the sky. How old are you?'

The kid told him.

'The same age as my younger grandson, Gebre.'

'Yes, I met him here once, with you. Where is he now?'

Gabriel attempted a smile. 'He is travelling.'

30 Rattling Cages

DATELINE: Stockwell Road, London SW9, February 8 2011

Carver was in bed, his laptop balanced on his belly, re-reading his notes. He'd been back in England for seventy-two hours and he hadn't left the flat. He'd slept, he'd eaten takeaway food and he'd read everything he could find on Quadrel Engineering & Defence, on export licences, international law regulating the sale of CS gas, definitions of internal repression – the works. There was no shortage of reading material but none of it would silence the nagging voice in his head – the one telling him that he was wasting his time. For the story to fly he'd needed an eyewitness and some evidence and he'd managed to lose both. He pushed himself up into a sitting position, shut his laptop and looked over at his bedside table. Next to the goose-neck lamp, balanced on top of a precarious-looking pile of books, was last night's pizza box; he flipped it open with a finger – empty. He sighed, then grimaced – something in the room didn't smell very good. He eyed the wastepaper bin in the corner of the bedroom, which was full of foil cartons, polystyrene and pizza boxes the same as the one in front of him.

He was considering whether to get out of bed when his phone started buzzing from somewhere down in the duvet. Carver was about to press *reject call* when he saw who it was that was calling.

'Hello, Jean.'

'Missing me yet, are you?' Her voice was crystal clear; she could have been in the next-door room, not a couple of thousand miles away.

'I'm surviving.'

'Barely, I bet. I can smell the takeaway food from here. Have you even stepped out of your flat?'

''Course.'

'What's the weather like?'

Carver glanced towards the window; the curtains were closed. 'It's raining.' This seemed like a pretty good guess.

'Not according to the World Wide Web it isn't: from what I'm reading here it's the kind of *diem* you need to go *carpe*.'

Carver sighed. 'I'm doing some more research, reading up on—'

'Give me a break, Carver. You've read enough; you need to go rattle some cages. Me and Patrick are doing what we can.'

'You and Patrick?'

Jean filled Carver in on what they'd been up to since he left Cairo. Patrick had been door-knocking in the neighbourhood where Nawal had collected the tear gas canisters, trying to find someone else who'd been at the demo or at least seen it. Zahra had taken Jean to Nawal's flat, to a friend's apartment near Tahrir where she sometimes slept and to a lock-up on the edge of the city where Nawal kept a beaten-up old Fiat that the pair had planned to put back on the road some day. They hadn't found her collection of gas canisters, batons and bullets in any of these places but Jean said Zahra hadn't given up. She was trying to think of other possible hiding places.

'She's in a pretty bad way but as long as there's a chance of doing right by Nawal, I reckon she'll keep going.'

'I see.'

'Are you getting the message, Billy?'

'I think so.'

'You need to pull your finger out – stop Hamlet-ing around.'

Carver picked up the empty pizza box and Frisbeed it in the general direction of the bin. 'Okay, I have to go see my boss, Naomi, later. I'll beg a bit more time to spend on this.'

'Good man, but don't beg too much and don't take any shit from those people.'

Carver paused. 'I appreciate you doing this, Jean, alongside your own stuff, I mean. How's that profile of your priest coming along?' Down at the other end of the line he heard the sound of Jean lighting up another cigarette, a deep pull of breath.

'Yeah, that's the other thing. I've been busy fact-checking that piece. There're a few things about Father Rumbek that don't quite add up.'

The Way of Sorrows (xi)

Near Zuwara, northern Libya

Wanis brought the news. Gebre had woken early and was sitting on a white plastic picnic chair that he'd dragged up to the roof of the unfinished villa. On the horizon, behind the blocks of half-built and falling-down apartments, the sky was brightening, turning from purple into pink; the air was cool on Gebre's skin and he closed his eyes. The only sounds at this hour were the low rumble of the sea, pushing shingle up and down the shore and the high singsong of swallows. The birds swept and darted across the white rooftops in their dozens. As Gebre watched, a couple of the birds separated themselves from the group and took a rest, long tails bobbing, on a washing line that someone had strung between this villa and the next. They were facing him and Gebre had a sense that they were waiting; he slid off his chair and down on to his haunches and the birds took this as their cue. They launched themselves from the washing line, wings beating furiously and then stopping. Gebre turned his head in time to see the birds glide over a thicket of television aerials sprouting from the block behind his and up into the roof of a tall cylindrical water tank. Gebre squinted his eyes and saw that what he'd thought was a rusted water stain was in fact a swallow's nest.

'Hey, black man, better start getting your shit together – your boat ride is tomorrow night.' Wanis was smiling. 'Will you leave me your cigarettes?'

Gebre and Solomon packed and repacked several times before they were happy. Their most precious things: photographs, Gebre's exam certificates, their telephones and a torch were still inside the plastic waterproof pouch and they put the money they had left in there too. It was agreed that Solomon would wear the pouch on a string around his neck. Everything else was in the suitcase but Wanis had warned Gebre that this might be weighed before they were allowed to board and as a result they'd removed all but the most essential articles of clothing.

The next night, Wanis's uncle and half a dozen other men arrived to escort all the people in Gebre and Solomon's warehouse down to the beach. The operation began at half past midnight. It was a scene of chaos, with tired and confused children crying and being hushed by their desperate, anxious parents who in turn were being threatened by members of the gang. The smugglers insisted there must be no noise and no lights either and as a result there was much tripping and stumbling as the group made its way across open ground and down to the shoreline. Once there they were ordered to march in the direction of a small jetty around half a mile away. In the distance they saw the occasional flare of burning gas from the Mellitah oil terminal.

As they drew closer the brothers saw two fishing boats tethered to the wooden pier and knocking against each other in the ink-black sea. Gebre had decided that on balance it would be better to be first on to the boat rather than last and so the brothers tried to keep their place near the front of the ramshackle queue. Standing at the entrance to the jetty was a hollow-cheeked Libyan man with a handgun tucked into his jeans, black against his white Real

Madrid football shirt. The man was muttering the same few words over and over to every man, woman or child who approached him, in Arabic and Tigrinya: '*Hold up your bags. Hand them to me.*'

The man took anything he considered too heavy or bulky and threw it back behind him on to a growing pile on the beach. As they waited in line, Gebre saw a couple of people pleading with the man, detailing how essential or personally significant their possessions were to them, offering to open their luggage and find the item they were unwilling to lose. The man was not interested: '*Get on the boat, or stay behind.*'

Gebre sighed. 'It seems they want to rob us one more time before we are allowed to go.' As the pair approached the front of the queue, Solomon pushed ahead of Gebre. The man was not interested in their case, which he lifted easily before handing back, but Solomon's trainers did interest him.

'The Adidas. What number?'

Solomon looked down at his trainers and answered in his own language. 'Too big for you, little man.'

The Libyan did not understand, but he registered the murmur of approval from the other passengers who'd overheard the exchange and he didn't like it. He put his hand to his gun and was about to press his case when Gebre intervened.

'My brother says the trainers are fake, mister. Not good enough for you. But my shirt is real Adidas; perhaps you would like to have this?'

The smuggler stared at the T-shirt and nodded, watching with an amused grin on his face as Gebre took off his shirt and, bare-chested now, handed it over. He took it and jutted his chin in the direction of the boat. Behind him – on the beach – his colleague was going through the confiscated bags. He had a switchblade in his hand and a pen light between his teeth and he was systematically slicing each bag open and removing anything of value.

The brothers walked to the end of the jetty and joined the line of migrants waiting to board the fishing boat furthest from the shore and closest to open sea. The crew were busy transferring a load of large wooden crates from the deck of the boat to the jetty and the Libyan captain was supervising this operation. He wore a white shirt with dark trousers and was wandering the deck shoeless. Solomon stared at his feet – the man's toes were so long that they looked more like hands than feet. He was shouting at his men to stack the boxes neatly and not to mix them up.

Having got themselves into a position where they knew they'd be among the first to be allowed on to the boat, Gebre relaxed a little. Solomon opened their suitcase and pulled out one of his own T-shirts for his brother to wear. While Gebre put it on, Solomon unzipped the plastic pouch around his neck and got his phone out.

'What are you doing?'

'I want a picture. Almost everything that's happened since we left I want to forget, but I want to remember this.' He switched his phone on, checked the flash was off and holding the camera at waist height took a couple of surreptitious photos of his brother. Solomon was about to turn the phone off and put it away when it buzzed in his hand. He looked at Gebre. 'Now we get a signal!'

'What is it?'

'A few missed calls from Grandpa and a message.' He handed the phone to Gebre.

Beloved boys, if you receive this and you are still in Libya then try and reach me, it could be better to delay the crossing. G

The brothers looked at each other. The group around the first boat was growing and the queue had become a crowd.

Eventually Gebre spoke. 'It is all fine. He will have heard of people having trouble with bad boats but this boat is good. It is too late to change our minds anyway. I will reassure him.'

Solomon nodded and watched Gebre type.

'I will tell him that we will call him tomorrow. From Italy!' He smiled at his big brother. As soon as the message was sent, Gebre switched the phone off and Solomon put it back in the pouch.

They stood in silence, awaiting further instructions and listening to the sound of the two boats knocking together in the water. The noise reminded Gebre of a child's wooden xylophone. There were already at least a hundred people waiting alongside the first boat and Gebre could feel his brother getting edgy. Solomon lifted the suitcase and pulled out one of the lifejackets

'I think we should put these on now, Gebre; it will be more difficult once we're in the boat.'

Gebre nodded and the pair took turns helping each other into the bright orange jackets, both aware that their fellow passengers were watching them closely.

The wait was not a long one; once his men had finished unloading the crates the captain appeared from beneath the deck of their boat and ordered that the people be let on. He oversaw this process himself to start with and his calm demeanour inspired some confidence. So did his boat; it stank of fish and diesel petrol but it seemed solid – *seaworthy* was the word Gebre had heard. As the people poured on and moved around in an attempt to find a comfortable space, the captain moved to the side of his boat to see where it was sitting in the water. Gebre guessed that there were between two hundred and fifty and three hundred people on board when the captain finally called a halt. He started the engine and reversed slowly away from the jetty and out into open water.

31 Long Player

DATELINE: Stockwell Road, London SW9, February 8 2011

Carver showered, dressed and ran a comb through his hair. He'd agreed to meet Naomi in reception at old Broadcasting House at eleven. The Tube train emptied at Oxford Circus and he joined the crowd as it funnelled itself from the platform level up to the street via tunnels, staircases and escalators. The animated adverts on the station walls offered fly-drive holidays and ladies lingerie. Carver wanted a coffee.

Jean's weather forecast was proving to be uncannily accurate. A light morning cloud had cleared while he was underground and the day was bright now. Carver could feel his fellow Londoners' spirits lift and walking past the window boxes outside the Langham Hotel he even spotted a few yellow crocuses poking their heads tentatively up through the dark soil. He bought himself a black coffee at the café next to the new BBC extension then doubled back towards old BH. Outside All Souls Church, a homeless woman was folding the cardboard boxes that had served as her bed and bedroom back into a neat pile.

He was early and was sitting on a worn red leather banquette in the corner of reception for twenty minutes before the uniformed woman behind the desk waved him over, an apologetic look on her face.

'Mr Carver?'

He nodded.

'I'm sorry for leaving you sitting there. Miss Holder asked that you meet her up on the sixth floor. Do you know it?'

'Yep.'

Carver rode the old art deco lift up to the sixth – home to various BBC bosses and an oak-panelled conference room. As the lift doors opened Carver saw his boss sitting in a high-backed wooden chair, typing away at her phone. She was wearing a black trouser suit and had her legs crossed with the right foot swinging – dangling a shoe. Behind her was a flip chart covered in Day-Glo Post-it notes. He tapped on the doorframe.

'Hello?'

Naomi put her phone down, pushed it away from her across the table and stood. 'William, welcome. Come in.'

The room was situated at the very front of Broadcasting House and as a result was a slightly odd shape; sitting in it felt rather like sitting in the prow of a ship, as there were windows on all sides and plenty of oak and leather.

Carver took the seat facing hers and looked around. 'Last time I was in here, someone was trying to sack me.'

'Really? Who was that?'

William tried to remember. 'A small man, damp hands . . . Druce? Drice?'

Naomi nodded. 'Oh yeah, I remember. Julian Drice, he used to sit in on management meetings. He left last year, went back into consultancy – big bucks. I don't think he was ever planning to stay long at the Beeb. He used to tell me that serious people, ambitious people, needed to switch jobs every three years.' Naomi looked at Carver. 'Think there's anything in that?'

'I can see why it would make sense for Drice. Get out quick before people realise what a wanker you are. Though in his case that would mean changing jobs every couple of hours.'

Naomi smiled 'You didn't get along?'

'No.' He studied his boss. 'Is that why you wanted to see me? Is this going to be another redundancy offer?'

Naomi shook her head. 'No, it isn't. I know we had a few rows while you were away.' Carver shrugged. 'You rub people up the wrong way and you dumped me right in it leaving Cairo with no notice but you're still one of the best reporters I've got.' Carver opened his mouth to speak, then thought better of it. 'So I'm willing to put those disagreements behind us William, if you are?'

'I am. Willing that is.' He paused before jutting his chin in the direction of the flip chart. 'What's all that about?'

Naomi looked over her shoulder. 'Ah, we just had an hour of digital training. Don't worry, I'm not planning to make you sit through that either. I think you'd rather be made redundant, wouldn't you?'

'Probably.'

'There is *some* interesting stuff in there though. A few ideas about how to find new audiences, ways to measure interest, that kind of thing. I think the most relevant thing for us . . .'

Carver tried his best to listen, but before long he could feel his mind begin to wander; he looked past Naomi's shoulder, out of the window and over towards the Langham Hotel. In one of the rooms he could see a chambermaid in an old-fashioned black smock changing the bed. She unfolded a bright white sheet and flicked it out in front of her. Hands outstretched, she waved it across the bed. The window was open to air the room and the sheet billowed like a sail. Naomi cleared her throat, summoning William back to the room. He tried to remember what he'd half heard: something about how the technology could work out not just how many people read a story or clicked on it to listen, but how long they read or listened for as well. The words Naomi had used were *linger time*, and the average linger time was nine seconds.

'What do you think?'

'I think that if people are only willing to pay attention for nine seconds then we might as well all give up and go home.'

She nodded. 'Fair point. You're more an analogue, long-player kind of guy; my granddad's the same.'

Carver balked at being bracketed with Naomi's ancient grand-father. 'I'm not a complete Luddite. We did some of that Face-chat stuff from Cairo – me and Patrick.'

'FaceTime, yes, I saw that.' Naomi, along with much of the rest of the BBC, had watched Carver's FaceTime appearance. It had reminded her of a hostage video; she kept expecting the sweaty-faced Carver to hold up a copy of that day's *Cairo Times* and beg, half-heartedly, for his life. 'It's not your strong suit.'

'Maybe not.'

'But with a bit more help you—'

Naomi was interrupted by a sudden thud, loud enough to make both she and Carver jump in their seats. He looked across to see a pigeon fall, half-conscious, away from the window closest to where they sat. The bird had flown hard into the glass, hitting with enough force that it left a dusty outline of its body – turned head and two broad wings. Carver stood and walked over to get a better look and was surprised to see the pigeon standing, unsteady but still alive, on the stone mantle beneath them. The bird shook its head and tested its wings, recovering its equilibrium before flying stutteringly off into the blue. As Carver turned away he saw, from the corner of his eye, a feathery flash of brown. The hawk was in hot pursuit, but the pigeon had a decent head start. He sat back down.

'What was I saying, William?'

'You were talking about getting me some help.'

'Right, I—'

'But I don't need help, Naomi. I just need you to let me do what I'm good at.'

'Which is what?'

'Digging, hassling. Making a nuisance of myself. Analogue stuff mainly.'

Naomi smiled. 'Fair enough, you win. Go on then, what's the story?'

Carver gave her an unvarnished version: a respected British defence company breaching an export ban, selling kit that was used to tear-gas men, women and children. He'd seen some evidence but he didn't have it anymore, he'd spoken to a witness but he didn't have that either. Naomi listened and when it was clear he'd finished – she spoke.

'Right. So it's a single source story?'

'Yeah.'

'But the source is dead?'

'Yeah.'

'And the gas canister you saw, that's gone too?'

'The one I saw, yes. There's at least one other and we're looking for it.'

Naomi pulled a face. 'Who's *we*?' She held up a hand. 'No, on second thoughts, don't tell me who *we* is.' She reached across the table and spun her phone; they both watched and waited for it to stop spinning, and when it did, she went on. 'So, Rob Mariscal came to see me last week . . .'

Carver sighed. 'Oh yeah?'

'He warned me you might try and flog me this story.'

'Is that right?'

'Rob said the gas you're talking about *was* British made but it was old stock, that it ended up in Egypt by accident – through a third party. He told me this was a *Guardian* page four kind of story at best. But he said you'd go overboard – chase it all *hell for leather* and forget about the due diligence. He told me about Quadrel too – he says they're very litigious.'

'They are. He's right.' Carver studied his editor. 'So Rob Mariscal wants you to drop the story. What do you want to do?'

Naomi stared at Carver. She was remembering something else that Rob had told her, back at the beginning. He'd said that sometimes an editor had to trust gut instinct and take a punt. 'I don't like being warned off stories. I'll deal with the lawyers; I'm good with lawyers. I want you to go after it, William – *hell for leather . . .*'

Carver nodded. 'Right you are.'

32 A Daughter Hears

DATELINE: The Orchard Apartments, Matariya, Cairo, Egypt,
February 9 2011

Zahra racked her brains but nothing came. She'd run out of places
to look for Nawal's collection of gas canisters, batons and bullets.
She'd stopped going to Tahrir Square, ignored messages from
Nawal's friends and followers and barely even looked at the news.
Zahra worked, slept and ate – that was all she did, and she only
did this much because her family depended on her salary and her
mother stood over her at mealtimes until she had eaten at least a
mouthful or two.

Mr Akar, meanwhile, had decided that now was the time to press
his case. He had arrived uninvited at the family's flat with gifts
for Zahra's mother and father, then stayed to drink her father's
gift – a French brandy he remembered the old man saying he
liked. The two men got drunk together in the living room while
Zahra and her mother sat next door in the kitchen. Zahra heard
her boss talk about how important she was to him, how the hospitality industry would go from strength to strength once the young
people in Tahrir Square got tired and went home. Akar told her

father that he needed her at his side. As he left, he lowered his voice.

'I know your daughter, I know her history but I can turn the blind eye, I am modern. A little chicken blood on the sheet the morning after the first night and everyone's honour is restored – hers, mine. And yours of course. Talk to her, please. A daughter hears her father.'

Zahra had left for work even earlier than usual the following morning. She would rather listen to her father demean himself at the end of the day than at the beginning. But she knew that sooner or later she would have to hear it and she knew what her response had to be. Zahra had all but given up.

The first message arrived late that night. She'd worked a double shift at the hotel and was almost asleep when her phone buzzed beneath her pillow. More than likely it was Mr Akar, with another ham-fisted sweet nothing, but when she lifted the pillow and looked at the screen it read: *Nawal*.

Zahra's heart started to pound. She fumbled and dropped the phone in her haste to open the message.

Here in this square is what we should be, what we once were and could be again.

She started to message back, and then stopped herself. It was not real. It was some kind of trap. Or a cruel joke. Her first logical thought was that she should ignore it, forget the message, but she knew she could not do that. She sat up in bed and dialled Nawal's number. The man who answered sounded sheepish; his voice was vaguely familiar.

'I am sorry, it was a mistake.'

It was the same man who had found the phone and sim cards dumped out near Hykestep military base. He said he'd been trying to find something he'd saved and had accidentally sent one of the old messages that the previous owner had written.

'Old messages?'

'Yes, a few old ones that did not send. I am sorry, I will delete them now, I promise.'

'No!' Zahra swung her feet from the bed and stood. 'Don't delete them, send them to me. All of them.'

As Nawal's messages landed one by one in her inbox, Zahra copied them and emailed them back to herself. She was determined they wouldn't go missing again. Once she'd satisfied herself that every last word that Nawal had intended to send her was safe she started to read. *Here in this square is what we should be, what we once were and could be again.* This felt like a draft of something, a thought that Nawal had had and that she would've asked Zahra to turn into something longer. They often worked that way. The messages that followed this were more straightforward:

Z. I'm in museum with medic, no signal; pls post this when you get it.

Z. Medic taking museum injured away. Out soon.

Z. Medic gone, army guy asking me to stay. Says it's too dangerous to leave – Molotovs.

Z. Long wait. Got a bad feeling.

Zahra, I love you. No time to say the rest. I hope you know?

Zahra dried her eyes on her sleeve and read the final message. The last thing Nawal would ever write: *He is coming. Go here – ground-floor apt, 43 Sabry Street.*

Zahra recognised the street name, she knew the neighbourhood; it was halfway between the Seti Hotel and Tahrir Square, an hour or so from her apartment. She checked the time on her phone. It was past midnight; even if she went now, no one would answer. The thought of going alone at any time of day concerned her. She lay back on the bed, but sleep was out of the question. She could either lie awake all night or she could call someone. Zahra scrolled through her contacts until she found Jean's number.

33 Hell for Leather

DATELINE: Quadrel Engineering & Defence, Hyde Park, London W2, February 9 2011

The kid on reception at Quadrel Engineering & Defence was conducting a thorough investigation of his nose using his thumb. Carver was the first visitor of the day and although he'd stopped picking his nose by the time William was standing in front of him, he still hadn't managed to get his tie on. Carver waited while he clipped the thing to his shirt collar and made sure the stag beetle logo was facing outwards and not obscured by his lanyard, which had Temporary Staff stamped on it.

'I'm sorry for keeping you waiting, sir, how can I help you today?'

The line sounded rehearsed. Behind him, through a half-open door, Carver could see a smart-suited woman unpacking a tower of Tupperware and fixing her hair. This was the real receptionist, the kid was just the stand-in, but that suited Carver.

'Impressive offices you've got here.'

The boy glanced around the lobby, as though seeing it for the first time, then remembered his line: 'Thank you, yes. The Quadrel headquarters boasts one of the highest atriums in Europe. The marble's real. It's Italian.'

'No shit?'

The kid studied Carver a little more closely. 'Who did you say you were here to see, sir?'

'I didn't.'

'I beg your pardon?'

'I haven't told you who I'm here to see – not yet.'

'Right, well . . . would you like to tell me?'

'I'm here to see your boss.'

'Which one?'

'How many have you got?'

The boy grinned and when he spoke again his London accent was more obvious. 'I'm new, temporary. Pretty much everyone here's my boss.'

William nodded. 'I know the feeling.' He smiled. 'I'm here to see the big boss. Quadrel's president? Or the CEO, or the chairman?'

The boy grinned again. 'That's all the same bloke – Mr Bellquist.'

'Really? Well I guess it's him I want to see then.'

'Have you got an appointment?'

'Not in the conventional sense.'

The kid laughed and this noise served to summon the proper receptionist, who marched from behind the half-closed door, her heels ricocheting on the real Italian marble. She glanced first at her underling and then at Carver, who sensed the fun was probably over.

'Did I hear you say you were here to see Mr Bellquist, sir?'

'That's right.'

'What's your name please? Your name and the time of your appointment.'

'I don't have an appointment, not in the con—'

'He won't see you without an appointment, sir. He doesn't see anyone without an appointment. What's your name?'

'My name's William Carver, I'm a journalist. I work for BBC radio.' He watched the woman write these details down. 'I'm happy to wait. If you could just tell Mr Bellquist that I'd like to ask him why Quadrel are selling tear gas to a repressive Egyptian regime. Why they broke an export ban to do it.' She wrote this down too. Credit where it's due – she was thorough.

'I think it's probably our press and public relations team you need to talk to, Mr . . .' She looked down at her note. 'Carver. I can give you their number.'

'Thanks, I've got their number. I'd prefer to talk to Mr Bellquist. Like I said, I can wait. I'll just sit over there.' Carver pointed in the direction of an expensive-looking white leather sofa and along-side it a low glass table covered in magazines.

The woman shrugged. 'Of course, sir, wait if you like. But I'm afraid you might be wasting your time.' She didn't look overly concerned. 'I'll speak to the press and publicity team anyway – on your behalf.'

Carver sat down and helped himself to a few magazines. The choice was pretty good: *Foreign Policy Review*, *GQ*, *Vanity Fair* plus all the main trade magazines for the defence sector. He started with a copy of the Quadrel Annual Report for the previous year. It was a glossy affair, perfect-bound and filled with facts, figures and photographs of impressive-looking hardware. It also included eye-wateringly awful descriptions of the company's achievements and aims – a mix of jargon, acronym and hyperbole that was so horrible Carver found it difficult to read more than a couple of lines at a time. Maybe that was the point?

There was a lot of different kit mentioned in the annual report – but no CS gas.

William had been waiting for a couple of hours when, glancing up from his reading, he saw the frosty receptionist pointing in his direction. The woman covered her mouth with her hand and whispered some instructions to her hapless apprentice. Then she picked up her pile of Tupperware and headed out the door for an early lunch. Carver waited until she was out of sight before approaching the desk. When he cleared his throat, the boy glanced up from his book, an anguished-looking smile on his face.

'Hello again, sir.'

'Hello. I hope your day's going better than mine.'

The kid shrugged.

'I guess they must pay you pretty well here, don't they?'

'I'm temporary, a trainee. I get the minimum wage.'

'Eight quid?'

The boy gave a mirthless laugh. 'I'm not twenty-one yet. It's more like five – and they take tax off that.'

'Really? Do you know how much this lot made last year? Its overall profit I mean?'

The kid shook his head.

'Two point one billion pounds.'

The boy frowned as he tried to conceive of a number that big.

'Do you know what your boss, Mr Bellquist, was paid?'

'No, sir.'

'Eighteen million pounds. Eighteen million, that's thirty-four thousand pounds a week. *You'd* have to work here for' – Carver did the sum in his head – 'two or three *years* to make what he makes in a week.'

'It doesn't seem very fair.'

'No, it doesn't. I think I might ask Mr Bellquist about that too. When I get to talk to him.'

The young man glanced past Carver, in the direction of the front door, then leaned across the desk. 'You're wasting your time sitting there, sir. Mr Bellquist never comes in or out the front door, not unless it's for show. He arrives and leaves by the back door; his Jag waits for him outside the Cardigan Arms. Out across the plaza and round to the right.'

Carver thanked the boy.

He gathered up his things, including a couple of the more interesting-looking trade magazines, and left. The plaza in front of Quadrel's headquarters was just as soulless as the building it was designed to showcase. Looking back at the space from the safety of the pavement, Carver realised what the problem was – it looked too much like the architect's model that had no doubt inspired it: the crisp lines of steel and stone were too straight. Even the people seemed to have been designed and carefully placed: seated in pairs, suited and smart. Two by the abstract sculpture, two on a bench beside an over-pollarded tree.

Carver ambled round the corner. The Jag was exactly where the kid had said it would be, parked outside the Cardigan Arms in a disabled bay. Carver walked up to the driver's door and tapped on the window; as the man behind the wheel opened it, he got a whiff of the pine-scented air freshener that was hanging from the rear-view mirror and underneath that the stink of stale cigar smoke.

'You can't park here. It's for blue badge holders only.'

The man behind the wheel wore a dark suit and black tie, and his hair was combed and Brylcreemed. He had a funereal look about him, like he'd be more at home driving a hearse. Carver watched as he reached into the glove compartment and retrieved a blue badge and a certificate. He held the piece of paper up for Carver to see.

'It's all legit – you can take the number and check it with Westminster Council if you like.'

'Don't worry, I will.'

The undertaker studied Carver. 'You don't look like a parking warden. Where's your . . . you know? Badge? Peaked cap? All that?'

'I'm undercover.'

'You're an undercover parking warden?'

'Yep.'

'I'm not sure I buy that.'

Carver nodded. 'You're quite right, I'm not really a parking warden. I'm a journalist. William Carver's the name. What time will Mr Bellquist be out, d'you think?'

'It depends, could be six, could be later.'

Carver could see that the man regretted answering this question the moment the words had past his lips.

'But I'm not s'posed to talk to journalists.' He coughed nervously.

'Fair enough, can I just give you this?' William retrieved a slightly dog-eared BBC business card from his wallet and handed it over; as he did so he caught another whiff of old cigar. 'You know, they've just done a load of new research on second-hand smoking and lung cancer? It's pretty scary stuff. You should check it out.'

The driver's window closed with a soft purring sound and Carver considered his options. It didn't take him long to decide to have a half in the Cardigan Arms.

Inside the pub, he bought his drink and some pork scratchings and sat down at a table next to the window. From there he had a good view of the street and the red Jag. He saw the driver take his phone from his pocket and hold it out in front of him. For a moment he thought the man was going to try and take a picture of him but it soon became clear that he was just long-sighted. Most likely he was Googling passive smoke and lung cancer.

Carver got the defence industry trade magazines out and started reading; if it was a waiting game that was required Carver was as good at that as anyone. The chair was comfortable enough, the beer was decent and the smell of roast chicken drifting from the Cardigan Arms kitchen tempting. Perhaps that kid on reception would appreciate a plate of food and a pint?

The Way of Sorrows (xii)

Nine nautical miles north of Zuwara

The passengers' relief at being under way was short-lived. After half an hour of slow progress, crawling through the black water and away from the Libyan coast, the captain cut the engine. He let the current take the overloaded boat and they drifted. Before long the coastline was swallowed in mist and a collective anxiety spread among the people on board; a few tried to ask members of the crew what was going on, only to be told to shut up.

The sea was still and the smallest sound carried. Gebre heard the dinghy long before he saw it. The captain was listening too and he and his crew shushed their anxious cargo to be quiet as the two boats drew closer. What Gebre could hear was a man calling out in a strange sort of shouted whisper in a language and with a guttural accent that was foreign to him, though he thought he caught the odd word of Arabic. Before long the two vessels had found each other and the man in the dinghy threw a couple of thick ropes up to the crew of the fishing boat so they could tether the two side by side. Gebre studied the dinghy: it was plastic, bright yellow and the word Zodiac was stamped on one end – it was the opposite of seaworthy. His fellow passengers were panicking now and the crew were having real trouble calming them; they wanted to know what was going on, what did the arrival of the dinghy mean? Gebre didn't need to ask, he knew: despite the huge amount of money he'd been paid, the man with feet like hands was not willing to risk losing his boat to the Italian or Libyan coastguard or whoever else might find this shipload of unfortunates. Instead he was going to decant his passengers into dinghies like this one and let them find their own way to Italy. His men had placed planks of wood across the floor of the Zodiac, to make the flimsy boat a little more solid.

The crew started herding the men, women and children standing closest to the dinghy over the side of the fishing boat and down a short ladder. They were received by another man whose job it was to position them properly. One person was ordered to sit with their back against the side of the yellow Zodiac and then open their legs so the next person could be fitted in between. The crew assembled the human jigsaw with surprising speed; women with children in arms were allowed a few extra inches. Before long there were nearly eighty people squeezed into the boat.

Gebre watched the operation closely, weighing up whether it would be better to be in this first dinghy or a subsequent one when he heard the captain calling out his and Solomon's names. Gebre raised his hand and the captain pushed through the crowd.

'You two are Hassen brothers?'

They nodded.

'This first boat is yours.'

'Why?'

The captain shrugged. 'We need some strong ones in each boat, this is yours. Get in.'

Gebre sensed that Solomon was ready to argue and put a hand on his brother's arm. Perhaps his friend Wanis had arranged for them to be placed in the first boat? There was no reason to believe that the next dinghy that arrived would be any improvement on this one and a good chance that it could be even worse. At least this one appeared to have a working outboard motor and one of the crew was teaching a middle-aged Ethiopian how to start the motor and hold the tiller steady. He also handed the man a clear plastic bag containing a couple of boxy-looking electronic devices; the Ethiopian looked reasonably competent and was listening attentively to his instructions. Gebre and Solomon were among the last to climb down the wooden ladder from the fishing boat into the Zodiac. As they did, a thought occurred to Gebre and he shouted up at the captain.

'Sir, sir, we will need more food.'

The Libyan shook his head. 'No, you will be fine. You will be sitting down with a big plate of pasta in a few hours' time!' The man gave them a gap-toothed grin but Gebre noticed that the younger man next to him, similar in features but slighter in build, was not smiling.

'At least leave us some water, sir, we will need water.'

The young man pulled at the captain's sleeve and whispered a few urgent words close to his ear. The older man snarled back but then nodded and his son disappeared below deck, returning moments later with a packet of biscuits tucked under his arm and a five-litre bottle of water in each hand. The captain grabbed one of the large water bottles from him, swearing loudly at the boy before jutting his chin in the direction of the ladder. The young man lay belly down on the deck of the boat and passed the biscuits and the bottle of water he'd been allowed to keep hold of down into the dinghy. Solomon took them with a nod of gratitude and a few words of thanks, but Gebre noticed that the young man could not look his brother in the eye.

34 Crooked Wood

DATELINE: The Embankment, London SW1, February 10 2011

Bellquist was on foot and bang on time. He walked once past the bench where Rob Mariscal was sitting then circled back and sat down next to him.

'Morning.'

'Good morning.'

'Glorious, isn't it?'

It wasn't quite seven. The sky was cloudless and the palest shade of blue. To their left, the sun was rising over Docklands – strong and bright despite the early hour. It lit London, turning the river molten.

Bellquist sighed. 'Well done on getting the right bench.'

Rob shrugged.

'And thank you for agreeing to see me.'

'My boss didn't give me a lot of choice.'

Bellquist smiled. 'No, I suppose not. So, Rob . . .' Bellquist paused. 'Is it Rob or Robert?'

'Either. Rob probably. Only my mother and the permanent secretary call me Robert.'

Bellquist smiled. 'Then it's Rob, I'm not your mother. More like a friendly big brother. So, what are you like with your Greek fables? Remember much from school?'

'A bit.'

'Are you familiar with the story of Androcles?'

'Vaguely.'

'I'll remind you: your man Androcles removes a thorn from the huge lion's paw and in return he gets a big old reward.'

Rob nodded; he was pretty sure the story was more complicated than that.

'That's what we're dealing with here: I'm the lion, your friend William Carver is the troublesome thorn and you? You get to be the hero.'

'I see. Well, William's not really my—'

'Carver's started hanging around my HQ – upsetting people. Do you know my offices?'

Rob shook his head.

'They're very neat. Clean lines, lots of marble. We've got the tallest atrium in the world, it's really beautiful.'

'Right, well—'

'He was there most of yesterday, making the place look untidy. He even went and talked to my driver, Andrew. I've had my driver a long time.' Bellquist glanced right down Embankment towards Westminster. A jogger in bright Day-Glo colours was approaching; he lowered his head and let her stride by. 'Anyway, he upset Andrew.'

'I understand. And this is still about the tear gas, is it? He's asking more questions?'

'He is, though God knows why; we gave him the statement. The gas was old stock, it was all above board when we sold it.'

'And that's true?'

'More or less. Anyway we gave him the statement, we sent the same statement to his boss but he still keeps sniffing around. He's got no evidence, no interviews.'

'How do you know?'

'I just know. He's got nothing. So why is he still banging away at this?'

'That's what he does.'

Bellquist shook his head, he didn't like this answer. 'I'm getting my lawyer to send his editor a letter. They do a nice line in terrifying letters and that's worked before. Sometimes I don't even need the letter, I just get the lawyer to phone up and tell them how litigious I am.'

Rob shook his head. 'I spoke to his editor, I told her all that.'

'And it didn't work?'

'It doesn't sound like it.'

'Why not?'

'She's a better hack than I gave her credit for.'

Bellquist pulled a face. 'Allow me to tell you something about myself, Rob, something that not that many people know. I'm actually a very cautious person, all the *hail fellow well-met* stuff is largely for show. I am *careful*.'

'I understand.'

'William Carver's timing is bad. There are a lot of things in play right now. New opportunities opening up and I can't afford to take risks.' The jogger was making a return pass, and both men lowered their heads as though in prayer. 'So here's what I'd like you to do. I'd like you to talk to him, persuade him to drop it.'

Rob smiled. 'You make it sound very simple.'

'It is simple. Sit down with him, offer him something.'

Mariscal tried and failed to stifle a laugh. 'Offer him something? Like what? Money?'

'Everyone has their price.'

'Not Carver.'

'Everyone. You just have to work out what it is and then decide whether you're willing to pay it.'

Rob shook his head. 'I'm afraid you don't know William, he has no interest in—'

'He values his reputation.'

'What?'

Bellquist pulled an envelope from his pocket 'So how about you try offering him this.' He handed the manila envelope to Mariscal.

'What is it?' Rob took a look inside the envelope and saw some sheets of paper and a memory stick.

'It's his reputation. It's a copy of every password he uses for every device and bank account. All his little password-protected projects too. Plus a copy of his entire hard drive.'

'You hacked into his home computer.'

'If he follows me, I'm going to follow him – physically, digitally, whatever. Imagine how horrible it would be if we found out that William had loads of really unpleasant material all over his hard drive, and his laptop and his phone. I mean the kind of images the worst sort of paedophiles pass around. The police take that sort of thing very seriously these days. And the papers love that kind of story, don't they?' Bellquist smiled at Rob. 'You know that better than me.'

Mariscal stuffed the envelope into his coat pocket and tried to rub some of the cold from his hands. 'I see.'

'It can destroy a man, that kind of thing. I've seen it happen – several times. So talk to Carver, explain the situation. Can you do that for me, Rob?'

'I suppose I can.'

Bellquist nodded. 'Good man.' He stood and turned, looking down at Mariscal. 'Do you know how much I pay the chap who does my press work?'

Rob shook his head.

'You remember Paul? You sat opposite him at that dinner at the Tower.'

Rob nodded.

'Paul gets two hundred and fifty thousand pounds a year; that's quite a lot of money. Maybe I should sack him and give *you* the job?'

Rob smiled politely.

'We upped your salary before, maybe we could double it this time?'

The *we* in this sentence snagged on Rob's ear. He was aware that Bellquist's blue eyes were studying him.

'School fees are expensive and so are new babies, mortgages and maintenance payments and credit card fees. I'm sure it all adds up.'

This deliberately vague but completely accurate thumbnail sketch of Rob's main outgoings took him by surprise but he did a pretty good job of hiding it. 'I'll speak to Carver. I'll do my best.'

Bellquist nodded. 'No man can ask more.'

Craig was waiting for Rob halfway down the long corridor that led from the MOD entrance to Mariscal's office. As Rob came closer the permanent secretary pointed a finger at the gloomy-looking portrait in front of him.

'You remember what I told you before? About the frock-coats.'

Rob looked at the painting: thickly spread oils and almost no light in the thing apart from in the rich red of the man's face and the white of his mutton-chop sideburns.

'Henry Brooks,' the permanent secretary said.

'Right. Was he a good Secretary of State?'

'Henry Brooks is the artist. I don't know who this other fellow is.' Craig pointed again. There at the bottom of the flaking, cara-melised lacquer frame was a small rectangle, lighter in colour. 'His nameplate appears to have fallen off. Shall we talk upstairs?'

'Of course.'

They took the lift to the top floor and walked once more to the part of the building where the renovation work was being done. The workmen hadn't arrived yet but progress had been made: new sash windows were in place on the river side and the room smelled of fresh sawn wood. Craig glanced up at the ceiling, which was newly plastered but hung with bare light bulbs.

'How was Mr Bellquist then?'

'He's . . . worried, I would say.'

'Worried, I see. And he wants you to help ease his worries?' Rob nodded.

'By putting some sort of pressure on your friend William Carver no doubt?'

Mariscal nodded. 'Yes, although he's a former friend really.'

Craig noted this. 'What exactly does Bellquist want?'

Rob gave his boss as concise a summary of the conversation as he thought he could get away with. As he heard himself speak, he realised he was already trying to minimise the seriousness of the plan. Perhaps he'd already decided what he was going to do? Perhaps Craig could help him decide?

'What do you think?'

The civil servant shook his head. 'What do I think of black-mail? I don't like it. I think that Mr Bellquist has overstepped the mark.'

'I see.'

'You refused of course?'

Rob paused. 'I didn't exactly refuse.'

Craig frowned. 'You thought that *I* might desire that you do this thing?'

'I suppose so. Yes.'

'Well, I do not. Absolutely not. I am too old to rage, and too compromised as well. But I still have one or two principles left. What Bellquist is proposing is far beyond the pale.' The permanent secretary glanced around the room – half a dozen workbenches and planks of wood stacked according to its length and thickness.

'Did he give you any clue as to why he thinks something so extreme is necessary?'

Rob had no trouble recalling the details. 'He said there were a lot of things in play right now.'

Craig harrumphed. 'There is no arguing with that.'

'He said that new opportunities were opening up, he couldn't afford to take any risks.'

Craig nodded slowly. 'Did he? Well, that's interesting.' Craig paused. '*Out of the crooked timber of humanity, no straight thing was ever made*: do you know that one?'

Rob shook his head.

'Immanuel Kant.' Craig was rolling back and forth on the balls of his feet, thinking. 'I fear that Mr Bellquist is playing us for a fool. Will you accompany me back down to my office, Robert? I promise I won't take too much more of your time.'

On the way down the permanent secretary spoke little and what he did say was obscure, almost gnomic.

'We opened a door and he simply walked through it. Or rather, I opened the door. Under instruction of course, but that is no excuse.'

They were at Craig's office and he was about to turn the brass doorknob when he stopped. 'I wonder, Robert, did Bellquist mention anything about *your* future? A doubling of your salary or something similar?'

Rob gazed down at the carpet; the pattern had been worn clean away. 'He did mention something like that, yes.'

'Mr Bellquist is clever, he knows that dangling a lure like that can do things to a man's judgement. His moral compass.'

'Yes.'

Craig was watching him, his hand still on the doorknob and still not turning it. 'Imagining what life might be like with twice the money you have now is unsettling. You're not the first person Bellquist has talked to in this way, you won't be the last.'

Mariscal nodded. 'He said that every man has his price. You just have to find out what it is and then decide whether you are willing to pay it.'

Craig smiled. 'I see, so you're probably wondering whether that includes me? Do I have a price and if I do – has Bellquist paid it?'

'Has he?'

'No, Bellquist hasn't bought me. Not yet . . .' The permanent secretary paused and then pushed the door open and walked in, followed by Rob. 'But he's tried.'

'How?'

Craig sighed. 'I mentioned it to you once: Kinbane Head. It's a spot near Ballycastle. Me and my old dad used to go fishing there every summer; we holidayed nearby.'

Mariscal nodded.

'The best house on the Head came up for sale a few years back. I didn't really have the money but I tried to buy it anyhow. I got close; right up to the very end of the auction I was ahead and I thought I had it. Then I was outbid, hugely outbid – by telephone.' Craig went and sat down behind his desk. 'Victor Bellquist bought the property, or someone acting on his behalf. Using company money I have no doubt. He got the house and the wee piece of land around it too.'

Mariscal looked at Craig; sitting behind the desk he appeared smaller now, vulnerable. 'I'm sorry.' He searched for something to say. 'You wanted to sit and watch the sunset?'

Craig lifted his head. 'Wrong coast.'

'What?'

'The house is on the other coast. The sun comes up right outside the front door, that's what I wanted. I've been working on British defence and foreign policy for forty years – it's been nothing but sunsets. A long string of unsatisfactory and unimpressive sunsets. I wanted to watch the sun rise.'

'I see.'

Craig shuffled some papers around on his desk. 'Every few months Mr Bellquist mentions the house and every few months I ignore him. Look at all this here' – he pointed at the papers – 'the latest list of exports that I am supposed to turn my blind eye to. Hard to believe that our Egyptian friends would have need of all this, but I turn the blind eye. Like the loyal Cyclops I am.' Craig covered one eye with his chubby hand and forced a smile. He glanced at the papers and then at Rob. 'Will you excuse me for a moment, Robert? I need to go and check whether Miriam is here.'

'Of course.' Rob sat in the chair opposite Craig's. He had a clear view of the papers on the permanent secretary's desk; he started reading, then looked away. Craig was gone some time.

'No sign yet, never mind. Well, I shouldn't detain you any longer.'

Mariscal stood and turned to leave, then stopped. 'Mr Craig?'

The civil servant raised both eyebrows. 'Yes, Robert?'

'These offers that Mr Bellquist makes?'

'Yes?'

'Do you think he honours them?'

Craig studied Rob. 'I'm sure he does, but . . .' He paused then took the papers from his desk and banged them back into a tidy pile.

'But?'

'Nothing.' He waved Mariscal away. 'Close the door, on your way out, will you?'

35 Sabry Street

DATELINE: The Orchard Apartments, Matariya, Cairo, Egypt,
February 10 2011

Zahra woke early. Only her mother was awake – awake and busy
preparing breakfast in the small kitchen. Zahra was keen to get
going and not at all hungry, but her mum insisted she wait and
have something.

'Sit, sit. One minute it will take.'

Zahra sat. The flickering TV screen in the corner of the kitchen
was showing the President's most recent public address – another
attempt to calm the people and save his skin. He was standing at
the entrance to a grand, gilded ballroom and, just behind him, a
few feet away, Zahra saw a familiar face – Abdul Balit. The
President was reassuring his people that he was listening, acknow-
ledging that mistakes had been made and promising that change
was on the way. Outside the open window, Zahra heard a few
boos and whistles coming from the neighbouring flats.

As she watched, it seemed to Zahra that Colonel Balit was edging
closer to the centre of the TV screen – closer to the President
and the thicket of microphones. Closer to power.

311

She kissed her mother and hurried from the apartment, breakfast in hand. As she walked round the stairwell and down half a dozen flights to the courtyard she checked her phone. She'd arranged to meet Jean Fitzgerald outside the Sabry Street address at eight. Setting off now she was certain to be early but she could decide whether to wait or go in by herself once she got there. Jean had urged caution and said she planned to assemble a posse.

Zahra strode through her neighbourhood in the direction of the bus station; it was a bright morning and the smell of fresh bread was in the air. She heard a bicycle bell and looked as a boy in a red T-shirt went coasting past her down the hill – feet lifted. She felt well for the first time in a long while. She was doing something positive, something that Nawal would have been proud of.

As she rounded the corner into Sabry Street, Zahra stopped. She saw, to her slight annoyance, that one of Jean's posse had arrived before her. An Egyptian by the looks of him.

'Hey.'

He turned sharply and stared at Zahra but said nothing.

'Are you here with Miss Jean?'

The man nodded slowly. 'Yes.'

'Is that number forty-three?'

He nodded again.

Zahra wondered how he'd managed to find it; looking around she could see no sign of any street numbers. She walked closer. The guy was tall and wore jeans and a purple shirt, and had a burlap bag slung across his shoulder. 'So do we wait for Jean and the others or just go in?'

The tall man smiled, stretching the thick scar that ran down the left side of his face from ear to jaw. 'Just go in. Two is enough.'

He let Zahra move past him and watched while she hesitated before knocking on the thick wooden door.

The man laughed. 'That door is open already.'

Zahra pulled it wide open and walked in with the tall man following close behind.

'Number forty-three is on the left.' He had lowered his voice and moved even closer. Zahra could feel him at her back. She turned and glared at him and he took a step back. She knocked firmly on the apartment door and waited until she heard movement and then a voice from the other side of the door.

'Hello?'

It was a thin sound, an older woman's voice. Zahra explained who she was, she apologised for disturbing her and told her about Nawal and the message she'd sent her. She asked if the woman remembered meeting anyone who fitted Nawal's description and whether there was any chance that she could have left something in her apartment? As she spoke she could sense the man behind her becoming impatient, although he said nothing.

The old woman heard Zahra out then asked 'Are you alone?'

She turned and looked at the tall Egyptian, who nodded.

'No, no, I have a—'

Purple shirt knocked Zahra down with one knuckled punch to the side of the head. A firm kick at the door and he was inside the old woman's flat. He dragged Zahra's unconscious body in by her collar and laid her down next to the sofa. Her skirt had ridden up and this distracted him momentarily. Perhaps he would do something about that later. The old woman was standing by the kitchen door, holding her mangy dog back by its collar. The animal was barking furiously. Purple shirt reached into his bag and brought out a new hunting knife – bought with this dog in mind. He was readying himself for the animal to attack when the old woman did something strange. She pushed the dog gently but firmly back into the kitchen then jammed the door shut with a chair, locking the angry animal inside. She picked up an old-fashioned-looking telephone and threw it at him – missing by some margin.

He killed her quickly then set about searching her flat, turning drawers out and lifting the furniture until he found what he'd been sent to find. Wrapped inside an old bed sheet, tied into a parcel with yellow rope, was Nawal's collection of gas canisters, batons and bullets. The package had been hidden underneath one of the armchairs; he doubted the old woman even knew it was there.

Purple shirt was on his way out of the door when he heard the chair fall. Turning around, he saw that the dog had somehow forced his way from the kitchen. He barked furiously and took a few threatening steps in his direction before stopping and falling silent. The animal had seen the old woman – his owner – lying on the floor.

He pushed his muzzle gently into her face then turned again towards the man, teeth bared. Purple shirt stepped towards the dog, knife in hand. When he was an arm's length away, the dog stopped his growling. He lowered his head and turned away. Purple shirt pushed the hunting knife deep into the dog's neck. With his last breath, his last push of strength, the dog stepped away and died, lying across his owner's slippered feet.

There was silence and then some sound from the street; he glanced down at Zahra, who was exactly where he'd left her. The noise outside was getting louder – any plans he had for the girl would have to wait. He left, closing the flat door behind him and walking out on to the street, his bag high on his shoulder.

He saw a small crowd of people, deep in conversation. A couple of westerners – a curly-haired older woman in a loose-fitting headscarf and a younger man were talking with locals, asking about both flat number forty-three and their missing friend. He turned his back and was attempting to walk past the group when the woman in the headscarf noticed him and shouted.

'Hey you! Hold your horses, where'd you just come from?'

He stopped and turned, jutting his jaw in the direction of the flat. 'I live here.'

Just then Zahra appeared at the door, unsteady on her feet and with a face like fury. 'Yalla! Stop him. He has killed a woman.'

Purple shirt made to walk away but Jean was fast. He felt a hand on his arm, then two hands as Patrick grabbed his other arm.

'Not so fast there, mate.'

He was about to shove the crazy woman away and grab for his knife when a jolt of crippling pain passed through him. Looking down, he saw the woman's knee buried deep in his groin. His legs buckled and he collapsed to the pavement, swallowing for air.

Jean watched as he folded himself into a foetal position, his face a similar colour to his shirt. She looked over at Zahra. 'I haven't had to do that in a while.'

The Way of Sorrows (xiii)

Thirty-eight nautical miles north of the Libyan coast

The dinghy chugged through the dark, in the direction that the smugglers had instructed them to take, the direction – they hoped – of the Italian mainland. As well as a hasty lesson in operating an outboard motor, the Ethiopian man had been given a phone and a handheld satellite navigation device, though he seemed unsure how to use it.

As night turned to dawn and a smudge of light appeared on the horizon, Gebre was relieved to find that the position of the sun suggested they were moving, albeit slowly, in the right direction. This was the only piece of good news that Gebre could identify; the horror and discomfort that he'd experienced while crossing the desert were already paling into insignificance next to life on board this boat. The passengers had been warned by the smuggling crew not to move in case the dinghy tipped, and the risk was obvious: the Zodiac was sitting low in the water and felt extremely unstable. For that reason people had no choice but to defecate and urinate where they sat or lay and this is what they did, muttering an apology to their families or neighbours as they did so. By mid-morning of the first day the stink was dreadful – piss, shit and vomit pooled beneath the wooden slats and sloshed around. Gebre found some small relief by shuffling closer to the outboard motor and letting the smell of petrol fill his nostrils in place of the reek of his fellow travellers.

Then there was the heat. There was no shelter, no shade apart from the little you might find in the shadow of the man or woman or child sitting next to you. Gebre could feel his exposed skin becoming blistered by the sun as the long day wore on. He was sure that sunstroke played a part in the first significant casualty.

It was around three in the afternoon when from the middle of the dinghy there was shouting, a man began flailing his arms and screaming that he could see devils at work.

'Blue devils, they're climbing from the sea! Push them back down!' He pulled himself to his feet and, stepping between and over his fellow passengers, made his way to the side of the boat. He leaned over, pushing his hands out towards the water, pressing down on the heads of devils that only he could see. The people closest to the man tried to reason with him, they grabbed at his clothes as he leaned out further and further but to no avail; the man plunged headlong into the water. He vanished for several seconds before appearing again. One or two people sitting on that side of the dinghy tried to reach for the man as he bobbed up and down in the sea but he would not reach back. Soon he was being carried away by the waves and the current, out into darker, rougher water. Gebre watched all this from his place alongside Solomon; close to the outboard motor, he was one of several who argued with the Ethiopian holding the tiller that they should try and double back and rescue the man. But the louder, more nervous voices said otherwise, insisting the man was too mad to be saved, that he did not want saving. Gebre stared at the man – he could not help him, but he decided that he would not look away.

The cold water had shocked him back to sanity now and Gebre

watched him trying to paddle his way back to the dinghy. When he realised this was futile, he tried to roll on to his back and float, arms and legs outstretched, but the waves were too big, they were pulling him under. Through effort or instinct he managed to keep his mouth locked shut for some time as the water rolled over his head but he was drowning. As one large wave lifted him, his eyes found Gebre's and the man mouthed something, a handful of words. Gebre shaded his eyes and stared; the drowning man shouted again – two words, spitting water from his mouth, then shouting the same two words again and again. The man was shouting his own name. Gebre nodded, he had understood. He had his name. The last look he received from the drowning man before a final wave lifted him then took him down was something Gebre thought about for hours afterwards. It was not fear any more, instead a look of embarrassment and the hugest sadness.

36 The Old Ways

DATELINE: Caversham, Reading, England, February 10 2011

Carver got slightly lost on the walk from the bus stop to McCluskey's house. He was fine as far as the allotments and the field where the same old horse was busy cropping the grass, tearing up noisy mouthfuls, but he took a wrong turn just after that. A sign pointing towards the golf course and in the direction of McCluskey's estate took him the other way instead and he had to double back.

The message from Jemima McCluskey had been as cryptic as ever but Carver knew better than to ignore an invitation so he'd had his suit pressed and caught the train.

'Some little toerag turned the fingerpost around in its moorings. It's been confusing folk all week.' McCluskey was leaning on the flint wall at the front of her garden, obviously waiting for Carver. She had a pair of yellow rubber gloves on and was holding a thick black plastic sack. 'Now you're here, I need a wee hand with something.'

William held the sack open and as far from his face as possible while McCluskey shovelled the sediment from the bottom of her pond into the bag.

'God, it stinks!'

'It's fish shit, what did you expect it to smell like?'

William turned his face away. He hoped McCluskey hadn't summoned him here just to help with the chores.

'Hold the bag wider, you big sissy! I'll talk to you to take your mind off the smell.'

'Okay.'

'What do you know about the Horn of Africa – Somalia, Ethiopia, Eritrea, all of those?'

Carver shrugged. 'Same as you, probably. Dirt poor, fragile. A fair bit of nasty jihadi business with al-Shabaab but no serious warring for a while. It's mainly frozen conflicts down there.'

McCluskey looked up from her shovelling. 'Is that right? Well, they're not going to stay frozen much longer.'

Inside the house, Carver was put in charge of making the tea while McCluskey changed out of her gardening clothes. She reappeared at the kitchen door wearing a tweed skirt and green polo neck and holding a sheaf of handwritten notes. 'I've been listening to a fair bit of shortwave radio recently.'

Carver nodded. 'That's very old-fashioned of you.'

'Digital's getting too easy to search and bug. People are going back to the old ways.'

'What kind of people?'

'All sorts.' She waved the notes in his direction. 'Bring the tea through and I'll tell you all about it. You'll need to read all this, see if you can make some sense of it.'

It took that pot of tea and one more plus a plate of fondant fancies for Carver to digest McCluskey's notes. The information she'd collected was intriguing but confused. Carver felt like he was looking at a hundred pieces from half a dozen different jigsaws. When he'd finished reading he put the papers to one side and said as much.

'So someone's sending arms down through North Africa – to Sudan and Somalia.'

McCluskey nodded. 'There and beyond: Ethiopia, Eritrea.'

'But there are no names in any of this' – he pointed at her notes – 'or none that I saw.'

She tutted. 'I can't do bloody everything for you, Carver. That there gives you a pretty good idea of what's going on. The kit they're talking about is hard to get hold of and all of a sudden these characters are getting it by the truckload.'

'What kind of characters are we talking about? Who are you listening to?'

'All sorts: middlemen, warlords, rag-tag armies and some proper armies too, I reckon.'

'They're buying. Who's doing the selling?'

McCluskey shook her head. 'I don't know, not for sure. But there's no way that all this is coming from China or the Russians. Not moving the way it's moving.'

Carver nodded.

'And if it's not them – if it's European, or American – then they're breaking half a dozen international conventions, breaking the law.'

Carver picked up the papers again and flicked through them. An incredible amount of work must have gone into gathering all this. God knows how many hours McCluskey must have spent knob twiddling and listening.

'Have you shown this to anyone at Caversham?'

'No, I haven't. And you know fine well *why* I haven't. I'm showing them to you.'

'You think it's British?'

McCluskey finished her tea and said nothing.

'I'm looking into a firm that sent a few boxes of anti-insurgency kit out – broke the export ban, or at least I think they did. But nothing on this scale – nowhere near.'

'Maybe you need to think again.'

Carver picked up his plastic bag. 'Can I take all this away with me?'

"Course. I've made copies.'

He tucked the notes down at the bottom of his bag. Inside he saw a parcel, the present he'd brought her.

'I almost forgot. I got you something.' He hauled himself to his feet and handed her the gift – a snow globe inexpertly wrapped in the front and back pages of yesterday's *Daily Telegraph*.

She opened it. 'Cleopatra's needle?'

'That's the one.'

'With Waterloo Bridge in the background?'

'Yeah.'

'Where'd you get it?'

'Embankment Tube. I couldn't find one in Cairo.'

'How hard did you try?'

'Not very.'

Carver was on the train back from Reading to London when an untitled message landed in his Gmail account.

> *Buy yourself a pay-as-you-go and get the number to our mutual friend on reception.*

He bought the handset at Paddington and then waited for a group of Japanese tourists to take photos next to the row of red phone boxes outside the station before calling the Seti Hotel. When Zahra picked up, Carver kept it businesslike and so did she. He read his new phone number out twice to be on the safe side, told her that he hoped she was well and hung up.

He was back at home, sitting on the sofa watching the TV news with the pay-as-you-go phone balanced on the armrest next to him when it rang. The unfamiliar and overly loud sound made him jump.

'Hello?'

'Hey there, Billy, how you doing?'

Carver felt his pulse quicken at the sound of Jean's voice. 'I'm good, absolutely fine. Never mind me. How're you? How's Zahra?'

'We're okay. Battered but unbowed is what we are.'

'What's with the whole new phones thing?'

'We had some trouble today. Only explanation I can think of is our phones are bugged – mine, Zahra's, yours too I guess. But that's not the headline. The headline is we're making progress, I think you'll be impressed.'

Carver was more than impressed. Jean told him about Nawal's missing messages, how they'd found the stash of batons and bullets and crucially the other gas canister. They also had a witness, albeit an unwilling one. 'They're keeping the murdering bastard in a lock-up on the edge of the city. That seemed like a better idea than handing him over to the police or the army.'

'Agreed, especially since he's probably working for one or both.'

'Zahra's got a couple of Nawal's football hooligan friends keeping an eye on him.'

'Any clue exactly who might have hired him?'

'Not yet, but he might feel more like talking when he starts getting hungry. Zahra's told them no rough stuff.' She paused. 'So, what do you think?'

'What do I think? I think you're brilliant.'

'Wanna come back and show me how grateful you are? Pick up where you left off?'

Carver coughed. 'I do want to do that. But not quite yet, I'm making progress here too.'

'Tell me.'

Carver told Jean about the time he'd been spending at Quadrel's headquarters, about the kid he'd met who was trying to be helpful. 'I think I'm beginning to get under their skin.'

'I don't doubt it. You can be bloody annoying.'

'And there's something else. An old contact of mine at

Caversham. The listening station?' He gave Jean a rough outline of the material McCluskey had given him.

'This is turning into a proper dot-to-dot puzzle, isn't it?'

'I wanted to ask another favour, Jean, but I don't want to take the piss.'

'Bit late for that, Billy. Ask away, I'm fine. A bit of old-fashioned digging and a dose of hope is doing me more good than any of those pills I've been taking all these years.'

'It's about that priest of yours, Rumbek.'

The Way of Sorrows (xiv)

Forty-seven nautical miles SSW of Lampedusa

On the morning of the second day the engine failed. Neither the Ethiopian who'd been put in charge of the outboard nor anyone else in the dinghy seemed able to fix it. They began to drift in a direction different from the one they knew they needed to be heading in and an argument began over whether or when to make a distress call. Some of the people on board were scared of being 'rescued' by the Libyan coastguard and returned to Tripoli and prison or who knew what.

Gebre argued that this was unlikely; he remembered what Wanis had told him about the Libyans wanting to send a message to Europe – how they were the message. Even if the Libyan coastguard heard their distress call, he thought it was unlikely they'd answer it and more likely that they'd pass the problem on to the Italians or Greeks or someone else.

In the end a compromise was reached: the passengers agreed Gebre should try and call the Sudanese priest again. He made the call and Solomon read the coordinates from the navigation system to him twice and listened carefully as he repeated them to the priest. When he had finished the call he nodded and smiled at those close to him. 'He knows where we are now, he will speak to the Italian coastguard and they will send help. He believes they will bring us to Italy. He says we are not to worry, we will be fine.' Gebre turned to his brother. 'He said he would try and get a message to Grandfather too. He'll tell him and our mother not to worry.'

37 Missio

DATELINE: The Royal View Hotel, Tahrir Square, Cairo, Egypt,
February 11 2011

@bigbeartahrir
| It is departure day for the President.

@egyptismtahrir
| Freedom loading: 99%

@mohammedktahrir
| The people and the army. One hand.

Patrick looked up from his laptop; Jean Fitzgerald was standing
smoking on the balcony outside his room.

'Twitter seem to think today's the day. What does it look like
down there?'

Jean shrugged. 'It's full to bursting.' She stared down at Tahrir;
there was a carnival-like atmosphere without a doubt. She could
hear speeches and music coming from different corners of the
square. She turned to Patrick, who was sitting cross-legged on his

bed. 'Carver said he thought Tahrir could end up being the prettiest military coup he'd ever seen. You think there's something in that?'

Patrick shrugged. 'Most people still trust the army. Did you hear about the football match? The game between the protesters and the soldiers?'

Jean *had* heard about this, Carver had mentioned it, but she was interested to hear Patrick's account. 'Were you there?'

'Yeah, I was recording it for a piece. They called it *people versus army* and they agreed a prize: whoever won, would win a tank.'

'And the protesters won?'

'Yeah, the people won, but they refused the prize. They said that winning was enough. Good story, huh?'

'It's a good story. Carver must have heard your piece, Patrick, he mentioned it too.'

'What did he say?'

Jean smiled. 'He said he thought the people should've taken the tank. He said he's got a feeling they might end up needing it.' She stubbed her cigarette out on the balcony railing and stepped back into the room 'Any mention of my elusive priest on Twitter or Facebook?'

Patrick shook his head. 'Nothing yet. You want to try the phone again?'

'Nah, I've been calling him for days. I think Muhammad's going to have to go to the mountain on this one – or whatever the Catholic equivalent of that is.'

They found Father Rumbek not far from the Tahrir Square cinema. Patrick was the first to spot him – a tall man in a dark suit and pristine white dog collar, busily arranging a gaggle of Coptic Christians into a protective ring surrounding a group of Muslims as they performed their lunchtime prayers. As they got closer, Patrick noticed that there were also several TV crews in attendance. He pointed this out to Jean, who nodded.

'He's a bit of a boaster, our Father Rumbek. I'm sure the telly people aren't here by accident.' She walked straight up to the priest and tapped him on the shoulder.

'Miss Jean! What a joy to see you.'

'Really? I thought maybe you were avoiding me?'

'Not at all. Just *so* busy. No rest for the wicked nor for the good.' He smiled. 'What are these additional questions that you want to ask me?'

Jean told the priest that her newspaper wanted to syndicate the article she was writing about him, to sell it to American papers as well as publishing it in the UK. She wanted to clarify some of the religious terminology and a few other things. By the time she'd finished, Father Rumbek was nodding vigorously.

'Of course, of course I do not want to confuse our American cousins. We will talk. But first I must hold mass. You will wait?'

'Yes, happy to. That's why all the TV crews are here, is it?'

'It is.' The priest caught something in Jean's voice – a change in tone. 'The Holy Father himself often reminds us that Jesus used every method to spread the word. I am simply doing as he would, were he here in Tahrir.'

Father Rumbek smiled and went off to tend his flock and the expectant TV crews. Jean and Patrick watched from a short distance away as he arranged everyone. When he was done, Patrick nudged Jean's arm.

'He's got a good eye for a wide shot.'

'Yeah.'

Father Rumbek was in place and all ready to go when something crossed his mind. He removed his suit jacket and rolled up his sleeves and Jean had to admit that this added a certain something. Rumbek looked like he was off to chop wood, just as soon as he'd finished saying mass. The priest looked around and caught Jean's eye.

'Would you be kind enough to look after my jacket, Miss Jean?'

'Sure.'

Father Rumbek was halfway into the Eucharistic prayer when his phone began to vibrate inside his pocket. Jean let it ring out a couple of times but on the third call she stepped back into the crowd and took the phone from his jacket pocket. The screen showed several missed calls and one unread message. There was something vaguely familiar about the repeat caller's number. Jean stared through the crowd at Father Rumbek, who was in full flow. *'What would Jesus do?'*

She got her notebook out.

The Way of Sorrows (xv)

Thirty-eight nautical miles SW of Lampedusa

Gebre was the first to hear it. The faintest sound – an engine, he thought, and so hopefully a ship? He stood up slowly, using Solomon's shoulder for balance, and scanned the horizon but saw nothing. Still he felt sure the noise was getting closer; what's more he was sure he'd heard this type of engine before. He shaded his eyes with a thin hand and turned a slow three hundred and sixty degrees. There it was – not the sound of a propeller churning through water, but of blades chopping through air: a helicopter. It was approaching from the west and as it got closer it blocked out the sun, darkening the sky. Gebre could see a man with binoculars looking in their direction.

Having reached them, the helicopter stopped and hovered directly above the dinghy. People shouted up with joy and in desperation women held their babies and small children above their heads so that they might be better seen and sooner saved. Gebre soon became worried about the dinghy turning over; too much movement and they would tip over and there was no way eighty-one people would fit inside one helicopter. He and Solomon started urging people to be still.

'We are saved now, sister, but we must stay in this boat a while so we need to sit down again.'

Gebre knew the dull green colour meant that this was some kind of army helicopter but he could see no clue as to which military it belonged to. A man in uniform pulled open the side door of the helicopter and took pictures of the boat and the people on his mobile phone. As they waved up at him, he threw down some biscuits but when Solomon and others shouted for water in a variety of languages and mimed their thirst, he shrugged apologetically. After taking a few more pictures and turning away to consult with his colleagues the man waved once more and pulled the side door shut. The helicopter rose higher, circled the dinghy again then flew away, back in the direction from which it had come.

The people on the boat stared at each other in confusion; some shouted hopelessly in the direction of the red tail-light, disappearing fast into the distance.

Gebre got to his feet again and raised his voice: 'They could not take us all, the helicopter is too small. They have gone to get a ship to rescue us. They will tell others where we are and soon the ship will come.'

Solomon nodded as his brother spoke and soon other heads were nodding too, but once the boat was calmed Solomon nudged Gebre's arm.

'They could have taken some, they should have taken the children.'

'Maybe, but you cannot blame them' – he looked around the boat – 'it was not a big helicopter, probably they did not even have room for all the children. The boat they will send will have room for everyone.'

At that moment the Ethiopian man who had been put in charge

of the outboard motor did something that seemed to defy all logic or explanation. As Solomon watched, he took the phone and the navigation device from the clear plastic bag and, quite casually, dropped them over the side of the dinghy.

Solomon grabbed his arm. 'What are you doing? Are you mad?'

The Ethiopian shook his head. 'It was what the smugglers told me to do. Once we are found, drop the phone and the navigation into the sea. If the authorities find us with those then they will accuse me or you of being the smuggler and we will end up in jail. They told me to do this.'

Solomon uttered an oath but let go of the man's arm and looked over at his brother.

Gebre shook his head. 'Don't worry, Sol, they know where we are now. They will come.'

38 A Little Light Journalism

DATELINE: The Cardigan Arms, Hyde Park, London W2,
February 11 2011

'Your phone rang. Both your phones in fact.'

'Oh yeah?' Carver finished zipping up his flies and sat back down at the table.

His lunch companion was using a napkin dipped in water to try and remove a soup stain from his Quadrel tie. 'How many phones have you got?'

'At the moment, two.'

'How come?'

'It's complicated. Give me a mo while I listen to these messages, will you? Go and ask the barman for some soda water for your tie.'

'That works better, does it?'

'Sometimes. And get us two more pints as well, put it on my tab.'

The call he'd missed on his regular phone was from Rob Mariscal, the one on the pay-as-you-go phone was from Jean. He called her back and heard a long ringtone and then static. He still hadn't got the hang of the new phone. He fiddled with the side, trying to turn up the volume.

'. . . so he's got Balit's number on his phone.'

'Say all that again, Jean.'

'I wrote all the recent numbers down from Father Rumbek's phone. There was one I thought I recognised and that's because it belongs to Abdul Balit, it's his office line.'

Carver paused. 'Why would the head of Egyptian security be calling a Catholic priest?'

Jean laughed. 'Yeah, I've been trying to think of a good reason and I'm pretty sure there isn't one. I thought you might be able to think of a couple of *bad* ones?'

'I can.'

'So here's what I'm going to do. I'm going to go rattle Balit's cage and see what falls out.'

Carver could feel a headache building behind one eye. 'Hang on a second, Jean. I need to think this through.'

'I'm not planning to do anything stupid. A little light journalism, that's all. Balit's agreed to meet me – tomorrow, for lunch.'

'Tomorrow? That's quick. Where? In a public place?'

'I suggested the Café Riche – public as it gets.'

'Right, even so, I think Patrick—'

'Patrick's going to be there too. A neighbouring table is the plan, in case he won't let me record.'

'Which he won't.'

'Which he won't.'

Carver heaved a sigh. He checked his watch, wondering if there might be any space left on the evening flight. Or even the first one out tomorrow.

Jean was a step ahead. 'Even if you arrived in time, it wouldn't make any sense for you to be there, Billy. You'd scare him off.' She was right. 'And you're making headway there anyway; give me the latest.'

Carver told her about the kid on reception agreeing to make a copy of Bellquist's appointments. He also told her about the call from Rob Mariscal.

'What does he want?'

'To meet. No details yet. He's already tried to kill the story once so he's mixed up in this somehow.'

'You should see him, find out what he's got.'

'I guess so.'

39 Meetings

DATELINE: Scott's Club, Dean Street, Soho, London W1, February 12 2011

Carver glanced around Rob Mariscal's chosen venue, the private members' club that Rob had belonged to ever since William had known him. It was lunchtime – surely a peak time in London's clubland – but the place was not busy. It had always been a mystery to Carver how the owner – the legendary Maggie – managed to keep the club afloat. She'd even paid for some improvements since Carver's last visit, the old sticky carpet replaced with a new one and an expensive-looking chandelier for the dining room at the front. Looking around, Carver counted three people eating and one lonely soul sitting at the rear of the long narrow room, close to the bar.

Maggie spotted William the moment he walked in and greeted him warmly. 'Rob's down at the back.' She pointed a pink lacquered nail in that direction. 'He's been here a while, if you know what I mean?'

'Thanks, Maggie.'

'What are you drinking?'

Before he could answer, Mariscal had lumbered up, his arms wide and a broad smile on his face.

'He'll have the usual, Mags.'

'I'll have a half of cider please, Maggie.'

Rob grabbed Carver's hand and, having given it a good shake, led him to the back of the club. The assorted armchairs and sofas here were just as William remembered – a motley and threadbare collection of furniture but comfortable. He chose the high-backed armchair opposite Rob's sunken sofa and stowed his plastic bag underneath the low, glass-topped table that separated them. Maggie brought him the half of cider he'd asked for as well as a double measure of the whisky that he used to drink, back when a rendez-vous like this was a more regular occurrence. It seemed churlish to refuse it.

Despite the warm welcome and the single malt, Carver had doubts about this meeting. Mariscal had already tried to persuade Naomi Holder to spike the story once, so the idea that he might now want to help seemed far-fetched.

'What's this all about then, Rob?'

Mariscal frowned. 'What? No – *hello, how are you? How are the kids?* None of that?'

Carver shrugged. 'How are the kids?'

'I've no idea.'

'How are you?'

'Oh, you know, I live a life of well-remunerated pain. I oversee the turd production line, polishing turds from nine 'til nine.'

'Is that some kinda poem you're working on?'

Rob smiled, despite the circumstances; he'd been looking forward to seeing William. 'Yeah, well, more of a ballad actually. "Ballad of a Government Communications Man". I'm going to get Bob Dylan to record it. It'll break people's hearts. It's broken mine already.' Rob finished his drink and called for another. 'Blended for me please, Mags. With ice.'

As they waited for the whisky, Rob's mobile lit up in the gloom and started vibrating across the table. On the screen was a young woman with very white teeth.

Carver glanced at it. 'How is . . . er.' He sifted his memory for the name of Rob's girlfriend. 'Luci?'

Mariscal shook his head. 'Luci is my former missus. Lindy is the girlfriend.'

'Sorry.'

'Don't be. Stroke of genius on my part, hooking up with a woman whose name is almost the same as the ex-wife. I mix them up myself – last month I managed to do it halfway through a drunken fuck. Obviously, Lindy loved that.'

Carver smiled. 'How did Luci feel about it?'

'Ha. Yeah, I haven't told her yet, maybe I'll save that for her birthday.' He let the phone ring out then stuck it back in his pocket. 'I'm having a baby. With Lindy.'

'Congratulations.'

'Thanks.' Maggie handed him his whisky and he took a gulp. 'Expensive business, babies.'

'I'm sure.'

'The other kids aren't cheap either – private school, tutors, holidays . . . alimony.'

Carver got the impression that Rob ran through this list quite regularly.

'Then there's Lindy's bloody walk-in shower.'

'What?'

'Never mind.' He leaned forward, cupping his drink with both hands. 'So listen, how about you do everyone a favour and drop this tear gas thing?'

Carver stifled a laugh. 'How about I don't?' He stared at Rob – his old colleague, his old friend. 'Who are you working for these days, Rob?'

'You know who I'm working for.'

'I'm not sure I do. The Ministry of Defence – but not just them? Maybe Quadrel Engineering as well? Is it Victor Bellquist's turds you're polishing or flushing or whatever it is you're trying to do here?'

Rob's hand went to his collar; he undid the second button and felt better for it. 'It's complicated.'

'Try me.'

Mariscal tried. He explained that a good part of the MOD job was helping British companies compete. 'Win our share of those big international contracts. Create jobs and make money that ends up back in the public purse – paying our pensions and all of that. Maybe you haven't noticed, William, but we're not making a lot of widgets these days. We need the defence industry.'

Carver nodded his head. '*Weaponry and usury.*'

'What?'

'That's what you used to call the arms trade and financial services industry. Back when you didn't think they were the be-all and end-all. When you were doing your old job.'

'I don't remember saying that.'

'You remember your old job though, don't you, Rob? You remember what you were. Before you were this?'

Mariscal took another slurp of whisky, the ice from the drink rattling against his teeth. 'Vaguely.'

Carver shook his head. 'I was worried that this was what you were going to ask me, Rob. Though I've got to say, I thought you'd be more persuasive.'

Rob looked at William over the rim of his glass. 'I'm not finished yet.'

Jean and Patrick's plan had been carefully thought through. Patrick arrived at the Café Riche late morning; he was shown to his table by an old fellow in a dark blue robe with gold trim. Jean knew this man – something of a local legend who had started working at the café on the day that the battle of El Alamein ended. He'd agreed to seat Patrick just behind the colonel's usual table and to leave him there untroubled. Patrick's rucksack was underneath his chair, with the digital recorder and directional microphone on top, pointing back towards the table behind him and hidden beneath a thin linen shirt.

Jean would make sure that the colonel sat in the seat facing the mic and with luck the machine would pick up enough if not all of what he said. Jean's other job was to encourage Balit to say something interesting. She was sure that the colonel's men would check the café before their boss arrived and had ordered Patrick to ditch what she called his *baby war corr* outfit and dress like a tourist. He'd bought a T-shirt with a cartoon camel on and a pair of shorts from the market. While waiting, he flicked idly through his copy of the *Rough Guide to Cairo*. Patrick thought he'd nailed the look and was particularly pleased with the T-shirt. He'd bought it in XL so that Rebecca could use it as a nightshirt when he got back to London. Patrick checked his watch – Jean and Balit would be here soon.

'They asked me to offer you something.'

'Who did?'

'Bellquist. He asked me whether you were biddable money, property.'

Carver shook his head. 'And you told him what?'

'I told him *no*. But *no* isn't something that people like him hear very often. He gave me this . . .' Rob pulled a folded A4 manila envelope from his jacket pocket and placed it on the table.

William eyed it warily. 'What is it?'

'It's a list of all your personal passwords. Plus a copy of your hard drive. He can access everything, any time he likes. If you don't give this up, then they'll stuff every device you've got with the most horrible shit they can find – proper paedo stuff – and then they'll tell the police.'

'That's not very nice.' Carver opened the envelope and, ignoring the memory stick, pulled out a couple of sheets of A4. Sure enough, there was an alphabetical list of every password he could remember and a fair few he couldn't.

'You should think about buying a new computer. And sorting out your passwords' – Rob pointed at the piece of paper – 'especially the passwords: *William123*? I mean, fucking really?'

Carver shrugged. 'I only use that for my banking.' He'd lost interest in the list of passwords and was looking at the other sheet of paper. It was a handwritten list of some sort and the writing was like Rob's. 'What's this?'

'I'm not sure. It's either the broken remains of my moral compass, or it's my suicide note.' He took a gulp of watery whisky. 'Actually, come to think of it – it's probably both.'

Patrick felt the phone buzz in his pocket. He put his guidebook down and looked around. He had a strong suspicion that the middle-aged Egyptian in a striped business suit sitting two tables to his left was watching him. He finished his mint tea and called for the waiter. While the old fellow was taking his order – more mint tea, the chickpea salad with some bread and oil – Patrick sneaked a look at his phone. It was from Jean: she was on her way from the hotel, coming on foot. He texted her back a simple *okay*.

'If you won't take the bribe and you're not bothered about the blackmail then you might need that other stuff.'

'Okay.'

'It's not from me. Not really . . .'

Carver gave Rob a questioning look.

'You asked me who I'm working for.'

William nodded.

'Well, the bloke who gave me the job, the person I'd prefer to be working for is Leslie Craig.'

'The permanent secretary.'

'That's the one. He wanted me to give you this. At least I think he did.'

'Why?'

'He wants to keep his corner clean.'

'Eh?'

Rob had remembered a surprising amount of the information he'd read – upside down – in the papers on Craig's desk. Product names, quantities and costs.

Carver ran an eye down the list. 'There's enough here to kit out a whole army.'

'Several small armies.'

'Fighting where? Against who?'

'Sub Sahara mainly. Each other probably. It doesn't matter where or who. People like Bellquist don't really care who's fighting who, over what.'

Carver glanced at Rob. This list, together with what McCluskey had given him and what Jean and Zahra and Patrick had got . . . it could be enough.

It was the sports holdall that was making Patrick nervous. The middle-aged Egyptian had a suit and tie on, polished shoes. He should be carrying a smart leather briefcase or one of those laptop bags – not a tatty nylon sports holdall. Patrick didn't like the way the bloke kept checking his bag either – checking it for no good reason as far as Patrick could see. Then there was the noise, the sound of a crowd gathering, close to the café. Patrick got out his phone and checked his Twitter feed.

@bigbeartahrir
| Pro Presidential demo in Talaat Harb.

That was where he was. It was a good two blocks from Tahrir and not an obvious place for a demonstration in support of the President.

@bigbeartahrir
l Let us show them what a real demonstration looks like!

This explained both the crowd noise outside and the fact that both Colonel Balit and Jean were late; it was ten minutes past the agreed meeting time.

'Why are you doing this, Rob?'

'I've been wondering about that. I think it might be the baby. It's another chance, isn't it?'

Carver shrugged.

'The little bastard doesn't know what a fuck-up his old man is yet. And maybe I won't be. Maybe I can improve?'

Carver nodded. 'Maybe. Either way, thank you. Or thanks to you and to Craig.'

Rob shook his head. 'I'm not sure you should be thanking either of us, William.'

'How come?'

Rob took a gulp of his whisky and winced. 'Look at those numbers.'

Carver looked at the right-hand column of Rob's handwritten list.

'The people who are sending this stuff south, they're making 20 or 25 per cent on millions and millions of pounds. Anyone who's got a slice of that is going to fight like fuck to keep hold of it.' He looked at William. 'Bribes and blackmail are at the soft end of what these people will do. What I'm saying is – watch your back.'

Carver pushed his unfinished drink across the table and stood. 'I've got to go.' He grabbed his bag.

'Fair enough. Are you all right? You've gone a bit pale.'

'I need to make a call.'

Out on Dean Street, a shower of rain had put a shine on the pavement. It was raining still, but not hard. Carver walked as far as the nearest shop awning and pulled his phone from his pocket. He called Jean first but the number rang out. He didn't bother leaving a message but instead tried Patrick who answered after a couple of distant-sounding rings. He was whispering.

'William?'

'Yeah, is Jean there?'

'Not yet but—'

'What about Balit?'

'No, but—'

'Get out.'

'What?'

'Leave there. Find Jean. Do it now, Patrick, just pick up your stuff and leave. I'll stay on the line.'

Patrick looked over at the Egyptian in the striped business suit; he'd lifted the sports holdall from the floor and was cradling it in his lap.

Carver had his phone pressed hard to his ear listening for something, for anything. But the sounds he heard made no sense. Around him, his fellow Londoners were hurrying through the rain; he saw three people sharing one umbrella, laughing as they ran. On the other side of the street he watched a mother attaching a clear plastic covering to her toddler's pushchair.

Patrick made it to the door of the café and stopped. Through the window he saw Jean, who was working her way slowly through a crowd of protesters; she was being jostled and had one hand at the side of her head, holding her white headscarf in place. She was wearing a black trouser suit and a little lipstick. Patrick looked to his left, half expecting to see Colonel Balit arriving from the opposite direction – half ready to run back to his seat and continue with their well-worked-out plan. But there was no sign of the colonel. He pushed the door open, raised his hand and waved in Jean's direction. On seeing him she stopped, a look of confusion clouding her face. Patrick reached into his pocket for his phone: 'William? You still there?'

''Course I'm bloody here. Where are you?'

'I'm outside the café. There's no sign of Balit but Jean's here, we're both fine.'

Carver heaved a mighty sigh. 'Good, that's good. Give me to her.'

The bullet hit Jean in the side of the neck. It tore through the soft flesh, exploding the windpipe and severing the carotid artery.

She took two jerking steps towards Patrick, then toppled forward, her right hand reaching out. Patrick caught her as she fell, dropping the phone as he did so. He sank into a cross-legged position on the pavement and sat with her head in his hands. There was a lot of blood, too much. He took the white scarf from around her head and tried to stem the flow but it was no use.

Jean was trying to speak. Her lips moved but nothing came. Her legs felt cold, then her arms. Then everything felt cold. Terrifying and cold. She tried to focus. She thought about Carver and tried to remember what she'd said to him, the last time they'd spoken. She couldn't remember and she knew she had to think of other things. She thought about her mother and then, straight away – her dad. Her only dad. Jean was staring up at Patrick, but it was her father's face she saw. She smiled at Patrick and then she closed her eyes and died.

The soldier shuffled back from the edge of the roof on all fours then stood and stretched his legs. He'd been sitting in the same arse-numbing position for over an hour, his legs were stiff. He looked at his rifle, an old Lee Enfield with a polished wooden cheek rest and ten-round magazine – nine left now. Alongside the rifle were his radio and a roll of black cloth about a foot long containing his scopes, a silencer and two boxes of bullets. Propped against the radio was a passport-sized photograph of Jean Fitzgerald. He picked up the photo, took a lighter from his camo jacket pocket and – turning it face down – set fire to one corner. It burned easily. The soldier sat back down and turned his radio up so he could hear the static and chatter more clearly. He was waiting for his call sign and after that his next instruction.

The Way of Sorrows (xvi)

Forty-six nautical miles SE of Lampedusa

Gebre had promised his brother and his fellow passengers that help would come. But it didn't. No one came. Not that day or the following day or any day after that. The very young and the elderly died first and every time one among them died, prayers were muttered and the body was covered and lowered over the side of the dinghy and into the sea.

A few days into this ordeal, Gebre opened his eyes and looked around, unsure whether he was conscious or still dreaming. He saw a boatful of people in *pietà* pose: the weak cradling the weaker, the barely living holding the just dead. After a week, two-thirds of the original eighty-two passengers were dead, the food was gone and there was very little water left. Solomon was entrusted with keeping hold of the five-litre bottle and some nights they managed to collect a little condensation and replenish it, but it was not enough. Some died from drinking seawater to supplement their share of the clean water, others drank their own piss, or tried to keep their mouths damp by chewing on leather belts or shoes. The remaining eighteen all stayed alive for one full day thanks to a tube of toothpaste they found in the rancid, shit-filled fold at the side of the dinghy.

Everything they had they shared, but every day other than that day, one or more of their number died.

Gebre suspected Solomon of giving him a little more of the good water than any of the other men left alive on the boat, a charge that Solomon vehemently denied.

'It is just that everything about you is so small, even your mouth. A few drops fill your tiny mouth.'

Gebre smiled and his brother reached over and tugged at his sleeve.

'I have been meaning to talk to you about this, Gebre. I do not think that you should send for Martha when you get to Europe, she is too tall for you. I saw you trying to hug her outside the cinema once – you looked like a man trying to climb a tree.'

By the fourteenth day only Gebre, Solomon and one other man were left alive and the good water was all but gone. Solomon's seemingly inexhaustible strength was finally leaving him. It was too hot to move or talk during the day but as the sun began to set he reached over for Gebre.

'I do not want the birds to eat my eyes.'

Gebre glanced at his brother, then away. 'Don't be foolish.'

'I mean it. I have thought about it. I don't want the birds to eat my eyes. I want to keep my eyes.'

'Fine.'

'When the time comes, Gebre, put me in the water, I would rather lie down there in the cool. When it's time, I want you to put me down there, not keep me up here.'

Gebre shook his head. 'It is not relevant, it's not going to happen, be quiet.'

Solomon reached out a hand and found his brother's. 'Say it, say you will put me in the water.' There were tears in Solomon's eyes now.

'I can't, Sol. I can't.'

Solomon let go of Gebre's hand, pushing it away. 'I do everything for you, I always do everything. I am asking you for *one thing*.'

Gebre looked away. The sea was so many colours, that was one of the things he had come to know. That the sea was not blue the way it is when you draw it as a child. It is every colour. And right then, it was green, the most beautiful green . . .

PART FOUR

@egyptismtahrir
| Freedom loaded . . . 100%.

@bigbeartahrir
| Raise your head up U R an Egyptian!

@mohammedktahrir
| Liberated lands – Tunisia, Egypt. Next – Libya,
| Syria, Bahrain and maybe even Saudi!

@JohnBrandonBBC
| Heading home! One of the toughest gigs in a long
| time, but a job well done by all accounts.

40 Wishes

DATELINE: Stockwell Road, London SW9, February 14 2011

The delivery guy had taken to calling Carver by his first name and making small talk. William had done nothing to encourage this but still Axlam persisted. He was Somali and he was saving up for a moped; when Carver explained that he had no English money left to tip him, Axlam said he'd take whatever he had. The kid's uncle changed the money for him and Axlam enjoyed reporting back on the value of the various notes and coins Carver gave him.

'Yesterday lunchtime you tipped me five pence in Liberian coins.'

Carver shrugged.

'But in the evening, when I brought you the Chinese?'

'Yeah?'

'Those Brazilian notes were worth twenty-five pounds!' Carver had considered asking for some of the Brazilian cash back but rejected the idea in favour of finding some more Liberian coins. He'd handed these over in exchange for the pizza but when he flipped the top open he saw that Axlam had delivered the wrong pizza. He went after him and handed it back.

353

'This thing's got pineapple on it – and ham.'

Axlam had a look. 'I'm very sorry, William. I will swap it for the right one.' He shoved the unwanted pizza into his boxy backpack. 'Fifteen minutes I promise or I give the tip back.'

'Fine.'

Carver watched some news while he was waiting. Egypt wasn't the lead any more but it was still pretty high up the order. The President had gone, handing power to the military, who were promising an orderly handover and elections. The protesters were leaving Tahrir Square and there were pictures of tents being cleared.

Axlam was back in ten, ringing on the bell but when Carver opened the door, instead of pepperoni pizza he found Patrick, standing alongside a large suitcase.

'Hello, William.'

'Hello.'

'I've been calling.'

'I know. I'm on leave, I don't want to talk about work.'

'I wasn't going to talk about—'

'I don't want to talk about anything. If I did, I would've called you back, wouldn't I? What's with the suitcase?' He vaguely recognised it.

'It's er . . . Jean's. It's all her stuff. Zahra gave it to me, to give to you.'

'Right.' Carver stepped into the hall and rolled the case back into his flat.

'Anything else?'

'Not really, just . . . I'm sorry, William. I'm really sorry.' There was a catch in his throat. 'I wish it had been me – me and not her.'

Carver stared at Patrick. 'I wish that too. But it wasn't.' He closed the door.

*

He tried her medicines first, taking various combinations of Jean's impressive collection washed down with wine. Some of these pills seemed to help, others not. He slept a lot. He thought about having all her clothes dry-cleaned then decided against; he thought about giving everything to the local hospice shop, but he couldn't do that either. Eventually he returned everything to the suitcase and pushed it to the back of his cupboard. The only things he kept out were Jean's notebook, her painkillers and Nawal's gas canister. He started work.

The phone numbers that Jean had copied from Father Rumbek's mobile were written in the back of her notebook. She'd scribbled some words next to a few of the numbers: *Balit office. Balit mobile? Asmara code. Thuraya sat phone. London mobile.* There were ticks and double ticks next to some numbers, crosses next to others and it became clear to Carver that this was an indication of which numbers she'd called and which she hadn't. Jean had avoided calling any of the numbers that might belong to one of the key players. She didn't want to tip their hand. She had been working the margins and Carver knew he had to be similarly careful.

His eye kept going back to one number and words she'd scribbled next to it. It was a long mobile number and next to it Jean had written: *East African mobile. Link?*

He phoned it that evening. He had a form of words in his head and was ready to close the call down if he felt he was giving away more than he was learning. The phone rang for a long time without switching to a messaging service. For some reason William was sure that there *was* someone on the other end of the line. They were just taking a long time to decide whether or not to answer. The phone picked up.

'*Si?*' It was a young man's voice, wary.

'Hello, I found your number in a book belonging to Jean Fitzgerald. I think she called you, I think you spoke to her.'

'*Si*.'

'She left me your number. She wanted me to call you.'

'Where is she?'

'She's dead.'

The young man sighed. 'Where are you calling me from?'

'From London.'

'Is that where the lady was from?'

'No, but she lived here – for a long time. She was born in New Zealand but she left when she was seventeen. Where are you?'

There was a long pause. 'Roma.'

Epilogue

DATELINE: The Borghese Gardens, Rome, Italy, May 3 2011

'So this is hell.' He heard the anguished English voice coming from the front of the bus and walked in that direction. He felt sorry for the tourists, sitting on top of a double-decker in the noonday sun, but their discomfort was his business opportunity. It still mystified him why anyone would pay so much money to ride an old bus around Rome on a hot day like this, but they did and so here he was, standing at the Borghese Gardens bus stop shouting up at the tourists in a mix of English, French and Italian. He wore a stack of twenty hats on his head, a range of different styles and sizes for men and women. Every seller had hats, but he had bucket hats for kids with Disney characters on them and for the teenagers, blue sun visors with the Italian flag which didn't offer much protection but looked cool and sold well. All the vendors sold sun cream, but he sold sunblock – the brand that tourists knew; he had the bottled water they recognised too.

When he wasn't selling, he watched. He studied his customers carefully, put himself in their place then found the things he

357

thought they would need or like – he thought his grandfather would be proud of him. They cherished their mobile phones so he sold portable chargers with a full phone's worth of charge on them. They worried about their children – he had the sunblock and the hats but also colouring books and crayons. They fiddled with the cheap earphones the bus driver gave them so he sold them better ones. His most recent innovation was a paper hat made from the tourist maps that hotels handed out for free. He'd learned how to fold the maps into several different shapes: a Napoleonesque was the most popular; he did this while they watched and they paid three euros for something that cost him nothing.

He sold the English voice some water and a paper hat, catching the five-euro note she threw down deftly and tucking it away in his money belt. He was about to work the other side of the bus when a short Italian woman appeared and started shouting.

'Aooo. Hey you, shoo! Leave these people alone, my driver has warned you about this.' Her voice sounded stern but the woman was smiling broadly as she yelled and he grinned back. Carlotta was only doing this to keep her miserable boss happy. *'Guarda che te faccio beve!* I'll call the police . . .'

He held up his hands and backed away. He loved the way Carlotta spoke her language, he could have listened to her shout at him all day. The way she spoke Italian made it sound more like singing than speaking.

'I am sorry.'

She tutted loudly and turned on her heel, skirt swishing. He loved that too. The only thing he didn't like about her was the long tattoo of an Italian boy's name written in extravagant, calligraphic script up on the inside of her right arm. *Lorenzo* was the name of his rival and although he knew the tattoo was a bad sign, he also knew Lorenzo was away studying in America, whereas he was here in Rome and saw her every day. What's more, Carlotta had told him that he looked a lot like one of her favourite football players, a man who played for Roma and was even blacker than he was. He was trying to encourage the comparison by wearing his hair shaved short at the side and long on top, the way this footballer and Carlotta seemed to prefer it.

He checked his digital watch. He'd been working since six this morning; it was nearly one now and he was hungry but he didn't want to eat any of the snacks he carried with him to sell to tourists. He could wait; he was meeting the English journalist at the Marinella restaurant in just over an hour. William Carver would surely want to eat?

There was a large ceiling fan inside the Marinella restaurant but the room was too tall and the fan too slow for it to do much good; the old wooden contraption simply stirred the warm air. Carver was early but that was fine; he needed to check his recording equipment and maybe have a bite to eat while he did that. He'd just have a starter and the kid could catch up when he arrived. Carver picked up the menu and ran an eye down it; none of the starters appealed. He'd have the vongole – that was usually more starter-size anyway.

He looked around for the waiter – there only seemed to be one, despite a black and white photograph behind the till showing a dozen waiting staff and half that again in chef's hats and aprons. In time the man arrived; he had a grey toothbrush moustache and a short temper.

'*Cosa vuoi?*'

Carver's Italian was not great but he managed to make the man understand that he wanted a large glass of red wine with his vongole and some bread and olive oil. The vongole arrived – a mountain of spaghetti big enough to feed a family, rich in garlic and expertly cooked. Carver showered the lower slopes with Parmesan before attacking the summit in search of clams. It soon became clear that the generous helping of pasta was there to compensate for the marked absence of clam.

Carver had only unearthed six when he heard the brass bell on a spring on the back of the restaurant door ring softly. Glancing up from his meal, he saw a young African man looking in his direction. The kid walked nervously towards Carver's table; he was wearing a checked shirt and jeans and pulling a beaten-up, black canvas roll-along suitcase behind him. He was getting ready to speak when the waiter marched from the kitchen and started berating him in angry Italian. Carver didn't need to understand the language to catch the absolute contempt. He stood and put himself in between the waiter and his guest.

'It is okay. Thank you, I asked this young man to meet me here.'

The waiter shook his head. If this stupid Englishman wanted to be robbed or ripped off then so be it. He took the precaution of removing the silverware from the tables closest to Carver's unwelcome guest and returned to the kitchen.

William gave the kid an apologetic smile and offered his hand. 'Hello, I'm William Carver.'

The kid shook hands, a good hold. 'Hello. I am Solomon Hassen.'

'Good to meet you at last.'

While Carver set up his microphone and MiniDisc recorder, using the bread basket as a makeshift mic stand, Solomon looked at the menu.

Carver told him to order anything he wanted and he chose calamari alla griglia, risotto alla pescatora, a glass of orangeade and the tiramisu; all ordered in a polite and perfectly fluent Italian. As soon as the first plate arrived on the table Solomon began to eat and he ate hungrily. Carver watched.

'You've got a taste for Italian food already then?'

Solomon nodded. 'We have Italian food in Asmara but not like this; the chef here is very good. They throw a lot of food away. But this man' – he jabbed a thumb back over his shoulder in the

360

direction of the waiter – 'this man is not so good. He pours bleach on the old food so it cannot be eaten.'

While Solomon spoke, Carver checked the levels, shuffling the microphone around and adjusting the dial until the green lights on the front of his machine were doing the right thing.

Solomon was watching. 'You want to do the interview while I am eating?'

William nodded. 'I want you to tell me what you told me before, about some of the things that you and your brother saw on the journey.'

Solomon nodded.

'I'll ask you to repeat some of that later – to clarify stuff. But for now, we just talk . . .' Carver leaned back in his seat. 'How about we start in Asmara? I've always wanted to see that place; tell me about it.'

So Solomon told him – from the beginning to the end.

The Way of Sorrows (xvii)

Twenty-six nautical miles south of Lampedusa

Solomon was woken by the sound of shouting. An Italian fisherman had managed to attach a grappling hook to the dinghy's engine and was pulling the boat closer to his. Solomon pulled himself into a sitting position and tried to speak, but his voice was gone. Looking down, he saw Gebre's hand in his – he squeezed it now, to wake his brother.

Gebre had waited until Solomon was sleeping before shuffling over and lifting his heavy arm from around the near empty bottle. He opened it and poured the last inch of fresh water slowly into his brother's mouth. This done he lay back down, exhausted, and stared up into the night sky . . . so many stars. He reached out, took Solomon's hand and held it. He knew that he would see his brother again. He was certain of it – just not in this world.

When he finished his story, Solomon's eyes shone. He looked up from the microphone and stared straight at Carver. 'I have tried to remember the names of the people who died in our boat. Can I read these names into your recording machine?'

Carver nodded. 'Of course.'

Solomon listed the names of the dead, ending with Gebre's name. 'I can show you his photograph?'

'Please.'

Solomon got out his mobile phone and moved a thumb across the screen until he found the photos he was looking for. Two pictures of Gebre, standing on a jetty in the dark, smiling sheepishly.

'Your brother looks like a good man.'

Solomon nodded. 'Yes.'

Carver enlarged the picture. 'This is the night you left Libya?'

'That's right. I wanted to remember it.'

'Behind Gebre – on those boxes – what is that?' Carver felt his stomach shift. He passed the phone to Solomon.

'Pictures . . . of bugs. Bugs with horns. They were stamped on the boxes.' He handed the phone back but it slipped from Carver's sweating hand.

He retrieved it, enlarged the photograph some more and stared. 'I don't believe it.'

'What?'

'This picture.' He pointed at Solomon's phone. 'It's part of a puzzle. Something I've been working on.'

Carver stared up at the ceiling fan, turning slowly, stirring the air. With Solomon he had an eyewitness – someone who'd seen the weapons arrive and how they made their way south. From McCluskey and from Mariscal he had an idea of what these weapons were and where they were headed. He had Nawal's gas canister and the list of numbers that Jean had found on Father Rumbek's phone. And now – now he had a photograph: physical, dated evidence.

'It's enough.'

'What?'

'What you have given me, Solomon – you and Gebre – it's enough. Will you excuse me? I need to make a telephone call.'

Carver stepped out on to the street and dialled Zahra's number. She answered on the second ring and William told her everything. He was speaking too quickly, he was babbling but Zahra understood what it meant.

'You have what you need then?'

'I think so.' He was smiling. 'I can go after them for you now, Zahra.'

'For me?'

'For you. For Nawal.'

'For Jean.'

Carver paused. His throat ached with unshed tears. 'Yes, for Jean. I'm going to go after every fucking one of them.'

Acknowledgements

The following books were particularly helpful while researching *A Single Source*: Ahdaf Soueif's *Cairo, My City, Our Revolution*, Denison, Yu Ren and Gebremedhin's *Asmara: Africa's Secret Modernist City*, Rachel Aspden's *Generation Revolution*, Tom Chesshyre's *A Tourist in the Arab Spring*, Nadia Idle and Alex Nunns' *Tweets from Tahrir*, Charlotte McDonald-Gibson's *Cast Away*, Patrick Kingsley's *The New Odyssey*, Isobel Coleman's *Paradise Beneath Her Feet, How Women are Transforming the Middle East*, Migreurop's *Atlas of Migration in Europe* and Seb Emina and Malcolm Eggs' *The Breakfast Bible*.

I would also like to acknowledge the journalism of Kevin Connolly, Mary Harper and Lyse Doucet as well as the work Forensic Architecture have done in investigating the story of 'The Left to Die Boat'. Thank you to Richard Knight for pointing me in that direction and his support throughout. I am grateful to Matilda Harrison for the early reading and to Steve Ali, Mohamad Aljasem, and Deborah Dolce for help with the Arabic and Italian translations. I'm indebted to too many BBC radio people to thank them individually but I would like to acknowledge the support given by the Radio 4 *World Tonight* and World Service *Newshour* teams.

Lisa Highton and John Saddler have both been patient editorial guides as this 'difficult second book' slowly took shape. Finally, thank you to my family and most of all to Vic who read, re-read and re-re-read. Words are insufficient but they'll have to do in the absence of an appropriate emoticon. Thank you.

About the Author

Peter Hanington is the author of *A Dying Breed*. He has worked as a journalist for over twenty-five years, including fourteen years at the *Today Programme* and more recently *The World Tonight* and *Newshour* on the BBC World Service. He lives in London with his wife and has two grown-up children.

Read Peter Hanington's thrilling debut, *A Dying Breed*

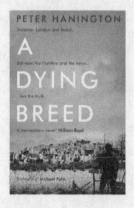

'What do you think's going to happen?'

'What?'

'In Afghanistan. What do you think will happen?'

William picked up his plastic bag. 'Dying. Dying is going to happen.'

Kabul, Afghanistan.

William Carver, a veteran but unpredictable BBC hack, is thrown into the unknown when a bomb goes off killing a local official. Warned off the story from every direction, Carver won't give in until he finds the truth.

London, England.

Patrick, a young producer, is sent out on his first foreign assignment to control the wayward Carver. As the story unravels, it seems the real story lies between the shadowy corridors of the BBC, the perilous streets of Kabul and the dark chambers of Whitehall.

Set in a shadowy world of dubious morality and political treachery, with echoes of Graham Greene and John le Carré, *A Dying Breed* is a gripping novel about journalism in a time of war and about the struggle to tell the stories that need to be told – even if it is much easier not to.